Slavic
Myths

Slavic Myths

Introduction by Ema Lakinska

General Editor: Jake Jackson

**FLAME TREE
PUBLISHING**

This is a FLAME TREE Book

FLAME TREE PUBLISHING
6 Melbray Mews
Fulham, London SW6 3NS
United Kingdom
www.flametreepublishing.com

First published 2023
Copyright © 2023 Flame Tree Publishing Ltd

25 27 26 24
3 5 7 9 8 6 4

ISBN: 978-1-80417-331-2

The stories 'The Devil and Spase the Shepherd', 'The Three Fates' and 'Silyan
the Stork' are printed with permission from and translated by Fay Thomev,
from the 10 volume collection: *Makedonski narodni umotvorbi vo X knigi* (Vol I–X)
by Marko Cepenkov, published by Makedonska kniga, Skopje, 1972.

The cover image is © copyright 2022 Flame Tree Publishing Ltd, based
on artwork courtesy of Shutterstock.com/AlexanderPavlov.

All inside images courtesy of Shutterstock.com and the following:
Tasha Romart, artdock and Limolida Design Studio.

Contributors, authors, editors and sources for this series include:
R. Nisbet Bain (editor/translator); Ivana Brlić-Mažuranić, translated
by F.S. Copeland; Marko K. Cepenkov, translated by Fay Thomev;
Jeremiah Curtin; Madame Elodie L. Mijatovich (translator); A. J. Glinski,
translated by Maude Ashurst Biggs; A.H. Wratislaw (translator).

Printed in China

Contents

Series Foreword

STRETCHING BACK to the oral traditions of thousands of years ago, tales of heroes and disaster, creation and conquest have been told by many different civilizations in many different ways. Their impact sits deep within our culture even though the detail in the tales themselves are a loose mix of historical record, transformed narrative and the distortions of hundreds of storytellers.

Today the language of mythology lives with us: our mood is jovial, our countenance is saturnine, we are narcissistic and our modern life is hermetically sealed from others. The nuances of myths and legends form part of our daily routines and help us navigate the world around us, with its half truths and biased reported facts.

The nature of a myth is that its story is already known by most of those who hear it, or read it. Every generation brings a new emphasis, but the fundamentals remain the same: a desire to understand and describe the events and relationships of the world. Many of the great stories are archetypes that help us find our own place, equipping us with tools for self-understanding, both individually and as part of a broader culture.

For Western societies it is Greek mythology that speaks to us most clearly. It greatly influenced the mythological heritage of the ancient Roman civilization and is the lens through which we still see the Celts, the Norse and many of the other great peoples and religions. The Greeks themselves learned much from their neighbours, the Egyptians, an older culture that became weak with age and incestuous leadership.

It is important to understand that what we perceive now as mythology had its own origins in perceptions of the divine and the rituals of the sacred. The earliest civilizations, in the crucible of the Middle East, in the Sumer of the third millennium BC, are the source to which many of the mythic archetypes can be traced. As humankind collected together in cities for the first time, developed writing and industrial scale agriculture, started to irrigate the rivers and attempted to control rather than be at the mercy of its environment, humanity began to write down its tentative explanations of natural events, of floods and plagues, of disease.

Early stories tell of Gods (or god-like animals in the case of tribal societies such as African, Native American or Aboriginal cultures) who are crafty and use their wits to survive, and it is reasonable to suggest that these were the first rulers of the gathering peoples of the earth, later elevated to god-like status with the distance of time. Such tales became more political as cities vied with each other for supremacy, creating new Gods, new hierarchies for their pantheons. The older Gods took on primordial roles and became the preserve of creation and destruction, leaving the new gods to deal with more current, everyday affairs. Empires rose and fell, with Babylon assuming the mantle from Sumeria in the 1800s BC, then in turn to be swept away by the Assyrians of the 1200s BC; then the Assyrians and the Egyptians were subjugated by the Greeks, the Greeks by the Romans and so on, leading to the spread and assimilation of common themes, ideas and stories throughout the world.

The survival of history is dependent on the telling of good tales, but each one must have the 'feeling' of truth, otherwise it will be ignored. Around the firesides, or embedded in a book or a computer, the myths and legends of the past are still the living materials of retold myth, not restricted to an exploration of origins. Now we have devices and global communications that give us unparalleled access to a diversity of traditions. We can find out about Native American, Indian, Chinese and tribal African mythology in a way that was denied to our ancestors, we can find connections, match the archaeology, religion and the mythologies of the world to build a comprehensive image of the human experience that is endlessly fascinating.

The stories in this book provide an introduction to the themes and concerns of the myths and legends of their respective cultures, with a short introduction to provide a linguistic, geographic and political context. This is where the myths have arrived today, but undoubtedly over the next millennia, they will transform again whilst retaining their essential truths and signs.

Jake Jackson
General Editor

Introduction to Slavic Myths

MYTHS AND LEGENDS commonly circulated throughout the Slavic tribes in Central and Eastern Europe, from Siberia in the East to the Balkans in the West, and were transferred to the younger generations in the form of folktales. The folktale, as a folkloric and literary genre, is present in all world cultures. Slavic folktales are short stories that include all the mythical creatures, deities and magical objects of Slavic mythology, and centre on moral lessons, adventure and magic. What differentiates them from other types of narrative forms is the uncanny, the strange and mystifying characteristics deeply rooted in their mythical basis, as well as the indeterminacy of plots in the setting of space and time. The difference between them and other literary forms is that the folktale puts an accent on the turning points and moments of crisis in the life of the protagonist. The Russian scholar Vladimir Propp was the first to introduce the Slavic term for this type of tale in 1928: he named it *скаска* (*skaska*). In modern Slavic languages, apart from the term *skaska*, the term *бајка* (*bajka*) is used as its synonym, defined by Croatian scholar Vladimir Biti in 1981.

The Slavs were tribes that started to migrate throughout the European continent in the sixth century CE. It is believed that their name came from the Proto-Slavic word *slovo*, meaning 'word', referring to 'people who understand each other'. In the first documents, which date from the ninth century and are written in Old Church Slavonic, these early tribes gave themselves the name *Slověne* (Словѣне). Thanks to Old Church Slavonic, myths and legends (disguised as folktales) started to disseminate orally across all Slavic tribes.

The alphabet of the Old Church Slavonic language, named the Glagolitic alphabet, was standardized for all Slavic peoples by Saint Cyril and Saint

Methodius in the ninth century CE, when the two missionaries (who were also brothers) created the script in order to translate the Bible into the Slavic languages. Later, it was transformed by Saint Clement of Ohrid to become what we know today as the Cyrillic alphabet. The two alphabets and Old Church Slavonic played an important role in oral and written dissemination of folktales: having a common language and an alphabet made it possible for stories to travel between tribes and circulate the continent. It also helped in the later creation of all Slavic languages and cultures as a whole, as well as in the spread of Christianity throughout Slavic countries.

With the beginning of the Great Migrations of Slavs into Eastern Europe and Western Asia in the late sixth century CE, the first Proto-Slavic tribes broke their group into three parts: East, West and South. Slavic tribes mixed their folklore and culture with that of the native tribes in the lands they occupied, making this mixture a common feature that would characterize each of these groups.

The Three Slavic Groups of Tribes

The East Slavs mainly settled in areas of today's Russia, Belarus and Ukraine. Occupying these geographical landscapes, they mixed with Finns and Balts. The Slavic languages that developed in this group were Russian, Belarussian, Ukrainian and Rusyn. Alphabet-wise, they all use their national versions of the Cyrillic alphabet. They are all Orthodox Christians. Modern countries in this group are Russia, Ukraine and Belarus.

The western Slavic tribes settled in Central Europe after the Germanic tribes left this area (and so mixed with Germanics, Hungarians, Celts and Old Prussians). Under the influence of the Western Roman Empire, they adopted Catholicism and the Latin alphabet. Slavic languages that belong to this group are Polish, Kashubian, Silesian, Polabian, Lower Sorabian, Upper Sorabian, Czech and Slovak. Modern countries in this group are Poland, the Czech Republic and Slovakia.

The South Slavs mixed with Proto-Balkan tribes such as Illyrian, Dacian, Thracian, Paeonian, Hellenic and Celtic. They also mixed with the Roman people who lived in the Byzantine Empire at the time of their arrival in the Balkans, as well as with itinerant tribes such as Huns, Avars, Goths and Bulgars. Due to the influence of the Byzantine Empire, these Slavic peoples adopted Orthodox Christianity as their religion and the Cyrillic alphabet for their writing. Some of the tribes like Torbeshi and Bosniaks adopted Islam as their religion, due to the influence of the Ottoman Empire. Slavic languages from this group are Slovene, Serbian, Croatian, Macedonian, Bulgarian, Bosnian and Montenegrin. Modern countries in this group are Slovenia, Croatia, Serbia, North Macedonia, Bosnia and Herzegovina, Montenegro and Bulgaria.

Cultural Fusion

In order to explain more vividly how this cultural fusion – which later influenced the interpretation of mythology of each separate Slavic tribe – occurred, we will take the example of the South Slavs, where the greatest synthesis took place. As Macedonian scholar Kiril Penusliski explains in *History of Macedonian Folklore* (2012), the rich mythology as part of the spiritual culture of the Slavs who inhabited the Balkan Peninsula was the basis for their oral literature. 'The Slavic tribes that settled in the territory of the Balkan Peninsula from the 6th century onwards continued for centuries to maintain the patriarchal way of life and preserve the benefits of their culture,' Penusliski writes. These people, fighting daily with animals, began to attribute magical powers to them, and even 'tried to propitiate them with prayers and spells, because they believed that some of their great-grandfathers, that is, patrons, were reincarnated in them'. Hence, folktales represent 'living reflections of the original beliefs and representations of the nature of our distant ancestors'. Vladimir Propp, in *The Historical Roots of the Wonder Tale* (1946), explains how initiation rituals of primitive tribes provide the basis of the folktale. He concludes that the evolution of folkloric forms took place according to the following schedule: ritual – myth – folktale. Myth arose on the basis of primitive rituals and rites, and when the influence of myth and religion began to weaken, mythic plots turned into folktales.

In the same line, Mircea Eliade points out in two of his works, *The Myth of the Eternal Return: Cosmos and History* (1949) and *Images and Symbols: Studies in Religious Symbolism* (1952), that symbol, myth and image are the foundation of spiritual life. Myth develops events that happened, as he says *in principio*, in a timeless fragment of *sacred* time. With the weakening influence of myths – as carriers of paganism, rituals and rites at their core – and with the increasing influence of religion, folktales were born. In today's world, folktales are a vivid example of how pagan or mythical traditions and Christianity can work together in a single literary form.

The reason the mythical and the religious did not erase one another in folktales is because the Slavic tribes showed high resilience to assimilation during the spread of Christianity, so instead there occurred amalgamations. For example, South Slavs living in small villages were never completely assimilated, as writes Nikos Chausidis in *The Mythical Images of the South Slavs* (1994). 'The basic cell of the system is the family, in which there is a strict set of customs that are passed down from generation to generation, and must not be interrupted or violated. Deep in the basis of food production lies the system of ritual-magical activities, with strictly fixed procedures that are determined by time and without which there is no successful harvest. All social institutions, such as marriage, family and tribe, are maintained by a set of rules and prohibitions, the basis of which is also mythical.' So, in order to protect themselves from the repressive way that the Byzantines were introducing Christianity, the South Slavs accepted 'all the formal Christian elements which did not mean changing the traditional system'. This process of changing the form and names of various deities, but not their functions, symbols or meanings, is present in both religion and mythology of all three groups of Slavs. And precisely because of this function of the myth to endlessly adapt and reshape itself into new forms, it has survived until modern times.

Regardless of the wide territory the Slavs occupied, or the amalgamations these three groups' settlements resulted in, these people share the same root – their common mythology. Given the differences of the amalgams of the three groups, their understanding and interpretation of the main mythical creatures and characters, as well as what they symbolize, may vary. In order to understand the mythology of the Slavs, it is important to explain some of their beliefs and cults, as well as the Slavic calendar and how they measured time. Also necessary is reviewing the most important characteristics of the Slavic mythical creatures, as well as the Slavic pantheon.

The Slavic Calendar

The Slavic calendar is a complex time counter that relies mainly on the weather and natural occurrences (sun, rain, harvest, etc.) This is mostly notable in the Slavic names of the months, where every Slavic nation has their own, describing the natural occurrences of the lands they settled in. The calendar is also at the core of the stories about their gods. Modern Orthodox holidays are also rooted in Slavic mythology. The Slavic calendar is a cosmogonic and a dualistic one, as presented in the story 'The Two Brothers' (*see* page 227), where a mother gives birth to two sons. As dualism holds the balance between the good and the bad, the night and the day, the warm and the cold, we find numerous examples in folktales: in the story 'The Golden-Haired Twins' (*see* page 221), we see a conflict between the old, wicked queen (personalization of the old year) and the new queen (personalization of the new year) who gives birth to golden-haired twins. Another example is the story 'The King of the Toads' (*see* page 200) when the young king, personalizing the new year, kills the old monarch, a character who lives on the bottom of the lake and is the image of the Underground, the realm of the dead.

Slavic Cults

The most widespread cult in Slavic mythology is the Cult of the Dead. Slavic people believed that after death (or even during sleep), the soul, or the spirit (*zduh*, *duh*) would leave the body. These spirits were considered to be different characters from the living being. They can be good, but also evil when they turn into Mora (*мора*), a male or female malevolent spirit that haunts the living. This is why Slavic mythology specifies strict rules regarding the rituals and handling of the dead. From the moment of cremation or burial, the graves of the dead need to be visited on strictly prescribed dates, when family members offer them food and drinks in order for the spirit to find a good place in heaven. In Slavic folktales, the spirits of the dead can also help the heroes, such as in the story 'Papalluga; or the Golden Slipper' (*see* page 171), the Slavic version of 'Cinderella', where the girl is helped on her journey by her dead mother. Mythical creatures such as vampires derive from this cult.

Aside from the cult for their dead, Slavic people had cults for every one of their gods where they would use rural practices to worship them. These cults were related to the Cult of the Trees, which might be the oldest Slavic cult. Silent whisperers were used to help people make confessions and pray to the tree. The most important tree in Slavic mythology was the oak tree – the tree of the gods Perun and Veles (*see* page 18) – which represented the world. They believed that their gods lived in the oak tree and considered it to be the home for all earthly beings. Its upper branches represented the heavens, the middle of the tree represented the realm of men, and the roots represented the Underworld. In rural practices, sometimes involving sacrifice, they would pray to the roots of the tree for the dead, and to its branches for the living. Mythical creatures such as fairies derive from this cult.

Mythical Creatures

Vampires are common in Slavic mythology. Vampires are believed to be dead people who rise from their graves at night and feast on the blood of their loved ones. According to Slavic mythology, the living can also be vampires, but in the form of *Wolkodlak* (or *wuldalak, verdilak, vukodlak*), a creature close to the French *lugaro* and the English *werewolf*. They were described as having fur, tails, sharp teeth and claws and would transform during the night only to return to their human form during the day. In Slavic folktales, these creatures are symbolic and represent the intuition of the protagonist like in the story 'Ivan Tsarevich, the Firebird and the Grey Wolf' (*see* page 67).

Other mythical creatures in Slavic folklore are the *vili*. The females are named *samovila* and represent mythical creatures close to fairies in the English tradition. The *samovila* derives its power from the Underworld and is usually an evil creature – much like the older iteration of fairies to be found in English folk songs, but unlike the more modern post-Victorian-era fairies with which we are more familiar, who are more benevolent and often exist to make someone's wish come true. The function of fairies in Slavic folktale traditions does not follow this later, more lighthearted vision.

It is believed that the *samovili* lived in the woods or near water, such as rivers, lakes, etc. They were very beautiful and could easily make a man fall in love with them and thereby manipulate him to achieve their plans. They were delightful singers and dancers and would use music to attract potential suitors. Sometimes in folktales, fairies are benefactors for girls such as in the story 'The Wood-Lady' (*see* page 32). In some folktales, they translate into mermaids, like in the story 'The Good Ferryman and the Water Nymphs' (*see* page 137), where the protagonist interacts with female and male fairies. The male version of the *samovila* is named *vilenik* and is not as frequent in Slavic mythology.

English and Slavic traditions also differ in another category of mythical creatures close to fairies – the *narechnici* (fates). They are described as three women who show up on the first night a child is born in order to foretell its future, such as in the story 'The Three Fates' (*see* page 176). Unlike fates in the English tradition, which shape the destiny of humans, the *narechnici* show up in folktales when heroes lose their paths, acting as fortune-tellers, sometimes as sorcerers or even witches. The most common one in Slavic mythology is Baba Yaga. She is present in the story 'The Feather of Bright Finist the Falcon' (*see* page 77), offering wisdom to the hero, and in 'The Cuirassier and the Horned Princess' (*see* page 100) where she gives magic objects to the protagonists.

Gods of the Slavic Pantheon

These Slavic mythical creatures, cults and beliefs wouldn't be the same without the gods of the Slavic pantheon. The most important gods in the Slavic pantheon include:

Perun – The God of Thunder

God of the Sky, more specifically God of Thunder and Lightning, Perun is the supreme god in the Slavic pantheon, and as such holds the highest place. He was believed to live in the high branches of the oak tree. In a dualistic pantheon where the good and the evil coexist together, Perun represents the good, the sky or the higher cosmic zones, often compared to Zeus in Greek mythology. As Slavic people were settlers and migrated frequently, he was also worshipped as the God of War – in some aspects like the Norse and Germanic Thor and Odin together. As the God of War, he is the God of Weapons as well, commonly invoked by Slavic fighters.

Perun is a heavily masculine figure: he represents activity in nature; he is the giver of rain that fertilizes the earth so that food is born. Symbolically, this is shown in the story 'Little Rolling-Pea' (*see* page 130), where a girl finds a pea in shallow waters and, after eating it, gives birth to a son of great intelligence and power.

As Perun was believed to live in the higher cosmic zones, the temples dedicated to him were always in high places, like mountaintops and groves of oak trees. He was worshipped by all Slavic tribes, and even by non-Slavic ones, as he appears as Perkunas in Baltic mythology. His name comes from the Proto-European root *per-* or *perk-* meaning 'to hit, to strike'. With the onset of Christianity, Perun was considered to have power equal to the new Christian God, who took his place. At this time, his archenemy Veles, with whom he had an eternal fight, was replaced by the Devil, and hence the duality of this pantheon exists until modern times.

Veles – The God of the Underworld, The Shapeshifter

Veles, or Volos, is the second most important god in the Slavic pantheon. He stands in opposition to Perun and represents a chthonic god. Veles is primarily the God of the Underworld, associated with deep waters, such as seas, oceans, rivers and floods. On the world's oak tree, Veles lives in the lower areas, among the roots.

He is found in the Ruthenian chronicle as *skotiy bog* which also makes him the God of Cattle, protector of the shepherds. In folktales he is outwitted by shepherds such as in the story 'The Devil and Spase the Shepherd' (*see* page 175). As cattle symbolize a family's wealth, he is also known as the God of Wealth.

He has the power to take different shapes, from animals to people, and is known to be the God of Magic, Commerce and Poetry. He is found in the shape of a wolf in the folktale 'The Iron Wolf' (*see* page 64), in the shape of a human in the folktale 'Oh: The Tsar of the Forest' (see page 56), and as the Tsar of the Sea in the folktale 'Vassilissa the Cunning and the Tsar of the Sea' (*see* page 117). His magic can also shapeshift the protagonists of the folktales such as in 'Stribor's Forest' (*see* page 212), where he gives wives the shape of serpents, and 'Oh: The Tsar of the Forest', 'The Biter Bit' (*see* page 108) and 'Silyan the Stork' (*see* page 231), where he shapeshifts heroes of bad morality into birds. He is considered to be a trickster deity, like Loki in the Norse pantheon, relying on sorcery and shamanism.

The popularity of Veles was great in all Slavic tribes, but especially in the south, where cities were named after him, such as the city of Veles in North Macedonia.

The Eternal Fight Between Perun and Veles

Essential to know when understanding the Slavic pantheon is the rivalry between Perun and Veles. As found in the Slavic cosmogonic myth, their conflict might be following the structural pattern of the primordial Indo-European rivalry between Mitra and Varuna in Hindu mythology.

According to Slavic legends, the cosmic battle between Perun and Veles began for two reasons. Perun and Veles each believed that the other had stolen his cattle – Perun because he was the God of Nature and Veles because he was the God of Cattle. In Indo-European mythology, the motif of stealing divine cattle is a common one, since cattle are a symbol of water. And thus Perun believed that Veles was stealing the heavenly water, or rain, from him and taking it to the Underworld.

The second reason for their rivalry was wife-theft. The sun was believed to be Perun's wife, whom Veles steals every night when she sets. And so, with the rising of the sun, Perun would be with his wife for half of the time, and the second half the sun would pass into the Underworld and be with Veles. If we interpret the symbols, we could say that this divine war was happening over the fertilization of the lands (given the divine cattle, the rain, the sun).

Svarog – The God of Fire

Svarog was the God of the Sun, often compared to the Greek god Hephaestus. He was the God of Celestial Fire as seen in the role of the Firebird in the story 'Ivan Tsarevich, the Firebird and the Grey Wolf'. Associated with smithcraft, he is believed to have created the world, and therefore to have created all gods as well. As such, he is considered to be the father of all gods, the original sky god of the Proto-Slavic pantheon.

According to Slavic legends, Svarog is sleeping and the real world we live in is his dream creation. If he awakens, the realm of men will be destroyed. His name is ancient, coming from the root *svar-* meaning 'bright' and *-og* that denotes a place. Svarog was the father of two sons: Svarogich, the God of Fire on Earth, and Dazbog, the God of Fire in the Sky, associated with the sun. Dazbog was worshipped throughout all the Slavic tribes, and Svarogich (a diminutive of Svarog's name) was worshipped by East Slavs, even after Christianization, and by the West Slavs, where he was considered to be the supreme god of the holy city of Radegast. Since Svarog was the predecessor of all gods, Svarogich might only be an epithet, meaning that all gods after Svarog (Perun, Veles, Dazbog, etc.) are all Svarogichs.

Dazbog – The God of Fortune

Dazbog, or Dzbog, the son of Svarog (and hence also known as Svarogich), like his father is known to be a solar deity, associated with fire and rain. In the story 'Vassilissa the Cunning and the Tsar of the Sea' he is an eagle that helps the hero by giving him a golden casket (wealth). He is the life-giver of the crops in the fields and, as food was considered fortune, he was named the God of Fortune. His name translates into *the giving god* ('daz' meaning 'to give' and 'bog' meaning 'god'). In Slavic culture he is the patron of the hearth fire, so people would offer him goods to maintain their fires through harsh winters.

In South Slavic folklore, Dazbog has two sides, one bright and one dark. During the day he is a benevolent deity that carries the sun across the sky in his chariot. During the night, Dazbog is a frightful deity who guards the doors of the Underworld, hence his connection with mining and precious metals.

Zorya – The Goddess of Dusk and Dawn

Acting in the middle area between the day and the night, Zorya is another representative in the Slavic pantheon who holds duality in her being. As Zorya Uternaya, she represents the morning star, the Goddess of Dawn, and was believed to open the doors of heaven every morning to allow the sun to rise. At dusk, she closes the doors, and therefore represents the evening star, or the Goddess of Dusk, when she was called Zorya Vechernaya.

In eastern Slavic tribes, Zorya Uternaya was known as Danica, and was believed to be the sun's sister. For some other tribes Zorya was the sun's mother – it is not always clear. Goddess Zorya is present in the story 'Fisherman Plunk and His Wife' (*see* page 155) as the Dawn-Maiden who helps Plunk on his journey.

Morana – The Goddess of Winter and Death

Morana, or Marzanna, is the Goddess of Winter and Death. She is believed to die along with all crops with the beginning of cold weather, to be reborn again in spring. According to West Slavs she is reborn as the Goddess Lada and becomes Morana again with the onset of the cold weather. This rebirth is depicted in the folktale 'Princess Miranda and Prince Hero' (*see* page 24) in the role of Princess Miranda. Slavs believed that during the last, cold months of the year, Goddess Morana turns into an old, terrible and evil goddess only to die by the end of the year. The majority of them believed that she was reborn on the night of the new year.

Slavic tribes close to Baltic mythology have constructed the myth that Morana was the wife and sister of the fertility and vegetation god Jarilo. In this myth she was the daughter of the sun and he was associated with the moon. They were taught to meet every spring, marry during the summer – hence the good harvest – and split during autumn when Jarilo would leave and go to the Underworld.

Lada – The Goddess of Love and Beauty

Compared to the Roman goddess Venus, Lada was the Goddess of Love and Beauty. She was the patron of weddings, and was believed to offer protection to married couples. Her activities went along with her brother Lado, and for some Slavic people they were considered to be two parts of the same deity. Lada is the Great Goddess or the Mother Goddess in the Slavic pantheon, especially to West Slavs. Similar to the Norse goddess Freya, Lada offers to her worshippers love and fertility.

Mokosh – The Goddess of Fertility

Mokosh, the Goddess of Fertility, was primarily worshipped by the East and South Slavs. For them, she was related to the cult of the Great Mother, and not Goddess Lada. She is the deity to help women give birth and assist them during their domestic duties. She is represented holding a phallus in each hand, as she is also the protector of male potency.

Triglav – The God of Vigilance, Sea and Storms

Triglav, the God of Vigilance, Sea and Storms, had three heads and was believed to have golden lips and eyes that he covered whenever people would sin in order not to see or hear them. The same as Perun, Triglav also is connected to the oak tree; he is believed to live on the upper branches as well. The trinity that he holds by having three heads is believed to combine three gods into one: God of the Sky, God of the Earth and God of the Underworld. Several places hold his name, including Mount Triglav in Slovenia and Trzyglow village in Poland.

Understanding Slavic Mythology

Given the great variety of mythical creatures, cults and beliefs in Slavic mythology, this book is divided into four thematic categories: Figures of Legend and Powerful Beings; Trials, Adventures and Adversity; Explorations of Morality; and Tales of the Uncanny. Each of these categories includes a short introduction that describes the core of the stories in each section, aiming to make it easier for the reader to dive into their meanings.

Unlike other mythologies, such as Greek, Norse, etc., Slavic folktales are stories about common people who have encounters with magic forces helping them in their moral voyages, and thus the main characters do not hold the names of the Slavic pantheon gods or mythical creatures, nor do their helpers. The recognition of the Slavic mythical creatures and deities depends on the reader's awareness of their powers, since their representations in folktales are symbolic.

Ema Lakinska is an associate researcher at the Institute of Macedonian Literature, part of the Ss. Cyril and Methodius University in Skopje, North Macedonia. As an INALCO-Paris alumnus and present PhD candidate, her research work focuses on Macedonian folktales and fairy tales. Her interpretations of literature follow the Jungian and psychoanalytic principle and go into the depths of every story, in order to discover its hidden and mystic meanings and place it closer to the readers.

Figures of Legend
& Powerful Beings

IN SLAVIC FOLKTALES gods and mythical creatures are present in a different form than the one we know of from the primordial myths. It is this metamorphosis that makes the folktales magical – and the trail exciting – since one character can personify more than one god or creature.

Such is the case with Princess Miranda, in the tale 'Princess Miranda and Prince Hero' (*see* page 24). She personifies the Goddess Morana in the beginning of the story when she turns all suitors into ice, and Goddess Lada later in the story when she finds Prince Hero. The eternal fight of good and bad is present in the folktale, with Kosciey, the king of the underground realm, actualizing aspects of Veles, the God of the Underworld, and Prince Hero actualizing aspects of Perun, the God of Thunder. This plurality of gods and mythical creatures in one story is visible in all the stories in this category. And so, the journey begins...

Princess Miranda and Prince Hero
(Polish)

FAR AWAY, IN THE WIDE OCEAN, there was once a green island where lived the most beautiful princess in the world, named Miranda. She had lived there ever since her birth, and was queen of the island. Nobody knew who were her parents, or how she had come there. But she was not alone; for there were twelve beautiful maidens, who had grown up with her on the island, and were her ladies-in-waiting.

But a few strangers had visited the island, and spoken of the princess's great beauty; and many more came in time, and became her subjects, and built a magnificent city, in which she had a splendid palace of white marble to live in.

And in the course of time a great many young princes came to woo her. But she did not care to marry any of them; and if anyone persisted, and tried to compel her by force to be his wife, she could turn him and all his soldiers into ice, by merely fixing her eyes upon them.

One day the wicked Kosciey, the king of the Underground realm, came out into the upper world and began to gaze all round it with his telescope. Various empires and kingdoms passed in review before him; and at last he saw the green island, and the rich city upon it; and the marble palace in this city, and in this palace the twelve beautiful young ladies-of-honour, and among them he beheld, lying on a rich couch of swansdown, the Princess Miranda asleep. She slept like an innocent child, but she was dreaming of a young knight, wearing a golden helmet, on a gallant steed, and carrying an invisible mace, that fought of itself…and she loved him better than life.

Kosciey looked at her; he was delighted with her beauty; he struck the earth three times and stood upon the green island.

Princess Miranda called together her brave army and led them into the field, to fight the wicked Kosciey. But he, blowing on them with his poisonous breath, sent them all fast asleep, and he was just going to lay hands upon the princess, when she, throwing a glance of scorn at him, changed him into a lump of ice and fled to her capital.

Kosciey did not long remain ice. So soon as the princess was away, he freed himself from the power of her glance, and regaining his usual form, followed her to her city. Then he sent all the inhabitants of the island to sleep, and among them the princess's twelve faithful damsels.

She was the only one whom he could not injure; but being afraid of her glances, he surrounded the castle – which stood upon a high hill – with an iron rampart, and placed a dragon with twelve heads on guard before the gate, and waited for the princess to give herself up of her own accord.

The days passed by, then weeks, then months, while her kingdom became a desert; all her people were asleep, and her faithful soldiers also lay sleeping on the open fields, their steel armour all rusted, and wild plants were growing over them undisturbed. Her twelve maidens were all asleep in different rooms of the palace, just where they happened to be at the time; and she herself, all alone, kept walking sadly to and fro in a little room up in a tower, where she had taken refuge – wringing her white hands, weeping, and her bosom heaving with sighs.

Around her all were silent, as though dead; only every now and then, Kosciey, not daring to encounter her angry glance, knocked at the door asking her to surrender, promising to make her queen of his Underground realm. But it was all of no use; the princess was silent, and only threatened him with her looks.

But, grieving in her lonely prison, Princess Miranda could not forget the lover of whom she had been dreaming; she saw him just as he had appeared to her in her dream.

And she looked up with her blue eyes to heaven, and seeing a cloud floating by, she said:

"O cloud! through the bright sky flying!
Stay, and hearken my piteous sighing!
In my sorrow I call upon thee;
Oh! where is my loved one? say!
Oh! where do his footsteps stray?
And does he now think of me?"

"I know not," the cloud replied. "Ask the wind."

And she looked out into the wide plain, and seeing how the wind was blowing freely, she said:

"O wind! o'er the wide world flying!
Do thou pity my grief and crying!
Have pity on me!
Oh! where is my loved one? say!
Oh! where do his footsteps stray?
And does he now think of me?"

"Ask the stars," the wind replied; "they know more than I do."
So she cried to the stars:

"O stars! with your bright beams glowing!
Look down on my tears fast flowing!
Have pity, have pity on me!
Oh! where is my loved one? say!
Oh! where do his footsteps stray?
And does he now think of me?"

"Ask the moon," said the stars; "who being nearer to the earth, knows more of what happens there than we do."

So she said to the moon:

"Bright moon, as your watch you keep,
From the starry skies, o'er this land of sleep,
Look down now, and pity me!
Oh! where is my loved one? say!
Where? where do his footsteps stray?
And does he now think of me?"

"I know nothing about your loved one, princess," replied the moon; "but here comes the sun, who will surely be able to tell you."

And the sun rose up in the dawn, and at noontide stood just over the princess's tower, and she said:

"Thou soul of the world! bright sun!
Look on me, in this prison undone!
Have pity on me!
Oh! where is my loved one? say!
Through what lands do his footsteps stray?
And does he now think of me?"

"Princess Miranda," said the sun; "dry your tears, comfort your heart; your lover is hastening to you, from the bottom of the deep sea, from under the coral reefs; he has won the enchanted ring; when he puts it on his finger, his army will increase by thousands, regiment after regiment, with horse and foot; the drums are beating, the sabres gleaming, the colours flying, the cannon roaring, they are bearing down on the empire of Kosciey. But he cannot conquer him by force of mortal weapons. I will teach him a surer way; and there is good hope that he will be able to deliver you from Kosciey, and save your country. I will hasten to your prince. Farewell."

The sun stood over a wide country, beyond the deep seas, beyond high mountains, where Prince Hero in a golden helmet, on a gallant horse, was drawing up his army, and preparing to march against Kosciey, the besieger of the fair princess. He had seen her three times in a dream, and had heard much about her, for her beauty was famous throughout the world.

"Dismiss your army," said the sun. "No army can conquer Kosciey, no bullet can reach him; you can only free Princess Miranda by killing him, and how you are to do it, you must learn from the old woman Jandza; I can only tell you where you will find the horse, that must carry you to her. Go hence towards the East; you will come to a green meadow, in which there are three oak trees; and among them you will find hidden in the ground an iron door, with a brazen padlock; behind this door you will find a battle charger, and a mace; the rest you will learn afterwards; ...farewell!"

Prince Hero was most surprised; but he took off his enchanted ring and threw it into the sea; with it all his great army vanished directly into mist, leaving no trace behind. He turned to the East and travelled onwards.

After three days he came to the green meadow, where he found the three oak trees, and the iron door, as he had been told. It opened upon a narrow, crooked stairway, going downwards, leading into a deep dungeon, where he found another iron door, closed by a heavy iron padlock. Behind this he heard a horse neighing, so loudly that it made the door fall to the ground, and at the same moment eleven other doors flew open and there came out a war-horse, which had been shut up there for ages by a wizard.

The prince whistled to the horse; the horse tugged at his fastenings and broke twelve chains by which he had been fettered. He had eyes like stars, flaming nostrils, and a mane like a thunder-cloud...he was a horse of horses, the wonder of the world.

"Prince Hero!" said the horse, "I have long waited for such a rider as you, and I am ready to serve you forever. Mount on my back, take that mace in your hand, which you see hanging to the saddle; you need not fight with it yourself, for it will strike wherever you command it, and beat a whole army. I know the way everywhere; tell me where you want to go, and you will presently be there."

The prince told him everything, took the self-fighting mace in his hand, and sprang on his back.

The horse reared, snorted, spurned the ground, and they flew over mountains and forests, higher than the flying clouds, over rapid rivers, and deep seas; but when they flew along the ground the charger's light feet never trampled down a blade of grass, nor raised an atom of dust on the sandy soil.

Before sunset Prince Hero had reached the primeval forest in which the old woman Jandza lived.

He was amazed at the size and age of the mighty oaks, pine trees and firs, where there reigned a perpetual twilight. And there was absolute silence – not a leaf or a blade of grass stirring; and no living thing, not so much as a bird, or the hum of an insect; only amidst this grave-like stillness the sound of his horse's hoofs.

The prince stopped before a little house, supported on crooked legs, and said:

"Little house, move
On your crooked legs free:

Turn your back to the wood,
And your front to me."

The house turned round, with the door towards him; the prince went in, and the old woman Jandza asked him, "How did you get here, Prince Hero, where no living soul has penetrated till now?"

"Don't ask me; but welcome your guest politely."

So the old woman gave the prince food and drink, made up a soft bed for him to rest on after his journey, and left him for the night.

Next morning he told her all, and what he had come for.

"You have undertaken a great and splendid task, prince; so I will tell you how to kill Kosciey. In the Ocean-Sea, on the island of Everlasting Life, there is an old oak tree; under this tree is buried a coffer bound with iron; in this coffer is a hare; under the hare sits a grey duck; this duck carries within her an egg; and in this egg is enclosed the life of Kosciey. When you break the egg he will die at once. Now goodbye, prince; and good luck go with you; your horse will show you the way."

The prince got on horseback, and they soon left the forest behind them, and came to the shore of the ocean.

On the beach was a fisherman's net, and in the net was a great fish, who when he saw the prince, cried out piteously, "Prince Hero! take me out of the net, and throw me back into the sea; I will repay you!"

The prince took the fish out of the net and threw it into the sea; it splashed in the water and vanished.

The prince looked over the sea and saw the island in the grey distance, far, far away; but how was he to get there? He leaned upon his mace, deep in thought.

"What are you thinking of, prince?" asked the horse.

"I am thinking how I am to get to the island, when I cannot swim over that breadth of sea."

"Sit on my back, prince, and hold fast."

So the prince sat firm on the horse's back and held fast by the thick mane; a wind arose, and the sea was somewhat rough; but rider and horse pushed on, through the billows, and at last came to shore on the island of Everlasting Life.

The prince took off his horse's bridle, and let him loose to feed in a meadow of luxuriant grass, and walked on quickly to a high hill, where grew the old oak tree. Taking it in both hands, he tugged at it; the oak resisted all his efforts; he tugged again, the oak began to creak, and moved a little; he mustered all his strength, and tugged again. The oak fell with a crash to the ground, with its roots uppermost, and there, where they had stood firmly fixed so many hundred years, was a deep hole.

Looking down he saw the iron-bound coffer; he fetched it up, broke open the lock with a stone, raised the lid, picked up the hare lying in it by its ears; but at that moment the duck, which had been sitting under the hare, took the alarm, and flew off straight to sea.

The prince fired a shot after her; the bullet hit the duck; she gave one loud quack and fell; but in that same instant the egg fell from her – down to the bottom of the sea. The prince gave a cry of despair; but just then a great fish came swimming, dived down to the depths of the sea, and coming to the shore, with the egg in its jaws, left it on the sand.

The fish swam away; but the prince, taking up the egg, mounted his horse once more; and they swam till they reached Princess Miranda's island, where they saw a great iron wall stretching all round her white marble palace.

There was only one entrance through this iron wall to the palace, and before this lay the monstrous dragon with the twelve heads, six of which kept guard alternately; when the one half-slept, the other six remained awake. If anyone were to approach the gate he could not escape the horrid jaws. Nobody could hurt the dragon; for he could only suffer death by his own act.

The prince stood on the hill before that gate and commanded his self-fighting mace, which also had the faculty of becoming invisible, to go and clear his entrance to the palace.

The invisible, self-fighting mace fell upon the dragon and began to thunder on all his heads with such force that all his eyes became bloodshot, and he began to hiss fiercely; he shook his twelve heads and stretched wide his twelve horrid jaws; he spread out his forest of claws; but this helped him not at all, the mace kept on smiting him, moving about so fast, that not a single head escaped, but could only hiss, groan, and shriek wildly! Now it had given a thousand blows, the blood gushed from a thousand wounds, and there was no help for the dragon; he raged, writhed about, and shrieked in despair; finally, as blow followed blow, and he could not see who gave them, he gnashed his teeth, belched forth flame, and at length turned his claws upon himself, plunging them deep into his own flesh, struggled, writhed, twisted himself round, and in and out; his blood flowed freely from his wounds...and now it was all over with the dragon.

The prince, seeing this, went into the courtyard of the palace, put his horse into the stable, and went up by a winding stair towards the tower, whence the Princess Miranda, having seen him, addressed him:

"Welcome, Prince Hero! I saw how you disposed of the dragon; but do be careful, for my enemy, Kosciey, is in this palace; he is most powerful, both through his own strength and through his sorceries; and if he kills you I can live no longer."

"Princess Miranda, do not trouble about me. I have the life of Kosciey in this egg." Then he called out, "Invisible self-fighting mace, go into the palace and beat Kosciey."

The mace bestirred itself quickly, battered in the iron doors, and set upon Kosciey; it smote him on the neck, till he crouched all together, the sparks flew from his eyes, and there was a noise of so many mills in his ears.

If he had been an ordinary mortal it would have been all over with him at once; as it was, he was horribly tormented and puzzled – feeling all these blows, and never seeing whence they came. He sprang about, raved, and raged, till the whole island resounded with his roaring.

At last he looked through the window, and behold there he saw Prince Hero. "Ah! that is all your doing!" he exclaimed and sprang out into the courtyard, to rush straight at him and beat him to a jelly! But the prince held the egg in one hand ready; and he squeezed it so hard that the shell cracked and the yolk and the white were all spilled together...and Kosciey fell lifeless!

And with the death of the enchanter all his charms were dissolved at once; all the people in the island who were asleep woke up and began to stir. The soldiers woke from sleep, and the drums began to beat; they formed their ranks, massed themselves in order, and began to march towards the palace.

And in the palace there was great joy; for Princess Miranda came towards the prince, gave him her white hand, and thanked him warmly. They went to the throne-room, and following the princess's example, her twelve waiting-maids paired off with twelve young officers of the army, and the couples grouped themselves round the throne, on which the prince and princess were sitting.

And then a priest, arrayed in all his vestments, came in at the open door, and the prince and princess exchanged rings and were married.

And all the other couples were married at the same time, and after the wedding there was a feast, dancing, and music, which it is a pleasure to think of. Everywhere there was rejoicing.

The Wood-Lady
(Czech)

BETTY WAS A LITTLE GIRL. Her mother was a widow, and she had no more of her property left than a dilapidated cottage and two she-goats. But Betty was, nevertheless, always cheerful. From spring to autumn she pastured the goats in the birch-wood. Whenever she went from home, her mother always gave her in a basket a slice of bread and a spindle, with the injunction, "Let it be full." As she had no distaff, she used to twine the flax round her head. Betty took the basket and skipped off singing merrily after the goats to the birch-wood. When she got there, the goats went after pasture, and Betty sat under a tree, drew the fibres from her head with her left hand, and let down the spindle with her right so that it just hummed over the ground, and therewith she sang till the wood echoed; the goats meanwhile pastured.

When the sun indicated midday, she put aside her spindle, called the goats, and after giving them each a morsel of bread that they mightn't stray from her, bounded into the wood for a few strawberries or any other woodland fruit that might happen to be just then in season, that she might have dessert to her bread. When she had finished her meal, she sprang up, folded her hands, danced and sang. The sun smiled on her through the green foliage, and the goats, enjoying themselves among the grass, thought, "What a merry shepherdess we have!" After her dance, she spun again industriously, and at even when she drove the goats home, her mother never scolded her for bringing back her spindle empty.

Once, when according to custom, exactly at midday, after her scanty dinner, she was getting ready for a dance, all of a sudden – where she came, there she came – a very beautiful maiden stood before her. She had on a white dress as fine as gossamer, golden-coloured hair flowed from her head to her waist, and on her head she wore a garland of woodland flowers. Betty was struck dumb with astonishment. The maiden smiled at her and said in an attractive voice, "Betty, are you fond of dancing?" When the maiden spoke so prettily to her, Betty's terror quitted her, and she answered, "Oh, I should like to dance all day long!" "Come, then, let's dance together. I'll teach you!" So spoke the maiden, tucked her dress up on one side, took Betty by the waist, and began to dance with her. As they circled, such delightful music sounded over their heads, that Betty's heart skipped within her. The musicians sat on the branches of the birches in black, ash-coloured, brown, and variegated coats. It was a company of choice musicians that had come together at the beck of the beautiful maiden – nightingales, larks, linnets, goldfinches, greenfinches, thrushes, blackbirds, and a very skilful mockingbird. Betty's cheek flamed, her eyes glittered, she forgot her task and her goats, and only gazed at her partner, who twirled before and round her with the most charming movements, and so lightly that the grass didn't even bend beneath her delicate foot. They danced from noon till eve, and Betty's feet were neither wearied nor painful. Then the beautiful maiden stopped, the music ceased, and as she came so she disappeared.

Betty looked about her; the sun was setting behind the wood. She clapped her hands on the top of her head, and, feeling the unspun flax, remembered that her spindle, which was lying on the grass, was by no means full. She took the flax down from her head, and put it with the spindle into her basket, called the goats, and drove them home. She did not sing on the way, but bitterly reproached herself for letting the beautiful maiden delude her, and determined that if the maiden should come to her again, she would never listen to her anymore. The goats, hearing no merry song behind them, looked round to see whether their own shepherdess was really following them. Her mother, too, wondered, and asked her daughter whether she was ill, as she didn't sing. "No, mother dear, I'm not ill, but my throat is dry from very singing, and therefore I don't sing," said Betty in excuse, and went to put away the spindle and the unspun flax. Knowing that her mother was not in the habit of reeling up the yarn at once, she intended to make up the next day what she had neglected to do the first day, and therefore did not say a word to her mother about the beautiful maiden.

The next day Betty again drove the goats as usual to the birch-wood and sang to herself again merrily. On arriving at the birch-wood the goats began to pasture, and she sat under the tree and began to spin industriously, singing to herself all the time, for work comes better from the hand while one sings. The sun indicated midday. Betty gave each of the goats a morsel of bread, went off for strawberries, and after returning began to eat her dinner and chatter with the goats. "Ah, my little goats, I mustn't dance today," sighed she, when after dinner she collected the crumbs from her lap in her hand and placed them on a stone that the birds might take them away. "And why mustn't you?" spoke a pleasing voice, and the beautiful maiden stood beside her, as if she had dropped from the clouds. Betty was still more frightened than the first time, and she closed her eyes that she might not even see the maiden. But when the maiden repeated the question, she answered modestly, "Excuse me, beautiful lady, I can't dance with you, because I should again fail to perform my task of spinning, and my mother would scold me. Today, before the sun sets, I must make up what I left undone yesterday." "Only come and dance – before the sun sets help will be found for you," said the maiden, tucked up her dress, and took Betty round the waist. The musicians sitting on the birch branches struck up, and the two dancers began to whirl. The beautiful maiden danced still more enchantingly. Betty couldn't take her eyes off her, and forgot the goats and her task. At last the dancer stopped, the music ceased, the sun was on the verge of setting. Betty clapped her hand on the top of her head, where the unspun flax was twined, and began to cry. The beautiful maiden put her hand on her head, took off the flax, twined it round the stem of a slender birch, seized the spindle, and began to spin. The spindle just swung over the surface of the ground, grew fuller before her eyes, and before the sun set behind the wood all the yarn was spun, as well as that which Betty had not finished the day before. While giving the full spool into the girl's hand the beautiful maiden said, "Reel, and grumble not – remember my words, 'Reel, and grumble not!'" After these words she vanished, as if the ground had sunk in beneath her. Betty was content, and thought on her way, "If she is so good and kind, I will dance with her again if she comes again." She sang again that the goats might step on merrily. But her mother gave her no cheerful welcome. Wishing in the course of the day to reel the yarn, she saw that the spindle was not full, and was therefore out of humour. "What were you doing yesterday that you didn't finish your task?" asked her mother reprovingly. "Pardon, mother, I danced a little too long," said Betty humbly, and, showing her mother the spindle, added, "Today it is more than full to make up for it." Her mother said no more, but went to milk the goats, and Betty put the spindle away. She wished to tell her mother of her adventure but bethought herself again. "No, not unless she comes again, and then I will ask her what kind of person she is, and will tell my mother." So she made up her mind and held her tongue.

The third morning, as usual, she drove the goats to the birch-wood. The goats began to pasture; Betty sat under the tree, and began to sing and spin. The sun indicated midday. Betty laid her spindle on the grass, gave each of the goats a morsel of bread, collected strawberries, ate her dinner, and while giving the crumbs to the birds, said, "My little goats, I will dance to you today!" She jumped up, folded her hands, and was just going to try whether she could manage to dance as prettily as the beautiful maiden, when all at once she herself stood before her. "Let's go together, together!" said she to Betty, seized her round the waist, and at the same moment the music struck up over their heads, and the maidens circled round with flying step. Betty forgot her spindle and her goats, saw nothing but the beautiful maiden, whose body bent in every direction like a willow-wand, and thought of nothing but the delightful music, in tune with which her feet bounded of their own accord. They danced from midday till even. Then the maiden stopped, and the music ceased. Betty looked round; the sun was behind the wood. With tears she clasped her hands on the top of her head and, turning in search of the half-empty spindle, lamented about what her mother would say to her. "Give me your basket," said the beautiful maiden. "I will make up to you for what you have left undone today." Betty handed her the basket, and the maiden disappeared for a moment, and afterwards handed Betty the basket again, saying, "Not now – look at it at home," and was gone, as if the wind had blown her away.

Betty was afraid to peep into the basket immediately, but half-way home she couldn't restrain herself. The basket was as light as if there was just nothing in it. She couldn't help looking to see whether the maiden hadn't tricked her. And how frightened she was when she saw that the basket was full – of birch leaves! Then, and not till then, did she begin to weep and lament that she had been so credulous. In anger she threw out two handfuls of leaves, and was going to shake the basket out; but then she bethought herself, "I will use them as litter for the goats," and left some leaves in the basket. She was almost afraid to go home. The goats again could hardly recognize their shepherdess. Her mother was waiting for her on the threshold, full of anxiety. "For Heaven's sake, girl! what sort of spool did you bring me home yesterday?" were her first words. "Why?" asked Betty anxiously. "When you went out in the morning, I went to reel. I reeled and reeled, and the spool still remained full. One skein, two, three skeins; the spool still full. 'What evil spirit has spun it?' said I in a temper; and that instant the yarn vanished from the spindle, as if it were spirited away. Tell me what the meaning of this is!" Then Betty confessed, and began to tell about the beautiful maiden.

"That was a wood-lady!" cried her mother in astonishment. "About midday and midnight the wood-ladies hold their dances. Lucky that you are not a boy, or you wouldn't have come out of her arms alive. She would have danced with you as long as there was breath in your body, or have tickled you to death. But they have compassion on girls, and often give them rich presents. It's a pity that you didn't tell me; if I hadn't spoken in a temper, I might have had a room full of yarn." Then Betty bethought herself of the basket, and it occurred to her that perhaps, after all, there might have been something under those leaves. She took out the spindle and unspun flax from the top and looked once more, and – "See, mother!" she cried out. Her mother looked and clapped her hands. The birch-leaves were turned into gold! "She ordered me: 'Don't look now, but at home!' but I did not obey." "Lucky that you didn't empty out the whole basket," thought her mother.

The next morning she went herself to look at the place where Betty had thrown out the two handfuls of leaves, but on the road there lay nothing but fresh birch-leaves. But the riches that Betty had brought home were large enough. Her mother bought a small estate; they had many cattle. Betty had handsome clothes and was not obliged to pasture goats; but whatever she had, however cheerful and happy she was, nothing ever gave her so great delight as the dance with the wood-lady. She often went to the birch-wood; she was attracted there. She hoped for the good fortune of seeing the beautiful maiden, but she never set eyes on her more.

Reygoch
(Croatian)

I

ONCE UPON A BEAUTIFUL SUMMER NIGHT, the men were watching their horses in the meadow. And as they watched, they fell asleep. And as they slept, the fairies flew out of the clouds to have some sport with the horses, as is the fairies' way. Each fairy caught a horse, mounted it, and then whipped it with her golden hair, urging it round and round the dewy meadow.

Among the fairies there was one quite young and tiny, called Curlylocks, who had come down to earth from the clouds for the first time that night.

Curlylocks thought it lovely to ride through the night like a whirlwind. And it so happened that she had got hold of the most spirited horse of all – a Black – small, but fierce as fire. The Black galloped round and round with the other horses, but he was the swiftest of all. Soon he was all in a lather of foam.

But Curlylocks wanted to ride faster still. She bent down and pinched the Black's right ear. The horse started, reared, and then bolted straight ahead, leaving behind the rest of the horses, the meadow and all, as he flew away like the wind with Curlylocks into the wide, wide world.

Curlylocks thoroughly enjoyed her lightning ride. The Black went like the wind, by field and by river, by meadow and mountain, over dale and hill. "Good gracious! what a lot of things there are in the world!" thought Curlylocks, full of delight as she looked at all the pretty sights. But what pleased her best was when they came through a country where there were mountains all covered with glorious forests, and at the foot of the mountains two golden fields like two great gold kerchiefs, and in the midst of them two white villages, like two white doves, and a little further on a great sheet of water.

But the Black would not stop, neither there nor anywhere, but rushed on and on as if he were possessed.

So the Black carried Curlylocks far and far away till at last they came to a great plain, with a cold wind blowing over it. The Black galloped into the plain, and there was nothing there but yellow sand, neither trees nor grass, and the further they went into that great waste, the colder it grew. But how large that plain is, I cannot tell you, for the good reason that the man does not live who could cross it.

The Black ran on with Curlylocks for seven days and seven nights. The seventh day, just before sunrise, they reached the centre of the plain, and in the centre of the plain they found the ruinous walls of the terribly great city of Frosten, and there it is always bitterly cold.

As the Black raced up to the ancient gates of Frosten, Curlylocks threw her magic veil on the wall, and so caught hold of the wall. The Black galloped away from under her, and so continued his wild career up to his old age to and fro between the huge walls of Frosten, till at last he found the northern gate and galloped out again into the plain – God knows whither!

But Curlylocks came down from the wall and began to walk about the city, and it was cold as cold! Her magic veil, without which she could not fly among the clouds, she wound about her shoulders, for she took great care of it. And so Curlylocks walked and walked about the city of Frosten, and all the time she felt as if she must come upon something very wonderful in this city, which was so marvellous and so great. However, nothing did she see but only great crumbling walls, and nothing did she hear but now and again a stone cracking with the cold.

Suddenly, just as Curlylocks had turned the corner of the very biggest wall, she saw, fast asleep at the foot of the wall, a huge man, bigger than the biggest oak in the biggest forest. The man was dressed in a huge cloak of coarse linen, and the strap he wore for a belt was five fathoms long. His head was as big as the biggest barrel, and his beard was like a shock of corn. He was so big, that man, you might have thought there was a church tower fallen down beside the wall!

This giant was called Reygoch, and he lived at Frosten. All he did was count the stones of the city of Frosten. He could never have finished counting them but for that huge head of his, as big as a barrel. But he counted and counted – he had counted for a thousand years and had already counted thirty walls and five gates of the city.

When Curlylocks spied Reygoch, she clasped her hands and wondered. She never thought there could be such an immense creature in the world.

So Curlylocks sat down by Reygoch's ear (and Reygoch's ear was as big as the whole of Curlylocks), and called down his ear, "Aren't you cold, daddy?"

Reygoch woke up, laughed, and looked at Curlylocks. "Cold? I should think I was cold," answered Reygoch, and his voice was as deep as distant thunder. Reygoch's big nose was all red with the cold, and his hair and beard were all thick with hoar-frost.

"Dear me!" said Curlylocks, "you're such a big man, and you aren't going to build yourself a roof to keep out of the cold?"

"Why should I?" said Reygoch, and he laughed again. "The sun will be out presently."

Reygoch heaved himself up so as to sit. He sat up. He clapped his left shoulder with his right hand, and his right shoulder he clapped with the left hand, so as to beat out the hoar-frost; and the hoar-frost came off each shoulder as if it were snow slipping off a roof!

"Look out! look out, daddy! you'll smother me!" cried Curlylocks. But Reygoch could scarcely hear her, because it was a long way from Curlylocks to his ear, so big was he when he sat up.

So Reygoch lifted Curlylocks onto his shoulder, told her his name and his business, and she told him how she had come.

"And here comes the sun," said Reygoch, and he pointed for Curlylocks to see.

Curlylocks looked, and there was the sun rising, but so pale and feeble, as if there were no one for him to warm.

"Well, you are silly, Reygoch!" said Curlylocks. "`you are really silly to live here and spend your life counting these tiresome stones of Frosten. Come along, Reygoch, and see how beautiful the world is, and find something more sensible to do."

Now it had never occurred to Reygoch to want a finer home for himself than Frosten city, nor had he ever thought that there might be better work than his in the world. Reygoch always thought, "I was meant to count the stones of Frosten," and had never asked for anything better.

Curlylocks, however, gave him no peace, but persuaded him to come out and see the world with her.

"I'll take you to a lovely country," said Curlylocks, "where there is an ancient forest, and beside the forest two golden fields."

Curlylocks talked for a long time. And old Reygoch had never had anybody to talk to, and so he couldn't resist persuasion.

"Well, let's go!" said he.

Curlylocks was mightily pleased with this.

But now they had to contrive something, so that Reygoch could carry Curlylocks, because Reygoch himself had nothing.

So Curlylocks drew out from her bosom a little bag of pearls. It was her mother who had given Curlylocks these pearls before allowing her to go down to earth, and she had told her, "If you ever should need anything, just throw down a pearl, and it will turn into whatever you want. Be very careful of those pearls, because there are so many things in the world that you will want more and more as you go on."

Curlylocks took out a tiny seed-pearl, threw it down, and lo, before their eyes there grew a little basket, just as big as Curlylocks, and the basket had a loop attached, just big enough to fit Reygoch's ear.

Curlylocks jumped into the basket; and Reygoch picked up the basket and hung it on his ear like an earring!

Whenever Reygoch laughed, whenever he sneezed or shook his head, Curlylocks rocked as if she were in a swing; and she thought it a capital way of travelling.

So Reygoch started to walk, and had already taken a ten-yard stride, when Curlylocks stopped him and begged, "Couldn't we go underground, perhaps, Reygoch dear, so that I might see what there is under the earth?"

"Why not?" answered Reygoch; for he could break into the earth as easy as fun, only it had never entered his head to look what might be underground.

But Curlylocks wanted to know everything about everything, and so they agreed to travel underground until they should arrive under the forest by the golden fields, and there they would come up.

When they had settled that, Reygoch began to break up the earth. He lifted up his great feet and stamped for the first time, and at that the whole of the great city of Frosten shook and a great many walls tumbled down. Reygoch raised his feet a second time and stamped again, and the whole plain quaked. Reygoch raised his feet a third time and stamped, and lo, half the world trembled, the solid earth gaped under Reygoch, and Reygoch and Curlylocks fell into the hole and down under the earth.

When they got there, they found the earth all honeycombed with pillars and passages on every side, and heaven alone knew where they all led to. And they could hear waters rushing and the moaning of the winds.

They followed one of the passages, and for a while they had light from the hole through which they had fallen. But as they went on it grew darker and darker – black darkness, such as there is nowhere save in the bowels of the earth.

Reygoch tramped calmly on in the dark. With his great hands he felt his way from pillar to pillar.

But Curlylocks was frightened by the great darkness.

She clung to Reygoch's ear and cried, "It's dark, Reygoch dear!"

"Well, and why not?" returned Reygoch. "The dark didn't come to us. It's we have come to it."

Then Curlylocks got cross, because Reygoch never minded anything and she had expected great things from so huge a man.

"I should be in a nice fix with you but for my pearls," said Curlylocks quite angrily.

Then she threw down another pearl, and a tiny lantern grew in her hand, bright as if it were lit with gold. The darkness crept back deeper into the earth, and the light shone far through the underground passages.

Curlylocks was delighted with her lantern, because it showed up all the marvels which had been swallowed by the earth in days of old. In one place she saw lordly castles, with doors and windows all fretted with gold and framed in red marble. In another place were warriors' weapons, slender-barrelled muskets and heavy scimitars studded with gems and precious stones. In a third place she saw long-buried treasures, golden dishes and silver goblets full of gold ducats, and the Emperor's very crown of gold three times refined. All these treasures had been swallowed up by God's will, and it is God's secret why so much treasure should lie there undisturbed.

But Curlylocks was quite dazzled with all these marvels; and instead of going straight ahead by the way they had settled upon, she begged Reygoch to put her down so that she might play about a little and admire all the strange things and gaze upon the wonders of God's secret.

So Reygoch set Curlylocks down, and Curlylocks took her little lantern and ran to the castles, and to the weapons, and to the treasure-hoards. And lest she might lose her little bag of pearls while she was playing, she laid it down beside a pillar.

As for Reygoch, he sat down to rest not far off.

Curlylocks began to play with the treasures; she looked at the beautiful things and rummaged among them. With her tiny hands she scattered the golden ducats, examined the goblets chased in silver, and put upon her head the crown of gold three times refined. She played about, looked round and admired, and at last caught sight of a very slender little ivory staff propped up against a mighty pillar.

But it was just that slender staff that kept the mighty pillar from collapsing, because the pillar was already completely hollowed out by the water. And therefore God had caused that little staff to fall down there, and the staff held up the pillar under the earth.

But Curlylocks wondered, "Why is that little staff just there?" And she went and picked up the staff to look at it.

But no sooner had Curlylocks taken the staff and moved it than the subterranean passages re-echoed with a terrible rumbling noise. The great pillar trembled, swayed and crashed down amid a whole mountain of falling earth, closing and blocking up the path between Reygoch and Curlylocks. They could neither see nor hear one another, nor could they reach one another...

There was the poor little fairy Curlylocks caught in the bowels of the earth! She was buried alive in that vast grave, and perhaps would never again see those golden fields for which she had set out, and all because she would not go straight on by the way they had intended, but would loiter and turn aside to the right and to the left to pry into God's secrets!

Curlylocks wept and cried, and tried to get to Reygoch. But she found that there was no way through, and that her plight was hopeless; and as for the bag of pearls, which might have helped her, it was buried under the landslide.

When Curlylocks realised this she stopped crying, for she was proud, and she thought, "There is no help for it, and I must die. Reygoch won't come to my rescue, because his wits are too slow even to help himself, let alone to make him remember to help me. So there is nothing for it, and I must die."

So Curlylocks prepared for death. But in case folk should ever find her in her grave she wanted them to know that she came of royal blood. So she set the crown of gold three times refined upon her head, took the ivory staff in her hand, and lay down to die. There was no one beside Curlylocks except her little lantern, burning as if it were lit with gold; and as Curlylocks began to grow cold and stiff, so the lantern burned low and dim.

Reygoch was really an old simpleton. When the pillar crashed down and there was the big landslide between him and Curlylocks he never moved, but sat still in the dark. Thus he sat for quite a long time, before it occurred to him to go and find out what had happened.

He felt his way in the dark to the spot where Curlylocks had been, groped about, and realised that the earth had subsided there and that the passage was indeed blocked.

"Eh, but that way is choked up now," considered Reygoch. And nothing else could he think of, but turned round, left the mound of fallen earth and Curlylocks beyond it, and went back by the road they had travelled from Frosten city.

* * *

Thus old Reygoch went his way, pillar by pillar. He had already gone a goodish bit; but there was all the time something worrying him. Reygoch himself couldn't imagine what it was that worried him.

He arranged the strap around his waist – perhaps it had been too tight; and then he stretched his arm – perhaps his arm had gone to sleep. Yet it was neither the one nor the other, but something else that worried him. Reygoch wondered what in the world it could be. He wondered, and as he wondered he shook his head.

And as Reygoch shook his head, the little basket swung at his ear. And when Reygoch felt how light the basket was, and that there was no Curlylocks inside, a bitter pang shot through his heart and breast, and – simpleton though he was – he knew well enough that he was grieved because he missed Curlylocks, and he realised also that he ought to save her.

It had taken Reygoch a lot of trouble to think out all that; but once he had thought it out, he turned like the wind and flew back to the place where the landslide was, to find Curlylocks behind the heap of earth. He flew, and he arrived just in time. Reygoch burrowed away with both hands, and in a little while he had burrowed a big hole, so that he could see Curlylocks lying there, the crown of fine gold on her head. She was already growing cold and rigid, with her little lantern beside her, and the flame of it as feeble as the tiniest little glow-worm.

If Reygoch had cried out in his grief the earth would have rocked, and the little lantern would have gone out altogether – even the little glow-worm light by the side of Curlylocks would have died away.

But Reygoch's throat was all tight with pain, so that he could not cry out. He put out his great big hand and gently picked up poor Curlylocks, who was already quite cold, and warmed her between the hollowed palms of his huge hands as you would warm a starved dicky-bird in winter. And lo! in a little while Curlylocks moved her little head, and at once the lantern burned a little brighter; and then Curlylocks moved her arm, and the lantern burned brighter still. At last Curlylocks opened her eyes, and the lantern burned as brightly as if its flame were pure gold!

Then Curlylocks jumped to her feet, caught hold of Reygoch's beard, and they both of them cried for pure joy. Reygoch's tears were as big as pears and Curlylocks' as tiny as millet-seed, but except for size they were both the same sort; and from that moment these two were mightily fond of one another.

When they had finished their cry, Curlylocks found her pearls, and then they went on. But they touched no more of the things they saw underground, neither the sunken ships with their hoards of treasure, which had worked their way down from the bottom of the sea, nor the red coral, nor the yellow amber which twined round the underground pillars. They touched nothing, but went straight along by the way that would take them to the golden fields.

When they had gone on thus for a long time, Curlylocks asked Reygoch to hold her up; and when he did so, Curlylocks took a handful of earth from above her head.

She took the earth, looked at her hand, and there, among the soil, she found leaves and fibres.

"Here we are, daddy, under the forest beside the golden fields," said Curlylocks. "Let's hurry up and get out."

So Reygoch stretched himself and began to break through the earth with his head.

II

And indeed they were under the forest, just underneath a wooded glen between the two villages and the two counties. No one ever came to this glen but the herd boys and girls from both villages and both counties.

Now there was bitter strife between the two villages – strife over the threshing-floors, and the pastures, and the mills, and the timber-felling, and most of all over the staff of headmanship, which one of the villages had long claimed as belonging to it by rights, and the other would not give up. And so these two villages were at enmity with one another.

But the herd boys and girls of both villages were just simple young folk, who understood nothing about the rights of their elders, and cared less, but met every day on the boundary between the two villages and the two counties. Their flocks mingled and fed together, while the boys played games, and over their games would often be late in bringing the sheep home of an evening.

For this the poor boys and girls would be soundly rated and scolded in both villages. But in one of the villages there was a great-grandfather and a great-grandmother who could remember all that had ever happened in either village, and they said, "Leave the children alone. A better harvest will spring from their childish games than ever from your wheat in the fields."

So the shepherds kept on coming, as before, with their sheep to the glen, and in time the parents stopped bothering about what the children did.

And so it was on the day when Reygoch broke through the earth at that very spot. The boys and girls happened to be all gathered together under the biggest oak, getting ready to go home. One was tying up his shoes, another fixing a thong to a stick, and the girls were collecting the sheep. All of a sudden they heard a dreadful thumping in the earth right underneath their feet! There was a thud, then a second, and at the third thud the earth gaped, and up there came, right in the midst of the shepherds, a fearsome large head as big as a barrel, with a beard like a shock of corn, and the beard still bristling with hoar-frost from Frosten city!

The boys and girls all screamed with fright and fell down in a dead faint – not so much because of the head as big as a barrel, but because of the beard, that looked for all the world like a shock of corn!

So the shepherds fainted away – all but young Lilio, who was the handsomest and cleverest among the lads of both villages and both counties.

Lilio kept his feet and went close up to see what sort of monster it might be.

"Don't be afraid, children," said Lilio to the shepherds. "The Lord never created that monstrous giant for evil, else he would have killed half the world by now."

So Lilio walked boldly up to Reygoch, and Reygoch lifted the basket with Curlylocks down from his ear and set it on the ground.

"Come – oh come quickly, boys!" cried Lilio. "There is a little girl with him, little and lovely as a star!"

The herd boys and girls got up and began to peep from behind each other at Curlylocks; and those who had at first been the most frightened were now the foremost in coming up to Curlylocks, because, you see, they were always quickest in everything.

No sooner had the herd boys and girls seen dear little Curlylocks than they loved her. They helped her out of her basket, led her to where the turf was softest, and fell to admiring her lovely robes, which were light as gossamer and blue as the sky, and her hair, which was shining and soft as the morning light; but most of all they admired her fairy veil, for she would wave it just for a moment, and then rise from the grass and float in the air.

The herd boys and girls and Curlylocks danced in a ring together, and played all kinds of games. Curlylocks's little feet twinkled for pure joy, her eyes laughed, and so did her lips, because she had found companions who liked the same things as she did.

Then Curlylocks brought out her little bag of pearls to give presents and pleasure to her new friends. She threw down a pearl, and a little tree grew up in their midst, all decked with coloured ribbons, silk kerchiefs and red necklaces for the girls. She threw down a second pearl, and from all parts of the forest came forth haughty peacocks; they stalked and strutted, they flew up and away, shedding their glorious feathers all over the turf, so that the grass fairly sparkled with them. And the herd boys stuck the feathers in their caps and doublets. Yet another pearl did Curlylocks throw out, and from a lofty branch there dropped a golden swing with silken ropes; and when the boys and girls got on the swing, it swooped and stooped as light as a swallow, and as gently as the grand barge of the Duke of Venice.

The children shouted for joy, and Curlylocks threw out all the pearls in her bag one after another, never thinking that she ought to save them; because Curlylocks liked nothing in the world better than lovely games and pretty songs. And so she spent her pearls down to the last little seed pearl, though heaven alone knew how badly she would need them soon, both she and her new friends.

"I shall never leave you anymore," cried Curlylocks merrily. And the herd boys and girls clapped their hands and threw up their caps for joy over her words.

Only Lilio had not joined in their games, because he was rather sad and worried that day. He stayed near Reygoch, and from there he watched Curlylocks in all her loveliness, and all the pretty magic she made there in the forest.

Meantime Reygoch had come out of his hole. Out he came and stood up among the trees of the forest, and as he stood there his head rose above the hundred-year-old forest, so terribly big was Reygoch.

Over the forest looked Reygoch, and out into the plain.

The sun had already set, and the sky was all crimson. In the plain you could see the two golden fields spread out like two gold kerchiefs, and in the midst of the fields two villages like two white doves. A little way beyond the two villages flowed the mighty River Banewater, and all along the river rose great grass-grown dykes; and on the dykes you could see herds and their keepers moving.

"Well, well!" said Reygoch. "And to think that I have spent a thousand years in Frosten city, in that desert, when there is so much beauty in the world!" And Reygoch was so delighted with looking into the plain that he just stood there with his great head as big as a barrel turning from right to left, like a huge scarecrow nodding above the tree-tops.

Presently Lilio called to him, "Sit down, daddy, for fear the elders of the villages should see you."

Reygoch sat down, and the two started talking, and Lilio told Reygoch why he was so sad that day.

"A very wicked thing is going to happen today," said Lilio. "I overheard the elders of our village talking last night, and this is what they said: 'Let us pierce the dyke along the River Banewater. The river will widen the hole, the dyke will fall, and the water will flood the enemy village; it will drown men and women, flood the graveyard and the fields, till the water will be level above them, and nothing but a lake to show where the enemy village has been. But our fields are higher, and our village lies on a height, and so no harm will come to us.' And then they really went out with a great ram to pierce the dyke secretly and at dead of night. But, daddy," continued Lilio, "I know that our fields are not so high, and I know that the water will overflow them too, and before the night is over there will be a lake where our two villages used to be. And that is why I am so sad."

They were still talking when a terrible noise and clamour arose from the plain.

"There!" cried Lilio, "the dreadful thing has happened!"

Reygoch drew himself up, picked up Lilio, and the two looked out over the plain. It was a sad sight to see! The dyke was crumbling, and the mighty Black Banewater rolling in two arms across the beautiful fields. One arm rolled towards the one village, and the second arm towards the other village. Animals were drowning, the golden fields disappeared below the flood. Above the graves the crosses were afloat, and both villages rang with cries and shouting. For in both villages the elders had gone out to the threshing-floors with cymbals, drums and fifes, and there they were drumming and piping away each to spite the other village, so crazed were they with malice, while over and above that din the village dogs howled dismally, and the women and children wept and wailed.

"Daddy," cried Lilio, "why have I not your hands to stop the water?"

Terrified and bewildered by the dreadful clamour in the plain, the herd boys and girls crowded round Reygoch and Lilio.

When Curlylocks heard what was the matter, she called out quick and sprightly, as befits a little fairy, "Come on, Reygoch – come on and stop the water!"

"Yes, yes, let's go!" cried the herd boys of both villages and both counties, as they wept and sobbed without stopping. "Come on, Reygoch, and take us along too!"

Reygoch stooped, gathered up Lilio and Curlylocks (who was still carrying her lantern) in his right hand, and all the rest of the herd boys and girls in his left, and then Reygoch raced with ten-fathom strides through the forest clearing and down into the plain. Behind him ran the sheep, bleating with terror. And so they reached the plain.

Through fog and twilight ran Reygoch with the children in his arms and the terrified flocks at his heels in frantic flight – all running towards the dyke. And out to meet them flowed the Black Banewater, killing and drowning as it flowed. It is terribly strong, is that water. Stronger than Reygoch? Who knows? Will it sweep away Reygoch, too? Will it drown those poor herd boys and girls also, and must the dear little Fairy Curlylocks die – and she as lovely as a star?

So Reygoch ran on across the meadow, which was still dry, and came all breathless to the dyke, where there was a great breach, through which the river was pouring with frightful force.

"Stop it up, Reygoch – stop it up!" wailed the boys and girls.

Not far from the dyke there was a little mound in the plain.

"Put us on that mound," cried Curlylocks briskly.

Reygoch set down Lilio and Curlylocks and the herd boys and girls on the hillock, and the sheep and lambs crowded round them. Already the hillock was just an island in the middle of the water.

But Reygoch took one mighty stride into the water and then lay down facing the dyke, stopping up the breach with his enormous chest. For a little while the water ceased to flow; but it was so terribly strong that nothing on earth could stop it. The water pressed forward; it eddied round Reygoch's shoulders; it broke through under him, over him, about him – everywhere – and rolled on again over the plain. Reygoch stretched out both arms and piled up the earth in great handfuls; but as fast as he piled it up, the water carried it away.

And in the plain the water kept on rising higher and higher; fields, villages, cattle, threshing-floors, not one of them could be seen anymore. Of both villages, the roofs and church steeples were all that showed above the flood.

Even around the hillock where the herd boys and girls were standing with Lilio and Curlylocks the flood was rising higher and higher. The poor young things were weeping and crying, some for their mothers, others for their brothers and sisters, and some for their homes and gardens; because they saw that both villages had perished, and not a soul saved – and the water rising about them, too!

So they crowded up higher and higher upon the hillock; they huddled together around Lilio and Curlylocks, who were standing side by side in the midst of their friends.

Lilio stood still and white as marble; but Curlylocks's eyes shone, and she held up her lantern towards Reygoch to give him light for his work. Curlylocks's veil rose and fluttered in the night wind and hovered above the water, as though the little fairy were about to fly away and vanish from among all these terrors.

"Curlylocks! Curlylocks! Don't go! Don't leave us!" wailed the herd boys, to whom it seemed as if there were an angel with them while they could look upon Curlylocks.

"I'm not going – I'm not going away!" cried Curlylocks. But her veil fluttered, as if it would carry her away of its own accord, over the water and up into the clouds.

Suddenly they heard a scream. The water had risen and caught one of the girls by the hem of her skirt and was washing her away. Lilio stooped just in time, seized the girl, and pulled her back onto the hillock.

"We must tie ourselves together," cried the herd boys. "We must be tied each to the other, or we shall perish."

"Here, children – here!" cried Curlylocks, who had a kind and pitiful heart.

Quickly she stripped her magic veil off her shoulders and gave it to the herd girls. They tore the veil into strips, knotted the strips into long ropes, and bound themselves together, each to other, round Lilio and Curlylocks. And round the shepherds bleated the poor sheep in terror of being drowned.

But Curlylocks was now among these poor castaways, no better off than the rest of them. Her pearls she had wasted on toys, and her magic veil she had given away and torn up out of the goodness of her heart, and now she could no longer fly, nor save herself out of this misery.

But Lilio loved Curlylocks better than anything else in the world, and when the water was already up to his feet he called, "Don't be afraid,

Curlylocks! I will save you and hold you up!" And he held up Curlylocks in his arms.

With one hand Curlylocks clung round Lilio's neck, and with the other she held up her little lantern aloft towards Reygoch.

And Reygoch, lying on his chest in the water, was all the time steadily fighting the flood. Right and left of Reygoch rose the ruins of the dyke like two great horns. Reygoch's beard was tousled, his shoulders were bleeding. Yet he could not stop the Banewater, and the flood round the hillock was rising and rising to drown the poor remnant there. And now it was night – yea, midnight.

All of a sudden a thought flashed through Curlylocks, and through all the sobbing and crying she laughed aloud as she called to Reygoch, "Reygoch, you old simpleton! why don't you sit between these two horns of the dyke? Why don't you dam the flood with your shoulders?"

The herd boys and girls stopped wailing at once. So dumbfounded were they at the idea that not one of them had thought of that before!

"Uhuhu!" was all you could hear, and that was Reygoch laughing. And when Reygoch laughs, mind you, it's no joke! All the water round him boiled and bubbled as he shook with laughter over his own stupidity!

Then Reygoch stood up, faced about, and – in a twinkling – he sat down between those two horns!

And then happened the most wonderful thing of all! For the Black Banewater stood as though you had rolled a wall into the breach! It stood, and could not rise above Reygoch's shoulders, but followed its usual course, as before, the whole current behind Reygoch's back. And surely that was a most marvellous rescue!

The boys and girls were saved from the worst of the danger; and Reygoch, sitting comfortably, took up earth in handfuls and all slow-and-surely rebuilt the dyke under himself and on either hand. He began in the middle of the night, and when the dawn broke, the job was finished. And just as the sun rose, Reygoch got up from the dyke with his work done, and started combing his beard, which was all caked with mud, twigs, and little fishes.

But the poor boys and girls were not yet done with their troubles; for where were they to go, and how were they to get there? There they stood on the top of the hillock. All around them was a waste of water. Nothing was to be seen of the two villages but just a few roofs – and not a soul alive in either. To be sure, the villagers might have saved themselves if they had taken refuge in their attics. But in both villages everybody had gone to the threshing-floor with cymbals and fifes to make merry, so that each could watch the destruction of the other. And when the water was up to their waists, they were still clanging their cymbals; and when it was up to their necks, they still blew their fifes for gratified spite. And so they were drowned, one and all, with their fifes and cymbals – and serve them right for their malice and uncharitableness!

So the poor children were left without a soul to cherish or protect them, all houseless and homeless.

"We're not sparrows, to live on the housetops," said the boys sadly, as they saw only the roofs sticking out of the water, "and we're not foxes, to live in burrows in the hills. If someone could clear our villages of the water, we might make shift to get along somehow, but as it is, we might as well jump into the water with our flocks and be drowned like the rest, for we have nowhere and no one to turn to."

That was a sad plight indeed, and Reygoch himself was dreadfully sorry for them. But here was an evil he could in no wise remedy. He looked out over the water and said, "There's too much water here for me to bale out or to drink up so as to clear your villages. Eh, children, what shall I do for you?"

But then up and spoke Lilio, that was the wisest lad in these parts: "Reygoch, daddy, if *you* cannot drink so much water, *the Earth can.* Break a hole in the ground, daddy, and drain off the water into the earth."

Dearie me! and wasn't that great wisdom in a lad no bigger than Reygoch's finger?

Forthwith Reygoch stamped on the ground and broke a hole; and the Earth, like a thirsty dragon, began to drink and to drink, and swallow, and suck down into herself all that mighty water from off the whole plain. Before long the Earth had gulped down all the water; villages, fields, and meadows reappeared, ravaged and mud-covered, to be sure, but with everything in its right place.

The young castaways cheered up at the sight, but none was so glad as Curlylocks. She clapped her hands and cried, "Oh, won't it be lovely when the fields all grow golden again and the meadows green!"

But hereupon the herd boys and girls were all downcast once more, and Lilio said, "Who will show us how to till the ground now that not one of our parents is left alive?"

And indeed, far and wide, there was not a soul alive older than that company of helpless young things in the midst of the ravaged plain, and none with them but Reygoch, who was so big and clumsy and simple that he could not turn his head inside one of their houses, nor did he know anything about ploughing or husbandry.

So they were all in the dumps once more, and most of all Reygoch, who was so fond of pretty Curlylocks, and now he could do nothing for her nor her friends!

And, worst of all, Reygoch was getting horribly homesick for his desolate city of Frosten. This night he had swallowed mud enough to last him a thousand years, and had seen more than enough of trouble. And so he was just dying to be back in his vast, empty city, where he had counted the stones in peace for so many hundred years.

So the herd boys were very crestfallen, and Lilio was crestfallen, and Reygoch the most crestfallen of all. And really it was sad to look upon all these poor boys and girls, doomed to perish without their parents and wither like a flower cut off from its root.

Only Curlylocks looked gaily about her, right and left, for nothing could damp her good spirits.

Suddenly Curlylocks cried out, "Look – oh look! What are those people? Oh dear, but they must have seen sights and wonders!"

All looked towards the village, and there, at one of the windows, appeared the heads of an aged couple – an old man and an old woman. They waved their kerchiefs, they called the young people by name, and laughed till their wrinkled faces all shone with joy. They were great-grandfather and great-grandmother, who had been the only sensible people in the two villages, and had saved themselves by taking refuge in the attic!

Oh dear! If the children had seen the sun at his rising and the morning star at that attic window, they would not have shouted so for joy. The very heavens rang again as they called out, "Granny! Grandad!"

They raced to the village like young whippets, Curlylocks in front, with her golden hair streaming in the wind, and after them the ewes and lambs. They never stopped till they reached the village, and there grandfather and grandmother were waiting for them at the gate. They welcomed them, hugged them, and none of them could find words to thank God enough for His mercy in giving grandad and grandma so much wisdom as to make them take refuge in the attic! And that was really a very good thing, because these were only quite simple villages, where there were no books nor written records; and who would have reminded the herd boys and girls of the consequences of wickedness if grandad and grandma had not been spared?

When they had done hugging each other, they remembered Reygoch. They looked round the plain, but there was no Reygoch. He was gone – gone all of a sudden, the dear huge thing – gone like a mouse down its hole.

And Reygoch had indeed gone like a mouse down its hole. For when grandpa and grandma appeared at the attic window, Reygoch got a fright such as he had never yet had in his life. He was terrified at the sight of their furrowed, wrinkled, withered old faces.

"Oh dear! oh dear! what a lot of trouble these old people must have been through in these parts to have come to look like that!" thought Reygoch; and in his terror he that very instant jumped down into the hole through which the Black Banewater had sunk down, and so ran away back to his desolate Frosten city.

* * *

All went well in the village. Grandad and Grandma taught the young folk, and the young folk ploughed and sowed. Upon the grandparents' advice they built just one village, one threshing-floor, one church, and one graveyard, so that there should be no more jealousy nor trouble.

All went well; but the best of all was that in the heart of the village stood a beautiful tower of mountain marble, and on the top of it they had made a garden, where blossomed oranges and wild olive. There lived Curlylocks, the lovely fairy, and looked down upon the land that had been so dear to her from the moment when she first came to earth.

And of an evening, when the field work was done, Lilio would lead the herd boys and girls to the tower, and they would sing songs and dance in a ring in the garden with Curlylocks, always lovely, gentle, and joyous.

But under the earth Reygoch once more fell in with the Black Banewater as it roared and burbled underneath, while he wrestled with it till he forced it deeper and deeper into the earth, and right down to the bottom of the Pit, so that it might never again serve the spite and envy of man. And then Reygoch went on to Frosten city. There he is sitting to this very day, counting the stones and praying the Lord never again to tempt him away from that vast and desolate spot, which is the very place for one so big and so simple.

Oh: The Tsar of the Forest
(Cossack)

THE OLDEN TIMES were not like the times we live in. In the olden times all manner of Evil Powers walked abroad. The world itself was not then as it is now: now there are no such Evil Powers among us. I'll tell you a *kazka* of Oh, the Tsar of the Forest, that you may know what manner of being he was.

Once upon a time, long long ago, beyond the times that we can call to mind, ere yet our great-grandfathers or their grandfathers had been born into the world, there lived a poor man and his wife, and they had one only son, who was not as an only son ought to be to his old father and mother. So idle and lazy was that only son that Heaven help him! He would do nothing, he would not even fetch water from the well, but lay on the stove all day long and rolled among the warm cinders. If they gave him anything to eat, he ate it; and if they didn't give him anything to eat, he did without. His father and mother fretted sorely because of him, and said, "What are we to do with thee, O son? for thou art good for nothing. Other people's children are a stay and a support to their parents, but thou art but a fool and dost consume our bread for naught." But it was of no use at all. He would do nothing but sit on the stove and play with the cinders. So his father and mother grieved over him for many a long day, and at last his mother said to his father, "What is to be done with our son? Thou dost see that he has grown up and yet is of no use to us, and he is so foolish that we can do nothing with him. Look now, if we can send him away, let us send him away; if we can hire him out, let us hire him out; perchance other folk may be able to do more with him than we can." So his father and mother laid their heads together and sent him to a tailor's to learn tailoring. There he remained three days, but then he ran away home, climbed up on the stove, and again began playing with the cinders. His father then gave him a sound drubbing and sent him to a cobbler's to learn cobbling, but again he ran away home. His father gave him another drubbing and sent him to a blacksmith to learn smith's work. But there too he did not remain long, but ran away home again, so what was that poor father to do? "I'll tell thee what I'll do with thee, thou son of a dog!" said he. "I'll take thee, thou lazy lout, into another kingdom. There, perchance, they will be able to teach thee better than they can here, and it will be too far for thee to run home." So he took him and set out on his journey.

They went on and on, they went a short way and they went a long way, and at last they came to a forest so dark that they could see neither earth nor sky. They went through this forest, but in a short time they grew very tired, and when they came to a path leading to a clearing full of large tree-stumps, the father said, "I am so tired out that I will rest here a little," and with that he sat down on a tree-stump and cried, "Oh, how tired I am!" He had no sooner said these words than out of the tree-stump, nobody could say how, sprang such a little, little old man, all so wrinkled and puckered, and his beard was quite green and reached right down to his knee. "What dost thou want of me, O man?" he asked. The man was amazed at the strangeness of his coming to light, and said to him, "I did not call thee; begone!" "How canst thou say that when thou didst call me?" asked the little old man. "Who art thou, then?" asked the father. "I am Oh, the Tsar of the Woods," replied the old man; "why didst thou call me, I say?" "Away with thee, I did not call thee," said the man. "What! thou didst not call me when thou saidst 'Oh'?" "I was tired, and therefore I said 'Oh'!" replied the man. "Whither art thou going?" asked Oh. "The wide world lies before me," sighed the man. "I am taking this sorry blockhead of mine to hire him out to somebody or other. Perchance other people may be able to knock more sense into him than we can at home; but send him whither we will, he always comes running home again!" "Hire him out to me. I'll warrant I'll teach him," said Oh. "Yet I'll only take him on one condition. Thou shalt come back for him when a year has run, and if thou dost know him again, thou mayst take him; but if thou dost not know him again, he shall serve another year with me." "Good!" cried the man. So they shook hands upon it, had a good drink to clinch the bargain, and the man went back to his own home, while Oh took the son away with him.

Oh took the son away with him, and they passed into the other world, the world beneath the earth, and came to a green hut woven out of rushes, and in this hut everything was green; the walls were green and the benches were green, and Oh's wife was green and his children were green – in fact, everything there was green. And Oh had water-nixies for serving-maids, and they were all as green as rue. "Sit down now!" said Oh to his new labourer, "and have a bit of something to eat." The nixies then brought him some food, and that also was green, and he ate of it. "And now," said Oh, "take my labourer into the courtyard that he may chop wood and draw water." So they took him into the courtyard, but instead of chopping any wood he lay down and went to sleep. Oh came out to see how he was getting on, and there he lay a-snoring. Then Oh seized him, and bade them bring wood and tie his labourer fast to the wood, and set the wood on fire till the labourer was burnt to ashes. Then Oh took the ashes and scattered them to the four winds, but a single piece of burnt coal fell from out of the ashes, and this coal he sprinkled with living water, whereupon the labourer immediately stood there alive again and somewhat handsomer and stronger than before. Oh again bade him chop wood, but again he went to sleep. Then Oh again tied him to the wood and burnt him and scattered the ashes to the four winds and sprinkled the remnant of the coal with living water, and instead of the loutish clown there stood there such a handsome and stalwart Cossack that the like of him can neither be imagined nor described but only told of in tales.

There, then, the lad remained for a year, and at the end of the year the father came for his son. He came to the self-same charred stumps in the self-same forest, sat him down, and said, "Oh!" Oh immediately came out of the charred stump and said, "Hail! O man!" "Hail to thee, Oh!" "And what dost thou want, O man?" asked Oh. "I have come," said he, "for my son." "Well, come then! If thou dost know him again, thou shalt take him away; but if thou dost not know him, he shall serve with me yet another year." So the man went with Oh. They came to his hut, and Oh took whole handfuls of millet and scattered it about, and myriads of cocks came running up and pecked it. "Well, dost thou know thy son again?" said Oh. The man stared and stared. There was nothing but cocks, and one cock was just like another. He could not pick out his son. "Well," said Oh, "as thou dost not know him, go home again; this year thy son must remain in my service." So the man went home again.

The second year passed away, and the man again went to Oh. He came to the charred stumps and said, "Oh!" and Oh popped out of the tree-stump again. "Come!" said he, "and see if thou canst recognize him now." Then he took him to a sheep-pen, and there were rows and rows of rams, and one ram was just like another. The man stared and stared, but he could not pick out his son. "Thou mayst as well go home then," said Oh, "but thy son shall live with me yet another year." So the man went away, sad at heart.

The third year also passed away, and the man came again to find Oh. He went on and on till there met him an old man all as white as milk, and the raiment of this old man was glistening white. "Hail to thee, O man!" said he. "Hail to thee also, my father!" "Whither doth God lead thee?" "I am going to free my son from Oh." "How so?" Then the man told the old white father how he had hired out his son to Oh and under what conditions. "Aye, aye!" said the old white father, "'tis a vile pagan thou hast to deal with; he will lead thee about by the nose for a long time." "Yes," said the man, "I perceive that he is a vile pagan; but I know not what in the world to do with him. Canst thou not tell me then, dear father, how

I may recover my son?" "Yes, I can," said the old man. "Then prythee tell me, darling father, and I'll pray for thee to God all my life, for though he has not been much of a son to me, he is still my own flesh and blood." "Hearken, then!" said the old man, "when thou dost go to Oh, he will let loose a multitude of doves before thee, but choose not one of these doves. The dove thou shalt choose must be the one that comes not out, but remains sitting beneath the pear-tree pruning its feathers; that will be thy son." Then the man thanked the old white father and went on.

He came to the charred stumps. "Oh!" cried he, and out came Oh and led him to his sylvan realm. There Oh scattered about handfuls of wheat and called his doves, and there flew down such a multitude of them that there was no counting them, and one dove was just like another. "Dost thou recognize thy son?" asked Oh. "An thou knowest him again, he is thine; an thou knowest him not, he is mine." Now all the doves there were pecking at the wheat, all but one that sat alone beneath the pear-tree, sticking out its breast and pruning its feathers. "That is my son," said the man. "Since thou hast guessed him, take him," replied Oh. Then the father took the dove, and immediately it changed into a handsome young man, and a handsomer was not to be found in the wide world. The father rejoiced greatly and embraced and kissed him. "Let us go home, my son!" said he. So they went.

As they went along the road together they fell a-talking, and his father asked him how he had fared at Oh's. The son told him. Then the father told the son what he had suffered, and it was the son's turn to listen. Furthermore the father said, "What shall we do now, my son? I am poor and thou art poor: hast thou served these three years and earned nothing?" "Grieve not, dear Dad, all will come right in the end. Look! there are some young nobles hunting after a fox. I will turn myself into a greyhound and catch the fox, then the young noblemen will want to buy me of thee, and thou must sell me to them for three hundred roubles – only, mind thou sell me without a chain; then we shall have lots of money at home, and will live happily together!"

They went on and on, and there, on the borders of a forest, some hounds were chasing a fox. They chased it and chased it, but the fox kept on escaping, and the hounds could not run it down. Then the son changed himself into a greyhound, and ran down the fox and killed it. The noblemen thereupon came galloping out of the forest. "Is that thy greyhound?" "It is." "'Tis a good dog; wilt sell it to us?" "Bid for it!" "What dost thou require?" "Three hundred roubles without a chain." "What do we want with *thy* chain, we would give him a chain of gold. Say a hundred roubles!" "Nay!" "Then take thy money and give us the dog." They counted down the money and took the dog and set off hunting. They sent the dog after another fox. Away he went after it and chased it right into the forest, but then he turned into a youth again and rejoined his father.

They went on and on, and his father said to him, "What use is this money to us after all? It is barely enough to begin housekeeping with and repair our hut." "Grieve not, dear Dad, we shall get more still. Over yonder are some young noblemen hunting quails with falcons. I will change myself into a falcon, and thou must sell me to them; only sell me for three hundred roubles, and without a hood."

They went into the plain, and there were some young noblemen casting their falcon at a quail. The falcon pursued but always fell short of the quail, and the quail always eluded the falcon. The son then changed himself into a falcon and immediately struck down its prey. The young noblemen saw it and were astonished. "Is that thy falcon?" "'Tis mine." "Sell it to us, then!" "Bid for it!" "What dost thou want for it?" "If ye give three hundred roubles, ye may take it, but it must be without the hood." "As if we want *thy* hood! We'll make for it a hood worthy of a Tsar." So they higgled and haggled, but at last they gave him the three hundred roubles. Then the young nobles sent the falcon after another quail, and it flew and flew till it beat down its prey; but then he became a youth again, and went on with his father.

"How shall we manage to live with so little?" said the father. "Wait a while, Dad, and we shall have still more," said the son. "When we pass through the fair I'll change myself into a horse, and thou must sell me. They will give thee a thousand roubles for me, only sell me without a halter." So when they got to the next little town, where they were holding a fair, the son changed himself into a horse, a horse as supple as a serpent, and so fiery that it was dangerous to approach him. The father led the horse along by the halter; it pranced about and struck sparks from the ground with its hoofs. Then the horse-dealers came together and began to bargain for it. "A thousand roubles down," said he, "and you may have it, but without the halter." "What do we want with *thy* halter? We will make for it a silver-gilt halter. Come, we'll give thee five hundred!" "No!" said he. Then up there came a gipsy, blind of one eye. "O man! what dost thou want for that horse?" said he. "A thousand roubles without the halter." "Nay! but that is dear, little father! Wilt thou not take five hundred with the halter?" "No, not a bit of it!" "Take six hundred, then!" Then the gipsy began higgling and haggling, but the man would not give way. "Come, sell it," said he, "with the halter." "No, thou gipsy, I have a liking for that halter." "But, my good man, when didst thou ever see them sell a horse without a halter? How then can one lead him off?" "Nevertheless, the halter must remain mine." "Look now, my father, I'll give thee five roubles extra, only I must have the halter." The old man fell a-thinking. "A halter of this kind is worth but three *grivni* and the gipsy offers me five roubles for it; let him have it." So they clinched the bargain with a good drink, and the old man went home with the money, and the gipsy walked off with the horse. But it was not really a gipsy, but Oh, who had taken the shape of a gipsy.

Then Oh rode off on the horse, and the horse carried him higher than the trees of the forest, but lower than the clouds of the sky. At last they sank down among the woods and came to Oh's hut, and Oh went into his hut and left his horse outside on the steppe. "This son of a dog shall not escape from my hands so quickly a second time," said he to his wife. At dawn Oh took the horse by the bridle and led it away to the river to water it. But no sooner did the horse get to the river and bend down its head to drink than it turned into a perch and began swimming away. Oh, without more ado, turned himself into a pike and pursued the perch. But just as the pike was almost up with it, the perch gave a sudden twist and stuck out its spiky fins and turned its tail toward the pike, so that the pike could not lay hold of it. So when the pike came up to it, it said, "Perch! perch! turn thy head toward me, I want to have a chat with thee!" "I can hear thee very well as I am, dear cousin, if thou art inclined to chat," said the perch. So off they set again, and again the pike overtook the perch. "Perch! perch! turn thy head round toward me, I want to have a chat with thee!" Then the perch stuck out its bristly fins again and said, "If thou dost wish to have a chat, dear cousin, I can hear thee just as well as I am." So the pike kept on pursuing the perch, but it was of no use. At last the perch swam ashore, and there was a Tsarivna whittling an ash twig. The perch changed itself into a gold ring set with garnets, and the Tsarivna saw it and fished up the ring out of the water. Full of joy she took it home and said to her father, "Look, dear Papa! what a nice ring I have found!" The Tsar kissed her, but the Tsarivna did not know which finger it would suit best, it was so lovely.

About the same time they told the Tsar that a certain merchant had come to the palace. It was Oh, who had changed himself into a merchant. The Tsar went out to him and said, "What dost thou want, old man?" "I was sailing on the sea in my ship," said Oh, "and carrying to the Tsar of my own land a precious garnet ring, and this ring I dropped into the water. Has any of thy servants perchance found this precious ring?" "No, but my daughter has," said the Tsar. So they called the damsel, and Oh began to beg her to give it back to him, "for I may not live in this world if I bring not the ring," said he. But it was of no avail, she would not give it up.

Then the Tsar himself spoke to her. "Nay, but, darling daughter, give it up, lest misfortune befall this man because of us; give it up, I say!" Then Oh begged and prayed her yet more, and said, "Take what thou wilt of me, only give me back the ring." "Nay, then," said the Tsarivna, "it shall be neither mine nor thine," and with that she tossed the ring upon the ground, and it turned into a heap of millet-seed and scattered all about the floor. Then Oh, without more ado, changed into a cock and began pecking up all the seed. He pecked and pecked till he had pecked it all up. Yet there was one single little grain of millet which rolled right beneath the feet of the Tsarivna, and that he did not see. When he had done pecking he got upon the window-sill, opened his wings, and flew right away.

But the one remaining grain of millet-seed turned into a most beauteous youth, a youth so beauteous that when the Tsarivna beheld him she fell in love with him on the spot and begged the Tsar and Tsaritsa right piteously to let her have him as her husband. "With no other shall I ever be happy," said she. "My happiness is in him alone!" For a long time the Tsar wrinkled his brows at the thought of giving his daughter to a simple youth; but at last he gave them his blessing, and they crowned them with bridal wreaths, and all the world was bidden to the wedding-feast. And I too was there, and drank beer and mead, and what my mouth could not hold ran down over my beard, and my heart rejoiced within me.

The Iron Wolf
(Cossack)

THERE WAS ONCE UPON A TIME a parson who had a servant, and when this servant had served him faithfully for twelve years and upward, he came to the parson and said, "Let us now settle our accounts, master, and pay me what thou owest me. I have now served long enough, and would fain have a little place in the wide world all to myself." "Good!" said the parson. "I'll tell thee now what wage I'll give thee for thy faithful service. I'll give thee this egg. Take it home, and when thou gettest there, make to thyself a cattle-pen, and make it strong; then break the egg in the middle of thy cattle-pen, and thou shalt see something. But whatever thou doest, don't break it on thy way home, or all thy luck will leave thee."

So the servant departed on his homeward way. He went on and on, and at last he thought to himself, "Come now, I'll see what is inside this egg of mine!" So he broke it, and out of it came all sorts of cattle in such numbers that the open steppe became like a fair. The servant stood there in amazement, and he thought to himself, "However in God's world shall I be able to drive all these cattle back again?" He had scarcely uttered the words when the Iron Wolf came running up, and said to him, "I'll collect and drive back all these cattle into the egg again, and I'll patch the egg up so that it will become quite whole. But in return for that," continued the Iron Wolf, "whenever thou dost sit down on the bridal bench, I'll come and eat thee." "Well," thought the servant to himself, "a lot of things may happen before I sit down on the bridal bench and he comes to eat me, and in the meantime I shall get all these cattle. Agreed, then," said he. So the Iron Wolf immediately collected all the cattle, and drove them back into the egg, and patched up the egg and made it whole just as it was before.

The servant went home to the village where he lived, made him a cattle-pen stronger than strong, went inside it and broke the egg, and immediately that cattle-pen was as full of cattle as it could hold. Then he took to farming and cattle-breeding, and he became so rich that in the whole wide world there was none richer than he. He kept to himself, and his goods increased and multiplied exceedingly; the only thing wanting to his happiness was a wife, but a wife he was afraid to take. Now near to where he lived was a General who had a lovely daughter, and this daughter fell in love with the rich man. So the General went and said to him, "Come, why don't you marry? I'll give you my daughter and lots of money with her." "How is it possible for me to marry?" replied the man. "As soon as ever I sit down on the bridal bench, the Iron Wolf will come and eat me up." And he told the General all that had happened. "Oh, nonsense!" said the General. "Don't be afraid. I have a mighty host, and when the time comes for you to sit down on the bridal bench, we'll surround your house with three strong rows of soldiers, and *they* won't let the Iron Wolf get at you, I can tell you." So they talked the matter over till he let himself be persuaded, and then they began to make great preparations for the bridal banquet. Everything went off excellently well, and they made merry till the time came when bride and bridegroom were to sit down together on the bridal bench. Then the General placed his men in three strong rows all round the house so as not to let the Iron Wolf get in; and no sooner had the young people sat down upon the bridal bench than, sure enough, the Iron Wolf came running up. He saw the host standing round the house in three strong rows, but through all three rows he leaped and made straight for the house. But the man, as soon as he saw the Iron Wolf, leaped out of the window, mounted his horse, and galloped off with the wolf after him.

Away and away he galloped, and after him came the wolf, but try as it would, it could not catch him up anyhow. At last, toward evening, the man stopped and looked about him, and saw that he was in a lone forest, and before him stood a hut. He went up to this hut and saw an old man and an old woman sitting in front of it, and said to them, "Would you let me rest a little while with you, good people?" "By all means!" said they. "There is one thing, however, good people!" said he. "Don't let the Iron Wolf catch me while I am resting with you." "Have no fear of that!" replied the old couple. "We have a dog called Chutko, who can hear a wolf coming a mile off, and he'll be sure to let us know." So he laid him down to sleep, and was just dropping off when Chutko began to bark. Then the old people awoke him and said, "Be off! be off! for the Iron Wolf is coming." And they gave him the dog, and a wheaten hearth-cake as provision by the way.

So he went on and on, and the dog followed after him till it began to grow dark, and then he perceived another hut in another forest. He went up to that hut, and in front of it were sitting an old man and an old woman. He asked them for a night's lodging. "Only," said he, "take care that the Iron Wolf doesn't catch me!" "Have no fear of that," said they. "We have a dog here called Vazhko, who can hear a wolf nine miles off." So he laid him down and slept. Just before dawn Vazhko began to bark. Immediately they awoke him. "Run!" cried they, "the Iron Wolf is coming!" And they gave him the dog, and a barley hearth-cake as provision by the way. So he took the hearth-cake, sat him on his horse, and off he went, and his two dogs followed after him.

He went on and on. On and on he went till evening, when again he stopped and looked about him, and he saw that he was in another forest, and another little hut stood before him. He went into the hut, and there were sitting an old man and an old woman. "Will you let me pass the night here, good people?" said he. "Only take care that the Iron Wolf does not get hold of me!" "Have no fear!" said they, "we have a dog called Bary, who can hear a wolf coming twelve miles off. He'll let us know." So he lay down to sleep, and early in the morning Bary let them know that the Iron Wolf was drawing nigh. Immediately they awoke him. "'Tis high time for you to be off!" said they. Then they gave him the dog, and a buckwheat hearth-cake as provision by the way. He took the hearth-cake, sat him on his horse, and off he went. So now he had three dogs, and they all three followed him.

He went on and on, and toward evening he found himself in front of another hut. He went into it, and there was nobody there. He went and lay down, and his dogs lay down also, Chutko on the threshold of the room door, Vazhko at the threshold of the house door, and Bary at the threshold of the outer gate. Presently the Iron Wolf came trotting up. Immediately Chutko gave the alarm, Vazhko nailed him to the earth, and Bary tore him to pieces.

Then the man gathered his faithful dogs around him, mounted his horse, and went back to his own home.

Ivan Tsarevich, the Firebird and the Grey Wolf
(Russian)

IN A CERTAIN KINGDOM, in a certain land, lived Tsar Vwislav Andronovich; he had three sons – Dmitri Tsarevich, Vassili Tsarevich, and Ivan Tsarevich. Tsar Vwislav had a garden so rich that in no land was there better. In the garden grew many precious trees, with fruit and without fruit.

Tsar Vwislav had one favourite apple tree, and on that tree grew apples all golden. The Firebird used to fly to the garden of Tsar Vwislav. She had wings of gold, and eyes like crystals of the East; and she used to fly to that garden every night, sit on the favourite apple tree, pluck from it golden apples, and then fly away.

The Tsar grieved greatly over that apple tree because the Firebird plucked from it many apples. Therefore he called his three sons and said, "My dear children, whichever one of you can catch the Firebird in my garden and take her alive, to him will I give during my life one half of the kingdom, and at my death I will give it all."

Then the sons cried out in one voice: "Gracious sovereign, our father, we will try with great pleasure to take the Firebird alive."

The first night Dmitri Tsarevich went to watch in the garden, and sat under the apple tree from which the Firebird had been plucking the apples. He fell asleep, and did not hear the Firebird when she came, nor when she plucked many apples.

Next morning Tsar Vwislav called his son Dmitri Tsarevich, and asked, "Well, my dear son, hast thou seen the Firebird?"

"No, gracious sovereign, my father, she came not last night."

The next night Vassili Tsarevich went to the garden to watch the Firebird. He sat under the same apple tree, and in a couple of hours fell asleep so soundly that he did not hear the Firebird when she came nor when she plucked apples.

Next morning Tsar Vwislav called him and asked, "Well, my dear son, hast thou seen the Firebird?"

"Gracious sovereign, my father, she came not last night."

The third night Ivan Tsarevich went to watch in the garden and sat under the same apple tree. He sat an hour, a second, and a third. All at once the whole garden was lighted up as if by many fires. The Firebird flew hither, perched on the apple tree, and began to pluck apples. Ivan stole up to her so warily that he caught her tail, but could not hold the bird, she tore off, flew away; and there remained in the hand of Ivan Tsarevich but one feather of the tail, which he held very firmly.

Next morning, the moment Tsar Vwislav woke from his sleep, Ivan Tsarevich went to him and gave him the feather of the Firebird. The Tsar was greatly delighted that his youngest son had been able to get even one feather of the Firebird. This feather was so wonderful and bright that when carried into a dark chamber it shone as if a great multitude of tapers were lighted in that place. Tsar Vwislav put the feather in his cabinet as a thing to be guarded forever. From that time forth the Firebird flew to the garden no more.

Tsar Vwislav again called his sons, and said, "My dear children, I give you my blessing. Set out, find the Firebird, and bring her to me alive; and what I promised at first he will surely receive who brings me the bird."

Dmitri and Vassili Tsarevich began to cherish hatred against their youngest brother because he had pulled the feather from the tail of the Firebird. They took their father's blessing, and both went to find the Firebird. Ivan Tsarevich too began to beg his father's blessing. The Tsar said to him, "My dear son, my darling child, thou art still young, unused to such a long and difficult journey. Why shouldst thou part from me? Thy brothers have gone; now, if thou goest too, and all three of you fail to return for a long time (I am old, and walk under God), and if during your absence the Lord takes my life, who would rule in my place? There might be rebellion too, or disagreement among our people, – there would be no one to stop it; or if an enemy should invade our land, there would be no one to command our men."

But no matter how the Tsar tried to detain Ivan Tsarevich, he could not avoid letting him go at his urgent prayer. Ivan Tsarevich took a blessing of his father, chose a horse, and rode away; he rode on, not knowing himself whither.

Riding by the path by the road, whether it was near or far, high or low, a tale is soon told, but a deed's not soon done. At last he came to the green meadows. In the open field a pillar stands, and on the pillar these words are written:

> "Whoever goes from the pillar straight forward will be hungry and cold; whoever goes to the right hand will be healthy and well, but his horse will be dead; whoever goes to the left hand will be killed himself, but his horse will be living and well."

Ivan read the inscription, and went to the right hand, holding in mind that though his horse might be killed, he would remain alive, and might in time get another horse.

He rode one day, a second, and a third. All at once an enormous grey wolf came out against him and said, "Oh! is that thou, tender youth, Ivan Tsarevich? Thou hast read on the pillar that thy horse will be dead. Why hast thou come hither, then?" The wolf said these words, tore Ivan Tsarevich's horse in two, and went to one side.

Ivan grieved greatly for his horse. He cried bitterly and went forward on foot. He walked all day and was unspeakably tired. He was going to sit down and rest, when all at once the Grey Wolf caught up with him and said, "I am sorry for thee, Ivan Tsarevich, thou art tired from walking; I am sorry that I ate thy good steed. Well, sit on me, the old wolf, and tell me whither to bear thee, and why."

Ivan Tsarevich told the Grey Wolf whither he had to go, and the Grey Wolf shot ahead with him swifter than a horse. After a time, just at nightfall, he brought Ivan Tsarevich to a stone wall not very high, halted, and said, "Now, Ivan Tsarevich, come down from the Grey Wolf, climb over that stone wall; on the other side is a garden, and in the garden the Firebird, in a golden cage. Take the Firebird, but touch not the cage. If thou takest the cage, thou'lt not escape; they will seize thee straightway."

Ivan Tsarevich climbed over the wall into the garden, saw the Firebird in the golden cage, and was greatly tempted by the cage. He took the bird out, and was going back; but changed his mind, and thought, "Why have I taken the bird without the cage? Where can I put her?" He returned, but had barely taken down the cage when there was a hammering and thundering throughout the whole garden, for there were wires attached to the cage. The watchmen woke up at that moment, ran to the garden, caught Ivan Tsarevich with the Firebird, and took him to the Tsar, who was called Dolmat. Tsar Dolmat was terribly enraged at Ivan, and shouted at him in loud, angry tones, "Is it not a shame for thee, young man, to steal? But who art thou, of what land, of what father a son, and how do they call thee by name?"

Ivan Tsarevich replied, "I am from Vwislav's kingdom, the son of Tsar Vwislav Andronovich, and they call me Ivan Tsarevich. Thy Firebird used to fly to our garden each night and pluck golden apples from my father's favourite apple tree, and destroyed almost the whole tree. Therefore my father has sent me to find the Firebird and bring it to him."

"Oh, youthful young man, Ivan Tsarevich," said Tsar Dolmat, "is it fitting to do as thou hast done? Thou shouldst have come to me, and I would have given thee the Firebird with honour; but now will it be well for thee when I send to all lands to declare how dishonourably thou hast acted in my kingdom? Listen, however, Ivan Tsarevich. If thou wilt do me a service – if thou wilt go beyond the thrice ninth land to the thirtieth kingdom and get for me from Tsar Afron the golden-maned steed, I will forgive thy offence and give thee the Firebird with great honour; if not, I will publish in all kingdoms that thou art a dishonourable thief."

Ivan Tsarevich went away from Tsar Dolmat in great grief, promising to obtain for him the golden-maned steed.

He came to the Grey Wolf and told him all that Tsar Dolmat had said.

"Oh! is that thou, youthful young man, Ivan Tsarevich? Why didst thou disobey my words and take the golden cage?"

"I have offended in thy sight," said Ivan to the Grey Wolf.

"Well, let that go; sit on me, and I will take thee wherever thou wilt."

Ivan Tsarevich sat on the back of the Grey Wolf. The wolf was as swift as an arrow, and ran, whether it was long or short, till he came at last to the kingdom of Tsar Afron in the night-time. Coming to the white-walled stables, the Grey Wolf said, "Go, Ivan Tsarevich, into these white-walled stables (the grooms on guard are sleeping soundly), and take the golden-maned steed. On the wall hangs a golden bridle; but take not the bridle, or it will go ill with thee."

Ivan Tsarevich entered the white-walled stables, took the steed, and was coming back; but he saw on the walls the golden bridle, and was so tempted that he took it from the nail. That moment there went a thunder and a noise throughout the stables, because strings were tied to the bridle. The grooms on guard woke up that moment, rushed in, seized Ivan Tsarevich, and took him to Tsar Afron. Tsar Afron began to question him. "Oh, youthful young man, tell me from what land thou art, of what father a son, and how do they call thee by name?"

To this Ivan Tsarevich replied, "I am from Vwislav's kingdom, the son of Tsar Vwislav, and they call me Ivan Tsarevich."

"Oh, youthful young man, Ivan Tsarevich!" said Tsar Afron, "was that which thou hast done the deed of an honourable knight? I would have given thee the golden-maned steed with honour. But now will it be well for thee when I send to all lands a declaration of how dishonourably thou hast acted in my kingdom? Hear me, however, Ivan Tsarevich: if thou wilt do me a service and go beyond the thrice ninth land to the thirtieth kingdom and bring to me Princess Yelena the Beautiful, with whom I am in love heart and soul for a long time, but whom I cannot obtain, I will pardon thy offence and give thee the golden-maned steed with honour. And if thou wilt not do me this service, I will declare in all lands that thou art a dishonourable thief."

Ivan Tsarevich promised Tsar Afron to bring Yelena the Beautiful, left the palace, and fell to crying bitterly.

He came to the Grey Wolf and told him all that had happened.

"Oh, Ivan Tsarevich, thou youthful young man," said the Grey Wolf, "why didst thou disobey me and take the golden bridle?"

"I have offended in thy sight," said Ivan Tsarevich.

"Well, let that go," replied the Wolf. "Sit on me; I will take thee wherever need be."

Ivan Tsarevich sat on the back of the Grey Wolf, who ran as swiftly as an arrow flies, and he ran in such fashion as to be told in a tale no long time; and at last he came to the kingdom of Yelena the Beautiful. Coming to the golden fence which surrounded her wonderful garden, the Wolf said, "Now, Ivan Tsarevich, come down from me and go back by the same road along which we came and wait in the field, under the green oak."

Ivan Tsarevich went where he was commanded. But the Grey Wolf sat near the golden fence, and waited till Yelena the Beautiful should walk in the garden.

Toward evening, when the sun was sinking low in the west, therefore, it was not very warm in the air, Princess Yelena went to walk in the garden with her maidens and court ladies. When she entered the garden and approached the place where the Grey Wolf was sitting behind the fence, he jumped out suddenly, caught the princess, sprang back again, and bore her away with all his power and might. He came to the green oak in the open field where Ivan Tsarevich was waiting, and said, "Ivan Tsarevich, sit on me quickly." Ivan sat on him, and the Grey Wolf bore them both along swiftly to the kingdom of Tsar Afron.

The nurses and maidens and all the court ladies who had been walking in the garden with the princess Yelena the Beautiful ran straightway to the palace and sent pursuers to overtake the Grey Wolf; but no matter how they ran, they could not overtake him, and turned back.

Ivan Tsarevich, while sitting on the Grey Wolf with princess Yelena the Beautiful, came to love her with his heart, and she Ivan Tsarevich; and when the Grey Wolf arrived at the kingdom of Tsar Afron, and Ivan Tsarevich had to take Yelena the Beautiful to the palace and give her to Tsar Afron, he grew very sad, and began to weep tearfully.

"What art thou weeping for, Ivan Tsarevich?" asked the Grey Wolf.

"My friend, why should I, good youth, not weep? I have formed a heartfelt love for Yelena the Beautiful, and now I must give her to Tsar

Afron for the golden-maned steed; and if I yield her not, then Tsar Afron will dishonour me in all lands."

"I have served thee much, Ivan Tsarevich," said the Grey Wolf, "and I will do yet this service. Listen to me. I will turn myself into a princess, Yelena the Beautiful. Do thou give me to Tsar Afron and take from him the golden-maned steed; he will think me the real princess. And when thou art sitting on the steed and riding far away, I will beg of Tsar Afron permission to walk in the open field. When he lets me go with the maidens and nurses and all the court ladies, and I am with them in the open field, remember me, and I will come to thee."

The Grey Wolf spoke these words, struck the damp earth, and became a princess, Yelena the Beautiful, so that it was not possible in any way to know that the wolf was not the princess. Ivan Tsarevich told Yelena the Beautiful to wait outside the town, and took the Grey Wolf to the palace of Tsar Afron.

When Ivan Tsarevich came with the pretended Yelena the Beautiful, Tsar Afron was greatly delighted in his heart that he had received a treasure which he had long desired. He took the false maiden and gave Ivan Tsarevich the golden-maned steed.

Ivan Tsarevich mounted the steed and rode out of the town, seated Yelena the Beautiful with him, and rode on, holding his way toward the kingdom of Tsar Dolmat.

The Grey Wolf lived with Tsar Afron a day, a second, and a third, instead of Yelena the Beautiful. On the fourth day he went to Tsar Afron, begging to go out in the open field to walk, to drive away cruel grief and sorrow. Then Tsar Afron said, "Oh, my beautiful princess Yelena, I will do everything for thee; I will let thee go to the open field to walk!" And straightway he commanded the nurses, the maidens, and all the court ladies to go to the open field and walk with the beautiful princess.

Ivan Tsarevich was riding along his road and path with Yelena the Beautiful, talking with her; and he had forgotten about the Grey Wolf, but afterward remembered. "Oh, where is my Grey Wolf?"

All at once, from wherever he came, the wolf stood before Ivan, and said, "Ivan Tsarevich, sit on me, the Grey Wolf, and let the beautiful princess ride on the golden-maned steed."

Ivan Tsarevich sat on the Grey Wolf, and they went toward the kingdom of Tsar Dolmat. Whether they journeyed long or short, when they had come to the kingdom they stopped about three versts from the capital town; and Ivan Tsarevich began to implore, "Listen to me, Grey Wolf, my dear friend. Thou hast shown me many a service, show me the last one now; and the last one is this: Couldst thou not turn to a golden-maned steed instead of this one? for I do not like to part with this horse."

Suddenly the Grey Wolf struck the damp earth and became a golden-maned steed. Ivan Tsarevich, leaving princess Yelena in the green meadow, sat on the Grey Wolf and went to the palace of Tsar Dolmat. The moment he came, Tsar Dolmat saw that Ivan Tsarevich was riding on the golden-maned steed, and he rejoiced greatly. Straightway he went out of the palace, met the Tsarevich in the broad court, kissed him, took him by the right hand, and led him into the white stone chambers. Tsar Dolmat on the occasion of such joy gave orders for a feast, and they sat at the oaken table at the spread cloth. They ate, they drank, they amused themselves, and rejoiced exactly two days; and on the third day Tsar Dolmat gave Ivan Tsarevich the Firebird together with the golden cage. Ivan took the Firebird, went outside the town, sat on the golden-maned steed together with Yelena the Beautiful, and went toward his own native place, toward the kingdom of Tsar Vwislav.

Tsar Dolmat the next day thought to take a ride through the open field on his golden-maned steed. He ordered them to saddle him; he sat on the horse and rode to the open field. The moment he urged the horse, the horse threw Tsar Dolmat off his back, became the Grey Wolf as before, ran off, and came up with Ivan Tsarevich. "Ivan Tsarevich," said he, "sit on me, the Grey Wolf, and let Yelena the Beautiful ride on the golden-maned steed."

Ivan sat on the Grey Wolf, and they went their way. When the Grey Wolf had brought Ivan to the place where he had torn his horse, he stopped and said, "I have served thee sufficiently, with faith and truth. On this spot I tore thy horse in two; to this spot I have brought thee. Come down from me, the Grey Wolf: thou hast a golden-maned steed; sit on him, and go wherever thou hast need. I am no longer thy servant."

The Grey Wolf said these words and ran to one side. Ivan wept bitterly for the Grey Wolf, and went on with the beautiful princess.

Whether he rode long or short with the beautiful princess, when he was within twenty versts of his own kingdom he stopped, dismounted, and he and the beautiful princess rested from the heat of the sun under a tree; he tied the golden-maned steed to the same tree, and put the cage of the Firebird by his side. Lying on the soft grass, they talked pleasantly, and fell soundly asleep.

At that time the brothers of Ivan Tsarevich, Dmitri and Vassili Tsarevich, after travelling through many lands without finding the Firebird, were on their way home with empty hands, and came unexpectedly upon their brother with the beautiful princess. Seeing the golden-maned steed and the Firebird in the cage, they were greatly tempted, and thought of killing their brother Ivan. Dmitri took his own sword out of the scabbard, stabbed Ivan Tsarevich, and cut him to pieces; then he roused the beautiful princess and asked, "Beautiful maiden, of what land art thou, of what father a daughter, and how do they call thee by name?"

The beautiful princess, seeing Ivan Tsarevich dead, was terribly frightened; she began to shed bitter tears, and in her tears she said, "I am Princess Yelena the Beautiful. Ivan Tsarevich, whom ye have given to a cruel death, got me. If ye were good knights, ye would have gone with him into the open field and conquered him there; but ye killed him when asleep, and what fame will ye receive for yourselves? A sleeping man is the same as a dead one."

Then Dmitri Tsarevich put his sword to the heart of Yelena the Beautiful and said, "Hear me, Yelena the Beautiful, thou art now in our hands; we will take thee to our father, Tsar Vwislav; thou wilt tell him that we got thee and the Firebird and the golden-maned steed. If not, we will give thee to death this minute." The princess, afraid of death, promised them, and swore by everything sacred that she would speak as commanded. Then they began to cast lots who should have Yelena the Beautiful, and who the golden-maned steed; and the lot fell that the princess should go to Vassili, and the golden-maned steed to Dmitri.

Then Vassili Tsarevich took the princess and placed her on his horse; Dmitri sat on the golden-maned steed and took the Firebird to give to their father, Tsar Vwislav; and they went their way.

Ivan Tsarevich lay dead on that spot exactly thirty days. Then the Grey Wolf ran up, knew Ivan by his odour, wanted to aid him, to bring him to life, but knew not how. Just then the Grey Wolf saw a raven with two young ones who were flying above the body and wanted to eat the flesh of Ivan Tsarevich. The wolf hid behind a bush; and when the young ravens had come down and were ready to eat the body, he sprang out, caught one, and was going to tear it in two. Then the raven came down, sat a little way from the Gray Wolf, and said: "Oh, Grey Wolf, touch not my young child; it has done nothing to thee!"

"Listen to me, raven," said the Grey Wolf. "I will not touch thy child; I will let it go unharmed and well if thou wilt do me a service. Fly beyond the thrice ninth land to the thirtieth kingdom, and bring me the water of death and the water of life."

"I will do that, but touch not my son." Having said these words, the raven flew away and soon disappeared from sight. On the third day the raven returned, bringing two vials, in one the water of life, in the other the water of death, and gave them both to the Grey Wolf. The wolf took the vials, tore the young raven in two, sprinkled it with the water of death; the little raven grew together, he sprinkled it with the water of life, and the raven sprang up and flew away.

The Grey Wolf sprinkled Ivan Tsarevich with the water of death: the body grew together; he sprinkled it with the water of life: Ivan Tsarevich stood up and exclaimed, "Oh, how long I have slept!"

"Thou wouldst have slept forever, had it not been for me. Thy brothers cut thee to pieces and carried off Princess Yelena with the golden-maned steed and the Firebird. Now hurry with all speed to thy own country; Vassili Tsarevich will marry thy bride today. To reach home quickly, sit on me; I will bear thee."

Ivan sat on the Grey Wolf; the wolf ran with him to the kingdom of Tsar Vwislav, and whether it was long or short, he ran to the edge of the town.

Ivan sprang from the Grey Wolf, walked into the town, and found that his brother Vassili had married Yelena the Beautiful, had returned with her from the ceremony, and was sitting with her at the feast.

Ivan Tsarevich entered the palace; and when Yelena the Beautiful saw him, she sprang up from the table, kissed him, and cried out, "This is my dear bridegroom, Ivan Tsarevich, and not that scoundrel at the table."

Then Tsar Vwislav rose from his place and asked the meaning of these words. Yelena the Beautiful told the whole truth – told how Ivan Tsarevich had won her, the golden-maned steed, and the Firebird; how his elder brother had killed him while asleep; and how they had terrified her into saying that they had won everything.

Tsar Vwislav was terribly enraged at Dmitri and Vassili, and cast them into prison; but Ivan Tsarevich married Yelena the Beautiful, and lived with her in harmony and love, so that one of them could not exist a single minute without the other.

The Feather of Bright Finist the Falcon
(Russian)

THERE LIVED AN OLD MAN with his old wife. They had three daughters. The youngest was such a beauty that she could neither be told of in a tale nor described with a pen. Once the old man was going to town to the fair, and he said, "My dear daughters, say what ye want; I will buy all ye wish at the fair."

The eldest said, "Father, buy me a new dress." The second said, "Father, buy me a shawl kerchief." But the youngest said, "Buy me a red flower."

The old man laughed at his youngest daughter. "Oh, little dunce! what dost thou want of a red flower? Great good in it for thee; better I'll buy thee clothes."

No matter what he said, he could not persuade her. "Buy me a little red flower, nothing but that." The old man went to the fair, bought the eldest daughter a dress, the second a shawl kerchief; but in the whole town he could not find a red flower. Only as he was coming home did an unknown old man happen in his way. The old man had a red flower in his hand. "Sell me thy flower, old man."

"It is not for sale, it is reserved. If thy youngest daughter will marry my son, Bright Finist the Falcon, I will give the flower as a gift."

The father grew thoughtful. Not to take the flower was to grieve his daughter, and to take it was to give her in marriage, God knows to whom! He thought and thought; still he took the flower. "What harm?" said he to himself. "They will come with proposals by and by. If he is not the right man, why, we can refuse." He came home, gave the eldest daughter her dress, the second her shawl, and to the youngest he gave the flower, saying, "I like not thy flower, my dear daughter; greatly I like it not." And then he whispered in her ear, "The flower was reserved, and not for sale. I took it from a strange man for the promise to give thee in marriage to his son, Bright Finist the Falcon."

"Be not troubled, father, he is so good and kind; he flies as a bright falcon in the sky, and when he strikes the damp earth he is a hero of heroes."

"But dost thou know him?"

"I know him, father. Last Sunday he was at Mass, and looked at me all the time. I talked to him – he loves me, father."

The old man shook his head, looked at his daughter very sharply, made the sign of the cross on her, and said, "Go to thy room, my dear daughter, it is time to sleep. The morning is wiser than the evening; we will talk this matter over hereafter."

The daughter shut herself up in her room, put the red flower in water, opened the window, and looked into the blue distance. Wherever he came from, Bright Finist the Falcon of Flowery Feathers wheeled before her, sprang in through the window, struck the floor, and became a young man. The maiden was frightened; but when he spoke it became one knows not how joyous and pleasant at her heart. They talked till dawn – I know not indeed of what; I know only that when day began to break, Bright Finist the Falcon of Flowery Feathers kissed her and said, "Every night as soon as the bright little flower is placed on the window I will fly to thee, my dear. But here is a feather from my wing. Shouldst thou wish for robes, go out on the balcony and wave it on the right side; in a moment all that thy soul desires will appear before thee." He kissed her once more, turned into a bright falcon, and flew away beyond the dark forest.

The maiden looked after her fated one, closed the window, and lay down to sleep. From that time every night, as soon as she placed the little red flower at the window, the good youth, Bright Finist the Falcon, flew to her.

Well, Sunday came. The elder sisters began to dress for Mass. "But what art thou going to wear? Thou hast nothing new," said they to the youngest one.

She answered, "Never mind; I can pray even at home."

The elder sisters went to church, and the youngest sat at the window in an old dress and looked at the orthodox people going to church. She bided her time, went out on the porch, waved her coloured feather on the right; and from wherever they came there appeared before her a crystal carriage, blooded horses, servants in gold, robes, and every ornament of precious stones. In one moment the beautiful maiden was dressed, sat in the carriage, and dashed off to church. The people looked, admiring her beauty. "It is clear that some Tsar's daughter has come," said they among themselves.

As soon as "Dostoino" was sung, she went out of the church, sat in the carriage, and was whirled back home. The orthodox people went out to look at her, to see where she would go; but nothing of the sort – her trace had grown cold long ago.

Our beauty had barely come to the court when she waved her bright feather on the left side; in a moment the maidens undressed her and the carriage vanished. She was sitting as if nothing had happened, looking out through the window to see how the orthodox people go home from church.

The sisters too came home. "Well, sister," said they, "what a beauty was at church today! Just a sight, neither to be told in a tale nor described with a pen. It must be that she is some Tsar's daughter from another land, so splendidly dressed, wonderfully!"

The second and third Sundays came; the beautiful maiden mystified the orthodox people, and her sisters, her father, and her mother. But the last time when she undressed she forgot to take out of her hair the diamond pin. The elder sisters came from the church and told her of the Tsar's daughter; but when they looked at the youngest sister the diamonds were blazing in her hair.

"Oh, sister, what is this?" cried they. "Why, just such a pin was in the hair of the Tsar's daughter today. Where didst thou get it?"

The beautiful maiden was confused, and ran to her chamber. There was no end of guesses and whispers, but the youngest sister said nothing and laughed in secret. The elder sisters began to watch her and to listen in the night at her chamber; and they overheard one time her conversation with Bright Finist the Falcon, and saw with their own eyes at daybreak how he sprang from the window and flew off beyond the dark forest.

The elder sisters were clearly malicious. They planned to put hidden knives for the evening on the window of their sister's room, so that Bright Finist the Falcon might cut his coloured wings. They did this straightway; the youngest sister knew nothing of the matter. She put her red flower on the window, lay down on the couch, and fell asleep soundly. Bright Finist the Falcon flew to the window, and as he was springing in cut his left foot; but the beautiful maiden knew nothing of this; she was sleeping so sweetly, so calmly. Angrily did Bright Finist the Falcon rise to the sky and fly beyond the dark forest.

In the morning the maiden woke up. She looked on every side; it was daylight already, and the good youth was not there. She looked at the window, and on the window were two sharp knives across each other, and red blood was dripping from them to the flower. Long did the maiden shed bitter tears; many sleepless nights did she pass by the window of her chamber. She waved the bright feather in vain; Bright Finist the Falcon flies no longer himself, and sends not his servants.

At last she went to her father with tears in her eyes and begged his blessing, gave orders to forge three pairs of iron shoes, three iron staves, three iron caps, and three iron Easter cakes; she put a pair of shoes on her feet, the cap on her head, took a staff in her hand, and went toward that point from which Bright Finist the Falcon had flown to her. She goes through slumbering forests, she goes over stumps, over logs. One pair of iron shoes are trodden out, one iron cap is worn off, one staff is breaking up, one cake is gnawed away, and the beautiful maiden walks on, walks all the time, and the forest grows darker, grows denser.

All at once she sees standing before her an iron hut on hen's legs, and it turns without ceasing.

"Hut, hut!" said she. "Stand with thy back to the forest, thy front to me."

The hut turned its front to her. She entered the hut, and in it was lying a Baba-Yaga from corner to corner, her lips on the crosspiece, her nose in the loft.

"Tfu-tfu-tfu! in former days nothing of Russia was seen with sight nor heard with hearing; but now the odor of Russia goes through the wide world invisible seeming, runs to one's nose. Where dost thou hold thy way, beautiful maiden? Art flying from labour, or seekest labour?"

"Oh, grandmother dear, I had Bright Finist the Falcon of Flowery Feathers; my sisters did harm him! Now I am seeking for Bright Finist the Falcon."

"Oh, my child, thou hast far to go; thrice nine lands must yet be passed! Bright Finist the Falcon of Flowery Feathers lives in the fiftieth kingdom in the eighteenth land, and is now betrothed to the daughter of a Tsar."

The Baba-Yaga nourished and fed the maiden with what God had sent, and put her to bed. Next morning, when the light was just coming, she roused her, gave her a present for the road – a small golden hammer and ten little diamond nails – and said, "When thou comest to the blue sea, the bride of Bright Finist the Falcon will come out on the shore to walk; take the golden hammer and drive the diamond nails. She will try to buy them of thee; but, beautiful maiden, take no pay, only ask to see Bright Finist the Falcon. Now go, with God, to my second sister."

Again the fair maiden goes through the dark forest, goes farther and farther; the forest is darker and deeper, the tree-tops wind up to the sky. Now almost the second pair of shoes are trodden out, the second cap worn away, the second iron staff breaking, the iron cake gnawed away; before the maiden is an iron hut on hen's legs, and it turns without ceasing.

"Hut, oh, hut!" said she. "Stop with thy back to the trees and thy front to me, so that I may creep in and eat."

The hut turned its back to the trees and its front to the maiden. She entered. In the hut lay a Baba-Yaga from corner to corner, her lips on the crosspiece, her nose in the loft.

"Tfu-tfu-tfu! in former days nothing of Russia was seen with sight or heard with hearing; but now the odour of Russia goes through the wide world. Whither dost hold thy way, fair maiden?"

"Grandmother, dear, I am seeking Bright Finist the Falcon."

"Oh! he is going to marry; they have the maiden's party tonight," said the Baba-Yaga.

She gave her to eat and drink, and put the maiden to sleep. At daybreak next morning she roused her, gave her a golden plate with a diamond ball, and enjoined on her most firmly, "When thou comest to the shore of the blue sea, roll the diamond ball on the golden plate. The bride of Bright Finist the Falcon of Flowery Feathers will try to buy the plate and ball; but take nothing for it, only ask to see Bright Finist the Falcon. Now go, with God, to my eldest sister."

Again the fair maiden goes through the dark forest, goes farther and farther; the forest grows darker and deeper. Now are the third pair of shoes almost trodden out, the third cap is wearing off, the third staff is breaking, and the last cake is gnawed away. On hen's legs stands an iron hut and turns about.

"Hut, oh, hut!" cried she. "Stand with thy back to the trees and thy face to me; I must creep in and eat bread."

The hut turned. In the hut lay another Baba-Yaga from corner to corner, her lips on the crosspiece, her nose in the loft.

"Tfu-tfu-tfu! in former times nothing of Russia was seen with sight nor heard with hearing; but now the odour of Russia goes through the wide world. Where, beautiful maiden, dost thou hold thy way?"

"Grandmother, dear, I am seeking Bright Finist the Falcon."

"Oh, fair maiden, he has married a Tsar's daughter! Here is my swift steed; sit on him, and go, with God."

The maiden sat on the steed and shot away farther. The forest grew thinner and thinner.

Behold, the blue sea is before her; broad and roomy is it spread, and there in the distance, like fire, burn the golden summits above the lofty, white-walled chambers. That is the kingdom of Bright Finist the Falcon. She sat then on the movable sand of the shore and hammered with hammer the diamond nails. All at once the Tsar's daughter goes with her nurses and maidens and trusty serving-women along the shore; she stops, and wants to buy the diamond nails and the golden hammer.

"Tsar's daughter, let me but look at Bright Finist the Falcon. I will give them for nothing," answered the maiden.

"Bright Finist the Falcon is sleeping at present, and has ordered that none be admitted; but give me thy beautiful nails and hammer. I will show him to thee."

She took the hammer and nails, ran to the palace, stuck into the clothes of Bright Finist the Falcon a magic pin, so that he should sleep more soundly and not wake; then she commanded her nurses to conduct the beautiful maiden through the palace to her husband, and went herself to walk.

Long did the maiden struggle, long did she weep over her dear one; she could not wake him in any way. When she had walked to her pleasure, the Tsar's daughter came home, drove her away, and pulled out the pin.

Bright Finist the Falcon woke. "Oh, how long I have slept! Someone was here," said he, "and wept over me all the time, talking the while; but I could not open my eyes, I felt so heavy."

"Thou wast only dreaming," said the Tsar's daughter. "No one was here."

Next day the beautiful maiden sat again on the shore of the blue sea and was rolling a diamond ball on a golden plate.

The Tsar's daughter went out to walk; she saw them and said, "Sell them to me."

"Let me look at Bright Finist the Falcon, and I will give them for nothing."

The Tsar's daughter agreed, and again she pierced the clothes of Bright Finist the Falcon with a magic pin. Again the fair maiden wept bitterly over her dear one, but could not rouse him.

The third day she sat on the shore of the blue sea, so sad and sorrowful, she was feeding her steed with glowing coals. The Tsar's daughter, seeing that the steed was eating fire, wanted to buy him.

"Let me look on Bright Finist the Falcon, and I'll give the steed for nothing."

The Tsar's daughter agreed, ran to the palace, and said to her husband, "Let me look in thy head." She sat down to look in his head, and stuck the pin in his hair; straightway he was in a deep sleep. Then she sent her nurses for the beautiful maiden.

The fair maiden came, tried to wake her dear, embraced him and kissed him, crying bitterly, bitterly herself; he wakes not. Then she began to look in his head, and out fell the magic pin.

Bright Finist the Falcon woke all at once; he saw the fair maiden and was glad. She told him everything as it was – how her malicious sisters had envied her, how she had wandered, and how she had exchanged with the Tsar's daughter. He loved her more than before, kissed her on the sweet lips, and gave command to call without delay boyars, princes, and people of every degree. Then he asked, "What is your judgment: with which wife should I spend my life – with her who sold me, or her who bought me?"

All the boyars, princes, and people of each degree decided in one voice to take the woman who had bought him; but the one who had sold him, to hang on the gate and shoot her. Bright Finist the Falcon of Flowery Feathers did this.

Water of Youth, Water of Life
and Water of Death
(Russian)

I N A CERTAIN KINGDOM IN A CERTAIN LAND there lived a Tsar; that Tsar had three sons – two crafty, and the third simple. Somehow the Tsar had a dream that beyond the thrice ninth land, in the thirtieth kingdom, there was a beautiful maiden, from whose hands and feet water was flowing, and that whoever would drink that water would become thirty years younger. The Tsar was very old. He summoned his sons and counsellors, and asked, "Can anyone explain my dream?"

The counsellors answered the Tsar: "We have not seen with sight nor heard with hearing of such a beautiful maiden, and how to go to her is unknown to us."

Now the eldest son, Dmitri Tsarevich, spoke up: "Father, give me thy blessing to go in all four directions, look at people, show myself, and make search for the beautiful maiden."

The Tsar gave his parental blessing. "Take," said he, "treasure as much as thou wishest, and all kinds of troops as many as are necessary."

Dmitri Tsarevich took one hundred thousand men and set out on the road, on the journey. He rode a day, he rode a week, he rode a month, and two and three months. No matter whom he asked, no one knew of the beautiful maiden, and he came to such desert places that there were only heaven and earth. He urged his horse on, and behold before him was a lofty mountain; he could not see the top with his eyes. Somehow he climbed the mountain and found there an ancient, a grey old man.

"Hail, grandfather!"

"Hail, brave youth! Art fleeing from labour, or seekest thou labour?"

"I am seeking labour."

"What dost thou need?"

"I have heard that beyond the thrice ninth land, in the thirtieth kingdom, is a beautiful maiden, from whose hands and feet healing water flows, and that whoever gets and drinks this water will grow thirty years younger."

"Well, brother, thou canst not go there."

"Why not?"

"Because there are three broad rivers on the road, and on these rivers three ferries: at the first ferry they will cut off thy right hand, at the second thy left foot, at the third they will take thy head."

Dmitri Tsarevich was grieved; he hung his stormy head below his shoulders, and thought, "Must I spare my father's head? Must I spare my own? I'll turn back."

He came down from the mountain, went back to his father, and said, "No, father, I have not been able to find her; there is nothing to be heard of that maiden."

The second son, Vassili Tsarevich, began to beg, "Father, give me thy blessing; perhaps I can find her."

"Go, my son."

Vassili Tsarevich took one hundred thousand men, and set out on his road, on his journey. He rode a day, he rode a week, he rode a month, and two, and three, and entered such places that there was nothing but forests and swamps. He found there Baba-Yaga, boneleg. "Hail, Baba-Yaga, boneleg!"

"Hail, brave youth! Art thou fleeing from labour, or seekest labour?"

"I am seeking labour. I have heard that beyond the thrice ninth land, in the thirtieth kingdom, is a beautiful maiden, from whose feet and hands healing water flows."

"There is, father; only thou canst not go there."

"Why not?"

"Because on the road there are three ferries: at the first ferry they will cut off thy right hand, at the second thy left foot, at the third off with thy head."

"It is not a question of saving my father's head, but sparing my own."

He returned, and said to his father, "No, father, I could not find her; there is nothing to be heard of that maiden."

The youngest son, Ivan Tsarevich, began to beg, "Give me thy blessing, father; maybe I shall find her."

The father gave him his blessing. "Go, my dear son; take troops and treasure all that are needed."

"I need nothing, only give me a good steed and the sword Kládyenets."

Ivan Tsarevich mounted his steed, took the sword Kládyenets, and set out on his way, on his journey. He rode a day, he rode a week, he rode a month, and two and three; and rode into such places that his horse was to the knees in water, to the breast in grass, and he, good youth, had nothing to eat. He saw a cabin on hen's feet, and entered. Inside sat Baba-Yaga, boneleg.

"Hail, grandmother!"

"Hail, Ivan Tsarevich! Art flying from labour, or seekest labour?"

"What labour? I am going to the thirtieth kingdom; there, it is said, lives a beautiful maiden, from whose hands and feet healing water flows."

"There is, father; though with sight I have not seen her, with hearing I have heard of her. But to her it is not for thee to go."

"Why so?"

"Because there are three ferries on the way: at the first ferry they will cut off thy right hand, at the second thy left foot, at the third off with thy head."

"Well, grandmother, one head is not much; I will go, whatever God gives."

"Ah! Ivan Tsarevich, better turn back; thou art still a green youth, hast never been in places of danger, hast not seen great terror."

"No," said Ivan, "if thou seizest the rope, don't say thou art not strong." He took farewell of Baba-Yaga and went farther.

He rode a day, a second, and a third, and came to the first ferry. The ferrymen were sleeping on the opposite bank. "What is to be done?" thought Ivan. "If I shout, they'll be deaf for the rest of their lives; if I whistle, I shall sink the ferry-boat." He whistled a half whistle. The ferrymen sprang up that minute and ferried him across the river.

"What is the price of your work, brothers?"

"Give us thy right hand."

"Oh, I want that for myself!" Then Ivan Tsarevich struck with his sword on the right, and on the left. He cut down all the ferrymen, mounted his horse, and galloped ahead. At the two other ferries he got away in the same fashion. He was drawing near the thirtieth kingdom. On the boundary stood a wild man, in stature tall as a forest, in thickness the equal of a great stack of hay; he held in his hands an enormous oak tree.

"Oh, worm!" said the giant to Ivan Tsarevich, "whither art thou riding?"

"I am going to the thirtieth kingdom; I want to see the beautiful maiden from whose hands and feet healing water flows."

"How couldst thou, little pigmy, go there? I am a hundred years guarding her kingdom, great, mighty heroes came here – not the like of thee – and they fell from my strong hand. What art thou? Just a little worm!"

Ivan Tsarevich saw that he could not manage the giant, and he turned aside. He travelled and travelled till he came to a sleeping forest; in the forest was a cabin, and in the cabin an old, ancient woman was sitting. She saw the good youth, and said, "Hail, Ivan Tsarevich! Why has God brought thee hither?"

He told her all without concealment. The old woman gave him magic herbs and a ball.

"Go out," said she, "into the open field, make a fire, and throw these herbs on it; but take care to stand on the windward. From these magic herbs the giant will sleep a deep sleep; cut his head off, then let the ball roll, and follow. The ball will take thee to those regions where the beautiful maiden reigns. She lives in a great golden castle, and often rides out with her army to the green meadows to amuse herself. Nine days does she stay there; then sleeps a hero's sleep nine days and nine nights."

Ivan Tsarevich thanked the old woman and went to the open field, where he made a fire and threw into it the magic herbs. The stormy wind bore the smoke to where the wild man was standing on guard. It grew dim in his eyes; he lay on the damp earth and fell soundly asleep. Ivan Tsarevich cut off his head, let the ball roll, and rode on. He travelled and travelled till the golden palace was visible; then he turned from the road, let his horse out to feed, and crept into a thicket himself. He had just hidden, when dust was rising in a column from the front of the palace. The beautiful maiden rode out with her army to amuse herself in the green meadows. The Tsarevich saw that the whole army was formed of maidens alone. One was beautiful, the next surpassed that one; fairer than all, and beyond admiration was the Tsarevna herself.

Nine days was she sporting in the green meadows, and the Tsarevich did not take his eyes from her, still he could not gaze his fill. On the tenth day he went to the golden palace. The beautiful maiden was lying on a couch of down, sleeping a hero's sleep; from her hands and feet healing water was flowing. At the same time her trusty army was sleeping as well.

Ivan Tsarevich took a flask of the healing water. His heroic heart could not withstand her maiden beauty. He tarried awhile, then left the palace, mounted his good steed, and rushed toward home.

Nine days slept the beautiful maiden, and when she woke her rage was dreadful. She stamped, and she screamed with a piercing voice, "What wretch has been here?" She sprang on to her fleet-flying mare, and struck into a chase after Ivan Tsarevich. The mare raced, the ground trembled; she caught up with the good hero, struck him with her sword, and straight in the breast did she strike. The Tsarevich fell on the damp earth; his bright eyes closed, his red blood stiffened. The fair maiden looked at him, and great pity seized her; through the whole world might she search, and not find such a beauty. She placed her white hand on his wound, and moistened it with healing water. All at once the wound closed, and Ivan Tsarevich rose up unharmed.

"Wilt thou take me as wife?" asked she.

"I will, beautiful maiden."

"Well, go home, and wait three years."

Ivan Tsarevich took farewell of his betrothed bride and continued his journey. He was drawing near his own kingdom; but his elder brothers had put guards everywhere, so as not to let him come near his father. The guards gave notice at once that Ivan Tsarevich was coming. The elder brothers met him on the road, drugged him, took the flask of healing water, and threw him into a deep pit. Ivan Tsarevich came out in the underground kingdom.

He travelled and travelled in the underground kingdom. When he came to a certain place, a great storm rose up, lightning flashed, thunder roared, rain fell. He went to a tree to find shelter, looked up, and saw young birds in that tree all wet. He took off his coat, covered them, and sat himself under the tree.

When the old bird flew to the tree, she was so large that she hid the light, and it grew dark as if night were near. When she saw her young covered, she asked, "Who has protected my little birds?" Then, seeing the Tsarevich, she said, "It is thou who didst this. God save thee! Whatever thou wishest, ask of me; I will do everything for thee."

He said, "Bear me out into the upper world."

"Make ready," said the bird, "a double box. Fill one half of it with every kind of game, and in the other half put water, so as to have something with which to nourish me."

The Tsarevich did all that was asked. The bird took the box on her back, and the Tsarevich sat in the middle. She flew up; and whether it was long or short, she bore him to this upper world, took farewell of him, and flew home.

Ivan Tsarevich went to his father; but the old Tsar did not like him by reason of the lies which his brothers had told, and sent him into exile. For three whole years Ivan wandered from place to place. When three years had passed, the beautiful maiden sailed in a ship to the capital town of Ivan Tsarevich's father. She sent a letter to the Tsar, demanding the man who had stolen the water, and if he refused she would burn and destroy his kingdom utterly.

The Tsar sent his eldest son; he went to the ship. Two little boys, grandsons of the Tsar, saw him, and asked their mother, "Is that our father?"

"No, that is your uncle."

"How shall we meet him?"

"Take each one a whip and flog him back home."

The eldest Tsarevich returned, looking as if he had eaten something unsalted.

The maiden continued her threats, demanded the guilty man. The Tsar sent his second son, and the same thing happened to him as to the eldest. Now the Tsar gave command to find the youngest Tsarevich.

When the Tsarevich was found, his father wished him to go on the ship to the maiden. But he said, "I will go when a crystal bridge is built to the ship, and on the bridge there shall be many kinds of food and wine set out."

There was no help for it; they built the bridge, prepared the food, brought wines and meat.

The Tsarevich collected his comrades. "Come with me, attend me," said he. "Eat ye and drink, spare nothing."

While he was walking on the bridge the little boys cried out, "Mother, who is that?"

"That is your father."

"How shall we meet him?"

"Take him by the hands and lead him to me."

They did so; there was kissing and embracing. After that they went to the Tsar, told him all just as it had been. The Tsar drove his eldest sons from the castle and lived with Ivan – lived on and gained wealth.

Trials, Adventures & Adversity

THE JOURNEY OF A HERO often begins at a point of crisis in his life, when morality and good need to prevail in order for him to arrive at his final destination. The folktales in this category offer examples for our own battles as well, teaching the difference between right and wrong.

Once we dive into the deeper meanings and qualities of Slavic folktales, we see that they offer good examples of the message that we shouldn't fall into despair when a situation doesn't look good – that things are not always as bad as they seem. Such is the case of the frog in the folktale 'The Frog Princess' (*see* page 92), who is a princess in disguise. Although the journey of the hero holds many obstacles, luckily, magical creatures are there to help, and to teach with their wisdom in order to aid the hero in achieving his goals, and thus give the reader a positive example and an enjoyable experience.

The Frog Princess
(Polish)

THERE WAS ONCE A KING, who was very old; but he had three grown-up sons. So he called them to him, and said, "My dear sons, I am very old, and the cares of government press heavily upon me. I must therefore give them over to one of you. But as it is the law among us, that no unmarried prince may be King, I wish you all to get married, and whoever chooses the best wife shall be my successor."

So they determined each to go a different way, and settled it thus. They went to the top of a very high tower, and each one at a given signal shot an arrow in a different direction to the others. Wherever their arrows fell they were to go in search of their future wives.

The eldest prince's arrow fell on a palace in the city, where lived a senator, who had a beautiful daughter; so he went there, and married her.

The second prince's arrow struck upon a country house, where a very pretty young lady, the daughter of a rich gentleman, was sitting; so he went there, and proposed to her, and they were married.

But the youngest prince's arrow shot through a green wood and fell into a lake. He saw his arrow floating among the reeds, and a frog sitting thereon, looking fixedly at him.

But the marshy ground was so unsafe that he could not venture upon it; so he sat down in despair.

"What is the matter, prince?" asked the frog.

"What is the matter? Why, I cannot reach that arrow on which you are sitting."

"Take me for your wife, and I will give it to you."

"But how can you be my wife, little frog?"

"That is just what has got to be. You know that you shot your arrow from the tower, thinking that where it fell, you would find a loving wife; so you will have her in me."

"You are very wise, I see, little frog. But tell me, how can I marry you, or introduce you to my father? And what will the world say?"

"Take me home with you, and let nobody see me. Tell them that you have married an Eastern lady, who must not be seen by any man, except her husband, nor even by another woman."

The prince considered a little. The arrow had now floated to the margin of the lake; he took the arrow from the little frog, put her in his pocket, carried her home, and then went to bed, sighing very deeply.

Next morning the king was told that all his sons had got married; so he called them all together, and said, "Well children, are you all pleased with your wives?"

"Very pleased indeed, father and king."

"Well, we shall see who has chosen best. Let each of my daughters-in-law weave me a carpet by tomorrow, and the one whose carpet is the most beautiful shall be queen."

The elder princes hastened at once to their ladies; but the youngest, when he reached home, was in despair.

"What is the matter, prince?" asked the frog.

"What is the matter? My father has ordered that each of his daughters-in-law shall weave him a carpet, and the one whose carpet proves the most beautiful shall be first in rank. My brothers' wives are most likely working at their looms already. But you, little frog, although you can give back an arrow, and talk like a human being, will not be able to weave a carpet, as far as I can see."

"Don't be afraid," she said; "go to sleep, and before you wake the carpet shall be ready."

So he lay down, and went to sleep.

But the little frog stood on her hind-legs in the window and sang:

"Ye breezes that blow, ye winds that sigh,
Come hither on airy wing;
And all of you straight to my dwelling hie,
And various treasures bring.
Two fleeces I crave of the finest wool,
And of the loveliest flowers a basketful;

From the depths of the ocean bring sands of gold,
And pearl-drops of lustre manifold;
That so I may fashion a carpet bright,
Adorned with fair flow'rets and gems of light,
And weave it in one short day and night,
When my true love's hands must the treasure hold."

There was a gentle murmur of the breezes, and from the

sunbeams descended seven lovely maidens, who floated into the room, carrying baskets of various coloured wools, pearls, and flowers. They curtsied deeply to the little frog, and in a few minutes they wove a wonderfully beautiful carpet; then they curtsied again, and flew away.

Meanwhile the wives of the other princes bought the most beautifully coloured wools and the best designs they could find, and worked hard at their looms all the next day.

Then all the princes came before the king and spread out their carpets before him.

The king looked at the first and the second; but when he came to the third, he exclaimed, "That's the carpet for me! I give the first place to my youngest son's wife; but there must be another trial yet."

And he ordered that each of his daughters-in-law should make him a cake next day; and the husband of the one whose cake proved the best should be his successor.

The youngest prince came back to his frog wife; he looked very thoughtful, and sighed deeply.

"What is the matter, prince?" she asked.

"My father demands another proof of skill; and I am not so sure that we shall succeed so well as before; for how can you bake a cake?"

"Do not be afraid," she said. "Lie down, and sleep; and when you wake you will be in a happier frame of mind."

The prince went to sleep; and the frog sprang up to the window, and sang:

"Ye breezes that blow, ye winds that sigh,
Come hither on airy wing;
And all of you straight to my dwelling hie,

94

These various gifts to bring.
From the sunbeams bright
Bring me heat and light;
And soft waters distil
From the pure flowing rill.
From the flowers of the field
The sweet odours they yield.
From the wheatfields obtain
Five full measures of grain,
That so I may bake
In the night-time a cake,
For my true love's sake."

The winds began to rise, and the seven beautiful maidens floated down into the room, carrying baskets, with flour, water, sweetmeats, and all sorts of dainties. They curtsied to the little frog, and got the cake ready in a few minutes; curtsied again, and flew away.

The next day the three princes brought their cakes to the king. They were all very good; but when he tasted the one made by his youngest son's wife, he exclaimed, "That is the cake for me! light, floury, white, and delicious! I see, my son, you have made the best choice; but we must wait a little longer."

The two elder sons went away much depressed; but the youngest greatly elated. When he reached home he took up his little frog, stroked and kissed her, and said, "Tell me, my love, how it was that you, being only a little frog, could weave such a beautiful carpet, or make such a delicious cake?"

"Because, my prince, I am not what I seem. I am a princess, and my mother is the renowned Queen of Light, and a great enchantress. But she has many enemies, who, as they could not injure her, were always seeking to destroy me. To conceal me from them she was obliged to turn me into a frog; and for seven years I have been forced to stay in the marsh where you found me. But under this frog-skin I am really more beautiful than you can imagine; yet until my mother has conquered all her enemies I must wear this disguise; after that takes place you shall see me as I really am."

While they were talking two courtiers entered, with the king's orders to the young prince, to come to a banquet at the king's palace, and bring his wife with him, as his brothers were doing by theirs.

He knew not what to do; but the little frog said, "Do not be afraid, my prince. Go to your father alone; and when he asks for me, it will begin to rain. You must then say that your wife will follow you; but she is now bathing in May-dew. When it lightens say that I am dressing; and when it thunders, that I am coming."

The prince, trusting to her word, set out for the palace; and the frog jumped up to the window, and standing on her hind-legs, began to sing:

"Ye breezes that blow, ye winds that sigh,
Come hither on airy wing;
And all of you straight to my dwelling hie,
These several gifts to bring.
My beauty of yore;
And my bright youth once more;
All my dresses so fair;
And my jewels so rare;
And let me delight
My dear love by the sight."

Then the seven beautiful damsels, who were the handmaidens of the princess – when she lived with her mother – floated on the sunbeams into the room. They curtsied, walked three times round her, and pronounced some magical words.

Then the frog-skin fell off her, and she stood among them a miracle of beauty, and the lovely princess she was.

Meanwhile the prince, her husband, had arrived at the royal banquet-hall, which was already full of guests. The old king welcomed him warmly, and asked him, "Where is your wife, my son?"

Then a light rain began to fall, and the prince said, "She will not be long; she is now bathing herself in May-dew."

Then came a flash of lightning, which illuminated all the palace, and he said, "She is now adorning herself."

But when it thundered, he ran to the door exclaiming, "Here she is!"

And the lovely princess came in, seeming to bring the sunshine with her. They all stood amazed at her beauty. The king could not contain his delight; and she seemed to him all the more beautiful, because he thought her the very image of his long-deceased queen. The prince himself was no less astonished and overjoyed to find such loveliness in her, whom he had only as yet seen in the shape of a little frog.

"Tell me, my son," said the king, "why you did not let me know what a fortunate choice you had made?"

The prince told him everything in a whisper; and the king said, "Go home then, my son, at once, and pick up that frog-skin of hers; throw it in the fire, and come back here as fast as you can. Then she will have to remain just as she is now."

The prince did as his father told him, went home, and threw the frog-skin into the fire, where it was at once consumed.

But things did not turn out as they expected; for the lovely princess, on coming home, sought for her frog-skin, and not finding it, began to cry bitterly. When the prince confessed the truth, she shrieked aloud, and taking out a green poppy-head, threw it at him. He went to sleep at once; but she sprang up to the window, sang her songs to the winds; upon which she was changed into a duck, and flew away.

The prince woke up in the morning, and grieved sadly, when he found his beautiful princess gone.

Then he got on horseback, and set out to find her, inquiring everywhere for the kingdom of the Queen of Light – his princess's mother – to whom he supposed she must have fled.

He rode on for a very, very long time, till one day he came into a wide plain, all covered with poppies in full flower, the odour of which so overpowered him, that he could scarce keep upright in his saddle. Then he saw a queer little house, supported on four crooked legs. There was no door to the house; but knowing what he ought to do, he said:

*"Little house, move
On your crooked legs free;
Turn your back to the wood,
And your front door to me."*

The hut with the crooked legs made a creaking noise and turned round, with its door towards the prince. He went straight in, and found an old fury, whose name was Jandza, inside; she was spinning from a distaff, and singing.

"How are you, prince?" she said, "what brings you here?"

So the prince told her, and she said, "You have done wisely to tell me the truth. I know your bride, the beautiful daughter of the Queen of Light; she flies to my house daily, in the shape of a duck, and this is where she sits. Hide yourself under the table, and watch your opportunity to lay hold of her. Hold her fast, whatever shapes she assumes; when she is tired she will turn into a spindle; you must then break the spindle in two, and you will find that which you are seeking."

Presently the duck flew in, sat down beside the old fury, and began to preen her feathers with her beak. The prince seized her by the wing. The duck quacked, fluttered, and struggled to get loose. But seeing this was useless, she changed herself into a pigeon, then into a hawk, and then into a serpent, which so frightened the prince, that he let her go; on which she became a duck again, quacked aloud, and flew out of the window.

The prince saw his mistake, and the old woman cried aloud, "What have you done, you careless fellow! you have frightened her away from me forever. But as she is your bride, I must find some other way to help you. Take this ball of thread, throw it before you, and wherever it goes follow after it; you will then come to my sister's house, and she will tell you what to do next."

So the prince went on day and night, following the ball of thread, till he came to another queer little house, like the first, to which he said the same rhyme, and going in, found the second old fury, and told her his story.

"Hide under the bench," she exclaimed. "Your bride is just coming in."

The duck flew in, as before, and the prince caught her by the wing; she quacked and tried to get away. Then she changed herself into a turkey, then into a dog, then into a cat, then into an eel, so that she slipped through his hands, and glided out of the window.

The prince was in despair; but the old woman gave him another ball of thread, and he again followed it, determining not to let the princess escape again so easily. So going on after the thread, as it kept unwinding, he came to a funny little house, like the two first, and said:

"Little house, move
On your crooked legs free;
Turn your back to the wood,
And your front door to me."

The little house turned round, so that he could go in, and he found a third old fury inside; much older than her sisters, and having white hair. He told her his story and begged for help.

"Why did you go against the wishes of your clever and sensible wife?" said the old woman. "You see she knew better than you what her frog-skin was good for; but you must needs be in such a hurry to display her beauty, to gain the world's applause, that you have lost her; and she was forced to fly away from you."

The prince hid himself under the bench. The duck flew in and sat at the old woman's feet, on which he caught her by the wings.

She struggled hard; but she felt his strength was too great for her to resist; so she turned herself into a spindle at once. He broke it across his knee...And lo! and behold! instead of the two halves of the spindle he held the hands of his beautiful princess, who looked at him lovingly with her beautiful eyes, and smiled sweetly.

And she promised him that she would always remain as she was then, for since her mother's enemies were all dead she had nothing to fear.

They embraced each other, and went out of the old fury's hut. Then the princess spoke some magical spells; and in the twinkling of an eye there appeared a wonderful bridge, reaching from where they stood hundreds of miles, up to the very gallery of the palace, belonging to the prince's father. It was all made of crystal, with golden hand-rails and diamond bosses upon them.

The princess spoke some more magical words, and a golden coach appeared, drawn by eight horses, and a coachman, and two tall footmen, all in golden liveries. And there were four outriders on splendid horses, riding by the side of the coach, and an equerry, riding in front, and blowing a brazen trumpet. And a long procession of followers, in splendid dresses, came after them.

Then the prince and princess got into the golden coach and drove away, thus accompanied, along the crystal bridge, till they reached home, when the old king came out to meet them, and embraced them both tenderly. He appointed the prince his successor; and such magnificent festivities were held on the occasion, as never were seen or heard of before.

The Cuirassier and the Horned Princess
(Czech)

I N A CERTAIN TOWN were encamped a regiment of cuirassiers, and they had a very unpleasant life. Twelve men of them agreed to desert – three sergeants and nine from the ranks. They carried out their plan; and when they had gone a good distance, one said to the rest, "Let us look, brothers, and see if we are not pursued." Another dismounted and climbed a high tree. "Oh! they are searching; but they will not overtake us, for we are far in advance of them." Then he came down, mounted his horse, and all rode rapidly on – rode till dusk. Then the chief man said, "Where shall we go for the night, brothers? Around here we see nothing but mountains and forests."

One of them climbed a tree again to look for a light. He saw one, and called to his comrades, "Look out! We will ride in the direction in which I throw this sword, for I see a light there."

All rode toward the light, and came to a very large building in the wild mountains. At the first glance they saw it was an enormous castle, which was open. They entered the court, led their horses to the stable – where oats were ready for twelve horses – and then went themselves into a hall where a table was laid for twelve persons, so that all might sit down and eat; but there was not a living soul to be seen.

"Brothers," said one of them, "may we touch this food and drink?"

"Why not?" said the chief. "What if we have to pay a few ducats for the entertainment?"

They sat down and ate with good relish. After they had eaten and drunk, an old sorceress slipped in and saluted them, saying, "Good evening, gentlemen. I greet you in this our famous castle. Did the supper taste well?"

"We ate with pleasure," answered one in the name of all, "only we were a little afraid how it would end."

"Fear not, fear not, I am glad ye are strengthened after the long ride," said the sorceress; and then she said further, "Now of course ye will need good beds, so as to refresh yourselves with grateful sleep. In the next chamber are twelve beds and twelve caskets. Lie on the beds prepared for you, but let no man dare, on pain of great punishment, to look at the caskets, which are unlocked."

All went to the next chamber; the sorceress gave them good-night and went out through the opposite door. In the morning when they rose everything was well prepared for them – basins with water and towels, and food for each man. After breakfast they spoke of the good cheer which they had not expected to find in the castle. They spoke of various subjects till they came to the caskets, and the splendid things that must be therein. Some expressed great curiosity; some were heard to say that they could not refrain till evening from looking in the caskets; others warned their comrades not to do that which they might regret.

They had a pleasant time all day at the castle, an excellent dinner, a good lunch, a splendid supper. After supper they went to bed. The sun was shining brightly through the windows next morning, but no man was stirring.

The chief rose and called the others, saying, "It is time to be up." Only two gave answer; the rest did not move. These three went to the beds and found their comrades lifeless. All were terrified, and went to the stable to look at their horses. In the stable they found the nine dead horses, of the nine dead men.

"What shall we do?" asked one of them. "We must leave this place where our comrades have perished; nothing can comfort us again."

They returned to the hall where breakfast was ready for only three. They sat down and ate. After eating, the sorceress came again, and said, "Ye see, my friends, that sinful curiosity has cost those nine men their lives. They could withstand it no longer, rose at midnight, opened the caskets, and looked at the contents; scarcely had they lain down again when sudden death overtook them. Had they followed my advice, as ye have, all might have had a pleasant time, and lived joyously here a whole year. Now I see by your faces that nothing can comfort you here, and that ye would gladly go away."

"Yes," answered one, "we fear to remain longer in this place, where our comrades died a sudden death."

"There is nothing to fear," said the sorceress, "but since it is unpleasant for you, I will not keep you. Go where ye like, but before going each may look without fear or danger in his casket, and take the things inside to remember me by; they may be useful."

The men were afraid at first to open the caskets, having before their eyes the sad example of their comrades; but when the sorceress assured them again and again that they might open them without fear and take out the contents, they grew bold and opened them. The first took from his casket a cap, which the sorceress said had such power that whoever put it on his head no man could see him. The second drew from his casket a mantle, and whoever put it on, the sorceress said, could fly through the air as high as he wished. The third took a purse which had the power that whenever it was shaken ten ducats were in it.

The sorceress bade them goodbye. They thanked her for the hospitality and useful presents and, saddling their horses, rode away from that castle with the Lord God.

They travelled long, and on the road kept telling what a good time they would have with their gifts. At last they came to a large town, took up their lodging at an inn, and asked what there was strange in the place. The innkeeper answered, "Nothing, unless it be that we have a princess immeasurably fond of playing cards, and who says that no one is able to play with her. She vanquishes every comer, and then has him flogged out of the castle."

The man who had the purse thought, "Wait a while, I'll settle thy play." He made ready straightway, and went to the castle. He had himself announced, and declared that he wished to play with the princess. Meanwhile the other two ate and drank well in the inn.

The princess was glad to find someone again with whom to play cards and whom she might overcome. She had him brought in without delay. The game began. The man lost; but he didn't mind that, for whenever he lost he shook the purse and had ten ducats again. So he kept losing and shaking the purse till the princess was astonished, and thought to herself, "Where dost thou get all these ducats, good man? Thou hast not a treasury at thy side, and still thou hast plenty of money. How dost thou get it?"

She watched him and saw that he shook the purse on his knee, from which he took the ducats. She had already won a great bag of ducats, but still was not able to win all he had. She kept thinking how to get that magic purse. "Now let us rest a little," said she, and went to the next room, from which she brought two goblets of wine. One she gave him and drank the other herself, for they were tired and needed refreshment. Her wine was pure, but in his she put a sleeping-powder. She drank to his health, and he emptied his goblet at a draught. After a while he was so very drowsy that he slipped from the seat, dropped under the table, and fell soundly asleep. That was his misfortune. The princess took the magic purse and gave him one like it containing ten ducats.

When he woke up the princess said to him, "Now let us play again." They played while he had ducats. When the ducats were gone he shook and shook the purse, but in vain. The princess said, "Well, my dear man, since thou hast no money, go. But that disgrace which I have put on others I will not put on thee. I will not have thee flogged out of the castle because I have won much money from thee; go in peace."

He went to his friends in great trouble. They greeted him from afar, and called out, "Well, how didst thou prosper?"

"Oh, badly, very badly, brothers; I no longer have the purse; I lost that."

"Oh, comrade, that is bad; how shall we live now? We are in debt for food and drink, and have nothing to pay with."

The one who had the magic mantle said, "Do ye know what, brothers? I'll take a good vengeance on that wicked woman!"

"But how?" was the question.

He answered, "This is how I'll do it. Let me have thy cap so that no one may see me, and I'll take my mantle. When the princess is going to church I'll seize her, fly with her through the air to desert regions, so far away that she will never be able to come home again."

"Yes, that will be a just punishment for her," said the two others. The third one immediately took the cap, wrapped the mantle around him, and waited for the princess. As she was going along the street he seized her, flew far away with her to wild mountains, and let her down there on the ground near a pear tree. On that tree were beautiful pears.

The princess begged the man to climb the tree and shake it, so that she might have some of the fruit to eat. "I'll gratify thee just once," said he. But he was so cunning that he did not leave the cap or magic mantle on the ground, but took them up on the tree, hung them both on a limb, and shook the tree with all his might. The cap and the mantle fell to the ground before the pears. The princess put the cap on her head at once, wrapped the mantle around her, and was off in an instant, sooner than the man on the tree had recovered from his fright.

He was now alone in the wild mountains. What was he to do? He stood motionless as the tree at his side, as if senseless from a thunderbolt; he had no longer magic cap or magic mantle. "Oh, where shall I go?" groaned he, and walked around on the mountains. In his trouble and fright he picked up some pears and ate them. Then other terrible miseries came upon him, for he had barely eaten the pears when unheard-of gigantic horns grew out of his head, so that he could not walk through the woods nor turn around; the horns stopped him everywhere; he could barely crawl forward.

With great care and much struggling, he dragged himself over a bit of road and came to a deep ravine, in which a hermit lived whose name was Wind.

"Oh, friend," said the man, "help me from the mountain, and take me home."

Said Wind, "I am not strong enough to bear thee to thy home, but go to my brother; he is the strongest of us. He will take thee home quickly."

"I should like to go to him, but I cannot move."

"He is not far from here – there, on that side; but go as well as thou art able. He will rid thee of those horns."

The man pushed through as best he could, and came, covered with sweat, to another cave, in which the eldest Wind brother was living. He fell on his knees before Wind and cried imploringly, "Be so kind as to bear me home!"

"I should like to help thee, my friend; but it is not so easy as may seem to thee. I must go to the Lord to ask with what force Wind may blow. If Wind may blow so trees will be torn out with their roots, thou canst reach home; if Wind blows but weakly, thou wilt not go there, for 'tis far. Wait a while; I'll come back soon."

Wind went to ask the Lord how hard he might blow, and the Lord commanded him to blow mightily.

When he returned, the man asked, "How is it?"

"Well," said Wind, "I must blow mightily; thou wilt reach home. But knowest thou there is an apple tree over there? Climb it, pluck an apple, cut it into four parts, and eat; thy great horns will fall off."

The man was glad, climbed the apple tree quickly, but the horns hindered him much. He plucked an apple and ate it; how soon was he free of the horns! He came down from the tree like a squirrel, and thought, "Oh, brother, thou'lt get back thy things!" As he was coming down he took more apples and put them in his pocket, then went to the pear tree and took pears. Soon Wind caught him up, bore him off swiftly, and in a short time put him down in front of the inn where his friends were waiting impatiently. They were all very glad.

"Where wert thou?" asked they.

"Oh, I was where ye will not be to your dying day, brothers!"

"How didst thou prosper?"

"Badly, badly."

"Where hast thou the cap and the mantle?"

"Oh, that woman took them from me!"

"Woe to us – woe, passing woe! Now we have neither the purse, the cap, nor the mantle. We are beggared beyond reckoning."

The innkeeper would not let them go because of their debt.

"What will become of us?" asked they in one voice.

The man whom Wind bore home said, "I have here noble and wonderful fruit which I brought from the wild mountains. One of you will take these pears to the street and sell them; but do not dare to sell them to anyone save the princess when she is going home from church. For the people thou must put such a price that they will not buy; for the princess reduce the price so that she may buy."

One of the men put the pears in a clean basket, covered them with a neat cloth, and went to the square through which the princess was wont to go to church and return. Soon she was coming out of the church, her servant following some steps behind. She saw the uncommonly beautiful pears from a distance, came up herself, and asked, "How many dost thou give for a copper?"

"Oh, these pears are not sold for copper coin! They are so splendid, and have such a flavour, that I can give only three for a ducat."

The princess bought all and gave them to her servant to carry; she had barely reached home, and sat near the table, when she took a golden knife, pared and ate with great relish a number of pears. She ate with such pleasure that she saw not how horns began to grow on her head after the first pear; and in a little while they had grown so much that she could not remain in the room. She went to the great supper-hall, but even there was forced to lie down on the floor, so broad and so lofty were her horns. She gave herself up to fearful lamentation and tears, so that all the servants and the king, her father, with the queen, her mother, ran in. All were horrified and wrung their hands, seeing the princess disfigured.

The king sent quickly for the doctors, who came in all haste from each corner and town. The servants ran to every place; each one in his excitement brought whomsoever he knew. The doctors met and shook their heads one after another; each said that in his life he had never seen nor had experience of such a case. They held a consultation, and at last decided to saw off the horns. They went to work, but in vain; they had barely sawed a piece, when it grew on again quickly, so that fright seized everyone. The princess was so horrified and ashamed that she would have preferred to be out of the world; no man could help her. Then the king made proclamation that whoso would free the princess from the horns would get her in marriage, and with her the whole kingdom.

Who was so glad now as the man with the apples? "Wait," thought he. "My little bird, thou'lt sing as I whistle – no man can help thee but me."

He had fine clothes brought and, dressed as a doctor, had himself announced at the palace. He was soon admitted, and began to speak to the princess, saying, "You must have angered God greatly, must have committed grievous sins, for which you are punished in this way. I expect to give you real help; but first of all you must tell me sincerely what you have done – my aid has to be rendered in view of that."

She confessed with weeping that she had been fond of playing cards; had outplayed all men, then had them flogged from the castle. The last time she had played with a stranger, from whom she had stolen a magic purse; and afterward she had stolen from another man a magic cap and mantle. No doubt the Lord had now punished her for that.

"Before we can think of a cure," said the unknown physician, "you must return the stolen property."

The princess had all the above-mentioned articles brought at once, and gave them gladly to the doctor, who promised to deliver them to the owners. "I will carry them away," said he, "and bring my medicine, through which you will be freed from the horns."

Half an hour later he returned, took her by the hand, looked at her tongue, and said, "Charming woman, you have eaten something, I suppose, from which these horns grew."

The princess answered, "I don't know that I have eaten anything harmful. I ate a few beautiful pears; with that exception I have never eaten any common food."

"You must have eaten something," said the doctor. "I have good medicine that will not fail, but I can only help you on condition that I receive the whole kingdom, with you in marriage, as our lord the king has proclaimed."

The king and princess promised then that the proclamation would be carried out if he would free her from the horns. After these words he set about the cure. He took from his pocket an apple and cut it into four parts; he told her to lie down, and gave her the first fourth of the apple. She was not able, however, to lie with comfort by reason of the horns. When she had eaten all the four quarters of the apple, the horns fell off at a blow. Then there was mighty gladness throughout the whole castle; everyone rejoiced that the princess, the only daughter of the king, was free of her horns.

The king had the marriage contract drawn up, and soon after they celebrated the wedding, at which the two friends of the young king were present; and he promised that while they lived they should remain at his court as the very first lords.

There was eating and drinking at the wedding; and among other things they ate bread made from rye. But, Mark tell thou no lie.

The Biter Bit
(Serbian)

O NCE UPON A TIME there was an old man who, whenever he heard anyone complain how many sons he had to care for, always laughed and said, "I wish that it would please God to give me a hundred sons!"

This he said in jest; as time, however, went on he had, in reality, neither more nor less than a hundred sons.

He had trouble enough to find different trades for his sons, but when they were once all started in life they worked diligently and gained plenty of money. Now, however, came a fresh difficulty. One day the eldest son came in to his father and said, "My dear father, I think it is quite time that I should marry."

Hardly had he said these words before the second son came in, saying, "Dear father, I think it is already time that you were looking out for a wife for me."

A moment later came in the third son, asking, "Dear father, don't you think it is high time that you should find me a wife?" In like manner came the fourth and fifth, until the whole hundred had made a similar request. All of them wished to marry, and desired their father to find wives for them as soon as he could.

The old man was not a little troubled at these requests; he said, however, to his sons, "Very well, my sons, *I* have nothing to say against your marrying; there is, however, I foresee, one great difficulty in the way. There are one hundred of you asking for wives, and I hardly think we can find one hundred marriageable girls in all the fifteen villages which are in our neighbourhood."

To this the sons, however, answered, "Don't be anxious about that, but mount your horse and take in your sack sufficient engagement-cakes. You must take, also, a stick in your hand so that you can cut a notch in it for every girl you see. It does not signify whether she be handsome or ugly, or lame or blind, just cut a notch in your stick for every one you meet with."

The old man said, "Very wisely spoken, my sons! I will do exactly as you tell me."

Accordingly he mounted his horse, took a sack full of cakes on his shoulder and a long stick in his hand, and started off at once to beat up the neighbourhood for girls to marry his sons.

The old man had travelled from village to village during a whole month, and whenever he had seen a girl he cut a notch in his stick. But he was getting pretty well tired, and he began to count how many notches he had already made. When he had counted them carefully over and over again, to be certain that he had counted all, he could only make out seventy-four so that still twenty-six were wanting to complete the number required. He was, however, so weary with his month's ride, that he determined to return home. As he rode along, he saw a priest driving oxen yoked to a plough, and seemingly very deep in anxious thought about something. Now the old man wondered a little to see the priest ploughing his own corn-fields without even a boy to help him, he therefore shouted to ask him why he drove his oxen himself. The priest, however, did not even turn his head to see who called to him, so intent was he in urging on his oxen and in guiding his plough.

The old man thought he had not spoken loud enough, so he shouted out again as loud as he could, "Stop your oxen a little, and tell me why you are ploughing yourself without even a lad to help you, and this, too, on a holy-day?"

Now the priest – who was in a perspiration with his hard work – answered testily, "I conjure you by your old age, leave me in peace! I cannot tell you my ill-luck."

At this answer, however, the old man was only the more curious, and persisted all the more earnestly in asking questions to find out why the priest ploughed on a Saint's day. At last the priest, tired with his importunity, sighed deeply and said, "Well, if you *will* know, I am the only man in my household, and God has blessed me with a hundred daughters!"

The old man was overjoyed at hearing this, and exclaimed cheerfully, "That's very good! It is just what I want, for *I* have a hundred sons, and so, as you have a hundred daughters, we can be friends!"

The moment the priest heard this he became pleasant and talkative, and invited the old man to pass the night in his house. Then, leaving his plough in the field, he drove the oxen back to the village. Just before reaching his house, however, he said to the old man, "Go yourself into the house whilst I tie up my oxen."

No sooner, however, had the old man entered the yard than the wife of the priest rushed at him with a big stick, crying out, "We have not bread enough for our hundred daughters, and we want neither beggars nor visitors," and with these words she drove him away.

Shortly afterwards the priest came out of the barn, and, finding the old man sitting on the road before the gate, asked him why he had not gone into the house as he had told him to do. Whereupon the old man replied, "I went in, but your wife drove me away!"

Then the priest said, "Only wait here a moment till I come back to fetch you." He then went quickly into his house and scolded his wife right well, saying, "What have you done? What a fine chance you have spoiled! The man who came in was going to be our friend, for he has a hundred sons who would gladly have married our hundred daughters!"

When the wife heard this she changed her dress hastily, and arranged her hair and head-dress in a different fashion. Then she smiled very sweetly, and welcomed with the greatest possible politeness the old man, when her husband led him into the house. In fact, she pretended that she knew nothing at all of anyone having been driven away from their door. And as the old man wanted much to find wives for his sons, he also pretended that he did not know that the smiling house-mistress and the woman who drove him away with a stick were one and the self-same person.

So the old man passed the night in the house, and next morning asked the priest formally to give him his hundred daughters for wives for his hundred sons. Thereupon the priest answered that he was quite willing, and had already spoken to his daughters about the matter, and that they, too, were all quite willing. Then the old man took out his "engagement-cakes" and put them on the table beside him, and gave each of the girls a piece of money to *mark* them. Then each of the engaged girls sent a small present by him to that one of his sons to whom she was thus betrothed. These gifts the old man put in the bag wherein he had carried the "engagement-cakes". He then mounted his horse and rode off merrily homewards.

There were great rejoicings in his household when he told how successful he had been in his search, and that he really had found a hundred girls ready and willing to be married; and these hundred, too, a priest's daughters.

The sons insisted that they should begin to make the wedding preparations without delay, and commenced at once to invite the guests who were to form part of the wedding procession to go to the priest's house and bring home the brides.

Here, however, another difficulty occurred. The old father must find two hundred *brideleaders* (two for each bride) one hundred *kooms* (first witnesses); one hundred *starisvats* (second witnesses); one hundred *chaious* (running footmen who go before the processions) and three hundred *vojvodes* (standard-bearers); and, besides these, a respectable number of other guests.

To find all these persons the father had to hunt throughout the neighbourhood for three years; at last, however, they were all found, and a day was appointed when they were to meet at his house and go thence in procession to the house of the priest.

On the appointed day all the invited guests gathered at the old man's house. With great noise and confusion, after a fair amount of feasting, the wedding procession was formed properly, and set out for the house of the priest, where the hundred brides were already prepared for their departure for their new home.

So great was the confusion, indeed, that the old man quite forgot to take with him one of the hundred sons, and never missed him in the greeting and talking and drinking he was obliged, as father of the bridegrooms, to go through. Now the young man had worked so long and so hard in preparing for the wedding-day that he never woke up till long after the procession had started and everyone had had, like his father, too much to do and too many things to think of to miss him.

The wedding procession arrived in good order at the priest's house, where a feast was already spread out for them. Having done honour to the various good things, and having gone through all the ceremonies usual on such occasions, the hundred brides were given over to their "leaders," and the procession started on its return to the old man's house. But, as they did not set off until pretty late in the afternoon, it was decided that the night should be spent somewhere on the road. When they came, therefore, to a certain river named "Luckless," as it was already dark, some of the men proposed that the party should pass the night by the side of the water without crossing over. However, some others of the chief of the party so warmly advised the crossing the river and encamping on the other bank, that this course was at length, after a very lively discussion, determined on; accordingly the procession began to move over the bridge.

Just, however, as the wedding party were half-way across the bridge its two sides began to draw nearer each other, and pressed the people so close together that they had hardly room to breathe – much less could they move forwards or backwards.

They were kept for some time in this position, some shouting and scolding, others quiet because frightened, until at length a black giant appeared, and shouted to them in a terribly loud voice, "Who are you all? Where do you come from? Where are you going?"

Some of the bolder among them answered, "We are going to our old friend's house, taking home the hundred brides for his hundred sons; but unluckily we ventured on this bridge after nightfall, and it has pressed us so tightly together that we cannot move one way or the other."

"And where is your old friend?" inquired the black giant.

Now all the wedding guests turned their eyes towards the old man. Thereupon he turned towards the giant, who instantly said to him, "Listen, old man! Will you give me what you have forgotten at home, if I let your friends pass over the bridge?"

The old man considered some time what it might be that he had forgotten at home, but at last, not being able to recollect anything in particular that he had left, and hearing on all sides the groans and moans of his guests, he replied, "Well, I will give it you, if you will only let the procession pass over."

Then the black giant said to the party, "You all hear what he has promised, and are all my witnesses to the bargain. In three days I shall come to fetch what I have bargained for."

Having said this, the black giant widened the bridge and the whole procession passed on to the other bank in safety. The people, however, no longer wished to spend the night on the way, so they moved on as fast as they could, and early in the morning reached the old man's house.

As everybody talked of the strange adventure they had met with, the eldest son, who had been left at home, soon began to understand how the matter stood, and went to his father saying, "O my father! you have sold *me* to the black giant!"

Then the old man was very sorry and troubled; but his friends comforted him, saying, "Don't be frightened! nothing will come of it."

The marriage ceremonies were celebrated with great rejoicings. Just, however, as the festivities were at their height, on the third day, the black giant appeared at the gate and shouted, "Now, give me at once what you have promised."

The old man, trembling all over, went forward and asked him, "What do you want?"

"Nothing but what you have promised me!" returned the black giant.

As he could not break his promise, the old man, very much distressed, was then obliged to deliver up his eldest son to the giant, who thereupon said, "Now I shall take your son with me, but after three years have passed you can come to the Luckless River and take him away."

Having said this the black giant disappeared, taking with him the young man, whom he carried off to his workshop as an apprentice to the trade of witchcraft.

From that time the poor old man had not a single moment of happiness. He was always sad and anxious, and counted every year, and month, and week, and even every day, until the dawn of the last day of the three years. Then he took a staff in his hand and hurried off to the bank of the river

Luckless. As soon as he reached the river, he was met by the black giant, who asked him, "Why are you come?" The old man answered that he had come to take home his son, according to his agreement.

Thereupon the giant brought out a tray on which stood a sparrow, a turtle-dove, and a quail, and said to the old man, "Now, if you can tell which of these is your son, you may take him away."

The poor old father looked intently at the three birds, one after the other, and over and over again, but at last he was forced to own that he could not tell which of them was his son. So he was obliged to go away by himself, and was far more miserable than before. He had hardly, however, got half-way home when he thought he would go back to the river and take one of the birds which he remembered had looked at him intently.

When he reached the river Luckless he was again met by the black giant, who brought out the tray again, and placed on it this time a partridge, a tit-mouse, and a thrush, saying, "Now, my old man, find out which is your son!"

The anxious father again looked at one bird after the other, but he felt more uncertain than before, and so, crying bitterly, again went away.

Just as the old man was going through a forest, which was between the river Luckless and his house, an old woman met him, and said, "Stop a moment! Where are you hurrying to? And why are you in such trouble?" Now, the old man was so deeply musing over his great unhappiness that he did not at first attend to the old woman; but she followed him, calling after him, and repeating her questions with more earnestness. So he stopped at last, and told her what a terrible misfortune had fallen upon him. When the old woman had listened to the whole story, she said cheerfully, "Don't be cast down! Don't be afraid! Go back again to the river, and, when the giant brings out the three birds, look into their eyes sharply. When you see that one of the birds has a tear in one of its eyes, seize that bird and hold it fast, for it has a human soul."

The old man thanked her heartily for her advice, and turned back, for the third time, towards the Luckless River. Again the black giant appeared, and looked very merry whilst he brought out his tray and put upon it a sparrow, a dove, and a woodpecker, saying, "My old man! find out which is your son!" Then the father looked sharply into the eyes of the birds, and saw that from the right eye of the dove a tear dropped slowly down. In a moment he grasped the bird tightly, saying, "This is my son!" The next moment he found himself holding fast his eldest son by the shoulder, and so, singing and shouting in his great joy, took him quickly home and gave him over to his eldest daughter-in-law, the wife of his son.

Now, for some time they all lived together very happily. One day, however, the young man said to his father, "Whilst I was apprentice in the workshop of the black giant, I learned a great many tricks of witchcraft. Now I intend to change myself into a fine horse, and you shall take me to market and sell me for a good sum of money. But be sure not to give up the halter."

The father did as the son had said. Next market-day he went to the city with a fine horse which he offered for sale. Many buyers came round him, admiring the horse, and bidding large sums for it, so that at last the old man was able to sell it for two thousand ducats. When he received the money, he took good care not to let go the halter, and he returned home far richer than he ever dreamt of being.

A few days later, the man who had bought the horse sent his servant with it to the river to bathe, and, whilst in the water, the horse got loose from the servant and galloped off into the neighbouring forest. There he changed himself back into his real shape and returned to his father's house.

After some time had passed, the young man said one day to his father, "Now I will change myself into an ox, and you can take me to market to sell me; but take care not to give up the rope with which you lead me."

So next market-day the old man went to the city leading a very fine ox, and soon found a buyer, who offered him ten times the usual price paid for an ox. The buyer asked also for the rope to lead the animal home, but the old man said, "What do you want with such an old thing? You had better buy a new one!" and he went off taking with him the rope.

That evening, whilst the servants of the buyer were driving the ox to the field, he ran away into a wood near, and, having taken there his human shape, returned home to his father's house.

On the eve of the next market-day, the young man said to his father, "Now I will change myself into a cow with golden horns, and you can sell me as before, only take care not to give up the string."

Accordingly he changed himself next morning into a cow, and the old man took it to the market-place, and asked for it three hundred crowns.

But the black giant had learnt that his former apprentice was making a great deal of money by practicing the trade he had taught him, and, being jealous at this, he determined to put an end to the young man's gains.

Therefore, on the third day he came to the market himself as a buyer, and the moment he saw the beautiful cow with golden horns he knew that it could be no other than his former apprentice. So he came up to the old man, and, having outbid all the other would-be purchasers, paid at once the price he had agreed on. Having done this, he caught the string in his hand, and tried to wrench it from the terrified old man, who called out, "I have not sold you the string, but the cow!" and held the string as fast as he could with both hands.

"Oh, no!" said the buyer, "I have the law and custom on my side! Whoever buys a cow, buys also the string with which it is led!" Some of the amused and astonished lookers-on said that this was quite true, therefore the old man was obliged to give up the string.

The black giant, well satisfied with his purchase, took the cow with him to his castle, and, after having put iron chains on her legs, fastened her in a cellar. Every morning the giant gave the cow some water and hay, but he never unchained her.

One evening, however, the cow, with incessant struggles, managed to get free from the chains, and immediately opened the cellar-door with her horns and ran away.

Next morning the black giant went as usual into the cellar, carrying the hay and water for the cow; but seeing she had got free and run away, he threw the hay down, and started off at once to pursue her.

When he came within sight of her, he turned himself into a wolf and ran at her with great fury; but his clever apprentice changed himself instantly from a cow into a bear, whereupon the giant turned himself from a wolf into a lion; the bear then turned into a tiger, and the lion changed into a crocodile, whereupon the tiger turned into a sparrow. Upon this the giant changed from the form of a crocodile into a hawk, and the apprentice immediately changed into a hare; on seeing which, the hawk became a greyhound. Then the apprentice changed from a hare into a falcon, and the greyhound into an eagle; whereupon the apprentice changed into a fish. The giant then turned from an eagle into a mouse, and immediately the apprentice, as a cat, ran after him; then the giant turned himself into a heap of millet, and the apprentice transformed himself into a hen and chickens, which very greedily picked up all the millet except one single seed, in which the master was, who changed himself into a squirrel; instantly, however, the apprentice became a hawk, and, pouncing on the squirrel, killed it.

In this way the apprentice beat his master, the black giant, and revenged himself for all the sufferings he had endured whilst learning the trade of witchcraft. Having killed the squirrel, the hawk took his proper shape again, and the young man returned joyfully to his father, whom he made immensely rich.

Vassilissa the Cunning and the Tsar of the Sea
(Russian)

A PEASANT SOWED RYE, and the Lord gave him a wonderful harvest. He could barely bring it in from the field. He drew the bundles home, threshed the grain, and poured it into bins; his granary was full to the brim. When he was pouring it in, he thought, "Now I shall live without trouble."

A mouse and a sparrow used to visit that peasant's barn; every one of God's days they came about five times, ate all they could, and then went out. The mouse would spring into her hole, and the sparrow fly away to his nest. They lived together in this way in friendship for three whole years and ate up all the grain; there remained only a mere trifle, about eight bushels, not more.

The mouse saw that the supply was drawing to an end and began to contrive how to deceive the sparrow and get possession of all that was left. And the mouse succeeded. She came in the dark night-time, gnawed a great hole in a plank, and let all the rye down through the floor to the last grain. Next morning the sparrow came to the granary to have breakfast and looked; there was nothing! The poor fellow flew out hungry and thought to himself, "Oh, the cursed creature, she has deceived me! I will fly now to her sovereign, the lion, and present a petition against the mouse; let the lion pass judgment on us in justice."

So he started and flew to the lion. "Lion, Tsar of beasts," said the sparrow, beating to him with the forehead, "I lived with one of thy beasts, the strong-toothed mouse. We lived for three years in one barn and had no dispute. But when the supply began to come to an end, she went to playing tricks, gnawed a hole through the floor, and let all the grain down to herself – left me, poor fellow, to be hungry. Judge us in truth; if not, I will fly to seek justice and reparation from my own Tsar, the eagle."

"Well, fly off, with God!" said the lion.

The sparrow rushed with his petition to the eagle and related the whole offence, how the mouse had stolen and the lion had upheld her. The eagle grew fiercely angry, and sent a swift courier to the lion straightway: "Come tomorrow with thy army of beasts to such and such a field; I will assemble all the birds and give battle."

Nothing to be done, the lion made a great call and summoned the beasts to battle. There were assembled of them seen and unseen. As soon as they came to the open field, the eagle flew upon them with his winged warriors like a cloud from heaven. A great battle began. They fought for three hours and three minutes, and the eagle Tsar conquered; he covered the whole field with bodies of beasts. Then he sent his birds to their homes, and flew himself to a slumbering forest, sat on a lofty oak, bruised and wounded, and began to think seriously how to regain his former strength.

This was a long time ago. There lived then a merchant with his wife, and they had not a single child. The merchant rose up one morning and said to his wife, "I have had a bad dream. I thought that a great bird fastened on me – one that eats a whole ox at a meal and drinks a pailful;

and it was impossible to get rid of the bird, impossible not to feed it. I'll go to the forest; mayhap the walk will cheer me."

He took his gun and went to the forest. Whether he wandered long or short in that forest, he wandered till he came to an oak-tree, saw an eagle, and was going to shoot it.

"Kill me not, good hero," said the eagle, in a human voice. "If thou kill me, small will be thy profit. Better take me home, feed me for three years, three months, and three days. I shall recover at thy house, shall let my wings grow, regain my strength, and repay thee with good."

"What pay can one expect from an eagle?" thought the merchant, and aimed a second time. The eagle spoke as at first. The merchant aimed a third time, and again the eagle begged, "Kill me not, good hero! Feed me three years, three months, and three days; when I have recovered, when my wings have grown and I have regained my strength, I'll repay thee with good."

The merchant took pity on the eagle, carried him home, killed an ox, and poured out a pailful of mead. "This will serve the eagle for a long time," thought he; but the eagle ate and drank all at one meal. A bad time to the merchant; from the unbidden guest utter ruin.

The eagle saw the merchant's loss and said, "Hear me, my host! Go to the open field. Thou wilt find there many beasts killed and wounded. Take their rich furs, bear them to the town to sell. Get food for thyself and me, and there will be some left for a supply."

The merchant went into the open field and saw many animals lying there, some slain and some wounded. He took the dearest furs, carried them to town to sell, and sold them for much money.

A year passed. The eagle said, "Bear me to that place where the lofty oaks are standing."

The merchant got his wagon ready and took him to that place. The eagle rose above the clouds, and when he swooped down, he struck a tree with his breast, the oak was split in two. "Well, merchant, good hero," said the eagle, "I have not regained my former strength; feed me another round year."

Another year passed. Again the eagle rose beyond the dark clouds, shot down from above, struck the tree with his breast, split the oak into small pieces. "Merchant, good hero, thou must feed me another whole year; I have not regained my former strength!"

When three years, three months, and three days had passed, the eagle said to the merchant, "Take me again to the same place – to the lofty oaks." The merchant carried him to the lofty oaks. The eagle soared higher than before; like a mighty whirlwind he struck from above the largest oak, broke it into small bits from the top to the root – indeed, the forest was reeling all around. "God save thee, merchant, good hero!" said the eagle. "Now all my former strength is with me. Leave thy horse, sit on my wings; I will bear thee to my own land, and pay thee for all the good thou hast done." The merchant sat on his wings, the eagle bore him out on the blue sea, and he rose high, high. "Look now," said he, "on the blue sea. Is it wide?"

"As a cart-wheel," answered the merchant.

The eagle shook his wings and threw the merchant, let him fall, gave him to feel mortal terror, and caught him before he had reached the water – caught him, and rose still higher. "Look on the blue sea. Is it great?"

"As a hen's egg."

The eagle shook his wings, threw the merchant, let him fall, but did not let him reach the water, caught him, and rose up higher than ever. "Look on the blue sea. Is it great?"

"As a poppy seed."

A third time the eagle shook his wings and threw the merchant from under the heavens; still he didn't let him reach the water, caught him, and asked, "Well, merchant, good hero, hast thou felt what mortal terror is?"

"I have," said the merchant. "And I thought I was lost forever."

"And so did I when thou wert pointing thy gun at me."

The eagle flew with the merchant beyond the sea, straight to the copper kingdom. "Behold, my eldest sister lives here!" said the eagle. "When we shall be guests with her, and she brings presents, take nothing, but ask for the copper casket." The eagle said this, struck the damp earth, and turned into a gallant hero.

They went through the broad court. The sister saw him and was delighted. "Oh, my own brother, how has God brought thee? I have not seen thee for three years and more; I thought thou wert lost forever. How can I entertain thee? How can I feast thee?"

"Entertain not me, my dear sister, I am at home in thy house; but entreat and entertain this good hero. He gave me meat and drink for three years – did not let me die of hunger."

She seated them at the oaken table, at the spread cloth; she feasted and entertained them, then led them to her treasure-chambers, showed treasures incalculable, and said to the merchant, "Good hero, here are gold, silver, and precious stones; take what thy soul desires."

The merchant gave answer: "I need neither gold, silver, nor precious stones. Give me the copper casket."

"Thou'lt not get it; that is not the boot for thy foot."

The brother was angry at his sister's words; he turned into an eagle – a swift bird – caught the merchant, and flew away.

"Oh, my own brother, come back!" cried the sister. "I'll not stand for the casket."

"Thou art late, sister!"

The eagle flew through the air. "Look, merchant, good hero, what is behind us and what before?"

"Behind, a fire is in sight; before us flowers are blooming."

"That is the copper kingdom in flames, and the flowers are blooming in the silver kingdom of my second sister. When we are her guests, and she offers gifts, take nothing, but ask for the silver casket." The eagle came, struck the damp earth, and became a good hero.

"Oh, my own brother," said his sister, "whence hast come; where wert thou lost; why hast thou been so long without visiting me; with what can I serve thee?"

"Entreat me not, entertain me not, my dear sister, I am at home with thee; but entreat and entertain this good hero, who gave me meat and drink for three years, and did not let me die of hunger."

She seated them at the oaken tables at spread cloths, entertained and feasted them, then led them to treasure-chambers. "Here are gold and silver and precious stones; take, merchant, what thy soul desires."

"I want neither gold, silver, nor precious stones. Give me only the silver casket."

"No, good hero, thy desire is not for the right morsel; thou mightest choke thyself."

The eagle brother was angry, caught up the merchant, and flew away.

"Oh, my own brother, come back! I will not stand for the casket."

"Thou art late, sister!"

Again the eagle flew under the heavens. "See, merchant, good hero, what is behind us, what is before?"

"Behind us a fire is blazing; before us are flowers in bloom."

"That is the silver kingdom in flames; but the flowers are blooming in the golden kingdom of my youngest sister. When we are her guests, and she offers gifts, take nothing; ask only for the golden casket." The eagle came to the golden kingdom and turned into a good hero.

"Oh, my own brother," said the sister, "whence hast thou come? Where hast thou vanished so long that thou hast not visited me? With what shall I feast thee?"

"Entreat me not, feast me not, I am at home; but entreat and feast this merchant, good hero. He gave me meat and drink for three years – saved me from hunger."

She seated them at the oaken table, at the spread cloth, entertained them, feasted them, led the merchant to her treasure-chambers, offered him gold, silver, and precious stones.

"I need nothing; give me only the golden casket."

"Take it for thy happiness. Thou didst give meat and drink to my brother for three years, and didst save him from hunger; I regret nothing that is spent on my brother."

So the merchant lived and feasted a while in the golden kingdom, till the time came for parting, for taking the road.

"Farewell," said the eagle; "think not on me with harsh feeling, but see that the casket is not opened till thou art at home."

The merchant journeyed homeward. Whether it was long or short, he grew tired and wished to rest. He stopped in a strange meadow on the land of the Tsar of the Sea; he looked and looked at the golden casket, couldn't endure, opened it. That moment, wherever it came from, there stood before him a great castle all painted. A multitude of servants appeared, inquiring, "What dost thou wish for; what dost thou want?" The merchant, good hero, ate his fill, drank enough, and lay down to sleep. The Tsar of the Sea saw that there was a great castle on his land, and he sent messengers: "Go see what sort of an insolent fellow has come and built a castle on my land without leave; let him go off at once in health and safety."

When such a threatening word came to the merchant he began to think and conjecture how to put the castle into the casket as before; he thought and thought – no, he could do nothing. "I should be glad to go away," said he, "but how, I can't think myself."

The messengers returned and reported all to the Tsar of the Sea. "Let him give me what he has at home but knows it not; I will put his palace in the golden casket."

There was no other way, and so the merchant promised with an oath to give what he had at home but knew it not. The Tsar of the Sea put the palace in the golden casket at once. The merchant took the casket and went his way. Whether it was long or short, he came home, and his wife met him. "Oh, be thou hearty, my world. Where wert thou lost?"

"Well, where I was I am not now."

"But while thou wert gone the Lord gave us a son."

"Ah! that is what was at home and I knew it not," thought the merchant, and he grew very sad and sorrowful.

"What is the matter? Art thou not glad to be here?" insisted his wife.

"Not that," said the merchant; and he told her all that had happened to him, and they grieved and wept together. But people of course cannot cry all their lives. The merchant opened his golden casket, and before them stood a great castle cunningly adorned, and he began to live with his wife and son and gain wealth.

Ten years passed and more; the merchant's son grew up, became wise, fine-looking, a splendid fellow. One morning he rose up in sadness and said to his father, "My father, I had a bad dream last night. I dreamed of the Tsar of the Sea; he commanded me to come to him. 'I am waiting long,' said he, 'it is time to know thy honour.'"

The father and mother shed tears, gave him their parental blessing, and let him go to a strange land. He went along the road, along the broad road; he walked over clear fields and wide steppes, and came to a dreamy forest. It was empty all around, not a soul to be seen; but there stood a small cabin by itself, with front to the forest and back to Ivan. "Cabin,

cabin," said he, "turn thy back to the forest, thy front to me." The cabin obeyed and turned its back to the forest, its front to Ivan. He entered the cabin; inside was Baba-Yaga, boneleg, lying from corner to corner. Baba-Yaga saw him and said, "Before now, nothing of Russia was heard with hearing or seen with sight, but now Russia runs to our eyes. Whence dost thou come, good hero, and where dost thou bear thy way?"

"Oh, thou old hag, thou hast given neither meat nor drink to a wayfaring man, and art asking for news!"

Baba-Yaga put drink on the table and various meats; she fed him, she gave him to drink, and put him to rest. Early next morning she roused him, and then she put questions. Ivan the merchant's son told the whole secret, and said, "Teach me, grandmother, how to go to the Tsar of the Sea."

"It is well that thou hast come to me; hadst thou not, thou wouldst have lost thy life, for the Tsar of the Sea is terribly angry because thou didst not go to him long ago. Listen to me: go by this path; thou wilt come to a lake. Hide behind a tree and wait a while. Three beautiful doves, maidens, will fly there – they are the daughters of the Tsar of the Sea. They will loose their wings, undress, and bathe in the lake. One will have many-coloured wings. Watch the moment, seize the wings, and do not give them up till she consents to marry thee. Then all will be right."

Ivan the merchant's son took farewell of Baba-Yaga and travelled the path she had shown, walked and walked, saw the lake, and hid himself behind a thick tree. After a time three doves came flying, one with many-coloured wings; they struck the earth, turned into beautiful maidens, removed their wings, and took off their dresses. Ivan the merchant's son kept his eyes open; he crept up in silence and took the many-coloured wings. He watched to see what would happen. The fair maidens bathed, came out of the water, two of them dressed straightway, put on their wings, turned into doves, and flew away. The third remained to find her wings. She searched, singing the while: "Tell who thou art, thou who hast taken my wings! If an old man, thou wilt be a father to me; if of middle years, my uncle dear; if a good youth, I will marry thee."

Ivan the merchant's son came from behind the tree. "Here are thy wings!"

"Now tell me, good youth, betrothed husband, of what stock or race art thou, and whither dost thou bear thy way?"

"I am Ivan the merchant's son, and I am going to thy own father, to the Tsar of the Sea."

"And my name is Vassilissa the Cunning."

Now, Vassilissa was the favourite daughter of the Tsar, and was first in mind and beauty. She showed her bridegroom how to go to the Tsar of the Sea, sprang away as a dove, and flew after her sisters.

Ivan the merchant's son came to the Tsar of the Sea, who made him serve in the kitchen, cut wood, and draw water. Chumichka, the cook, did not like him, and told lies to the Tsar. "Your Majesty," said he, "Ivan the merchant's son boasts that in one night he can cut down a great dense forest, pile the logs in heaps, dig out the roots, plough the land, sow it with wheat, reap that wheat, thresh it, grind it into flour, make cakes of the flour, and give these cakes to your Majesty at breakfast next morning."

"Well," said the Tsar, "call him to me."

Ivan the merchant's son came.

"Why art thou boasting that in one night thou canst cut down a thick forest, plough the land just like a clean field, sow it with wheat, reap the wheat, thresh it, and make it into flour, the flour into cakes for my breakfast next morning? See that by tomorrow morning this is all done; if not, I have a sword, and thy head leaves thy shoulders."

No matter how Ivan protested, it was no use. The order was given; it had to be carried out. He went away from the Tsar and hung his stormy head from grief. Vassilissa the Cunning, the daughter of the Tsar, saw him, and asked, "Why art thou grieved?"

"What is the use in telling thee? Thou couldst not cure my sorrow!"

"How knowest? Maybe I can."

Ivan the merchant's son told her what task the Tsar had put on him.

"What task is that! That is a pleasure – the task is ahead. Go thy way; pray to God and lie down to rest. The morning is wiser than the evening; toward daylight all will be ready."

Just at midnight Vassilissa the Cunning went out on the great porch and cried in a piercing voice. In one moment labourers ran together from every side – myriads of them; one was felling a tree, another digging out roots, another ploughing the land. In one place they were sowing, in another reaping and threshing. A pillar of dust went up to the sky, and at daybreak the grain was ground, the cakes baked. Ivan took the cakes to the breakfast of the Tsar.

"Splendid fellow!" said the Tsar; and he gave command to reward him from his own treasure.

Chumichka the cook was angrier than ever at Ivan, and began to talk against him again. "Your Majesty, Ivan the merchant's son boasts that in one night he can make a ship that will fly through the air."

"Well, call him hither."

They called Ivan the merchant's son.

"Why boast to my servants that in one night thou canst make a wonderful ship that will fly through the air, and say nothing to me? See this ship is ready by morning; if not, I have a sword, and thy head leaves thy shoulders."

Ivan the merchant's son from sorrow hung his stormy head lower than his shoulders, and went from the Tsar beside himself. Vassilissa the Cunning said to him, "Of what art thou grieving; why art thou sad?"

"Why should I not be sad? The Tsar of the Sea has commanded me to build in one night a ship that will fly through the air."

"What sort of task is that? That is not a task, but a pleasure; the task is ahead. Go thy way; lie down and rest. The morning is wiser than the evening; at daybreak all will be done."

At midnight Vassilissa the Cunning went out on the great porch, cried in a piercing voice. In a moment carpenters ran together from every side; they began to pound with their axes, and the work was seething quickly. Toward morning all was ready.

"A hero!" said the Tsar. "Come, now we will take a trip."

They sat on the ship together and took as a third companion Chumichka the cook; and they flew through the air. When they were flying over the place of wild beasts the cook bent over the side to look out. Ivan the merchant's son pushed him from the ship that moment. The savage beasts tore him into little bits. "Oh," cried Ivan the merchant's son, "Chumichka has fallen off!"

"The devil be with him," said the Tsar of the Sea. "To a dog, a dog's death!" They came back to the palace. "Thou art skilful, Ivan," said the Tsar. "Here is a third task for thee. Break my unridden stallion so that he will go under a rider. If thou wilt break him I will give thee my daughter in marriage; if not, I have a sword, and thy head leaves thy shoulders."

"Now that is an easy task," thought Ivan the merchant's son. He went away from the Tsar laughing. Vassilissa the Cunning saw him and asked about everything; he told her.

"Thou art not wise, Ivan," said she. "Now a difficult task is given thee – no easy labour. That stallion will be the Tsar himself. He will carry thee through the air above the standing forest, below the passing cloud, and scatter thy bones over the open field. Go quickly to the blacksmiths, order them to make for thee an iron hammer three poods in weight, and when thou art sitting on the stallion hold firmly and beat him on the head with the iron hammer."

Next day the grooms brought out the unridden stallion. They were barely able to hold him; he snorted, rushed, and reared. The moment Ivan sat on him he rose above the standing forest, below the passing cloud, flew through the air more swiftly than strong wind. The rider held firmly, beating him all the time on the head with the hammer. The stallion struggled beyond his power, and dropped to the damp earth. Ivan the merchant's son gave the stallion to the grooms, drew breath himself, and went to the palace. The Tsar of the Sea met him with bound head.

"I have ridden the horse, your Majesty."

"Well, come tomorrow to choose thy bride. But now my head aches."

Next morning Vassilissa the Cunning said to Ivan the merchant's son, "There are three sisters of us with our father; he will turn us into mares and make thee select. Be careful, take notice; on my bridle one of the spangles will be dim. Then he will let us out as doves. My sisters will pick buckwheat very quietly, but I will not – I will clap my wings. The third time he will bring us out as three maidens, one like the other in face, in stature, and hair. I will shake my handkerchief; by that thou mayest know me."

The Tsar brought out the three mares, one just like the other, and put them in a row. "Take the one that pleases thee," said the Tsar.

Ivan the merchant's son examined them carefully. He saw that on one bridle a spangle had grown dim. He caught that bridle and said, "This is my bride."

"Thou hast taken a bad one; thou mayest choose a better."

"No use, this will do for me."

"Choose a second time."

The Tsar let out three doves just alike, and scattered buckwheat before them. Ivan saw that one of them was shaking her wings all the time. He caught her by the wing and said, "This is my bride."

"Thou hast not taken the right piece; thou wilt choke thyself. Choose a third time."

He brought out three maidens, one like the other in face, in stature, and hair. Ivan the merchant's son saw that one waved her handkerchief; he seized her by the hand. "This is my bride."

There was nothing to be done. The Tsar could not help himself, and gave Vassilissa the Cunning to Ivan, and they had a joyous wedding.

Not much nor little time had passed when Ivan thought of escaping to his own country with Vassilissa the Cunning. They saddled their horses and rode away in the dark night. In the morning the Tsar discovered their flight and sent a pursuing party.

"Drop down to the damp earth," said Vassilissa the Cunning to her husband. "Perhaps thou wilt hear something."

He dropped to the earth, listened, and answered, "I hear the neighing of horses."

Vassilissa turned him into a garden, and herself into a head of cabbage. The pursuers returned to the Tsar empty-handed. "Your Majesty, there is nothing to be seen in the open country; we saw only a garden, and in the garden a head of cabbage."

"Go on, bring me that head of cabbage; that is their tricks."

Again the pursuers galloped on; again Ivan dropped down to the damp earth. "I hear," said he, "the neighing of horses." Vassilissa the Cunning made herself a well, and turned Ivan into a bright falcon. The falcon was sitting on the brink, drinking water. The pursuers came to the well. There was no road beyond, and they turned back.

"Your Majesty, there is nothing to be seen in the open country; we saw only a well, and a bright falcon was drinking water out of that well."

The Tsar himself galloped a long time to overtake them.

"Drop down to the damp earth; perhaps thou wilt hear something," said Vassilissa the Cunning to her husband.

"There is a hammering and thundering greater than before."

"That is my father chasing us. I know not, I cannot think what to do."

Vassilissa the Cunning had three things – a brush, a comb, and a towel. She remembered them and said, "God is yet merciful; I have still defence before the Tsar." She threw the brush behind her; it became a great drowsy forest. A man could not put his hand through, could not ride around it in three years. Behold, the Tsar of the Sea gnawed and gnawed the drowsy forest, made a path for himself, burst through it, and was again in pursuit. He was drawing near them, had only to seize them with his hand. Vassilissa threw her comb behind, and it became such a great lofty mountain that a man could neither pass over it nor go around it.

The Tsar of the Sea dug and dug in the mountain, made a path, and again chased after them. Then Vassilissa the Cunning threw the towel behind her, and it became a great, great sea. The Tsar galloped up to the sea, saw the road was stopped, and turned homeward.

Ivan the merchant's son was near home, and said to Vassilissa the Cunning, "I will go ahead, tell my father and mother about thee, and do thou wait here."

"See to it," said Vassilissa the Cunning, "when thou art home, kiss all but thy godmother; if thou kiss her thou'lt forget me."

Ivan came home, kissed all in delight, kissed his godmother, and forgot Vassilissa. She stood there, poor thing, on the road, waited and waited; Ivan did not come for her. She went to the town and hired to do work for an old woman.

Ivan thought of marrying; he found a bride, and arranged a feast for the whole world.

Vassilissa heard this, dressed herself as a beggar, and came to the merchant's house to beg alms.

"Wait," said the merchant's wife; "I'll bake thee a small cake instead of cutting the big one."

"God save thee for that, mother!" said Vassilissa.

But the great cake got burnt, and the small one came out nicely. The merchant's wife gave Vassilissa the burnt cake and put the small one on the table. They cut that cake, and immediately two pigeons flew out.

"Kiss me," said the cock-pigeon to the other.

"No, thou wilt forget me, as Ivan the merchant's son forgot Vassilissa the Cunning."

And the second and the third time he asked, "Kiss me."

"No, thou'lt forget me, as Ivan the merchant's son forgot Vassilissa the Cunning."

Ivan remembered then; he knew who the beggar was, and said to his father and mother, "This is my wife."

"Well, if thou hast a wife, then live with her."

They gave rich presents to the new bride, and let her go home; but Ivan the merchant's son lived with Vassilissa the Cunning, gained wealth, and shunned trouble.

Little Rolling-Pea
(Belarusian)

IN A CERTAIN EMPIRE and a certain province, on the ocean sea, on the island of Bujan, stood a green oak, and under the oak a roasted ox, and by its side a whetted knife. Suddenly the knife was seized. Be so good as to eat! This isn't a story (*kazka*), but only a preface to a story (*prikazka*): whoever shall listen to my story, may he have a sableskin cloak, and a horseskin cloak, and a very beautiful damsel, a hundred roubles for the wedding, and fifty for a jollification!

There was a husband and wife. The wife went for water, took a bucket, and after drawing water, went home, and all at once she saw a pea rolling along. She thought to herself, "This is the gift of God." She took it up and ate it, and in course of time became the mother of a baby boy, who grew not by years, but by hours, like millet dough when leavened. They nursed and petted him in a way that couldn't be improved upon, and put him to school. What others learnt in three or four years he understood in a single year, and the book was not sufficient for him. He came from the school to his father and mother. "Now, then, Daddy and Mammy, thank my teachers, for already many come to school to me. Thank God, I know more than they."

Well, he went into the street to amuse himself, and found a pin, which he brought to his father and mother. He said to his father, "Here's this piece of iron; take it to a smith, and let him make me a mace of seven poods weight." His father didn't say a single word to him, but only thought in his own mind, "The Lord has given me a child different from other people; I think he has a middling understanding, but he is now making a fool of me. Can it possibly be that a seven-pood mace can be made out of a pin?" His father, having a considerable sum of money in gold, silver, and paper, drove to the town, bought seven poods of iron, and gave them to a smith to make a mace of. They made him a seven-pood mace, and he brought it home.

Little Rolling-pea came out from the attic, took his seven-pood mace, and, hearing a storm in the sky, threw it into the clouds. He went up into his attic. "Mother, look in my head before I start; a nasty thing is biting me, for I am a young lad." Well, rising from his mother's knees, he went out into the yard and saw the clouds. He fell down with his right ear to the broad ground, and on rising up called his father, "Father, come here: see what is whizzing and humming; my mace is coming to the ground." He placed his knee in the way of his mace; the mace struck him on the knee and broke in halves. He became angry with his father. "Well, father, why did you not have a mace made for me out of the iron that I gave you? If you had done so, it would not have broken, but only bent. Here is the same iron for you, go and get it made; don't add any of your own." The smiths put the iron in the fire and began to beat it with hammers and pull it, and made a seven-pood mace.

Little Rolling-pea took his seven-pood mace and got ready to go on a journey, a long journey; he went and went, and Overturn-hill met him. "I salute you, brother Little Rolling-pea! Whither are you going? Whither are you journeying?" Little Rolling-pea also asked him a question: "Who are you?" "I am the mighty hero Overturn-hill." "Will you be my comrade?"

said Little Rolling-pea. He replied, "Possibly I will be at your service." They went on together.

They went and went, and the mighty hero Overturn-oak met them. "God bless you, brothers! Good health to you! What manner of men are you?" inquired Overturn-oak. "Little Rolling-pea and Overturn-hill." "Whither are you going?" "To such a city. A dragon devours people there, so we are going to smite him." "Is it not possible for me to join your company?" "It is possible," said Little Rolling-pea. They went to the city, and made themselves known to the emperor. "What manner of men are you?" "We are mighty heroes!" "Is it in your power to deliver this city? A dragon is ravenous and destroys many people. He must be slain." "Why do we call ourselves mighty heroes, if we do not slay him?"

Midnight came, and they went up to a bridge of guelder-rosewood over a river of fire. Lo! up came a six-headed dragon, and posted himself upon the bridge, and immediately his horse neighed, his falcon chattered, and his hound howled. He gave his horse a blow on the head: "Don't neigh, devil's carrion! Don't chatter, falcon! And you, hound, don't howl! For here is Little Rolling-pea. Well now," said he, "come forth, Little Rolling-pea! shall we fight or shall we try our strength?" Little Rolling-pea answered, "Not to try their strength do good youths travel, but only to fight." They began the combat. Little Rolling-pea and his comrades struck the dragon three blows at a time on three heads. The dragon, seeing that he could not escape destruction, said, "Well, brothers, it is only little Rolling-pea that troubles me. I'd settle matters with you two." They began to fight again, smashed the dragon's remaining heads, took the dragon's horse to the stable, his falcon to the mews, and his hound to the kennel; and Little Rolling-pea cut out the tongues from all six heads, took and placed them in his knapsack, and the headless trunk they cast into the river of fire. They came to the emperor and brought him the tongues as certain proof. The emperor thanked them. "I see that you are mighty heroes and deliverers of the city, and all the people. If you wish to drink and eat, take all manner of beverages and eatables without money and without tax." And from joy he issued a proclamation throughout the whole town, that all the eating-houses, inns, and small public-houses were to be open for the mighty heroes. Well, they went everywhere, drank, amused themselves, refreshed themselves, and enjoyed various honours.

Night came, and exactly at midnight they went under the guelder-rose bridge to the river of fire, and speedily up came a seven-headed dragon. Immediately his horse neighed, his falcon chattered, and his hound howled. The dragon immediately struck his horse on the head. "Neigh not, devil's carrion! chatter not, falcon! howl not, hound! for here is Little Rolling-pea. Now then," said he, "come forth, Little Rolling-pea! Shall we fight or try our strength?" "Good youths travel not to try their strength, but only to fight." And they began the combat, and the heroes beat off six of the dragon's heads; the seventh remained. The dragon said, "Give me breathing time!" But Little Rolling-pea said, "Don't expect me to give you breathing time." They began the combat again. He beat off the last head also, cut out the tongues, and placed them in his knapsack, but threw the trunk into the river of fire. They came to the emperor and brought the tongues for certain proof.

The third time they went at midnight to the bridge of guelder-rose and the river of fire; speedily up came to them a nine-headed dragon. Immediately his horse neighed, his falcon chattered, and his hound howled. The dragon struck his horse on the head. "Neigh not, devil's carrion! falcon, chatter not! hound, howl not! for here is Little Rolling-pea. And now come forth, Little Rolling-pea! Shall we fight or try our strength?" Little Rolling-pea said, "Not to try their strength do good youths travel, but only to fight." They began the combat, and the heroes beat off eight heads; the ninth remained. Little Rolling-pea said, "Give us breathing time, unclean power!" It answered, "Take breathing time or not, you will not overcome me; you slew my brothers by craft, not by strength." Little Rolling-pea not only fought, but thought how to delude the dragon. All at once he thought of a plan, and said, "Yes, there's still much of your brother behind – I'll take you all." Hastily the dragon looked round, and he cut off the ninth head also, cut out the tongues, put them into his knapsack, and threw the trunk into the river of fire. They went to the emperor. The emperor said, "I thank you, mighty heroes! live with God, and with joy and courage, and take as much gold, silver, and paper money as you want."

After this the wives of the three dragons met together and took counsel together. "Whence did those men come who slew our husbands? Well, we *shall* be women if we don't get rid of them out of the world." The youngest said, "Now then, sisters! let us go by the highroad, where they will go. I will make myself into a very beautiful wayside seat, and if, when wearied, they sit down upon it, it will be death to them all." The second said to her, "If you do nothing to them, I will make myself into an apple tree beside the highroad, and when they begin to come up to me, the agreeable odour will attract them; and if they taste the apples, it will be death to them all." Well, the heroes came up to the beautiful wayside seat. Little Rolling-pea thrust his sword into it up to the hilt – blood poured forth! They went on to the apple tree. "Brother Little Rolling-pea," said the heroes, "let us each eat an apple." But he said, "If it is possible, let us eat; if it is not possible, let us go on further." He drew his sword and thrust it into the apple tree up to the hilt, and blood poured forth immediately. The third she-dragon hastened after them, and extended her jaws from the earth to the sky.

Little Rolling-pea saw that there was not room for them to pass by. How were they to save themselves? He looked about and saw that she specially aimed at him, and threw the three horses into her mouth. The she-dragon flew off to the blue sea to drink water, and they proceeded further. She pursued them again. He saw that she was near, and threw the three falcons into her mouth. Again the she-dragon flew to the blue sea to drink water, and they proceeded further. Little Rolling-pea looked round; the she-dragon was again pursuing him, and seeing his danger, he took and threw the three hounds into her mouth. Again she flew off to the blue sea to drink water; while she drank her fill, they proceeded still further. He looked round and saw that she was catching them up again.

Little Rolling-pea took his two comrades and threw them into her mouth. The she-dragon flew to the blue sea to drink water, and he went on. Again she overtook him; he looked round, saw that she was not far off, and said, "Lord, protect me and save my soul!" He saw before him an iron workshop, and fled into the smithy. The smith said to him, "Why, stranger, are you so cowardly?" "Honourable gentlemen! protect me from an unclean power, and save my soul!" They took and shut the smithy completely up. "Give up to me what is mine!" said the she-dragon. Then the smiths said to her, "Lick the iron door through, and we will place him on your tongue." She licked the door through, and placed her tongue in the centre. The smiths seized her tongue three at a time with red-hot pincers, and said, "Come, stranger, do with her what you will!" He went out into the yard, and began to pound the she-dragon, and pounded her skin to the bones, and her bones to the marrow; then took her with her whole carcase and buried her seven fathoms deep. Then, and not till then, did he live and eat morsels; but we ate bread, for he had none. I was there, too, and drank honey-wine; it flowed over my beard, but didn't get into my mouth.

Explorations of Morality

IN SLAVIC FOLKTALES, when a moral lesson is not learned, there is a regression in the hero's position. Regardless of whether the hero is male or female, in this situation mythical creatures help them explore morality in order to make them stronger, braver and wiser.

Such is the case in the story 'The Bear in the Forest Hut' (*see* page 146) when the heroine is left in the forest by her father, having been blamed by her stepmother, only to be found, protected and raised by a bear. This bear, holding attributes of Perun (the God of Thunder), keeps the girl safe in his forest hut, and after every job well done gives her presents. It is the work she does that helps her explore her morality, and the bear assures her that after every successful lesson she earns a treat. The results of the lessons learned are the happy endings in the folktales of this section.

The Good Ferryman and the Water Nymphs
(Polish)

T HERE WAS ONCE AN OLD MAN, very poor, with three sons. They lived chiefly by ferrying people over a river; but he had had nothing but ill-luck all his life. And to crown all, on the night he died, there was a great storm, and in it the crazy old ferry-boat, on which his sons depended for a living, was sunk.

As they were lamenting both their father and their poverty, an old man came by, and learning the reason of their sorrow said, "Never mind; all will come right in time. Look! there is your boat as good as new."

And there was a fine new ferry-boat on the water, in place of the old one, and a number of people waiting to be ferried over.

The three brothers arranged to take turns with the boat and divide the fares they took.

They were, however, very different in disposition. The two elder brothers were greedy and avaricious, and would never take anyone over the river without being handsomely paid for it.

But the youngest brother took over poor people, who had no money, for nothing; and moreover, he frequently relieved their wants out of his own pocket.

One day at sunset, when the eldest brother was at the ferry, the same old man, who had visited them on the night their father died, came and asked for a passage.

"I have nothing to pay you with but this empty purse," he said.

"Go and get something to put in it then first," replied the ferryman, "and be off with you now!"

Next day it was the second brother's turn; and the same old man came and offered his empty purse as his fare. But he met with a like reply.

The third day it was the youngest brother's turn; and when the old man arrived and asked to be ferried over for charity, he answered, "Yes, get in, old man."

"And what is the fare?" asked the old man.

"That depends upon whether you can pay or not," was the reply, "but if you cannot, it is all the same to me."

"A good deed is never without its reward," said the old man, "but in the meantime take this empty purse; though it is very worn and looks worth nothing. But if you shake it, and say:

'For his sake who gave it, this purse I hold,
I wish may always be full of gold;'

it will always afford you as much gold as you wish for."

The youngest brother came home, and his brothers, who were sitting over a good supper, laughed at him, because he had taken only a few copper coins that day, and they told him he should have no supper. But when he began to shake his purse and scatter gold coins all about, they jumped up from the table and began picking them up eagerly.

And as it was share and share alike, they all grew rich very quickly. The youngest brother made good use of his riches, for he gave away money freely to the poor. But the greedy elder brothers envied him the possession of the wonderful purse, and contrived to steal it from him. Then they left their old home; and the one bought a ship, laded it with all sorts of merchandize, for a trading voyage. But the ship ran upon a rock, and everyone on board was drowned. The second brother was no more fortunate, for as he was travelling through a forest with an enormous treasure of precious stones, in which he had laid out his wealth, to sell at a profit, he was waylaid by robbers, who murdered him and shared the spoil among them.

The youngest brother, who remained at home, having lost his purse, became as poor as before. But he still did as formerly, took pay from passengers who could afford it, ferried over poor folks for nothing, and helped those who were poorer than himself so far as he could.

One day the same old man with the long white beard came by; the ferryman welcomed him as an old friend, and while rowing him over the river, told him all that had happened since he last saw him.

"Your brothers did very wrong, and they have paid for it," said the old man, "but you were in fault yourself. Still, I will give you one more chance.

Take this hook and line; and whatever you catch, mind you hold fast, and not let it escape you, or you will bitterly repent it."

The old man then disappeared, and the ferryman looked in wonder at his new fishing-tackle – a diamond hook, a silver line, and a golden rod.

All at once the hook sprang of itself into the water; the line lengthened out along the river current, and there came a strong pull upon it. The fisherman drew it in, and beheld a most lovely creature, upwards from the waist a woman, but with a fish's tail.

"Good ferryman, let me go," she said. "Take your hook out of my hair! The sun is setting, and after sunset I can no longer be a water-nymph again."

But without answering, the ferryman only held her fast and covered her over with his coat, to prevent her escaping. Then the sun set, and she lost her fish-tail.

"Now," she said, "I am yours; so let us go to the nearest church and get married."

She was already dressed as a bride, with a myrtle garland on her head, in a white dress, with a rainbow-coloured girdle, and rich jewels in her hair and on her neck. And she held in her hand the wonderful purse that was always full of gold.

They found the priest and all ready at the church, were married in a few minutes, and then came home to their wedding-feast, to which all the neighbours were invited. They were royally entertained, and when they were about to leave, the bride shook the wonderful purse and sent a shower of gold pieces flying among the guests; so they all went home very well pleased.

The good ferryman and his marvellous wife lived most happily together; they never wanted for anything, and gave freely to all who came. He continued to ply his ferry-boat; but he now took all passengers over for nothing, and gave them each a piece of gold into the bargain.

Now there was a king over that country, who a year ago had just succeeded to his elder brother. He had heard of the ferryman, who was so marvellously rich, and wishing to ascertain the truth of the story he had heard, came on purpose to see for himself. But when he saw the ferryman's beautiful young wife, he resolved to have her for himself, and determined to get rid of her husband somehow.

At that time there was an eclipse of the sun; and the king sent for the ferryman, and told him he must find out the cause of this eclipse, or be put to death.

He came home in great distress to his wife; but she replied, "Never mind, my dear. I will tell you what to do, and how to gratify the king's curiosity."

So she gave him a wonderful ball of thread, which he was to throw before him, and follow the thread as it kept unwinding – towards the East.

He went on a long way, over high mountains, deep rivers, and wide regions. At last he came to a ruined city, where a number of corpses were lying about unburied, tainting the air with pestilence.

The good man was sorry to see this, and took the pains to summon men from the neighbouring cities, and get the bodies properly buried. He then resumed his journey.

He came at last to the ends of the earth. Here he found a magnificent golden palace, with an amber roof, and diamond doors and windows.

The ball of thread went straight into the palace, and the ferryman found himself in a vast apartment, where sat a very dignified old lady, spinning from a golden distaff.

"Wretched man! what are you here for?" she exclaimed, when she saw him. "My son will come back presently and burn you up."

He explained to her how he had been forced to come out of sheer necessity.

"Well, I must help you," replied the old lady, who was no less than the Mother of the Sun, "because you did Sol that good turn some days ago, in burying the inhabitants of that town, when they were killed by a dragon. He journeys every day across the wide arch of heaven, in a diamond car drawn by twelve grey horses with golden manes, giving heat and light to the whole world. He will soon be back here, to rest for the night...But... here he comes; hide yourself, and take care to observe what follows."

So saying, she changed her visitor into a lady-bird, and let him fly to the window.

Then the neighing of the wonderful horses and the rattling of chariot wheels were heard, and the bright Sun himself presently came in and, stretching himself upon a coral bed, remarked to his mother, "I smell a human being here!"

"What nonsense you talk!" replied his mother. "How could any human being come here? You know it is impossible."

The Sun, as if he did not quite believe her, began to peer anxiously about the room.

"Don't be so restless," said the old lady, "but tell me why you suffered eclipse a month or two ago."

"How could I help it?" answered the Sun. "When the dragon from the deep abyss attacked me, and I had to fight him? Perhaps I should have been fighting with the monster till now, if a wonderful mermaid had not come to help me. When she began to sing, and looked at the dragon with her beautiful eyes, all his rage softened at once; he was absorbed in gazing upon her beauty, and I meanwhile burnt him to ashes, and threw them into the sea."

The Sun then went to sleep, and his mother again touched the ferryman with her spindle; he then returned to his natural shape, and slipped out of the palace. Following the ball of thread, he reached home at last, and next day went to the king and told him all.

But the king was so enchanted at the description of the beautiful sea-maiden that he ordered the ferryman to go and bring her to him, on pain of death.

He went home very sad to his wife, but she told him she would manage this also. So saying, she gave him another ball of thread to show him which way to go, and she also gave him a carriage-load of costly lady's apparel, jewels, and ornaments – told him what he was to do, and they took leave of one another.

On the way the ferryman met a youth riding on a fine grey horse, who asked, "What have you got there, man?"

"A woman's wearing apparel, most costly and beautiful." He had several dresses, not simply one.

"I say, give me some of those as a present for my intended, whom I am going to see. I can be of use to you, for I am the Storm-wind. I will come, whenever you call upon me thus:

'Storm-wind! Storm-wind! come with speed!
Help me in my sudden need!'"

The ferryman gave him some of the most beautiful things he had, and the Storm-wind passed.

A little further on he met an old man, grey-haired, but strong and vigorous-looking, who also said, "What have you got there?"

"Women's garments costly and beautiful."

"I am going to my daughter's wedding; she is to marry the Storm-wind; give me something as a wedding present for her, and I will be of use to you. I am the Frost; if you need me call upon me thus:

'Frost, I call thee; come with speed;
Help me in my sudden need!'"

The ferryman let him take all he wanted and went on.

And now he came to the sea-coast; here the ball of thread stopped, and would go no further.

The ferryman waded up to his waist into the sea, and set up two high poles, with cross-bars between them, upon which he hung dresses of various colours, scarves, ribbons, gold chains, diamond earrings and pins, shoes, and looking-glasses, and then hid himself, with his wonderful hook and line ready.

As soon as the morning rose from the sea, there appeared far away on the smooth waters a silvery boat, in which stood a beautiful maiden with a golden oar in one hand, while with the other she gathered together her long golden hair, all the while singing so beautifully to the rising sun, that, if the ferryman had not quickly stopped his ears, he would have fallen into a delicious reverie, and then asleep.

She sailed along a long time in her silver boat, and round her leaped and played golden fishes with rainbow wings and diamond eyes. But all at once she perceived the rich clothes and ornaments hung up on the poles, and as she came nearer, the ferryman called out:

"Storm-wind! Storm-wind! come with speed!
Help me in my sudden need!"

"What do you want?" asked the Storm-wind.

The ferryman without answering him, called out:

"Frost, I call thee; come with speed,
Help me in my sudden need!"

"What do you want?" asked the Frost.

"I want to capture the sea-maiden."

Then the wind blew and blew, so that the silver boat was capsized, and the frost breathed on the sea till it was frozen over.

Then the ferryman rushed up to the sea-maiden, entangling his hook in her golden hair, lifted her on his horse, and rode off as swift as the wind after his wonderful ball of thread.

She kept weeping and lamenting all the way. But as soon as they reached the ferryman's home, and saw his wife, all her sorrow changed into joy; she laughed with delight, and threw herself into her arms.

And then it turned out that the two were sisters.

Next morning the ferryman went to court with both his wife and sister-in-law, and the king was so delighted with the beauty of the latter that he at once offered to marry her. But she could give him no answer until he had the Self-playing Guitar.

So the king ordered the ferryman to procure him this wonderful guitar, or be put to death.

His wife told him what to do, and gave him a handkerchief of hers, embroidered with gold, telling him to use this in case of need.

Following the ball of thread, he came at last to a great lake, in the midst of which was a green island.

He began to wonder how he was to get there, when he saw a boat approaching, in which was an old man with a long white beard, and he recognized him with delight as his former benefactor.

"How are you, ferryman?" he asked. "Where are you going?"

"I am going wherever the ball of thread leads me, for I must fetch the Self-playing Guitar."

"This guitar," said the old man, "belongs to Goldmore, the lord of that island. It is a difficult matter to have to do with him; but perhaps you may succeed. You have often ferried me over the water; I will ferry you now."

The old man pushed off, and they reached the island.

On arriving the ball of thread went straight into a palace, where Goldmore came out to meet the traveller, and asked him where he was going and what he wanted.

He explained, "I am come for the Self-playing Guitar."

"I will only let you have it on condition that you do not go to sleep for three days and nights. And if you do, you will not only lose all chance of the Self-playing Guitar, but you must die."

What could the poor man do but agree to this?

So Goldmore conducted him to a great room and locked him in. The floor was strewn with sleepy-grass, so he fell asleep directly.

Next morning in came Goldmore, and on waking him up said, "So you went to sleep! Very well, you shall die!"

And he touched a spring in the floor, and the unhappy ferryman fell down into an apartment beneath, where the walls were of looking-glass, and there were great heaps of gold and precious stones lying about.

For three days and nights he lay there; he was fearfully hungry. And then it dawned upon him that he was to be starved to death!

He called out, and entreated in vain. Nobody answered, and though he had piles of gold and jewels about him, they could not purchase him a morsel of food.

He sought in vain for any means of exit. There was a window of clearest crystal, but it was barred by a heavy iron grating. But the window looked into a garden whence he could hear nightingales singing, doves cooing, and the murmur of a brook. But inside he saw only heaps of useless gold and jewels, and his own face, worn and haggard, reflected a thousand times.

He could now only pray for a speedy death, and took out a little iron cross, which he had kept by him since his boyhood. But in doing so he also drew out the gold-embroidered handkerchief, given him by his wife, and which he had quite forgotten till now.

Goldmore had been looking on, as he often did, from an opening in the ceiling to enjoy the sight of his prisoner's sufferings. All at once he recognized the handkerchief as belonging to his own sister, the ferryman's wife.

He at once changed his treatment of his brother-in-law, as he had discovered him to be, took him out of prison, led him to his own apartments, gave him food and drink, and the Self-playing Guitar into the bargain.

Coming home, the ferryman met his wife half-way.

"The ball of thread came home alone," she explained, "so I judged that some misfortune had befallen you, and I was coming to help you."

He told her all his adventures, and they returned home together.

The king was all eagerness to see and hear the Self-playing Guitar; so he ordered the ferryman, his wife, and her sister to come with it to the palace at once.

Now the property of this Self-playing Guitar was such that wherever its music was heard, the sick became well, those who were sad merry, ugly folks became handsome, sorceries were dissolved, and those who had been murdered rose from the dead and slew their murderers.

So when the king, having been told the charm to set the guitar playing, said the words, all the court began to be merry and dance – except the king himself! For all at once the door opened, the music ceased, and the figure of the late king stood up in his shroud, and said, "I was the rightful possessor of the throne! And you, wicked brother, who caused me to be murdered, shall now reap your reward!"

So saying, he breathed upon him, and the king fell dead – on which the phantom vanished.

But as soon as they recovered from their fright, all the nobility who were present acclaimed the ferryman as their king.

The next day, after the burial of the late king, the beautiful sea-maiden, the beloved of the Sun, went back to the sea, to float about in her silvery canoe, in the company of the rainbow fishes, and to rejoice in the sunbeams.

But the good ferryman and his wife lived happily ever after as king and queen. And they gave a grand ball to the nobility and to the people. The Self-playing Guitar furnished the music, the wonderful purse scattered gold all the time, and the king entertained all the guests right royally.

The Bear in the Forest Hut
(Polish)

THERE WAS ONCE AN OLD MAN who was a widower, and he had married an old woman who was a widow. Both had had children by their first marriage; and now the old man had a daughter of his own still living, and the old woman also had a daughter.

The old man was an honest, hard-working, and good-natured old fellow, but too much under his wife's thumb. This was very unfortunate, because she was wicked, cunning, and sly, and a bad old witch.

Her daughter was only too like her in disposition, but she was her mother's darling.

But the old man's daughter was a very good sweet girl. Nevertheless her stepmother hated her; she was always tormenting her, and wishing her dead.

One day she had beaten her very cruelly, and pushed her out of doors, then she said to the old man, "Your wretched daughter is always giving me trouble; she is such an ill-tempered, spoilt hussy, that I cannot do anything with her. So if you wish for peace in the house, you must put her into your waggon, drive her away into the forest, and come back without her."

The old man was very sorry to have to do this; for he loved his own little daughter most dearly. But he was so afraid of his wife that he dared not refuse. So he put the poor girl into his waggon, drove a long way into the forest, took her out, and left her there alone.

She wandered about a long time, gathering wild strawberries to eat with a little piece of bread, which her father had given her. Towards evening she came to the door of a hut in the forest, and knocked at the door.

Nobody answered her knock. So she lifted the latch, went in, and looked round – there was nobody there.

But there was a table in one corner, and benches all round the walls, and an oven by the door. And near the table, close to the window, was a spinning-wheel and a quantity of flax.

The girl sat down to the spinning-wheel and opened the window, looked out, and listened; but nobody came.

But as it grew dusk she heard a rustle not far off, and from somewhere not far from the hut a voice was heard, singing:

"Wanderer, outcast, forsaken!
Whom the night has overtaken;
If no crime your conscience stain,
In this hut tonight remain."

When the voice ceased, she answered:

"I am outcast and forsaken;
Yet unstained by crime am I:
Be you rich, or be you poor;
For this night here let me lie!"

Once more there was a rustle in the branches; the door opened, and there came into the room – a bear!

The girl started up, very frightened, but the bear only said, "Good evening, pretty maiden!"

"Good evening to you, whoever you are," she replied, somewhat reassured.

"How did you come here?" he asked. "Was it of your own free will, or by compulsion?"

The maiden told him all, weeping; but the bear sat down beside her, and stroking her face with his paw, replied, "Do not cry, pretty one; you shall be happy yet. But in the meantime you must do just what I tell you. Do you see that flax? You must spin it into thread; of that thread you must weave cloth, and of that cloth you must make me a shirt. I shall come here tomorrow at this same time, and if the shirt is ready I will reward you. Goodbye!"

So saying the bear made her a parting bow, and went out. At first the girl began to cry, and said to herself, "How can I do this in only twenty-four hours – spin all that flax, weave it into cloth, and make a shirt out of it? Well! I must set to work! and do what I can…He will at least see that my will was good, though I was unable to perform the task."

Thus saying, she dried her tears, ate some of her bread and strawberries, sat down to the spinning-wheel, and began to spin by the light of the moon.

The time went by quickly as she worked, and it was daylight before she knew.

And there was no more flax left; she had spun out the last distaff-full.

She was astonished to see how fast the work had gone, and began to wonder how she was to weave the thread without any loom.

Thinking, she fell asleep.

When she woke, the sun was already high in the heavens. There was breakfast ready on the table and a loom under the window.

She ran down to the neighbouring brook, washed her face and hands, came back, said grace, and ate her breakfast; then she sat down to the loom.

The shuttle flew so fast that the cloth was all ready by noon.

She took it out into a meadow, sprinkled it from the brook, spread it out in the sun, and in one hour the cloth was bleached.

She came back with it to the hut, cut out the shirt, and began to stitch at it diligently.

The twilight was falling, and she was just putting in the last stitch when the door opened, and the bear came in and asked, "Is the shirt ready?"

She gave it to him.

"Thank you, my good girl; now I must reward you. You told me you had a bad stepmother; if you like, I will send my bears to tear her and her daughter in pieces."

"Oh! don't do that! I don't want to be revenged; let them live!"

"Let it be so then! Meanwhile make yourself useful in the kitchen; get me some porridge for supper. You will find everything you want in the cupboard in the wall; but I will go and fetch my bedding, for I shall spend tonight at home."

The bear left the room, and the maiden made up the fire in the oven, and began to get the porridge ready.

Just then she heard a sound under the bench, and there ran out a poor, lean little mouse, which stood up on its hind-legs, and said in human tones:

"Mistress! help me lest I die
A poor weak, little mouse am I!
I am hungry, give me food;
And to you will I be good."

The girl was sorry for the mouse, and threw it a spoonful of porridge. The mouse ate it, thanked her, and ran away to its hole.

The bear soon came in with a load of wood and stones; these he laid upon the stove and, having eaten a basin of porridge, he climbed upon the stove, and said, "Here, girl, is a bunch of keys on a steel ring. Put out the fire; but you must walk about the room all night, and keep on jingling these keys, till I get up; and if I find you alive in the morning you shall be happy."

The bear began snoring directly, and the old man's daughter kept walking about the hut, jingling the keys.

Soon the mouse ran out of its hole, and said, "Give me the keys, mistress, I will jingle them for you; but you must hide yourself behind the stove, for the stones will soon be flying about."

So the mouse began to run up and down by the wall, under the bench. The maiden hid behind the oven, and about midnight the bear woke up, and threw out a stone into the middle of the room.

But the mouse kept running about and jingling the keys. And the bear asked, "Are you alive?"

"I am," replied the girl from behind the oven.

The bear began to throw stones and billets of wood, thick and fast from the stove, and every time he did so, he asked, "Are you alive?"

"I am," replied the girl's voice from behind the oven, and the mouse still ran up and down, jingling the keys.

With the dawn the cocks began to crow, but the bear did not wake. The mouse gave up the keys, and ran back to its hole; but the old man's daughter began to walk about the room and jingled the keys.

At sunrise the bear came off the stove and said, "O daughter of the old man! you are blest of heaven! For here was I, a powerful monarch, changed by enchantment into a bear, until some living soul should spend two nights in this hut. And now I shall soon become a man again and return to my kingdom, taking you for my wife. But before this comes to pass, do you look into my right ear."

The old man's daughter threw back her hair, and looked into the right ear of the bear. And she saw a beautiful country, with millions of people, with high mountains, deep rivers, impenetrable forests, and pastures covered with flocks, well-to-do villages, and rich cities.

"What seest thou?" asked the bear.

"I see a lovely country."

"That is my kingdom. Look into my left ear."

She looked, and could not enough admire what she saw – a magnificent palace, with many carriages and horses in the courtyard, and in the carriages rich robes, jewels, and all kinds of rarities.

"What do you see?" asked the bear.

She described it all.

"Which of those carriages do you prefer?"

"The one with four horses," she replied.

"That is yours then," answered the bear as he opened the window.

There was a sound of wheels in the forest, and a golden carriage presently drew up before the cottage drawn by four splendid horses, although there was no driver.

The bear adorned his beloved with a gown of cloth-of-gold, with diamond earrings, a necklace set with various precious stones, and diamond rings, saying, "Wait here a little while; your father will come for you presently, and in a few days, when the power of the enchantment is over, and I am a king again, I will come for you, and you shall be my queen."

So saying, the bear disappeared into the forest, and the old man's daughter looked out of the window to watch for her father's coming.

The old man, having left his daughter in the wood, came home very sad. But on the third day he harnessed his waggon again, and drove into the forest to see if she were alive or dead, and if she were dead at least to bury her.

Towards evening the old woman and her own daughter looked out of the window, and a dog, the favourite of the old man's daughter, suddenly rushed to the door, and began to bark:

"Bow! wow! wow! the old man's here!
Bringing home his daughter dear,
Decked with gold and diamonds' sheen,
Gifts to please a royal queen."

The old woman gave the dog an angry kick. "You lie, you big ugly dog! Bark like this!

"Bow! wow! wow! the old man's come!
His daughter's bones he's bringing home!"

So saying she opened the door, the dog leaped forth, and she went with her daughter into the courtyard. They stood as if transfixed!

For in drove the carriage with four galloping horses, the old man sitting on the box, cracking his whip, and his daughter sat inside, dressed in cloth of gold and adorned with jewels.

The old woman pretended she was overjoyed to see her, welcomed her with many kisses, and was anxious to know where she got all these rich and beautiful things.

The girl told her that they were all given to her by the bear in the forest hut.

Next day the old woman baked some delicious cakes, and gave them to her own daughter, saying to the old man, "If your wretched, worthless daughter has had such good luck, I am sure my sweet, pretty darling will get a deal more from the bear, if he can only see her. So you must drive her out in the waggon, leave her in the forest, and come back without her."

And she gave the old man a good push to hasten his departure, shut the door of the cottage in his face, and looked out of the window to see what would happen.

The old man went to the stable, got out the waggon, put the horse to, helped his stepdaughter in, and drove away with her into the forest.

There he left her, turned his horse's head, and drove quickly home.

The old woman's daughter was not long in finding out the hut in the forest. Confident in the power of her charms, she went straight into the little room. There was nobody within, but there was the same table in one corner, the benches round the walls, the oven by the door, and the spinning-wheel under the window with a great bundle of flax.

She sat down on one of the benches, undid her bundle, and began eating the cakes with great relish, looking from the window all the time.

It soon began to get dark, a strong wind began to blow, and a voice was heard singing outside:

"Wanderer! outcast, forsaken!
Whom the night has overtaken;
If no crime your conscience stain,
Here this night you may remain."

When the voice ceased she answered:

"I am outcast and forsaken;
Yet unstained by crime am I:
Be you rich, or be you poor,
For this night here let me lie."

Then the door opened, and the bear walked in.

The girl stood up, gave him a winning smile, and waited for him to bow first.

The bear looked at her narrowly, made a bow, and said, "Welcome, maiden...but I have not much time to stay here. I must go back to the forest; but between now and tomorrow evening you must make me a shirt out of this flax; so you must set at once about spinning, weaving, bleaching, washing, and then about sewing it. Goodbye!"

So saying, the bear turned and went out.

"That's not what I came here for," said the girl, so soon as his back was turned, "to do your spinning, weaving, and sewing! You may do without a shirt for me!"

So saying, she made herself comfortable on one of the benches and went to sleep.

Next day, at evening twilight, the bear came back, and asked, "Is the shirt ready?"

She made no answer.

"What's this? the distaff has not been touched."

Silence as before.

"Get me ready my supper at once. You will find water in that pail, and the groats in that cupboard. I must go and fetch my bedding, for tonight I will sleep at home."

The bear went out, and the old woman's daughter lit the fire in the stove, and began to prepare the porridge. Then the little mouse came out, stood on its hind-legs, and said:

"Mistress! help me, or I die!
A poor, weak little mouse am I!
I am hungry, give me food;
And to you will I be good."

But the unkind girl only caught up the spoon with which she was stirring the porridge and flung it at the poor mouse, which ran away in a fright.

The bear soon came back with a huge load of stones and wood; instead of a mattress he arranged a layer of stones on the top of the stove, and covered this with the wood in place of a sheet. He ate up the porridge, and said, "Here! take these keys; walk all night about the hut, and keep on jingling them. And if, when I get up tomorrow, I find you still alive, you shall be happy."

The bear was snoring at once, and the old woman's daughter walked up and down drowsily, jingling the keys.

But about midnight the bear woke up and flung a stone towards the quarter whence he heard the jingling. It hit the old woman's daughter.

She gave one shriek, fell, and expired instantly.

Next morning the bear descended from the top of the oven, looked once at the dead girl, opened the cottage door, stood upon the threshold, and stamped upon it three times with all his force. It thundered and lightened, and in one moment the bear became a handsome young king, with a golden sceptre in his hand and a diamond crown on his head.

And now there drew up before the cottage a carriage, bright as sunshine, with six horses. The coachman cracked his whip till the leaves fell from the trees, and the king got into the carriage and drove away from the forest to his own capital city.

The old man, having left his stepdaughter in the forest, came home rejoicing in his daughter's joy. She was expecting the king every day. In the meantime he busied himself with looking after the four splendid horses, cleaning the golden carriage, and airing the costly horse-clothes.

On the third day after his return, the old woman came down upon him and said, "Go and fetch my darling; she is no doubt all dressed in gold by this time, or married to a king; so I shall be a queen's mother."

The old man, obedient as ever, harnessed the waggon and drove off.

When evening came the old woman gazed from the window; when the dog began to bark:

"Bow! wow! wow! the old man's come!
Your daughter's bones he's bringing home!"

"You lie!" exclaimed the old woman. "Bark like this:

'Bow! wow! wow! the old man's here!
Driving home your daughter dear,
Decked in gold and diamonds' sheen,
Gifts to please a royal queen.'"

So saying, she ran out of the house to meet the old man coming back in the waggon. But she stood as if thunderstruck, sobbed, and wept, and was hardly able to articulate, "Where is my sweetest daughter?"

The old man scratched his head and replied, "She has met with a great misfortune; this is all I have found of her – a few bare bones and blood-stained garments; in the wood, in the old hut…she has been devoured by wolves."

The old woman, wild with grief and despair, gathered up her daughter's bones, went to some neighbouring cross-ways, and when a number of people had gathered together, she buried them there with weeping and lamentation; then she fell face-downward on the grave – and was turned to stone.

Meanwhile a royal carriage drew up in the courtyard of the old man's cottage, bright as the sun, with four splendid horses, and the coachman cracked his whip till the cottage fell to pieces with the sound.

The king took both the old man and his daughter into the carriage, and they drove away to his capital, where the marriage soon took place.

The old man lived happily in his declining years as the father-in-law of a king, and with his sweet daughter, who had once been so miserable, a queen.

Fisherman Plunk and His Wife
(Croatian)

I

FISHERMAN PLUNK WAS SICK AND TIRED of his miserable life. He lived alone by the desolate sea-shore, and every day he caught fish with a bone hook, because they didn't know about nets in those parts at that time. And how much fish can you catch with a hook, anyhow?

"What a dog's life it is, to be sure!" cried Plunk to himself. "What I catch in the morning I eat up at night, and there's no joy for me in this world at all, at all."

And then Plunk heard that there were also rich sheriffs in the land, and men of great power and might, who lived in luxury and comfort, lapped in gold and fed on truffles. Then Plunk fell a-thinking how he too might come to look upon such riches and live in the midst of them. So he made up his mind that for three whole days he would sit still in his boat on the sea and not take any fish at all, but see if that spell would help him.

So Plunk sat for three days and nights in his boat on the face of the sea – three days he sat there, three days he fasted, and for three days he caught no fish. When the third day began to dawn, lo and behold, a silver boat arose from the sea – a silver boat with golden oars – and in the boat, fair as a king's daughter, stood the Pale Dawn-Maiden.

"For three days you have spared my little fishes' lives," said the Dawn-Maiden, "and now tell me what you would like me to do for you?"

"Help me out of this miserable and dreary life. Here am I all day long slaving away in this desolate place. What I catch during the day I eat up at night, and there is no joy for me in the world at all, at all," said Plunk.

"Go home," said the Dawn-Maiden, "and you will find what you need." And as she spoke, she sank in the sea, silver boat and all.

Plunk hurried back to the shore and then home. When he came to the house, a poor orphan girl came out to meet him, all weary with the long tramp across the hills. The girl said, "My mother is dead, and I am all alone in the world. Take me for your wife, Plunk."

Plunk hardly knew what to do. "Is this the good fortune which the Dawn-Maiden has sent me?" Plunk could see that the girl was just a poor body like himself; on the other hand, he was afraid of making a mistake and turning away his luck. So he consented, and took the poor girl to be his wife; and she, being very tired, lay down and slept till the morning.

Plunk could scarcely await the next day for wondering how his good fortune would show itself. But nothing happened that day except that Plunk took his hook and went out fishing, and the woman went up the hill to gather wild spinach. Plunk came home at night, and so did the woman, and they supped upon fish and wild spinach. "Eh, if that is all the good luck there is to it, I could just as well have done without," thought Plunk.

As the evening wore on, the woman sat down beside Plunk to tell him stories, to wile away the time for him. She told him about nabobs and kings' castles, about dragons that watch treasure-hoards, and kings' daughters who sow their gardens with pearls and reap gems. Plunk listened, and his heart within him began to sing for joy. Plunk forgot that he was poor; he could have sat and listened to her for three years together. But Plunk was still better pleased when he considered: "She is a fairy wife. She can show me the way to the dragons' hoards or the kings' gardens. I need only be patient and not make her angry."

So Plunk waited; and day after day went by, a year went by, two years passed. A little son was born to them; they called him little Winpeace. Yet all went on as usual. Plunk caught fish, and his wife gathered wild spinach in the mountains. In the evening she cooked the supper, and after supper she rocked the baby and told Plunk stories. Her stories grew prettier and prettier, and Plunk found it harder and harder to wait, till at last, one evening, he had had enough of it; and just as his wife was telling him about the immense treasures of the Sea King, Plunk jumped up in a rage, shook her by the arm and cried, "I tell you I'll wait no longer. Tomorrow in the morning you shall take me down to the Sea King's Castle!"

The woman was quite frightened when Plunk jumped up like that. She told him that she did not know where the Sea King had his Castle, but Plunk began to beat his poor wife most unmercifully, and threatened to kill her unless she told him her fairy secret.

Then the poor girl understood that Plunk had taken her for a fairy. She burst into tears and cried, "Truly I am no fairy, but a poor orphan girl who knows no spells nor magic. And for the tales I have told you, I had them from my own heart to beguile your weariness."

Now this only put Plunk all the more in a rage, because he had lived in a fool's paradise for over two years; and he angrily bade the woman go away next morning ere dawn with the child, along the sea-shore to the right-hand side, and he, Plunk, would go to the left, and she was not to come back again till she had found the way to the Sea King's Castle.

When the dawn came, the woman wept and begged Plunk not to send her away. "Who knows where one of us may be destroyed on this desolate sea-shore?" said she. But Plunk fell upon her again, so that she took up her child and went away crying whither her husband had bidden her. And Plunk went off in the opposite direction.

So the woman went on with her baby, little Winpeace. She went on for a week; she went on for a fortnight, and nowhere did she find the way to the Sea King. She grew so terribly tired that one day she fell asleep on a stone beside the sea. When she woke up, her baby was gone – her little Winpeace.

Her grief was so great that the tears froze fast in her heart, and not a word could she speak for sorrow, but became dumb from that hour.

So the poor dumb creature wandered back along the sea-shore and home. And next day Plunk came home, too. He had not found the way to the Sea King, and he came back disappointed and cross.

When he got home, there was no baby Winpeace, and his wife had gone dumb. She could not tell him what had happened, but was all haggard with the great trouble.

And so it was with them from that day forward. The woman neither wept nor complained, but did her housework and waited upon Plunk in silence; and the house was still and quiet as the grave. For some time Plunk stood it, but in the end he got thoroughly weary. He had just felt almost sure of the Sea King's treasure, and lo! all this trouble and worry had come upon him.

So Plunk made up his mind to try his sea-spell once more. Again for three whole days he sat in his boat on the sea, for three days he fasted, for three days he caught no fish. At the third day, at daybreak, the Dawn-Maiden arose before him.

Plunk told her what had happened, and complained bitterly.

"I'm worse off than ever before. The baby is gone, the wife is dumb, and my house dreary as the grave, and I'm just about bursting with trouble."

To this the Dawn-Maiden said never a word, but just asked Plunk a question: "What do you want? I will help you just this once more."

But Plunk was such a zany that he couldn't think of anything else but just this, that he was set on seeing and enjoying the Sea King's treasure; and so he didn't wish for his child back again, or that his wife should regain the power of speech, but he begged the Dawn-Maiden: "Fair Dawn-Maiden," said he, "show me the way to the Sea King."

And again the Dawn-Maiden said nothing, but very kindly set Plunk on his way. "When day dawns at the next New Moon, get into your boat, wait for the wind, and then drift eastward with the wind. The wind will carry you to the Isle Bountiful, to the stone Gold-a-Fire. And there I shall be waiting for you to show you the way to the Sea King."

Plunk went joyfully home.

When it was about the New Moon (but he never told his wife anything) he went out at the streak of dawn, got into his boat, waited for the wind, and let the wind carry him away toward the east.

The wind caught the boat and carried it along to the Unknown Sea, to the Isle Bountiful. Like a green garden the fruitful island floats upon the sea. The grass grows rank, and the meadows lush, the vines are full of grapes and the almond trees pink with blossom. In the midst of the island there is precious stone, the white blazing stone Gold-a-Fire. One half of the stone sheds its glow upon the island, and the other half lights up the sea under the island. And there on the Isle Bountiful, on the stone Gold-a-Fire, sits the Dawn-Maiden.

Very kindly did the Dawn-Maiden receive Plunk, and very kindly did she set him on his way. She showed him a mill-wheel drifting on the sea towards the island, and the mermaids dancing in a ring around the wheel. Then she told him – always very kindly – how he must ask the mill-wheel politely to take him down to the Sea King and not let the Dark Deeps of the Sea swallow him.

Last of all the Dawn-Maiden said, "Great store of gold and treasure will you enjoy in the Sea King's domain. But mark – to earth you cannot return, for three terrible watchers bar the way. One troubles the waves, the second raises the storm, and the third wields the lightning."

But Plunk was happy as a grig in his boat as he paddled towards the mill-wheel, and thought to himself, "It's easy to see, fair Dawn-Maiden, that you've never known want in this world. I shan't hanker back after this earth, where I'm leaving nothing but ill-luck behind!"

So he paddled up to the mill-wheel, where round the mill-wheel the mermaids were playing their foolish games. They dived and chased each other through the water; their long hair floated on the waves, their silver fins glittered, and their red lips smiled. And they sat on the mill-wheel and made the sea all foamy around it.

The boat reached the mill-wheel, and Plunk did as the Dawn-Maiden had told him. He held his paddle aloft so that the Dark Deeps should not swallow him, and he politely asked the mill-wheel, "Round wheel giddy-go-round, please take me down, either to the Dead Dark Deep or to the Sea King's Palace."

As Plunk said this, the mermaids came swishing along like so many silver fish, swarmed round the mill-wheel, seized the spokes in their snowy hands, and began to turn the wheel – swiftly, giddily.

An eddy formed in the sea – a fierce eddy, a terrible whirlpool. The whirlpool caught Plunk; it swept him round like a twig and sucked him down to the Sea King's fastness.

Plunk's ears were still ringing with the swirl of the sea and the mermaids' silly laughter when he suddenly found himself sitting on beautiful sand – fine sand of pure gold.

Plunk looked round and cried out, "Ho, there's a wonder for you! A whole field of golden sand."

Now what Plunk had taken to be a big field was only the great Hall of the Sea King. Round the Hall stood the sea like a marble wall, and above the Hall hung the sea, like a glass dome. Down from the stone Gold-a-Fire streamed a bluish glare, livid and pale as moonlight. From the ceiling hung festoons of pearls, and on the floor below stood tables of coral.

And at the end – the far end, where slender pipes were piping and tiny bells tinkling – there lazed and lounged the Sea King himself; he stretched his limbs on the golden sand, raising only his great bullock's head, beside him a coral table, and behind him a golden hedge.

What with the quick, shrill music of the pipes, the tinkling of the bells, and the sheen and glimmer all around him, Plunk wouldn't have believed there could be so much pleasure or wealth in the world!

Plunk went clean mad for pure joy – joy went to his head like strong wine; his heart sang; he clapped his hands; he skipped about the golden sand like a frolicsome child; he turned head over heels once, twice, and again – just like a jolly boy.

Now this amused the Sea King vastly. For the Sea King's feet are heavy – far too heavy – and his great bullock's head is heavier still. The Sea King guffawed as he lounged on the golden sand; he laughed so heartily that the golden sand blew up all round him.

"You're fine and light on your feet, my boy," said the Sea King, and he reached up and pulled down a branch of pearls and gave it to Plunk. And then the Sea King ordered the Under Seas Fairies to bring choice viands and honeyed drink in golden vessels. And Plunk had leave to sit beside the Sea King at the coral table, and surely that was a great honour!

When Plunk had dined, the Sea King asked him:

"Is there anything else you would like, my man?"

Now what should a poor man ask for, who had never known what it is to have a good time? But Plunk was hungry from his long journey, and he had made but a poor meal of it off the choice viands and the honeyed drinks. So he said to the Sea King, "Just as you were saying that, O King of the Sea, I was wishing that I had a good helping of boiled wild spinach."

The Sea King was rather surprised, but he recovered himself quickly, laughed and said to Plunk, "Eh, brother of mine, wild spinach is very dear down here, dearer than pearls and mother-o'-pearl, because it's a long way from here to the place where it grows. But since you have just asked for it, I will send a Foam Fairy to bring you some from the land where the wild spinach grows. But you must turn three more coach-wheels for me."

As Plunk was already in the best of humours, he didn't find that hard either. Lightly he leapt to his feet, and quickly they all flocked round him, the mermaids and the tiny folk in the Palace, and all for to see that wonder!

Plunk took a run over the golden sand, turned a beautiful coach-wheel, then a second and a third, light as a squirrel, and the Sea King and all the tiny folk rocked with laughter at such cunning.

But heartiest of all laughed a little baby, and that was the little King whom the mermaids themselves had crowned King for fun and idle sport. The wee baby was sitting up in a golden cradle. His little shirt was of silk, the cradle was hung with tiny bells of pearl, and in his hands the child held a golden apple.

While Plunk was turning coach-wheels and the little King laughed so heartily, Plunk looked round at him. He looked at the little King, and then – Plunk started. It was his own baby boy, little Winpeace.

Well, Plunk was suddenly disgusted. He would never have guessed that he would grow sick of it so soon.

Plunk frowned; he was angry, and when he had got over his shock a bit he thought, "Look at him, the urchin, how he's got on, lording it here in idleness and sport, and his mother at home gone dumb with grieving!"

Plunk was vexed; he hated seeing himself or the child in this Palace, yet he dared not say a word lest they should part him from the boy. So he made himself the servant of his son, of little Winpeace, and thought to himself, "Perhaps I shall be left alone with him sometimes. Then I will remind the boy of his father and mother; I will run away with him; I will carry off the little brat and go back with him to his mother."

So thought Plunk, and one fine day, when he happened to be alone with the little King, he whispered to the child, "Come along, my boy, let's run away with father."

But Winpeace was only a baby, and what with living so long under the sea, he had quite forgotten his father. He laughed; the little King laughed. He thought, "Plunk is making fun," and he kicked Plunk with his little foot.

"You are not my father; you are the silly-billy who turns head-over-heels before the Sea King."

That stung Plunk to the heart, so that he well-nigh died with the pain of it. He went out and wept for sheer bitter sorrow. All the Sea King's attendants gathered round him and said one to the other, "Well, well, he must have been a great lord on earth, to weep amid such splendours."

"Upon my soul," cried Plunk wrathfully, "I was the same as your Sea King here. I had a son who tugged my beard, a wife who showed me marvels, and wild spinach, brothers, as much as you want – and no need to turn coach-wheels before anybody either."

The sea-folk marvelled at such magnificence, and left Plunk to mourn his lost greatness. But Plunk went on serving the little King. He did all he could to please the boy, thinking, "I shall get him somehow to run away with me." But the little King grew sillier and more wayward every day; the days passed, and every day the child only thought Plunk more than ever a zany.

II

Now all this time Plunk's wife was at home, all alone and grieving. The first evening she made up the fire and kept the supper hot for Plunk; but when she gave up expecting Plunk, she let the fire go out, nor did she kindle it again.

So the poor dumb soul sat on her threshold. She neither worked, nor tidied, nor wept, nor lamented, but just pined away with grief and sorrow.

She could not take counsel with anyone, because she was dumb; nor could she cross the sea after Plunk, because she was all broken up with grieving.

Where could she go, poor soul! but back one day to the far hills, where her mother lay buried. And as she stood by her mother's grave, a beautiful Hind up came to her.

And as the dumb animals speak, so the Hind spoke to the Woman: "You must not sit there and pine away, my daughter, for else your heart will break and your house will perish. But every evening you must get Plunk's supper ready for him, and after supper you must unpick some fine hemp. If Plunk does not come home, then you must take his supper in the morning and the fine hemp as well, and also the slender twin pipes, and go up into the rocky mountain. Play upon the twin pipes; the snakes and their young will come and eat up the supper, and the sea-fowl will line their nests with the hemp."

Full well the daughter understood all that her mother said, and as she was bid so did she do. Every evening she cooked supper, and after supper she unpicked hemp. Plunk did not come back; and so the woman took her little twin pipes in the morning, and carried both supper and hemp to the rocky mountain. And as she played on her little pipes, played softly on the right-hand pipe, lo, snakes and baby snakes came out of the rocks. They ate up the supper and thanked the woman in the dumb speech. And when she played on the left-hand pipe, lo, gulls great and small came flying, carried off the hemp to their nests, and thanked the woman.

For three months the woman went on in this way; thrice the moon waxed and waned, and still Plunk had not come home.

Again grief overcame the poor dumb soul, so that she went again to her mother's grave.

The Hind came up, and in dumb speech the woman said to her, "Well, Mother, I have done all you told me, and Plunk has not come back. I am weary of waiting. Shall I throw myself into the sea, or fling myself down from the cliffs?"

"Daughter of mine," said the Hind, "you must not fail in your trust. Your Plunk is in grievous trouble. Now listen and hear how you may help him. In the Unknown Sea there is a Big Bass, and that Bass has a golden fin, and on that fin grows a golden apple. If you catch that Bass by moonlight you will deliver your dear Plunk from his trouble. But on the road to the Unknown Sea you will have to pass three caverns of cloud. In the first there is a monstrous Snake, the Mother of All Snakes – it is she who troubles the sea and stirs up the waves; in the second there is a monstrous Bird, the Mother of All Birds – it is she who raises the storm; and in the third there is a Golden Bee – it is she who flashes and wields the lightning. Go, daughter dear, to the Unknown Sea, and take nothing with you but your bone hook and slender twin pipes, and if you should find yourself in great trouble, rip open your right-hand sleeve, all white and unhemmed."

The daughter gave good heed. Next day she took out the boat and put off to sea, taking nothing with her but her hook and the slender twin pipes.

She drifted and sailed on the face of the sea till the waters bore her to a far-off place, and there on the sea, lo, three terrible caverns of lowering cloud!

From the entrance of the first cavern peered the head of a fearsome Snake, the Mother of All Snakes. Her grisly head blocked up all the entrance, her body lay coiled along the cave, and with her monstrous tail she lashed the sea, troubling the waters and stirring up the waves.

The woman did not dare go near the terrible sight, but remembered her little pipes, and began to play upon the right-hand pipe. And as she played, there came from the far-off, rock-bound lands snakes and baby snakes galore swimming over the sea. Great coloured snakes and tiny little snakes all came hurrying up and scurrying up and begged the fearsome Snake –

"Let the woman take her boat through your cavern, Mother dear! She has done us a great good turn and fed us every day in the morning."

"Through my cavern I may not let her pass," answered the fearsome Snake, "for today I must stir up the waves of the sea. But if she did you such a good turn, I will repay it with another. Would she rather have a bar of gold or six strings of pearls?"

But a true wife is not to be beguiled with gold or pearls, and so the woman answered in dumb speech, "'Tis only for a small matter I have come here – for the Bass that lives in the Unknown Sea. If I have done you a good turn, let me pass through your cavern, fearsome Snake."

"Let her pass, Mother dear," said the snakes and baby snakes again. "Here are many of us whom she has fed – full many to whom she gave meat. You just lie down, Mother dear, and take a nap, and we'll stir up the waters for you."

Now the Snake couldn't very well disoblige such a big family, and she had been longing for sleep for a thousand years. So she let the woman through the cavern, and then curled up on the floor of the cavern and fell into a fearsome sleep. But before she fell asleep she reminded the snakes and baby snakes once more: "Now, stir me up the waters right properly, children dear, while I rest a little."

So the woman passed through the cavern, and the snakes and their young stayed in the cavern; but instead of stirring up the sea they soothed it and made it calm.

The woman sailed on, and came to the second cavern. And in the second cavern there was a monstrous Bird, the Mother of All Birds. She craned her frightful head through the opening, her iron beak gaped wide; she spread her vast wings in the cavern and flapped them, and whenever she flapped her wings she raised a storm.

The woman took up her twin pipes and sweetly played upon the left-hand pipe. And from the far shore came flying gulls great and small, and begged the monstrous bird to let the woman pass with her boat through her cavern, for that she had been a good friend to them and unpicked hemp for them every day.

"I can't let her pass through my cavern, for today I must raise a mighty storm. But if she was so kind to you, I will repay her with even greater kindness. From my iron beak I will give her of the Water of Life, so that the power of speech shall be restored to her."

Well, and wasn't it a sore temptation for the poor dumb creature who desired above all things that the power of speech should return to her? But she remained steadfast, and this is what she answered the Bird: "'Tis not for my own good that I came, but for a small matter – for the Bass that lives in the Unknown Sea. If I have done you a good turn, let me pass through your cavern."

Then the grey gulls all entreated the Mother Bird and also advised her to take a little nap, and they would meanwhile raise the storm for her. The

Mother Bird listened to her children's entreaty, clung to the wall of the cavern with her iron talons, and went to sleep.

But the gulls great and small, instead of raising the storm, calmed the wild winds and soothed them.

So the dumb woman sailed through the second cavern and came to the third.

In the third cavern she found the Golden Bee. The Golden Bee buzzed in the entrance; she wielded the fiery lightning and the rolling thunder. Sea and cavern resounded; lightnings flashed from the clouds.

Fear seized upon the woman when she found herself all alone with these terrors. But she remembered her right sleeve; she ripped it off, her sleeve all white and unhemmed, flung it over the Golden Bee and caught her in the sleeve!

The thunder and lightning were stilled at once, and the Golden Bee began to coax the woman: "Set me free, O woman! and in return I will show you something. Look out over the wide waters, and it's a joyful sight you will see."

The woman looked out over the wide waters. The sun was just on the horizon. The sky grew pink overhead, the sea grew crimson from the east, and from the sea arose a silver boat. And in the boat sat the Dawn-Maiden, pale and fair as a king's daughter, and beside her a little child in a silken shirt and with a golden apple in his hand. It was the Dawn-Maiden taking the little King for his morning sail on the sea.

The woman recognized her lost baby.

Now isn't that a wonder of wonders, that the sea should be so wide that a mother cannot encompass it, and the sun so high that a mother should not be able to reach it?

Her joy took hold of her like terror. She trembled like the slender aspen. Should she stretch out her hand to the child? Or call to him tenderly? Or should she just stand and look at him for ever and ever?

The silver boat glided over the crimson sea. It faded away in the distance; the boat sank under the waves, and the mother roused herself with a start.

"I will show you," said the Golden Bee to the woman, "how to get to the little King, your son, and live with him in joy and happiness. But first set me free, that I may wield the lightnings in the cavern – and through my cavern I cannot let you pass!"

A fierce pang overcame the poor mother, overwhelmed, and shook her. She had seen her darling; her eyes had beheld her heart's desire; she had seen and beheld him, but not hugged him, not kissed him! The pang shook her from head to foot. Should she be true to Plunk or no? Should she let the Bee go and win to her child, or pass through the cavern to the Unknown Sea for the sake of the Big Bass?

But even as the pang shot through the woman, the tears gushed forth from her heart; the power of speech returned to her, and 'twas in living words that she answered the Golden Bee: "Don't sting me, O Golden Bee! I shall not let you go, because I must pass through your cavern. I have wept for my child and buried him in my heart. I have not come here for my own happiness, but for a small matter – for the Big Bass that lives in the Unknown Sea."

Thus said the woman, and passed into the cavern. She rested in the cavern; she took her ease in the boat, and there she waited for nightfall and moonrise.

Eh, my dearie, but the sea was quiet that day, with the winds at rest in the sky, and the fearsome Snake asleep in the first cavern, and the monstrous Bird asleep in the second, and the wearied woman in the third!

So the day went quietly by; evening came, and the moon rose. When the moon rode high in the heavens, the woman sailed out upon the Unknown Sea at midnight, and in the midst of the Sea she let down her little bone hook.

III

That very evening the little King bade Plunk knit him a nice set of silken reins. "First thing tomorrow morning I shall harness you to my little carriage, and you shall give me a ride on the golden sands."

Dearie me, considered poor Plunk, and where was he to hide from the Dawn-Maiden when she would go down into the sea in the morning and behold him thus tomorrow harnessed to a cart by his own son?

All the Sea King's court slept. The Sea King slept. The wilful little King slept – only Plunk was awake and knitting away at the reins. He knitted fiercely, like one who is thinking hard. When it seemed to him that the strings were strong enough, Plunk said to himself, "I never asked anyone's counsel when I was making a fool of myself, nor shall I do so now that I have come to my senses."

And as he said this he went softly up to the cradle where his son lay fast asleep, wound the reins round and round the rockers of the cradle, lashed the cradle to his own back, and started to run away with his son.

Softly Plunk strode over the golden sand – strode through the mighty Hall, spacious as a wide meadow; slipped through the golden hedge, parting the branches of pearls; and when he came to where the sea stood up like a wall, nothing daunted, Plunk dived into the water with his boy.

But it is far – terribly far – from the Sea King's fastness to the world of day above! Plunk swam and swam; but how was a poor fisherman to swim when he was weighed down by the little King – golden cradle, golden apple and all – on his back?

Plunk felt as if the sea was piling itself up above him, higher and higher, and heavier and heavier!

And just as Plunk was at the last gasp, he felt something scrape along the golden cradle, something that caught in the rocker of the cradle; and when it had caught fast, it began to haul them along apace!

"Now it's all up with me!" said poor Plunk to himself. "Here's a sea-monster carrying me away on his tusk."

But it wasn't the tusk of a sea-monster; it was a bone fishhook, the very hook that Plunk's wife had let down.

When the woman felt that her hook had caught, she joyfully summoned all her strength, pulling and hauling with all her might, for fear of losing the great Big Bass.

As she began to haul in her catch the golden rocker began to show above the water. The woman could not distinguish it rightly by moonlight, but thought, "It is the golden fin of the Bass."

Next came up the child with the golden apple. Again the woman thought, "It is the golden apple on the fish's fin." And when at last Plunk's head came up, the woman cried out joyfully, "And here is the head of the great Big Bass."

And as she cried out she hauled in her catch, and when she had hauled it close alongside – why, dearie mine, how am I to tell you rightly how overjoyed were those three when they met again in the boat, all in the moonlight, in the middle of the Unknown Sea?

But they dare not lose any time. They had to pass through the three caverns ere the monstrous watchers should awaken. So they took out the oars and rowed with all their might and main.

But oh dear! the bad luck they had! When the little King awoke and saw his mummy, he remembered her at once. He threw both his little arms round his mummy's neck – and the golden apple fell out of his hand. Down fell the apple into the sea, down to the very bottom and into the Sea King's Castle, and hit the Sea King right on his shoulder!

The Sea King woke up and bellowed with rage. All the court jumped to their feet. They saw at once that the little King and his servant were missing!

They gave chase. The mermaids swam out under the moonlight; the light foam fairies flew out over the water; runners were sent out to rouse the watchers in the caverns.

But the boat had already passed through the caverns, and so they had to pursue it farther on. Plunk and the woman were rowing – rowing for dear life, their pursuers close in their wake. The mermaids whipped up the waters, the swift foam fairies darted after the boat, the angry waves rose up in wrath behind them, and the wind howled from the clouds. Nearer and nearer came the pursuers. The finest ship afloat would not have had a chance, and how could a tiny two-oared boat? For hours and hours the boat flew on before the tempest, and just as the day began to break, lo, terror gathered from all sides around the boat.

For the hurricane beat upon the boat, the crested billows towered above it, and the mermaids joined in a ring around it. The ring heaved and swayed around the boat, the mermaids raised their linked hands high to let the mountainous waves pass through, but never let the little craft escape the waves. Sea and storm whistled and roared.

The fear of death was upon Plunk, and in his dire need he cried out, "Oh, fair Dawn-Maiden, help!"

The Dawn-Maiden arose from the sea. She saw Plunk but never looked at him. She looked at the little King, but no gift had she for him; but to the faithful wife she swiftly gave her gift – a broidered kerchief and a pin.

Quickly they hoisted the kerchief, and it became a white sail, and the pin turned into a rudder. The wind filled the sail, so that it bulged like a ripe apple, and the woman gripped the rudder with a strong hand. The mermaids' ring round the boat was broken; the boat rode upon the azure sea like a star across the blue heavens! A wonder of wonders, it flew over the sea before its terrible pursuers; the fiercer the pursuit, the greater help it was to them; for the swifter the wind blew, the more swiftly yet flew the boat before the wind, and the swifter the sea, the more swiftly rode the boat upon the sea.

Already the rock-bound shore loomed afar, and upon the shore Plunk's little cottage and the bar of white sand before it.

As soon as the land hove in sight, the pursuit slackened. The foam fairies fear the shore; the mermaids keep away from the coast. Wind and waves stayed on the high seas, and only the boat flew straight ahead to land like a child to its mother's lap.

The boat flew to land over the white sand bar and struck on a rock. The boat split on the rock. Down went sail and rudder, down went the golden cradle, away flew the Golden-winged Bee, and Plunk and his wife and child were left alone on the beach outside their cottage.

When they sat down that night to their supper of wild spinach, they had clean forgotten all that had happened. And but for those twin pipes, there's not a soul would remember it now. But whoever starts to play on the pipes, the fat pipe at once begins to drone out about Plunk:

Harum-scarum Plunk would go
Where the pearls and corals grow;
There he found but grief and woe.

And then the little pipe reminds us of the woman:

Rise, O Dawn, in loveliness!
Here is new-born happiness;
Were it three times drown'd in ill.
Faith and Love would save it still!

And that is the twin pipes' message to the wide, wide world.

Papalluga, or The Golden Slipper
(Serbian)

A S SOME VILLAGE GIRLS WERE SPINNING whilst they tended the cattle grazing in the neighbourhood of a ravine, an old man with a long white beard – so long a beard that it reached to his girdle – approached them, and said, "Girls, girls, take care of that ravine. If one of you should drop her spindle down the cliff, her mother will be turned into a cow that very moment."

Having warned them thus, the old man went away again. The girls, wondering very much at what he had told them, came nearer and nearer to the ravine, and leant over to look in. Whilst doing so, one of the girls – and she the most beautiful of them all – let her spindle fall from her hand, and it fell to the bottom of the ravine.

When she went home in the evening she found her mother, changed into a cow, standing before the house; and from that time forth she had to drive this cow to the pasture with the other cattle.

In a little time the father of the girl married a widow, who brought with her into the house her own daughter. The stepmother immediately began to hate the stepdaughter, because the girl was incomparably more beautiful than her own daughter. She forbade her to wash herself, to comb her hair, or to change her clothes, and sought by every possible way to torment and scold her. One day she gave her a bag full of hemp and said, "If you do not spin all this well and wind it, you need not return home, for if you do I shall kill you."

The poor girl walked behind the cattle and spun as fast as possible; but at midday, seeing how very little she had been able to spin, she began to weep. When the cow, her mother, saw her weeping, she asked her what was the matter, and the girl told her all about it. Then the cow consoled her, and told her not to be anxious. "I will take the hemp in my mouth and chew it," she said, "and it will come out of my ear as thread, so that you can draw it out and wind it at once upon the stick." And so it happened. The cow began to chew the hemp, and the girl drew the thread from her ear and wound it, so that very soon they had quite finished the task.

When the girl went home in the evening, and took all the hemp, worked up, to her stepmother, she was greatly astonished, and next morning gave her yet more hemp to spin and wind. When at night she brought that home ready, the stepmother thought she must be helped by some other girls, her friends; therefore the third day she gave her much more hemp than before. But when the girl had gone with the cow to the pasture, the woman sent her own daughter after her to find out who was helping her. This girl went quietly towards her stepsister so as not to be heard, and saw the cow chewing the hemp and the girl drawing the thread from her ear and winding it, so she hastened home and told all to her mother. Then the stepmother urged the husband to kill the cow. At first he resisted, but, seeing his wife would give him no peace, he at last consented to do as she wished, and fixed the day on which he would kill it. As soon as the stepdaughter heard this she began to weep, and when the cow asked her why she wept, she told her all about it. But the cow said, "Be quiet; do not cry. Only when they kill me take care not to eat any of the meat, and be sure to gather all my bones and bury them behind the house, and whenever you need anything, come to my grave and you will find help." So when they killed the cow the girl refused to eat any of the flesh, saying she was not hungry, and afterwards carefully gathered all the bones and buried them behind the house, on the spot the cow had told her.

The real name of this girl was Mary, but as she had worked so much in the house, carrying water, cooking, washing dishes, sweeping the house, and doing all sorts of housework, and had very much to do about the fire and cinders, her stepmother and half-sister called her "Papalluga" (Cinderella).

One day the stepmother got ready to go with her own daughter to church, but before she went she spread over the house a basketful of millet, and said to her stepdaughter, "You, Papalluga! If you do not gather up all this millet and get the dinner ready before we come back from church, I will kill you."

When they had gone to church the poor girl began to weep, saying to herself, "It is easy to see after the dinner; I shall soon have that ready; but who can gather up all this quantity of millet!" At that moment she remembered what the cow had told her, that in case of need she should go to her grave and would there find help, so she ran quickly to the spot, and what do you think she saw there? On the grave stood a large box full of valuable clothes of different kinds, and on the top of the box sat two white doves, who said, "Mary, take out of this box the clothes which you like best and put them on, and then go to church; meanwhile we will pick up the millet seeds and put everything in order." The girl was greatly pleased, and took the first clothes which came to hand. These were all of silk, and, having put them on, she went away to church. In the church everyone, men and women, wondered much at her beauty and her splendid clothes, but no one knew who she was or whence she came. The king's son, who happened to be there, looked at her all the time and admired her greatly. Before the service was ended she stood up and quietly left the church. She then ran away home, and as soon as she got there took off her fine clothes and again laid them in the box, which instantly shut itself and disappeared.

Then she hurried to the hearth and found the dinner quite ready, all the millet gathered up, and everything in very good order. Soon after the stepmother came back with her daughter from the church, and was extremely surprised to find all the millet picked up and everything so well arranged.

Next Sunday the stepmother and her daughter again dressed themselves to go to church, and, before she went away, the stepmother threw much more millet about the floor, and said to her stepdaughter, "If you do not gather up all this millet, prepare the dinner, and get everything into the best order, I shall kill you." When they were gone, the girl instantly ran to her mother's grave, and there found the box open as before, with the two doves sitting on its lid. The doves said to her, "Dress yourself, Mary, and go to church; we will pick up all the millet and arrange everything." Then she took from the box silver clothes and, having dressed herself, went to church. In the church everyone, as before, admired her very much, and the king's son never moved his eyes from her. Just before the end of the service, the girl again got up very quietly and stole through the crowd. When she got out of church she ran away very quickly, took off the clothes, laid them in the box, and went into the kitchen. When the stepmother and her daughter came home, they were more surprised than before; the millet was gathered up, dinner was ready, and everything in the very best order. They wondered very much how it was all done.

On the third Sunday the stepmother dressed herself to go with her daughter to church, and again scattered millet about on the ground, but this time far more than on the other Sundays. Before she went out she said to her stepdaughter, "If you do not gather up all this millet, prepare the dinner, and have everything in order when I come from church, I will kill you." The instant they were gone, the girl ran to her mother's grave and found the box open with the two white doves sitting on the lid. The doves told her to dress herself and go to church and to have no care about the millet or dinner.

This time she took clothes all of real gold out of the box, and, having put them on, went away to the church. In the church all the people looked at her and admired her exceedingly. Now the king's son had resolved not to let her slip away as before, but to watch where she went. So, when the service was nearly ended, and she stood up to leave the church, the king's son followed her, but was not able to reach her. In pushing through the crowd, however, Mary somehow in her hurry lost the slipper from her right foot and had no time to look for it. This slipper the king's son found, and took care of it. When the girl got home, she took off the golden clothes and laid them in the box, and went immediately to the fire in the kitchen.

The king's son, having determined to find the maiden, went all over the kingdom, and tried the slipper on every girl, but in some cases it was too long, in others too short, and, in fact, it did not fit any of them. As he was thus going about from one house to the other, the king's son came at last to the house of the girl's father, and the stepmother, seeing the king's son coming, hid her stepdaughter in a wash-trough before the house. When the king's son came in with the slipper and asked if there were any girl in the house, the woman answered, "Yes," and brought out her own daughter. But when the slipper was tried it was found it would not go even over the girl's toes. Then the king's son asked if no other girl was there, and the stepmother said, "No, there is no other in the house." At that moment the cock sprung upon the wash-trough and crowed out "Cock-a-doodle-do! – here she is under the wash-trough!"

The stepmother shouted, "Go away! may the eagle fly away with you!" But the king's son, hearing that, hurried to the wash-trough and lifted it up, and what did he see there! The same girl who had been in the church, in the same golden clothes in which she had appeared the third time there, but lying under the trough, and with only one slipper on. When the king's son saw her he nearly lost his senses for the moment, he was so very glad. Then he quickly tried to place the slipper he carried on her right foot, and it fitted her exactly, besides perfectly matching with the other slipper on her left foot. Then he took her away with him to his palace and married her.

The Devil and Spase the Shepherd
(Macedonian)

"**GOOD MORNING, SPASE**," said the Devil.
"**My mornings are never wont to be bad**," answered Spase, "**so you've no need to make them good**."

"On my way here, I passed your house, Spase."

"The road brought you, so that's why you passed my house."

"And I saw your wife, Spase."

"Blind – you're not, so of course you saw her. That's why God gave you eyes."

"I heard when your wife bore a child, Spase."

"Deaf – you're not, so how could you not hear? My wife lay with a man, that's why she bore a child."

"Ah, and she bore two children, Spase, and both of them boys."

"Brother followed brother, that's why two were born."

"But one of them, Spase, died."

"The Lord giveth and the Lord taketh."

"And the other boy, Spase, also died."

"Brother after brother came, brother after brother went."

"But your wife too, Spase, died."

"Even so, God rest her soul, life will still go on. I can marry again."

"Ah, and your dappled bull died, Spase."

"He died, yes. Living creatures bear human burdens. They too nourish souls."

"The head of the bull, Spase, they left for you to eat."

"The head of the house eats the head."

"But the head got eaten by the bitch, Spase."

"Yes, she ate it, yes. Misfortune follows on the heels of evil deeds."

"But then they killed the bitch, Spase."

"She got what she gave."

"They threw her onto the dunghill, Spase."

"That was where she always liked to lie."

The Devil was at his wit's end. He could think of no other taunts to break Spase. In fury and frustration, the Devil burst like a roasting chestnut out of its skin.

The Three Fates
(Macedonian)

THERE WAS A VERY POOR MAN who had no house in which to live. Driven by this, he hiked out to a nearby mountain, found a good spot near the main road, and built himself a humble cottage in which he settled with his wife and children.

A very rich man was travelling on horseback along that road and was overtaken by night just near the cottage. As he rode along, he became more and more fearful as his saddlebags were full of money. He happened to peer towards the little house, where a fire was glowing invitingly, and he decided to see if he would be able to spend the night there. He backtracked, deciding to first find out what sort of people lived there; if they seemed decent, he'd stay, if not, he'd continue on his way. Scared or not, what else could he do on that lonely mountain?

When he looked through the window of the cottage, he saw that a man and his wife with several children were warming themselves around the fire.

"Thank goodness," said the rich man to himself. "This is a family home, just what I was hoping for." He called out, "Good evening, friends."

"Good evening to you," replied the poor man.

If it's possible, would you be able to put me up for the night, as it's too dark to keep travelling?" he asked.

"Of course, friend. There are no problems about that, but I'm sorry I can't offer you any dinner. There's no food in the house – we've eaten all we had. But as far as sleeping goes, you're welcome," offered the poor man.

"I don't expect you to provide me with food. I have plenty with me. I only want somewhere to lie down," said the rich traveller. "Thank you for your offer."

With that, he tethered his horses, took his things into the house and sat close to the fire to thaw out from the bitter cold outside. From his saddlebags, he shared out the food he was carrying and, together with the family, ate his dinner.

"It's as if you've been sent from heaven, noble sir," said his host. "You've arrived with all sorts of fine things to eat on this, the third night after the birth of our son. Hopefully it's a good-luck omen. We don't want him to suffer as much as we have."

"Congratulations. I hope it is for the best and that God grants him a good life," said the traveller.

They sat for a while, then, when the time came, they lay down to sleep. All of them dozed off, except for the rich man who just couldn't sleep. He suspected the poor man might be planning to rob and kill him during the night. So he was wide awake at midnight when the three Fates appeared to determine the new baby's destiny.

"What do you think, sister?" said the first Fate to the second. "What future should we write out for this baby, this son of a poor man?"

"What should we write? Why, we should that he should live for only forty days. Otherwise he'll be another burden on his poor father," she replied. "Yes, that's what we should do."

"But wouldn't it be better if we decided that he should live, and when he grows up, he should marry the daughter of this rich traveller who's staying here overnight?" suggested the third.

"Most fitting! What a good idea!" chorused the two others. "Yes, let's do that." They opened their Book of Destiny and wrote, "This boy will become the rich man's son-in-law and inherit all his property".

The rich man heard what the three Fates said, and he became so agitated that even by morning, he hadn't closed his eyes to sleep. He just lay there thinking up ways to get rid of the baby.

"Ha! The chances of this yokel's son becoming my son-in-law and getting his hands on my property are zilch!" he thought.

Morning arrived, and the rich man started preparing for his departure. As he did, he said to his poverty-stricken hosts, "Listen, friends. Why don't you give me the baby boy to adopt, seeing I have no children. I've got more assets than I know what to do with! Why, you already have four other children, long may they live."

"Oh no!" they exclaimed. "What mother and father can give up their baby, no matter how poor they are? You can't expect us to do that!"

The rich man then tried to convince them with money. "It's true that no parents would willingly give up their child, but somehow I think I can change your minds. Look, here's one hundred gold coins. They will enable you to buy a house in town where you can live comfortably. And your boy will live in even more comfort at my place."

When they heard that proposal and saw the gold, they reconsidered. They found some rags in which they wrapped the baby, gave him a fig that he could suck on like a dummy, and handed him over to the rich man to adopt. The rich man mounted his horse, cradling the baby in his arms, and started down the road, thinking all the while about how to do away with the poor child. He considered maybe murdering it by hurling it against some rocks, but that was too cruel. He wondered about just leaving it abandoned on the road, but he was worried lest someone find it. On he rode, thinking these thoughts, when he espied a cave not far off the road. He carried the baby into it and abandoned it there, believing that it would die alone without anyone knowing a thing.

That cave happened to be a bears' den, and in it there were two small cubs that had been recently born. When the rich man dumped the baby, it tumbled and rolled right across to where the cubs were. Because it was crying, the little cubs were curious and started to play with it, one passing it to the other and back again. Just then, the mother bear returned from grazing to find the baby crying. She felt sorry for it, so she fed it and nursed it to sleep. Thankfully, when God wills it, He can even inspire a bear to suckle a human baby rather than eat it. What with today and tomorrow, the bear nurtured the infant and raised it to a toddler. The little boy too started to wander out with the bear family in search of food, such as wild apples, berries and other things that grew on the mountain.

One day, as the boy was climbing a tree to gather fruit, he was spotted by some goat herders and coal merchants. They were amazed and wondered where that naked boy who roamed around with the mountain bears could be from. They started to track him to discover where he hid and lived. After many days, they saw him as he entered his cave and resolved to capture him. Many villagers equipped themselves with whatever they could find and concealed themselves around the bears' den.

When the mother bear headed out, the boy followed, and the villagers started to chase him. He ran – they pursued, till finally they grabbed him and took him to the village. But who should look after him? Who? They came to the decision to give him to a childless widow, who gratefully accepted him and raised him as her own till he grew into a fine young man. Then she found him an apprenticeship with an important businessman in town.

"But what's the boy's name, Granny?" asked the businessman.

"His name is Bearboy, sir, because he was found living with the mountain bears," she explained.

Bearboy had just settled in to his new job when, in order for the destiny pronounced by the three Fates to be fulfilled, the rich man who had "adopted" him came in to the office. He was in town for a few months on business and sat down to discuss some deal with Bearboy's employer.

"Bearboy, go and order some coffee for our visitor," instructed his boss. Bearboy ran off on his errand, and some dim memory prompted the rich visitor to ask, "Why do you call your apprentice Bearboy?"

"His story is quite incredible," replied the businessman.

"Why? What's so incredible about it? Tell me!" insisted his visitor.

"Alright. This lad was found by some villagers living in the mountains with the bears. Apparently, there was a bear cave near the main road and that's where he was trapped. They gave him to a widow who looked after him, and because she didn't know his name, she christened him Bearboy. So that's why I call him Bearboy too."

After hearing that story, the rich man was quite certain that Bearboy was the one and same child that he had thrown into the cave. He immediately figured out a plan to destroy him.

"Would you mind sending your apprentice to deliver a very important and urgent letter for me? It has to go as far as my house in the village and be given to my wife," he said.

"Of course! He can take it at once," replied Bearboy's employer.

The rich man sat far over on the other side and composed the letter for Bearboy to deliver to his house. Bearboy rushed the letter there and, luckily for him, the rich man's wife was not home, so he gave it to their daughter instead.

She opened it to read and, oh, you should have seen what he'd written! The rich man had instructed his wife to kill Bearboy, to either slaughter or poison him, because he claimed that Bearboy had caused him so much damage that they were nearly ruined.

When she read those awful words, the daughter was overcome with hatred for her father and filled with love for Bearboy. She decided to outsmart her father and win Bearboy for herself. It seemed that fate would run its course.

She grabbed another sheet of paper and wrote a very different message:

"Dear wife. The bearer of this letter is the finest and most intelligent man I've ever met. Accordingly, I want you to build a grand new house on our property and arrange that our daughter marries him. And the sooner the better, because it seems that we have been destined to be

united with a young man so remarkable, it would be impossible to find his match anywhere."

She sealed the letter, not a moment too soon, for her mother arrived home, and Bearboy handed the new letter to her. On reading it, the woman was delighted. She was taken with the handsome, young Bearboy, so straight away she summoned the builders and lost no time in organizing the marriage between Bearboy and her daughter.

Some three or four months later, the rich man finally was able to return to his village. He couldn't wait to find out how Bearboy had been done away with. As he neared his estate, he saw a brand-new house had been built.

"What the devil!" he exclaimed. "What's been going on here? What's this new house doing here?" He stormed up to his wife and demanded an explanation.

"But it's all in accordance with what you told me to do in the letter you sent with Bearboy. I did exactly as you said. I built the house and arranged for our daughter to marry him," she said.

When he heard that, the rich man was flabbergasted. "Ah, the devil take him. I'll fix that cur, that Bearboy, just wait! That bastard will soon find out what I have in store for him." He uttered these threats under his breath, but at the same time he pretended to his wife that indeed she had followed his instructions to the letter and praised her for carrying them out so well.

"Yes, that's right! You've done everything perfectly," he lied.

"I know what I'm doing," she answered happily. "It's all been so wonderful."

The rich man entered his house and was greeted by his daughter and her husband Bearboy, as well as his own son. They each shook his hand and welcomed him warmly. The rich man kept up his pretense, making out he was ever so fond of Bearboy, and congratulated him heartily for everything.

The next day, even before dawn had broken, the rich man headed out towards his sheep pens. He did this without anyone knowing. When he arrived there, he bullied the shepherd into digging a grave and gave him the following order:

"Listen here, shepherd. There's a job I want you to do, and once it's done, you can depend on me to look after you for the rest of your days.

This is what it is. Tomorrow morning a young man will come here asking you for a ram to roast. You are to kill him and bury him in this grave. Do not ask any questions and do not say a word to a soul about it. If anyone asks, you don't know anything, right? Is that all clear?"

"You can count on me, sir, I won't let you down," replied the shepherd.

The rich man hurried home and persuaded his wife to throw a big celebratory dinner party. The rich man's plan was that Bearboy would go to the shepherd the next morning to pick up the ram for roasting.

Even before the sun had risen, the rich man's wife tiptoed into Bearboy's bedroom to wake him for his errand, but he was fast asleep in her daughter's loving arms. She waited a little while, but decided she couldn't disturb him, so instead she went and woke up her own son and sent him in place of Bearboy.

The lad went off, and as soon as he asked the shepherd for a ram, he was grabbed and given a lot more than he asked for. The shepherd rammed his staff against his throat, and he dragged the lad's body over to the grave and pushed it in.

Later, the rich man rose from his bed and asked his wife whether she'd sent Bearboy to pick up the ram.

"No, I didn't send Bearboy in the end, because I felt sorry to wake him so early," she replied. "I sent our own son instead, because really, he's so much better at that sort of thing."

That reply had the same effect as a snake bite would. The rich man rushed to the sheep pens to see what the shepherd had done.

"What happened, shepherd? Did my boy come?"

"He came, alright, and I finished him off good and proper, sir!"

"Bravo. You did well," said the rich man through his tears, and he sobbed all the way home. "Ah, you cursed Fates. Will what you decreed really come true? Will all my efforts come to nothing? I refuse to let that yokel's son end up with all my hard-earned money. Just wait and see what I'm going to do to him now!"

With that, he hired a trained assassin for I don't know how high a price. The rich man arranged for the assassin to kill Bearboy. His instructions were that a man and his wife would be walking past a particular spot on the road to a certain village, and he was to shoot the man.

To set his plan in action, the rich man said to his wife, "Listen, let's all go out tonight and dine at such and such a restaurant, but I think it would be nice if Bearboy and his wife went early so they can have some time to themselves. We'll follow later to arrive just before dinner."

"Yes dear, what a good idea," she agreed.

The rich lady told Bearboy and her daughter of the plan, so the young couple got dressed and off they went. However, they got hot walking in the afternoon sun and decided to turn off into a field to rest under the cool shade of the trees. Both Bearboy and his wife stretched out, and before long they fell fast asleep.

Several hours later, as dusk was failing, they awoke to the sound of a gunshot nearby on the road. It was the sort of bang that a gun makes when it's fired into a piece of wood.

"I don't like the sound of that shot," said Bearboy. "It sounds to me as though someone's been hit."

They hurried along the road, when suddenly they came face to face with the rich man's wife, who was crying and running for all she was worth.

"What's happened? Why are you running, mother?" asked her daughter.

"Oh, it's too dreadful," she cried, "Your father has been shot! He's dead!"

"He dug a grave for Bearboy but fell into it himself," replied her daughter, unmoved. Only then, did she tell her mother about the original letter that Bearboy had delivered. After that, the rich man's strange behaviour became as clear as day to his widow.

So there, everything happens according to what the Fates decree.

Tales of the Uncanny

S THE UNCANNY – the strange and unsettling – accounts for the greatest difference between Slavic folktales and other genres, it also fulfils its deepest function. The understanding of the uncanny represents the moral lesson itself.

For example, in the folktale 'Silyan the Stork' (*see* page 231), the protagonist of low moral fibre turns into a stork when he drinks from the water in the well. The acceptance of his strange new form as a stork, and of finding himself in a new guise and with new functions, but also losing the old ones, is the path he must follow in order for him to absorb the moral lesson that he should appreciate what he used to be and have. In this case, it is by losing what is dearest to him that he learns to appreciate what he had. The path of learning moral lessons is also a journey of maturation and an entry into the world of adults.

The Mouse-Hole and
the Underground Kingdom
(Czech)

B EFORE TIMES LONG PAST there reigned a king somewhere, and he had three sons. When they had grown up, and were trained as befits princes, they came one day to their father and said, "Our kingly father, permit us to visit strange lands, since we know our own country well."

"Yes, it is proper," answered the king wisely, "for royal princes to know more than any of my subjects, and I permit what ye ask, but on one condition. Ye are all of an age in which almost every man seeks the partner of his life; and as far as I know, ye also will do the same. I have no wish to tell you what princesses to fall in love with, but I ask this: Return before a year and a day, and bring me some gift – not costly, but valued – from your chosen ones."

The princes were astonished that their father had guessed their thoughts so well, and agreed without thinking. Then they took their crossbows and went to the open field. The eldest son let the bow-string go, and the arrow flew to the east. The second let the string go, and the arrow flew to the west.

"And where am I to aim?" cried the youngest, whose name was Yarmil. That moment a mouse ran near him to its hole; he let the string go, and the arrow flew after the mouse.

"Oh, thoughtless fellow!" said the eldest prince in rebuke, "now thou must go to the mouse-hole."

"It is settled," answered Yarmil, and shrugged his shoulders.

They went home, prepared for the road, and next day started; the eldest to the east, the second to the west, and Yarmil to the mouse-hole. Up to that moment he had held it merely a jest; but how was he astonished when on nearing the place the earth opened so that he rode in conveniently and, sooner than he could think, was in an open country, in the middle of which stood a white marble castle. Nowhere did he see a living soul, and he felt sure then that he would find no one in the castle. But scarcely had he entered the gate when a lady came forth to meet him who had not only garments, but face, hair, eyes, in short everything, white as newly fallen snow. She held by the bridle a mettlesome white steed, and without saying a word, indicated to Yarmil to descend from his own horse and sit on the white one; but he had barely mounted the white steed when it rose with him through the air, and without heeding the bit, went on till it brought him to the earth before a splendid castle. Yarmil marvelled, for the castle was so brilliant that he could not look at it, such was the glitter of gold and precious stones. Around about, wherever the eye could see, was a beautiful garden, in which the most luxuriant trees were growing, the most beautiful flowers were in bloom, and birds of every colour were singing.

When he had recovered from the first surprise, Yarmil dismounted and wished to lead the steed to the castle; but it tore away, rose through the air, and vanished like a white dove in the clouds.

Full of expectation, Yarmil entered the castle. He struck on the gate; no answer, but it opened of itself. He went in on broad marble steps to the door of the first chamber. Again he knocked – no answer, but the door opened. He entered, but how did he wonder again! There was such splendour that he exclaimed, "My father is by far the richest king, but this chamber alone is worth more than his kingdom."

But if the first chamber was rich, the second was richer; and that splendour increased till he came to the eleventh, where there was a great crystal tub with golden hoops, into which, through a golden pipe, water still clearer than crystal was flowing. In the twelfth chamber were only four naked walls, an ordinary ceiling, and a common floor, but in the middle of the floor a diamond pan. When Yarmil examined more carefully, he saw written on it: "Whoever wishes to liberate me must carry me next to his body, and bathe me each day."

Urged by curiosity, Yarmil removed a diamond, then a golden, and finally, with great effort, a silver cover. But how was he frightened when under it appeared a great ugly toad! He wished to escape, but at that moment such terror seized him that in spite of himself he took the toad out of the pan and put it in his bosom. The toad chilled him, but in a moment he was as happy as if he had liberated someone from death. Straightway he went to the eleventh chamber, took the toad from his bosom, and washed it carefully; but to his great affliction he saw that it was a toad, and the more he washed the uglier it grew. When he had grown tired, he put it in his bosom again and went to the garden to cheer himself.

A sight of the trees and the flowers hitherto unnoticed, the odour of them, and the singing of the birds entertained him so that midday came before he knew it. He went back to the castle, and there, to his great surprise, saw in the first chamber a table covered with the most delicate dishes. He sat down with appetite, and when he had eaten to his content and drunk of the wine which an unseen hand had placed before him in a golden goblet, he confessed that he had never tasted at his father's table, or at the greatest festivals, such delicate dishes and such good wine.

Now he looked the room through with more care; the splendour did not charm him so much as at first, but the many musical instruments, writing implements, and beautiful books pleased him beyond measure, for he was skilled in every good art.

After the supper, which was as good as the dinner, he lay on a soft bed and slept soundly till morning; then he ate a good meal, which was on the table, and spent the time as he had the day before. He was annoyed at his lonely life, but he soon drove away trouble. He was grieved because the more the toad was washed the uglier it grew; still he washed it with care, and carried it in his bosom.

Now the year was nearing its end, when he had to return to his father with a gift from his bride. He walked like one deprived of reason through the castle and the garden; nothing could comfort him, but still he did not forget to bathe the toad each day, and with greater care. When the last day of the year had come, he knew not what to begin; but while walking through the room he saw on his writing-table a sheet of paper not there before. He seized it quickly, and on it was written in black letters:

DEAR YARMIL, – I love thee unspeakably; but be thou patient, as I am patient. A gift for thy father thou hast in the pan; give it to him, but tarry not long at home. Put me back in the pan.

Yarmil hastened with joy to the twelfth chamber, took from the pan a rich casket set with diamonds, and put the toad in the pan; then he ran out quickly, mounted the white steed which was waiting, and which rose in the air and flew regardless of bit, till it stopped before the white castle; there the white lady gave Yarmil his horse, took the white steed, and led it away.

In a short time Yarmil came to the great gate, and when he had ridden through and looked, there was nothing behind but a mouse-hole. Putting spurs to his horse, he rushed on at a gallop and came to the gate of his father's castle almost at the same moment as his brothers, so that all three were able to appear together before their father and say, "Here we are, according to thy command."

"But have ye brought gifts from your princesses?" asked the king.

"Of course," cried the elder brothers, proudly. Yarmil answered, as it were, timidly, with a nod; for he knew not what was in that casket taken from the pan.

The king had invited a great number of guests to look at the gifts. All were in the banqueting-hall. The king led his sons thither, and when the feast was ended, he said to the eldest, "Now give me the gift from thy princess."

"My love is the daughter of a great king," said the prince proudly, and he gave his father a casket containing a small mirror.

The king looked, and wondered not a little that he saw his whole person. Then he said, "Well, men's hands can do everything."

The second son gave him a still smaller mirror, but the king saw in it his whole person; still he only said, "Men's hands can do everything. But what has thy princess sent me?" asked he of Yarmil. In silence, and timidly, Yarmil gave him the casket. The king barely looked in it when he cried in amazement, "That princess of thine has wealth in abundance; these diamonds alone have more value than my kingdom." But he wondered when he took from the casket another such mirror, but smaller; and he was really frightened when in a twinkle a puppet sprang out and held the glass for him as soon as he looked at it, and the moment he stopped looking the puppet was gone.

"Oh," cried the king, "no hand of man could frame that." And, embracing Yarmil, he added with tenderness, "Thou hast brought me true joy, my son."

Yarmil called to mind the ugly toad and had no regret now that he had spent a whole year with it; but his brothers and his mother, who was a witch and hated Yarmil, were enraged though they dissembled.

When the feast was over and the princes were parting with their father, he said, "Go now with rejoicing, but return in a year and a day, and bring me portraits of your princesses."

The elder brothers promised with joy, but Yarmil barely nodded, for he feared what his father would say should he bring the toad's portrait; still he went with his brothers beyond the town, where he parted with them, and galloped on to the mouse-hole. He was just drawing near when the ground opened to give a good entrance. At the white castle, the white lady took his horse and gave him the white steed, which rose through the air and, regardless of bit, flew on till it reached the golden castle. Yarmil hurried to the twelfth chamber; the steed disappeared like a dove in the clouds.

In the castle nothing was changed, and the diamond pan was standing in the twelfth chamber. Yarmil removed the three covers, took out the toad and placed it in his bosom. Now he bathed it twice each day, but to his grief it grew uglier. How could he take the portrait of his princess to his father! He might paint the most beautiful lady, because he was very well skilled in painting, but he would not deceive his father. Only the hope that the toad would help him as before gave him strength to endure the dreary life.

At last the day was near in which he must return to his father. He looked continually on his writing-table till he saw to his great joy a sheet of paper on which was written in silver letters:

DEAR YARMIL, – I love thee unspeakably; be patient, as I am patient. Thou hast my portrait in the pan; give it to thy father, but tarry not long. Put me back in the pan.

Yarmil hastened to the twelfth chamber, found in the pan a casket still richer than the first. He took it quickly and put the toad in its place. Then he hurried forth, and sat on the white steed, which brought him to the white castle, where the white lady gave him his own horse. When he had ridden through the gate and looked back, he saw nothing behind but a mouse-hole. He put spurs to his horse, and rode to the gate of his father's castle at the same time with his brothers. They stood before their father and said, "Here we are, as thou hast commanded."

"Do ye bring me portraits of your princesses?" asked the king.

"Of course!" exclaimed the two elder brothers, full of pride. But Yarmil only answered with a nod, for he knew not what portrait the casket contained.

The king led them to the banqueting-hall, where the guests were assembled. When the banquet was over, he said to the eldest, "Now show me the portrait of thy princess."

The eldest brother gave a rich casket to his father. He opened it, took out a portrait, and looking at it from every side, said at last, "That is a beautiful lady; she pleases me. Still there are fairer than she in the world, but any man might love her." Then he gave the portrait to the guests, and said to his second son, "And the portrait of thy princess?"

The second son gave him promptly a richer casket and smiled with happiness. He thought doubtless that his father must be astonished at the beauty of his princess; but he looked on her with indifference and said, "A beautiful lady too, but there are more beautiful in the world; still any man might fall in love with her."

Then he nodded to Yarmil, who gave with trembling hand his diamond casket. Scarcely had the king looked at it when he exclaimed, "Thy princess must be rich beyond measure; thy casket is at any time worth twice my whole kingdom." But how was he astonished when he took out the portrait! He looked fixedly at it for a while, unable to utter a word. Then he said with the greatest enthusiasm, "No; such a lady cannot be found in the world."

All the guests crowded around the portrait, and in one voice agreed with the king. At last Yarmil drew near to look at his princess, unknown till that moment. Now he regretted no whit that he had spent two years in lone life and nursing a toad; but his brothers and his mother were raging, and envied him his princess.

Next day the princes were taking farewell, and the king said to them, "After this time I will not let you go again. In a year and a day I wish to see your princesses; then we will celebrate the weddings."

The two elder brothers were shouting with joy, but Yarmil answered no word. They took leave of their father and went together to the edge of the town, where they separated; the eldest went to the east, the second to the west, but Yarmil to the mouse-hole, which opened quickly to give him a convenient passage. At the white castle the white lady gave him the white steed, which flew to the golden castle regardless of bit. There Yarmil descended, and the steed vanished like a dove in the clouds.

Full of hope, Yarmil hastened to the twelfth chamber, for he trusted to find there his wondrous fair princess whose portrait he had taken to his father; but he found in the pan the ugly toad, which he put in his bosom, and now washed three times each day. In vain was all his labour, for the more he bathed the uglier grew the toad. Had it not been for the portrait he would have fled from the castle, and who knows what he might have done? Every day his strength decreased, and when the last day of the year drew near, it is a wonder that he did not despair; for the toad had become now not only ugly beyond measure, but all mangy, so that he shivered when he looked at it. And now he must bring this to his father as his chosen one.

"My father will kill me!" cried he with grief, and threw himself on the couch. He thought what to do, but could come to no resolve. At last he reached to his bosom to look once more at the toad, hoping that at sight of it a happy thought might come; but a new surprise – the toad was gone. Now he began to lament. He ran through the whole castle, searched every room, and in the garden every tree and bush, but no trace of the toad.

At last he remembered the dish in the twelfth chamber, ran thither, but stopped on the threshold as if thunderstruck; for that poor chamber had become a real paradise, and in the middle of it stood a lady as beautiful, if not still more beautiful, than the portrait which he had carried to his father. In speechless amazement he looked at her, and who knows how long he might have stood there had she not turned to him and said, "My dear, thou hast suffered much; but I am not yet entirely free, and my people are not. Hurry now to the cellar; here is the key, and do to a hair what I command, or it will go ill with us. When the door is opened, thou wilt hear a terrible wailing; but listen to nothing, and speak not a word. Go down on the steps; below thou wilt find on a table twelve burning tapers, and before each taper one shirt. Roll up the shirts, quench the tapers, and bring them all with thee."

Yarmil took the key. When he opened the door of the cellar he heard such wailing that it is a wonder his heart did not break; but mindful of what had been said by his bride, he went boldly, descended the steps, rolled up the twelve shirts, quenching at each one, one taper; then he took the shirts and the tapers and hurried back. But how did he wonder when he saw a man nailed to the door by his tongue! The man begged Yarmil by all things to set him free, so that there was a strange feeling in Yarmil's heart; but after short hesitation he mastered this feeling, and shut the door.

When he came to his bride and gave her the shirts with the tapers, she said, "These twelve shirts are my twelve skins, in which I was a toad; and these twelve tapers burned me continually. Now I am liberated, it is true; but it will be three years before I shall be completely free. Know that I am the daughter of a mighty king, whom that foul monster, who is nailed to the cellar door by the tongue, changed into a toad because I refused him my hand. He is a wizard; but there is a witch more powerful than he. To punish him, she nailed him to that door; I, too, am still in her power. Now promise that for three years thou wilt tell no living person into what creature I was enchanted; but especially tell not how many skins I had."

"Not even to my own mother!" exclaimed Yarmil with excitement.

"It is just from thy own mother that thou must hide it most, for she is a witch, and hates thee; she knows long since that thou art three years with me, and most carefully will she try to learn from thee just what I have forbidden thee to tell."

Yarmil was greatly grieved, but the princess soon cheered him, especially when she said, "It is now high time to go, so as to come to thy father's at the right moment." Then she took him by the hand and led him down the stairs. In front of the castle a carriage with four white horses was waiting; when they entered, the horses rushed off with such speed that soon they passed the white castle. Yarmil was going to ask who the white lady was, when the princess said, "That is my mother, who has aided in my liberation."

Soon they were at the great gate; and when they had passed it, and looked back, there was nothing but a mouse-hole. They arrived at the king's castle just in the same moment with the two elder brothers and their princesses. But no one looked at them, for the eyes of all were turned to Yarmil's bride.

The king was rejoiced most of all. He conducted the bride to the banqueting-hall, where there was a multitude of guests, and with tears of delight he exalted the happiness of his favourite son; but the elder princes and the queen were enraged, though they would not let it be known.

On the following day came the weddings of the three princes; though Yarmil and his bride were the last, still glory came only to them. At the banquet the guests drank continually to the health of his bride, so that the other princesses were purple from shame.

When Yarmil was almost reeling with delight, the queen drew near him, and praised with great flattery the beauty of his bride; but all at once she spoke of her origin, and in every way tried to discover whence she had come.

Yarmil at first evaded her questions; but when she urged him vehemently to tell from what land came his bride, he said, "Dear mother, I will do everything according to thy wish, but of this one thing ask me not."

"I know well whence she comes," smiled the queen. "I know, too, that thou didst not see her first in her present form."

"Of course not, but I am proud that I liberated her."

"Oh, my dear son!" exclaimed the queen compassionately. "I pity thee greatly for letting thyself be so duped; but dost thou know that that beauty of hers is pure deceit?"

"Why?" asked Yarmil in fright.

"Because she is a witch," whispered the queen in his ear, with an anxious look. "There is still time," continued she, when she saw that Yarmil as it were believed, "to extricate thyself from her snares; and I wish to aid thee in every way. But thou must tell me what form she had before."

Yarmil said that he would not tell, but the queen did not abandon her plan. When she could not discover from him directly, she began to name every kind of beast, looking with exceeding quickness at his face. Yarmil shook his head unceasingly, but was confused when she said "toad."

"Then she was a toad before," cried in horror the queen. "Ah! dear son, it is ill, very ill with thee; but it may be well yet if only I know in how many skins she was living."

Again Yarmil answered decidedly that he would not tell, but the queen tried so long that at last she discovered. Now she knew what she wanted, and went from Yarmil. It is a wonder that he was not suspicious, but he said nothing to the princess.

Next morning a number of guests went with the king and his sons to the chase, and stayed in the forest till evening; thus the queen could act freely.

While the three princesses and the remaining guests were walking in the garden, she stole into the chamber of Yarmil's bride, found the twelve shirts and the tapers, hid them in her own apartments, and in the evening, when the king had returned from the chase and all were sitting in the banqueting-hall at table, she went to the garden, where she burned the shirts and the tapers. At that moment Yarmil's bride felt great faintness, so that she went for fresh air in the garden.

Yarmil hurried after her, but he had scarcely gone through the door, when she cried, "Woe is me, Yarmil! Thou hast told what I forbade thee to tell. Forget me; I must now to the glass mountain, from which there is no liberation." Straightway she vanished in the darkness of night.

Yarmil remained a moment as if paralysed; then he ran through the garden as if he had lost his wits, and called his bride by the most endearing names, but in vain. The guests ran out at the sound of his lamentation, and were greatly terrified when Yarmil told his misfortune. The queen also came quickly, and listened as if with terrified wonder to what had happened.

"That was a witch," said she; "and 'tis well that other mishaps have not come."

But the king was grieved more than all, and put an end to the rejoicing. Next day the two elder brothers went away with their brides, and poor

Yarmil stayed home alone. In vain did his father try to comfort him; in vain did he promise that he would go himself to seek another bride for him. Yarmil was not to be consoled; and when the first onrush of sorrow had passed, he resolved to go to the glass mountain for his bride.

"In what direction wilt thou go?" objected his father. "While I live no one has heard of a glass mountain."

"Still I will go," said Yarmil, firmly. "It will come to the same whether I perish on the road or at home; in any event I shall die of disappointment."

The king tried in all ways to dissuade him from going, but Yarmil would not let him talk. He mounted his horse, dropped the reins, and let him go whithersoever he would. He travelled long in this objectless way, hither and thither; but at last he saw that he must act differently if he meant to reach the glass mountain. But now came his real trouble, for wherever he asked about the glass mountain, people stared at him and said that there was no such mountain in the world. Yarmil did not let himself be frightened, and now he galloped the more eagerly on his horse, and asked the more carefully everywhere. He had passed through towns without number, but still no one knew of a glass mountain. At last he heard the name.

In a certain town there was a juggler – a showman with every kind of wonder. Yarmil was just going past him at the moment when he cried out, "The witch with her twelve daughters on the glass mountain!"

Yarmil called the juggler aside and said, "Here are ten goldpieces, tell me where the glass mountain is."

"I am a poor man," said the juggler, honestly, "and need these goldpieces greatly; but I know nothing of the glass mountain."

"Nor in what country it is?" asked Yarmil, impatiently.

"I know that," answered the man. "It is in the east, but they say it is very far off; and besides, they say that no one can go within twenty miles of it."

Yarmil threw the ten goldpieces into the juggler's cap, and putting spurs to his horse galloped off to the east. Many a time did the sun rise and set before he reached the glass mountain. But what good did it do him to go there? Around the mountain flowed an immensely great river, and on the bridge which was across it stood on guard three very fierce giants.

Yarmil's courage fell. That moment the white lady from the white castle appeared suddenly before him and said, "Bind thy horse's hoofs with thy coat, and go very carefully over the bridge. The giant who stands on watch will see thee only when thou art in front of him, and will start after thee; but throw behind this dust and nothing will harm thee. Do the same for the second and third giant." She gave him three packages of dust and said, "Beyond the river is a mill in which they give a witch to grind. Ask the miller for a night's lodging; he will give it thee, and invite thee to supper. Towards the end of the supper the cook will bring him a roast cock, and to that he will not invite thee; he eats it all himself. The bones of it he leaves on the plate and the cook must throw them under the wheel; but tell her to hide them for thee. And when it will be midnight, go to the glass mountain and put the bones before thee; but be careful to save one till thou art on the summit, then throw that last one back over thy head."

The moment the lady had finished, she disappeared. Yarmil sprang from his horse, tore his coat into four pieces, and with them muffled the feet of his horse; then he mounted and rode cautiously to the bridge. The first giant was sitting with his back to him and dozing. Yarmil passed him safely; but that moment the giant woke, and howled with a terrible voice to him to come back. Here Yarmil threw the dust behind, and that moment there was such darkness that it hid the giant completely. The same happened with the second and third giant, and Yarmil crossed the river safely. Not far off was the mill, and the miller stood just on the threshold.

"What dost thou wish here?" growled he at Yarmil.

"Oh, grant me a night's lodging," said Yarmil; "I am a traveller from distant lands."

"I'll give thee nothing," answered the miller, roughly, "for if I did I should lose my place."

Yarmil begged again, and begged so long that the miller asked, "Whence art thou?" Yarmil told him; and the miller, meditating awhile, said, "Well, if thou art the son of so powerful a king, I will give thee a night's lodging; for we are from the same country, and I knew thy father very well."

Then he led him to a sitting-room; and since it was just dark, he asked him to supper. Yarmil watched continually to see if the cock would soon come to the table, and he had not long to wait. The miller grew sullen, and without speaking a word ate the cock. Yarmil went out and, pressing a few goldpieces into the hands of the cook, begged her to hide the bones of the cock for him. The moment the cook saw the goldpieces she was glad to agree.

When the miller had picked the cock, he called the cook and ordered her strictly to throw the bones under the wheel. The cook took the plate and, motioning as if she had thrown them into the water, put them very adroitly into her apron; when all were asleep she gave them to Yarmil. He waited quietly till the approach of midnight, then he went out cautiously and made for the glass mountain with his horse. Full of expectation, he took out the first bone and put it on the mountain; and behold! in a moment a step was made so that he could walk comfortably on it, and so it happened with every bone. Yarmil was already at the summit and only one bone remained to him; this he threw with all his power over his head, and in a twinkle there was a pleasant highway along which his horse ran after him with ease.

All wearied, Yarmil fell down at the castle, in which lived the sorceress with the twelve princesses, her daughters, and he soon fell asleep. When he woke the sun was high in the heavens; and before he could think what further to do, his own princess came to him.

"I told thee," said she reproachfully, "to forget me, but thou didst not obey."

"Hide me somewhere quickly from the sorceress. In the night we will flee."

"Simple man!" said the princess, smiling. "She knows long ago that thou art here. Rather go to her, but be polite beyond measure. At dinner, rise after each dish and walk through the room, otherwise thou wilt stay here for the ages."

Yarmil had to obey. When he came to the sorceress, he bowed low before her and said, "Great mighty lady, I have come for my bride."

"I will give her to thee," smiled the sorceress, "but first thou must serve me three years."

"I am glad to do everything thou mayest desire," said Yarmil, bowing. And the sorceress answered graciously, inviting him at once to the table, to which just then one of the princesses brought the first dish. Yarmil ate with a relish, but when he had finished he said to the sorceress, "Permit me, great mighty lady, to walk a little. I have travelled so much that I fear my legs will lose their power."

"Oh, walk if it please thee," answered the sorceress, but her eyes glittered with anger. And Yarmil did the same after each dish, and the sorceress was ready to split from rage. Next day she gave him a wooden axe and a saw, and said, "Thou must clear all that forest over there, or be the son of Death."

Yarmil took the axe and the saw, and went on. In the forest he threw himself on the ground and thought of death; for such a stretch of forest no man could clear alone, still less with such tools. At midday his princess brought him dinner.

"Ah!" scolded she, "thou art not working diligently."

"Why trouble myself for nothing?" sighed Yarmil.

"Only be of good courage," said the princess, comforting him. "It is not so bad today; it will be worse tomorrow."

Then she gave him dinner, and when Yarmil had eaten, he put his head on her lap and fell asleep soundly. Then the princess took out of her bosom some kind of powder and, muttering mysterious words, she threw it in the air. And wonder of wonders! in the twinkle of an eye invisible hands began to fell the aged trees, cut, split, and pile, so that in a short time the whole forest was felled.

Now Yarmil woke up, and hurried with the princess to the castle. The sorceress praised him; she suppressed her rage with difficulty and said, "Thou hast worked out thy first year in order."

Next day the sorceress gave him a spade and a wheelbarrow, and said, "Thou must carry away that mountain out there, or be the son of Death."

Yarmil went with his tools to the hill, but when there he threw himself on the ground, for a thousand men would not have been able to carry off the hill in ten years. At midday his princess brought him dinner and said, "Oh, thou art working as diligently as yesterday!"

"I am," sighed Yarmil.

"Only be of good cheer," said the princess, comforting him. "Today it is not so bad; it will be worse tomorrow."

When Yarmil had eaten, he put his head on her lap and fell asleep. The princess again threw into the air a powder of some kind, muttering mysterious words; and straightway unseen hands began to work so vigorously that in a short time the hill was carried away.

Then Yarmil woke up, and hurried to the sorceress to tell her he had done what she had commanded. She flamed up in anger, but nevertheless said, "Thou hast worked the second year of thy service in order."

Next day she gave him a tailor's thimble and said, "Thou must bail out that fish-pond, or be the son of Death."

Yarmil took the thimble and went. At the fish-pond, however, he threw himself on the ground and waited for the princess. She came sooner than usual; and when Yarmil, strengthened with food, had fallen asleep with his head on her lap, she threw powder in the air, muttering mysterious words. Soon the water began to disappear from the fish-pond. Now she roused Yarmil and said to him, "Draw thy sword, and give good care. When all the water is gone from the pond the sorceress will take the shape of a rainstorm and try to destroy us. But look well at the darkness, and where it is blackest strike there with thy sword."

Yarmil promised to do so, and had barely drawn his sword when a black darkness rushed from the castle – but almost on the ground, so that Yarmil could strike the blackest spot with ease. At that moment the darkness turned into the sorceress, and Yarmil's sword stuck in her heart. With fearful cursing, she fell to the earth and died. Yarmil hurried to the castle with the princess, mounted his horse, and rushed off at a swift gallop.

He had to travel far before he came to his father's castle; but to make up, there was joy unspeakable at the happy meeting. The queen was terrified when she saw them, and she had reason; for when Yarmil told all to his father the king gave her to be burned without mercy.

When the feasting was over, Yarmil set out with his wife on the journey to their kingdom. When they came to the mouse-hole it was no longer a mouse-hole, but a magnificent gate leading to a great city, in the middle of which stood a golden castle on a hill; and in that city there were multitudes of people everywhere, and in the castle throngs of courtiers and servants, who greeted with mighty applause their master and mistress, thanking Yarmil at the same time for their liberation.

Now followed feasting, which lasted for eight whole days; and when the feasting was over, they all lived happily beyond measure, because the royal pair were goodness itself.

The King of the Toads
(Czech)

MANY AND MANY A YEAR AGO there was a cottage by the sea, and in this cottage lived a fisherman who caught fish in the sea. By the king's command he was allowed to take fish, not when he liked, but only once a week, and that on Mondays. He was anxious, therefore, to catch many on that day. Fish, of course, are not so crafty as men, but still they know enough to see that there is no fun in being caught. What is to be done with them afterwards they don't know; still, they must suspect that it can hardly be for their amusement. It is no wonder then that they did not crowd into the fisherman's net.

The fisherman worked every Monday till the sweat streamed down his face; and this all the more, since, come what might, he was obliged to bring fish to the king's kitchen each Monday. Once he worked the whole forenoon without catching even a white fish. "I will try once more," thought the tired fisherman; "I will throw everything into the water, and jump around to frighten the fish, they are so stubborn."

He threw the net deeply, and when he pulled it was very heavy. "Now there will be fish," thought he, joyfully; but what was his astonishment when, instead of fish, he drew out a great copper kettle.

The kettle was so well fastened that the fisherman had to work long before he could take off the cover. But how he was frightened! Scarcely had he removed the cover when out of the kettle rushed black smoke, which grew thicker and thicker, till at last it changed to a fiery man.

"Thou hast helped me, and I will help thee," said he to the terrified fisherman, "but in my own way I will destroy thee."

The fisherman lost his head but, soon recovering, said, "Oh, I don't care, I am already tired of this world; still thou must do something for me, since I freed thee. I can't understand how thou wert able to live in such a small place, and under the water too, and then change so quickly."

"I'll show thee in a moment," said the fiery man, and he began to turn into black smoke, and in no long time he was packed into the kettle again.

"Dost see me?" inquired he of the fisherman.

"I see thee," answered the fisherman, laughing. "I see thee, but thou'lt not see me anymore."

The cover was already on the kettle and fastened firmly. The fiery man by no means expected to find such cunning among people and, considering his condition in the kettle, began to beg of the fisherman: "Let me out and I will reward thee."

"Swear that thou wilt never destroy me," said the fisherman.

The spirit answered with a solemn voice, "I swear."

The fisherman removed the cover, and black smoke rolled out, growing thicker and thicker, till at last it turned into a fiery man.

"Follow me," said he to the fisherman, and the latter followed without thinking.

In a short time they came to a high cliff, in which steps were cut in the stone. The fiery man bent to the earth, plucked an herb, and, giving it to the fisherman, said, "Keep this with thee always. Put thy foot on this step; immediately after thou wilt be on a high mountain, from which thou wilt see a great lake. In the lake is a wealth of fish, and thou hast the right to catch as many of them as may please thee, but only once a week, on Mondays. When thou hast the wish to come down, climb to the top, and soon thou wilt be at the bottom."

Thereupon the fiery man vanished, but the fisherman went on the steps cut in the rock. In one moment a mighty wind caught him, and in a twinkle he was on a high mountain, from which he saw an altogether unknown country covered with dark forests, in the midst of which was a broad lake. Only here and there was a grass-plot to be seen; there were neither hills nor the dwellings of men.

The fisherman went down from the mountain, and when he had reached the lake he found a boat with all the fishing-tackle, as if made ready for him. He went to work willingly, threw in the net, and drew out nothing; he threw it in a second time, drew out as much as before. "That fiery man has fooled me," thought he, "but the third throw is always the best." He cast his net again and drew out three fish. When he saw them in the net, he said bitterly, "Well, this is a wealth of fish! If it goes on in this way, I'll soon leave the place; besides, I don't like travelling by wind." But when he looked at the fish more carefully and took them in his hand, he found that in all his life he had never seen anything like them. "These are not for me," muttered he. "I must give them to the king; he will soon try them." With that he left the boat, went to the mountain, and had barely touched the summit when a mighty wind seized him and placed him on level land. He set out for home, and it was time, for his wife had already cooked the dinner and was waiting. As soon as he saw her before the door, he hurried his steps, and when she was in the cottage he began to run. And why did he run, because he feared her? Not at all. He cared nothing for her, as he said himself; but he loved domestic peace, and did everything his wife wanted, but always did it in such fashion that she might not know what he was doing; this was to preserve his own importance in her eyes. He went into the house slowly, and said at the door, "Well, my dear, I have caught a few fish today; but I had much trouble, or I should have been home long ago."

"Time for thee," snapped his wife. "If thou art late again I'll eat alone, leave nothing, and thou wilt find out that I am not thy slave to wait and suffer hunger."

"Oh well, things are not so bad today," said the fisherman. "Better come and see these wonderful fish."

"They are just like any other fish," cried the woman, "only they look a little different, that's all."

"And for that very reason thou wilt take them to the king. He will pay us well for them; we should not be able to use them."

"Oh, thou couldst soon do away with them," replied his wife, "but that's why I'll take them to the king; besides, we are up to our ears in fish."

After dinner the fisherman's wife hurried to the king with the fish. When she came to the palace, she asked the first man she met where the king was, but got as answer: "I don't keep the king!" She went farther, making confusion everywhere until all the servants came together, but no one said anything to her. At last she reached the guard who stood before the king's chamber; she wanted to go without ceremony to his Kingly Grace. The guard pushed her back sharply, but the fishwoman did not retreat so easily; she tried once more to break through the guards, but this time she was repulsed. One of the guards, as firm as a rock, and with as much hair on his face as a bear, caught her by the hand and pulled her so roughly that she almost fell to the floor. She screamed that they were killing her, and roused the whole palace; even the king came. She turned straight to him and cried out over the heads of the men, "Royal Grace, I am bringing fish, and these bears won't let me in."

The king, who was in good humour that day, beckoned her to come. "What kind of fish, and how many?" asked he when she approached.

"Royal Grace, only three, but so wonderful that I have not seen such as long as I live." With that she took a fish from the basket and handed it to the king.

"Wonderful, indeed," said the king, "but give them not to me, give them to my cook; and here is to thee for the road," giving her a handful of goldpieces.

The fishwoman, when she saw so much money, fell at the king's feet, and came near throwing him down; but he didn't mind. Then she took the fish to the kitchen, and ran headlong home.

After she had gone, the king went to the kitchen, looked at one of the fish, and said to the cook, "Thou must dress these fish in a special manner, and answer with thy head for the cooking."

"Royal Grace, in what manner?" asked the cook, trembling with terror when he heard of his head; for though he was a great hero at cutting off heads, he trembled like an aspen when his own head was in question.

"That's thy affair," replied the king. "I will send my chamberlain to thee to look after the fish."

The king went away, and presently the chamberlain appeared. The cook did not know how to prepare the fish, and lost his wits – but that was his luck, for he did everything without knowing it, and altogether different from his wont. At last when they had the fish on the pan and began to butter them, the whole palace trembled. Then followed a terrible shock; and before the cook or the chamberlain could think what it meant, they received each such a slap on the face from an invisible hand that they fell senseless to the floor. And while they were lying in such concord on the floor, they knew not that one of the fish stood on his tail in the pan and said to the other two, "Will ye serve me or be food for the king?"

"Serve thee," said both in one voice. With that all three of them vanished, and to this day no man knows whither they went.

The cook woke up from his involuntary slumber sooner than the chamberlain; he did not rise, however, but waited for the other. Then he rose, groaned heavily, complained, and both hurried to the fish; but they were gone. "The devil take the fish!" said the cook, "but what will the king say?"

It was no great joy for the chamberlain that the fish were gone; still he went to the king and told him of all that had happened in the kitchen.

"I cannot believe it," said the king, "but if thou canst get more fish like these, thou wilt be forgiven this time. Now go to the fisherman and tell him to get other fish like these."

The chamberlain hurried away with light heart and rejoiced at his easy escape. The fisherman said that he could catch fish only on Mondays. The chamberlain told this to the king; the king was very angry. But what could he gain by that?

There was joy in the fisherman's cottage by reason of so much money, and the fisherman's wife could hardly wait till Monday. She roused her husband early Monday morning, got him a holiday breakfast, and almost pushed him out of the house, so as to bring those strange fish with all speed. The fisherman obeyed, not his wife, however, but the king, and hastened to the cliff with the wonderful herb in his bosom. He had barely stood on the step, when he was carried to the mountain; and from there he rushed to the lake, where he found a boat waiting for him as before.

The first and second time he caught nothing; but the third time he drew out three fish. "Now my wife will be glad," thought he, and hurried up the mountain; from there he was taken to the valley in an instant, and ran home. His wife pulled the fish out of his hands, threw them into a basket, and ran to the king's palace. The guard was ordered to let her pass; and she went straight to the king, who came out to meet her and, looking at the fish to see if they were the same, gave her another handful of gold for her trouble. The fishwoman thanked him, took the fish to the kitchen, and went home leisurely, for she counted the money to see if there was the same as before; there was still more. Now there was joy in the cottage, and the fisherman was thankful in his heart to the fiery man, by whose action he had gained such peace in his household.

New orders were issued by the king to the cook, who was trembling with terror, thinking what would come of the fish. But the king, who did not believe even the chamberlain, sent his eldest son to watch both the chamberlain and the cook, lest they should eat the fish themselves. They all stood in great expectation around the pan in which the butter was melting under the fish; but as soon as they began to butter the fish, the castle was shaken more violently than before, a still louder shock followed, and the cook, chamberlain, and even the prince himself, received such slaps from an unseen hand that all three fell senseless to the floor. And while they were lying there, they did not know that one of the fish stood on its tail in the pan, and said to the other two, "Will ye be food for the king, or serve me?"

"Serve thee," answered the two in one voice; then all three vanished in an instant, and to this day no man knows whither.

The cook came to his senses first; but seeing the chamberlain and the prince still on the floor, he stayed where he was. The chamberlain followed his example; at last the prince jumped up and roused both. For a while they acted as if they had lost their wits, then rose to their feet slowly, and complained. When they looked in the pan they found it empty. The prince told all carefully to his father. The king was raging, and threatened them all with death. At last he was pacified, and sent the prince to the fisherman. The prince gave the king's order, but the fisherman said that he could catch those fish only on Mondays. When the king heard this he fell into a towering passion, though he knew himself that the fish could be caught only on Mondays. At last he grew calm, but resolved to be present next time they cooked these most wonderful fish.

On Monday the fisherman's wife pushed her husband out of the house at the dawn of day. The fisherman came to the top of the mountain as before, then hastened to the lake, where on the third cast of the net he drew out three fish. He hurried to the top of the mountain; next moment he was in the valley, and ran home as fast as his breath would let him. His wife shortened the journey for him: she ran to meet him and, pulling the fish out of his hands, rushed off to the palace like a crazy woman. The king was waiting, and ran out the moment he saw her. When he looked at the fish he gave her two handfuls of gold. She took the fish to the kitchen, and hurried away. When she came to the field she sat down and counted the money ten times.

In the king's kitchen the king, the prince, and the chamberlain watched the cook while he was preparing the fish. Because the king was present, great attention was paid to everything. This was done partly to make the king tired of being there; but he gave them to understand that he would wait till the fish were ready. After long preparation they got them on the pan; but as soon as the cook began to butter them the palace shook as in a tempest. Then came a shock as from a lightning-stroke, and in an instant all present received such slaps on the face that they fell senseless to the floor. While lying there without distinction of persons none of them knew, not even the king, that one of the fish stood on its tail in the pan and said to the other two, "Will ye serve me or be food for the king?"

"Serve thee!" answered both in one voice; and all three vanished.

After a long time the cook woke from his trance and, seeing the king prostrate, remained as he was. In like manner acted the chamberlain and the prince when they recovered. At last the king rose, walked around the pan quickly, saw no fish, wondered greatly, and went to his chambers in silence. When the king had gone, the prince, the chamberlain, and the cook sprang from the floor and shook themselves.

The king pondered long over these fish, weighed everything duly, and then sent for the fisherman. The fisherman came straightway; but how he wondered when he heard what had happened at the buttering of the fish! The king said, "Take me to that lake; I will examine everything carefully myself." The fisherman of course consented. The king took his bodyguard, and all moved toward the cliff, with the fisherman at the head. When they arrived there the fisherman gave the king some of the herb which he had received from the fiery man, took him by the hand, and stood on the stone step. In an instant a mighty wind seized them; the king and the fisherman flew through the air, but the bodyguard stood, as if fallen from heaven. They waited long; but when nothing came of it, they returned to the palace, and told the terrified people what they had seen.

In due time the king with the fisherman appeared on the summit of the mountain, from whence he saw the whole country. Although there was no palace, nor even a cottage, still it pleased him greatly at first sight.

"There," said the fisherman to the king, "is the lake where I catch the wonderful fish; I haven't gone farther yet in any direction."

"Very well," said the king, "let us go down."

On reaching the lake the king told the fisherman to catch the fish; but he went on himself to examine the place. The farther he went the thicker the grass, till at last he had hard work to get through; still he advanced till he came to a beautiful green meadow, having on one side the forest, and on the other the lake. Near the shore in a boat sat an old grandfather, whose head was as white as an apple tree in blossom.

"Wilt thou row me over, grandfather?" asked the king.

"Why should I not, since that is what I am here for?"

The king took a seat in the boat. The old man rowed without hurrying; but the boat moved lightly over the smooth water, like a fly through the blue sky. When they reached the middle of the lake the old man turned to one side. Then the king saw a grand castle half hidden in the dark forest.

"Oh, what a beautiful castle! Who reigns there?" asked the king.

"Thou wilt learn if thou enter," replied the old man. When they touched the shore he gave the king a green twig, and said, "Take this twig; it will be of use to thee. Goodbye, for thou wilt not see me again."

"But who will take me back?"

"No one. Thou wilt go back on dry land." And, turning aside, he disappeared.

The king went straight to the palace; and if he wondered at the words of the old man, he was still more astonished when he entered the principal gate and saw no living soul. Thoughtfully he ascended the broad steps, went through one chamber, then another, a third, and a fourth; but nowhere did he find a living creature. "This is some enchanted castle," thought the king to himself. "Who knows how I shall escape? But I will see all, and then find the way home." He examined the chambers further till he came to the last, and there in the middle of the room sat an old man, bent to the floor. "I said this was an enchanted castle," thought the king. "Here sits one man!"

The old man raised his head and, seeing the king, said, "Welcome; at last I see a human face!"

The king approached him and asked, "Who art thou, and what does this empty palace mean?"

"I am a king, but without subjects or power; another rules in my place," answered the old man bitterly.

"What is the cause of this?"

"The treason of my own wife."

"And is there no rescue?"

"Well, the same as none; therefore be off at once, otherwise my wife will kill thee when she returns from the King of the Toads."

"I am not afraid of a woman," said the king. "I want to stand before her; we shall see if there is no escape."

"If there were escape I should not be sitting here confined by the King of the Toads!"

"Who is this King of the Toads?"

"Listen; I will tell thee my whole sad story. The sun is yet high, and until it sets my wife will not return. Once I ruled over a powerful nation; around my palace was a great city, and near it a beautiful garden. All is changed into a dark forest and a lake. The fish in the lake are my former subjects. I was once happy, and the more so because I obtained as wife a beautiful and kind princess; but the King of the Toads got into the place where the lake now is, and he turned my wife's heart from me. I remonstrated, begged, threatened my wife with death, but in vain. Every day she went to meet the King of the Toads, and listened to his wheedling speech. Once I came upon them in the summer-house, and heard with my own ears their whispering and kissing. At last the King of the Toads said, 'I will find the nest of the magic bird, will take its eggs, and give them thee to eat; thou wilt become immortal and ever young; then we shall be altogether happy.' 'Deceitful serpent!' I cried, springing from my hiding-place; and with a sharp sword I cut the King of the Toads in two. My wife fell upon him, weeping, and he grew together again. Looking at me with venomous eye, he muttered words I could not understand, and that moment I felt my blood grow cold, and my veins stiffened so that I could not think of further struggle. I came home in misery and sat down on this chair to rest; but the King of the Toads froze me to my seat, and laid a spell upon the land. From that time I sit here, I know not how many years. My wife spends every day with her lover, and catches frogs for him out of the lake; in return, he promises her immortality and eternal youth. Now, thou canst see there is no aid for me; but escape thou before my wife kills thee."

"I will not flee," said the king, and drew his sword. "I'll cut off her head, the traitorous soul!"

"Foolish man," said the old king. "The King of the Toads saves her, and will not let her be hurt."

"Let him guard her; I must avenge thee," answered the king, and sat on a chair waiting for the deceitful queen, paying no attention to the old man, who begged him by everything in the world to escape.

As the sun was going down the queen came, and was not a little astonished when she saw the stately knight with her husband. The king drew his sword and ran towards her, but the moment the sword touched her clothing it broke in two. It would have been bad for the king now, if he had not remembered the twig which the boatman gave him. He pulled it out quickly, and struck the queen three times. The third time he struck she dropped on a seat, and was unable to move an eye.

"Sit there, like thy husband," said the king mockingly, and counselled with the old man what to do further.

"It would be better," said the old man, who gained courage when he saw his wife frozen to the chair, "to persuade the King of the Toads to free the kingdom and me from enchantment."

"I will try," answered the king and, going to the adjoining chamber, where the queen's wardrobe was, he dressed in her garments and came back to the old man. "Now I will go to the King of the Toads and pretend to be his love, thy virtuous wife. Then I will beg him; and if he does not do what I want, I'll freeze him with this twig, and stroke him with my sword till his heart softens."

"But beg of him first," said the old man.

The king made his way in silence to the King of the Toads; but as it was night he could not find him, and was obliged to call out. He changed his voice, which deceived the King of the Toads, who came quickly and wished to embrace him, thinking that he was the queen.

"No, my dear," said the king, "first thou must do something to please me. What good is it for us to live together if my former husband is troubling me? Either kill him altogether or give him back his former condition, so that he may die; if thou wilt take the spell from him, he will fall to dust and ashes."

"Let it be as thou wishest," said he, drawing nearer.

But she moved away, and said, "I have one more favour to ask, but this concerns us alone. As soon as my former husband dies thou wilt take his place and we shall reign together, but what sort of a reign would it be if the whole country were enchanted; therefore give back its former shape to the kingdom, and I will marry thee before the world."

"So let it be," replied the King of the Toads, and embraced his supposed love, who refused no longer. Scarcely had he touched her when he was struck three times with the twig, in the dark night, and the King of the Toads was frozen to the earth.

"Serpent of hell!" cried the king with his powerful voice, "now I'll enchant thee for the eternal ages." And with that he drew out his sword and cut him into countless pieces, which he threw into the water. Frogs rushed from every side with a terrible croaking, and greedily swallowed the bits of the body of their destroyer.

They had barely devoured him when the water began to run out of the lake; and the king saw by the light of the moon which had risen over the mountain summit, how the tree-tops were rising quickly from the water, higher and higher till the water disappeared altogether, and in the place of the lake was a splendid park, in which were multitudes of people who, praising the king, hurried to the castle. The king joined them, but before reaching the castle he had to pass through a large city; and only after travelling many streets did he arrive there. All the chambers were lighted up, and full of people, so that with difficulty did he find the old man, who was standing in the last chamber, and preventing the people from hewing the queen to pieces; but the king drew his sword and cut off her head. "She deserved it," said he to the old man, who dropped a few tears for his former wife.

Now universal rejoicings began, but the liberated king took no part in them. He called his deliverer and said, "My hours are numbered, I give the whole kingdom to thee; rule in my place."

The new king thanked the old one kindly, and when he rose in the morning, he heard that the old king was dead.

Our king mounted a fiery steed, rode to the city, and announced to the people the death and last will of their former ruler. They grieved for a moment, then with shouts of gladness greeted the new king.

After the burial of the old monarch, his successor examined the kingdom; and as everything pleased him greatly, he decided to stay there. Therefore he went to his former palace, but the road was far longer than when he had travelled it with the fisherman. He was obliged to ride several weeks before arriving there. No one knew him, for several years had passed while he was in the enchanted kingdom. At last an old grandfather came, who said, "I am one of the body-guard who went with thee to the cliff where thou didst leave us. Take me, I beg, into thy service again, for all my comrades are dead; I am alone."

The people believed quickly the grandfather's words, gathered around the king and kissed the hem of his garment. The king sold his castle, put everything he could into wagons, and made ready for the road. Now he remembered the fisherman, asked how he was getting on, and when he had returned home.

"Only yesterday," was the reply.

"Send for him," commanded the king; and straightway the fisherman was there.

When the king asked about his adventures, the fisherman answered, "Royal Grace, I have no fish, and God alone knows what happened in that place. All at once the water disappeared under my boat and I was on dry land. I left everything and ran away; but trees began to grow under me, and so quickly that every second branches struck my face. Since it was in the night I might have lost my senses. In the morning I wondered when I saw instead of a forest an enormous city, with a great palace. I hurried from that magic country, thinking to see my cottage soon; but I travelled one day, I travelled two, a week, a month, and then a year – no sign of my cottage. I gave up for a time, and only yesterday I came home safely. My wife was dead; I am all alone now in this wide world."

"Do not cry," said the king. "Thou hast me yet. Thou wilt stay with me."

The fisherman answered with tears, and all started off on their journey. They arrived safely at the new kingdom; and all lived happily till they died.

Stribor's Forest
(Croatian)

I

ONE DAY A YOUNG MAN went into Stribor's Forest and did not know that the Forest was enchanted and that all manner of magic abode there. Some of its magic was good and some was bad – to each one according to his deserts.

Now this Forest was to remain enchanted until it should be entered by someone who preferred his sorrows to all the joys of this world.

The young man set to and cut wood, and presently sat down on a stump to rest, for it was a fine winter's day. And out of the stump slipped a snake and began to fawn upon him. Now this wasn't a real snake, but a human being transformed into a snake for its sins, and it could only be set free by one who was willing to wed it. The snake sparkled like silver in the sun as it looked up into the young man's eyes.

"Dear me, what a pretty snake! I should rather like to take it home," said the young man in fun.

"Here's the silly fool who is going to help me out of my trouble," thought the sinful soul within the snake. So she made haste and turned herself at once out of a snake into a most beautiful woman standing there before the young man. Her sleeves were white and embroidered like butterflies' wings, and her feet were tiny like a countess's. But because her thoughts had been evil, the tongue in her mouth remained a serpent's tongue.

"Here I am! Take me home and marry me!" said the snake-woman to the youth.

Now if this youth had only had presence of mind and remembered quickly to brandish his hatchet at her and call out, "I certainly never thought of wedding a piece of forest magic," why, then the woman would at once have turned again into a snake, wriggled back into the stump, and no harm done to anybody.

But he was one of your good-natured, timid and shy youths; moreover, he was ashamed to say "No" to her, when she had transformed herself all on his account. Besides, he liked her because she was pretty, and he couldn't know in his innocence what had remained inside her mouth.

So he took the woman by the hand and led her home. Now that youth lived with his old mother, and he cherished his mother as though she were the image of a saint.

"This is your daughter-in-law," said the youth, as he entered the house with the woman.

"The Lord be thanked, my son," replied his mother, and looked at the pretty girl. But the mother was old and wise, and knew at once what was inside her daughter-in-law's mouth.

The daughter-in-law went out to change her dress, and the mother said to her son, "You have chosen a very pretty bride, my boy; only beware, lest she be a snake."

The youth was dumbfounded with astonishment. How could his mother know that the other had been a snake? And his heart grew angry within him as he thought, "Surely my mother is a witch." And from that moment he hated his mother.

So the three began to live together, but badly and discordantly. The daughter-in-law was ill-tempered, spiteful, greedy and proud.

Now there was a mountain peak there as high as the clouds, and one day the daughter-in-law bade the old mother go up and fetch her snow from the summit for her to wash in.

"There is no path up there," said the mother.

"Take the goat and let her guide you. Where she can go up, there you can tumble down," said the daughter-in-law.

The son was there at the time, but he only laughed at the words, simply to please his wife.

This so grieved the mother that she set out at once for the peak to fetch the snow, because she was tired of life. As she went her way she thought to ask God to help her; but she changed her mind and said, "For then God would know that my son is undutiful."

But God gave her help all the same, so that she safely brought the snow back to her daughter-in-law from the cloud-capped peak.

Next day the daughter-in-law gave her a fresh order: "Go out on to the frozen lake. In the middle of the lake there is a hole. Catch me a carp there for dinner."

"The ice will give way under me, and I shall perish in the lake," replied the old mother.

"The carp will be pleased if you go down with him," said the daughter-in-law.

And again the son laughed, and the mother was so grieved that she went out at once to the lake. The ice cracked under the old woman, and she wept so that the tears froze on her face. But yet she would not pray to God for help; she would keep it from God that her son was sinful.

"It is better that I should perish," thought the mother as she walked over the ice.

But her time had not yet come. And therefore a gull flew over her head, bearing a fish in its beak. The fish wriggled out of the gull's beak and fell right at the feet of the old woman. The mother picked up the fish and brought it safely to her daughter-in-law.

On the third day the mother sat by the fire, and took up her son's shirt to mend it. When her daughter-in-law saw that, she flew at her, snatched the shirt out of her hands, and screamed, "Stop that, you blind old fool! That is none of your business."

And she would not let the mother mend her son's shirt.

Then the old woman's heart was altogether saddened, so that she went outside, sat in that bitter cold on the bench before the house, and cried to God, "Oh God, help me!"

At that moment she saw a poor girl coming towards her. The girl's bodice was all torn and her shoulder blue with the cold, because the sleeve had given way. But still the girl smiled, for she was bright and sweet-tempered. Under her arm she carried a bundle of kindling-wood.

"Will you buy wood for kindling, Mother?" asked the girl.

"I have no money, my dear; but if you like I will mend your sleeve," sadly returned the old mother, who was still holding the needle and thread with which she had wanted to mend her son's shirt.

So the old mother mended the girl's sleeve, and the girl gave her a bundle of kindling-wood, thanked her kindly, and went on happy because her shoulder was no longer cold.

II

That evening the daughter-in-law said to the mother, "We are going out to supper with Godmother. Mind you have hot water for me when I come back."

The daughter-in-law was greedy and always on the look-out to get invited for a meal.

So the others went out, and the old woman was left alone. She took out the kindling-wood which the poor girl had given her, lit the fire on the hearth, and went into the shed for wood.

As she was in the shed fetching the wood, she suddenly heard something in the kitchen a-bustling and a-rustling – "Hist, hist!"

"Whoever is that?" called the old mother from the shed.

"Brownies! Brownies!" came the answer from the kitchen in voices so tiny, for all the world like sparrows chirping under the roof.

The old woman wondered what on earth was going on there in the dark, and went into the kitchen. And when she got there the kindling-chips just flared up on the hearth, and round the flame there were Brownies dancing in a ring – all tiny little men no bigger than half an ell. They wore little fur coats, their caps and shoes were red as flames, their beards were grey as ashes, and their eyes sparkled like live coal.

More and more of them danced out of the flames, one for each chip. And as they appeared they laughed and chirped, turned somersaults on the hearth, twittered with glee, and then took hands and danced in a ring.

And how they danced! Round the hearth, in the ashes, under the cupboard, on the table, in the jug, on the chair! Round and round! Faster and faster! They chirped and they chattered, chased and romped all over the place. They scattered the salt, they spilt the barm, they upset the flour – all for sheer fun. The fire on the hearth blazed and shone, crackled and glowed, and the old woman gazed and gazed. She never regretted the salt nor the barm, but was glad of the jolly little folk whom God had sent to comfort her.

It seemed to the old woman as though she were growing young again. She laughed like a dove, she tripped like a girl, she took hands with the Brownies and danced. But all the time there was the load on her heart, and that was so heavy that the dance stopped at once.

"Little brothers," said the mother to the Brownies, "can you not help me to get a sight of my daughter-in-law's tongue, so that when I can show my son what I have seen with my own eyes he will perhaps come to his senses?"

And the old woman told the Brownies all that had happened. The Brownies sat round the edge of the hearth, their little feet thrust under the grate, each wee mannikin beside his neighbour, and listened to the old woman, all wagging their heads in wonder. And as they wagged their heads, their red caps caught the glow of the fire, and you'd have thought there was nothing there but the fire burning on the hearth.

When the old woman had finished her story, one of the Brownies called out, and his name was Wee Tintilinkie: "I will help you! I will go to the sunshiny land and bring you magpies' eggs. We will put them under the sitting hen, and when the magpies are hatched your daughter-in-law will betray herself. She will crave for little magpies like any ordinary forest snake, and so put out her tongue."

All the Brownies twittered with joy because Wee Tintilinkie had thought of something so clever. They were still at the height of their glee when in came the daughter-in-law from supper with a cake for herself.

She flew to the door in a rage to see who was chattering in the kitchen. But just as she opened the door, the door went bang! The flame leapt; up jumped the Brownies, gave one stamp all round the hearth with their tiny feet, rose up above the flames, and flew up to the roof – the boards in the roof creaked a bit, and the Brownies were gone!

Only Wee Tintilinkie did not run away, but hid among the ashes.

When the flame leapt so unexpectedly and the door banged to, the daughter-in-law got a start, so that for sheer fright she plumped on the floor like a sack. The cake broke in her hand; her hair came down, combs and all; her eyes goggled, and she called out angrily, "What was that, you old wretch?"

"The wind blew up the flame when the door opened," said the mother, and kept her wits about her.

"And what is that among the ashes?" said the daughter-in-law again. For from the ashes peeped the red heel of Wee Tintilinkie's shoe.

"That is a live ember," said the mother.

However, the daughter-in-law would not believe her, but, all dishevelled as she was, she got up and went over to see close to what was on the hearth. As she bent down with her face over the ashes, Wee Tintilinkie quickly let out with his foot, so that his heel caught the daughter-in-law on the nose. The woman screamed as if she were drowning in the sea; her face was all over soot, and her tumbled hair all smothered with ashes.

"What was that, you miserable old woman?" hissed the daughter-in-law.

"A chestnut bursting in the fire," answered the mother, and Wee Tintilinkie in the ashes almost split with laughter.

While the daughter-in-law went out to wash, the mother showed Wee Tintilinkie where the daughter-in-law had set the hen, so as to have little chickens for Christmas. That very night Wee Tintilinkie fetched magpies' eggs and put them under the hen instead of hens' eggs.

III

The daughter-in-law bade the mother take good care of the hen and to tell her at once whenever the chickens were hatched. Because the daughter-in-law intended to invite the whole village to come and see that she had chickens at Christmas, when nobody else had any.

In due time the magpies were hatched. The mother told her daughter-in-law that the chickens had come out, and the daughter-in-law invited the village. Gossips and neighbours came along, both great and small, and the old woman's son was there too. The wife told her mother-in-law to fetch the nest and bring it into the passage.

The mother brought in the nest, lifted off the hen, and behold, there was something chirping in the nest. The naked magpies scrambled out, and hop, hop, hopped all over the passage.

When the Snake-Woman so unexpectedly caught sight of *magpies*, she betrayed herself. Her serpent's nature craved its prey; she darted down the passage after the little magpies and shot out her thin quivering tongue at them as she used to do in the Forest.

Gossips and neighbours screamed and crossed themselves, and took their children home, because they realized that the woman was indeed a snake from the Forest.

But the mother went up to her son full of joy.

"Take her back to where you brought her from, my son. Now you have seen with your own eyes what it is you are cherishing in your house." And the mother tried to embrace her son.

But the son was utterly infatuated, so that he only hardened himself the more against the village, and against his mother, and against the evidence of his own eyes. He would not turn away the Snake-Woman, but cried out upon his mother, "Where did you get young magpies at this time of year, you old witch? Be off with you out of my house!"

Eh, but the poor mother saw that there was no help for it. She wept and cried, and only begged her son not to turn her out of the house in broad daylight for all the village to see what manner of son she had reared.

So the son allowed his mother to stay in the house until nightfall.

When evening came, the old mother put some bread into her bag, and a few of those kindling-chips which the poor girl had given her, and then she went weeping and sobbing out of her son's house.

But as the mother crossed the threshold, the fire went out on the hearth, and the crucifix fell from the wall. Son and daughter-in-law were left alone in the darkened cottage. And now the son felt that he had sinned greatly against his mother, and he repented bitterly. But he did not dare to speak of it to his wife, because he was afraid. So he just said, "Let's follow Mother and see her die of cold."

Up jumped the wicked daughter-in-law, overjoyed, and fetched their fur coats, and they dressed and followed the old woman from afar.

The poor mother went sadly over the snow, by night, over the fields. She came to a wide stubble-field, and there she was so overcome by the cold that she could go no farther. So she took the kindling-wood out of her bag, scraped the snow aside, and fit a fire to warm herself by.

But lo! no sooner had the chips caught fire than the Brownies came out of them, just the same as on the household hearth!

They skipped out of the fire and all round in the snow, and the sparks flew about them in all directions into the night.

The poor old woman was so glad she could almost have cried for joy because they had not forsaken her on her way. And the Brownies crowded round her, laughed and whistled.

"Oh, dear Brownies," said the mother, "I don't want to be amused just now; help me in my sore distress!"

Then she told the Brownies how her silly son had grown still more bitter against her since even he and all the village had come to know that his wife truly had a serpent's tongue. "He has turned me away; help me if you can."

For a while the Brownies were silent, for a while their little shoes tapped the snow, and they did not know what to advise.

At last Wee Tintilinkie said, "Let's go to Stribor, our master. He always knows what to do."

And at once Wee Tintilinkie shinned up a hawthorn-tree; he whistled on his fingers, and out of the dark and over the stubble-field there came trotting towards them a stag and twelve squirrels!

They set the old mother on the stag, and the Brownies got on the twelve squirrels, and off they went to Stribor's Forest.

Away and into the night they rode. The stag had mighty antlers with many points, and at the end of each point there burned a little star. The stag gave light on the way, and at his heels sped the twelve squirrels, each squirrel with eyes that shone like two diamonds. They sped and they fled, and far behind them toiled the daughter-in-law and her husband, quite out of breath.

So they came to Stribor's Forest, and the stag carried the old woman through the forest.

Even in the dark the daughter-in-law knew that this was Stribor's Forest, where she had once before been enchanted for her sins. But she was so full of spite that she could not think of her new sins nor feel fear because of them, but triumphed all the more to herself and said, "Surely the simple old woman will perish in this Forest amid all the magic!" and she ran still faster after the stag.

But the stag carried the mother before Stribor. Now Stribor was lord of that Forest. He dwelt in the heart of the Forest, in an oak so huge that there was room in it for seven golden castles, and a village all fenced about with silver. In front of the finest of the castles sat Stribor himself on a throne, arrayed in a cloak of scarlet.

"Help this old woman, who is being destroyed by her serpent daughter-in-law," said the Brownies to Stribor, after both they and the mother had bowed low before him. And they told him the whole story. But the son and daughter-in-law crept up to the oak, and looked and listened through a wormhole to see what would happen.

When the Brownies had finished, Stribor said to the old woman, "Fear nothing, Mother! Leave your daughter-in-law. Let her continue in her wickedness until it shall bring her again to the state from which she freed herself too soon. As for yourself, I can easily help you. Look at yonder village, fenced about with silver."

The mother looked, and lo! it was her own native village, where she had lived when she was young, and in the village there was holiday and merry-making. Bells were ringing, fiddles playing, flags waving, and songs resounding.

"Cross the fence, clap your hands, and you will at once regain your youth. You will remain in your village to be young and blithe once more as you were fifty years ago," said Stribor.

At that the old woman was glad as never before in her life. She ran to the fence; already her hand was on the silver gate, when she suddenly bethought herself of something, and asked Stribor, "And what will become of my son?"

"Don't talk foolishness, old woman!" replied Stribor. "How would you know about your son? He will remain in this present time, and you will go back to your youth. You will know nothing about any son!"

When the old woman heard that, she considered sadly. And then she turned slowly away from the gate, went back to Stribor, bowed low before him, and said, "I thank you, kind lord, for all the favour you would show me. But I would rather abide in my misery and know that I have a son than that you should give me all the riches and happiness in the world and I forget my son."

As the mother said this, the whole Forest rang again. There was an end to the magic in Stribor's Forest, because the mother preferred her sorrows to all the joys of this world.

The entire Forest quaked, the earth fell in, and the huge oak, with its castles and its silver-fenced village, sank underground. Stribor and the Brownies vanished, the daughter-in-law gave a shriek, turned into a snake, wriggled away down a hole, and mother and son were left alone side by side in the middle of the Forest.

The son fell on his knees before his mother, kissed the hem of her garment and her sleeve, and then he lifted her up in his arms and carried her back to their home, which they happily reached by daybreak.

The son prayed God and his mother to forgive him. God forgave him, and his mother had never been angry with him.

Later on the young man married that poor but sweet girl who had brought the Brownies to their house. They are all three living happily together to this day, and Wee Tintilinkie loves to visit their hearth of a winter's evening.

The Golden-Haired Twins
(Serbian)

ONCE UPON A TIME, a long, long while ago, there lived a young king who wished very much to marry, but could not decide where he had better look for a wife.

One evening as he was walking disguised through the streets of his capital, as it was his frequent custom to do, he stopped to listen near an open window where he heard three young girls chatting gaily together.

The girls were talking about a report which had been lately spread through the city, that the king intended soon to marry.

One of the girls exclaimed, "If the king would marry me, I would give him a son who should be the greatest hero in the world."

The second girl said, "And if I were to be his wife, I would present him with two sons at once. Two twins with golden hair."

And the third girl declared that were the king to marry *her* she would give him a daughter so beautiful that there should not be her equal in the whole wide world!

The young king listened to all this, and for some time thought over their words, and tried to make up his mind which of the three girls he should choose for his wife. At last he decided that he would marry the one who had said she would bring him twins with golden hair.

Having once settled this in his own mind, he ordered that all preparations for his marriage should be made forthwith, and shortly after, when all was ready, he married the second girl of the three.

Several months after his marriage, the young king, who was at war with one of the neighbouring princes, received tidings of the defeat of his army, and heard that his presence was immediately required in the camp. He accordingly left his capital and went to his army, leaving the young queen in his palace to the care of his stepmother.

Now the king's stepmother hated her daughter-in-law very much indeed, so when the golden-haired twins were born, the old queen contrived to steal them out of their cradle, and put in their place two ugly little dogs. She then caused the two beautiful golden-haired boys to be buried alive in an out-of-the-way spot in the palace gardens, and then sent word to the king that the young queen had given him two little dogs instead of the heirs he was hoping for. The wicked stepmother said in her letter to the king that she herself was not surprised at this, though she was very sorry for his disappointment. As to herself, she had a long time suspected the young queen of having too great a friendship for goblins and elves, and all kinds of evil spirits.

When the king received this letter, he fell into a frightful rage, because he had only married the young girl in order to have the golden-haired twins she had promised him as heirs to his throne.

So he sent word back to the old queen that his wife should be put at once into the dampest dungeon in the castle, an order which the wicked woman took good care to see carried out without delay. Accordingly the poor young queen was thrown into a miserably dark dungeon under the palace, and kept on bread and water.

Now there was only a very small hole in this prison – hardly large enough to let in light and air – yet the old queen managed to cause a great many people to pass by this hole, and whoever passed was ordered to spit at and abuse the unhappy young queen, calling out to her, "Are you really the queen? Are you the girl who cheated the king in order to be a queen? Where are your golden-haired twins? You cheated the king and your friends, and now the witches have cheated you!"

But the young king, though terribly angry and mortified at his great disappointment, was, at the same time, too sad and troubled to be willing to return to his palace. So he remained away for fully nine years. When he at last consented to return, the first thing he noticed in the palace gardens were two fine young trees, exactly the same size and the same shape.

These trees had both golden leaves and golden blossoms, and had grown up of themselves from the very spot where the stepmother of the king had buried the two golden-haired boys she had stolen from their cradle. The king admired these two trees exceedingly, and was never weary of looking at them. This, however, did not at all please the old queen, for she knew that the two young princes were buried just where the trees grew, and she always feared that by some means what she had done would come to the king's ears. She therefore pretended that she was very sick, and declared that she was sure she should die unless her stepson, the king, ordered the two golden-leaved trees to be cut down, and a bed made for her out of their wood.

As the king was not willing to be the cause of her death, he ordered that her wishes should be attended to, although he was exceedingly sorry to lose his favourite trees.

A bed was soon made from the two trees, and the seemingly sick old queen was laid on it as she desired. She was quite delighted that the golden-leaved trees had disappeared from the garden; but when midnight came she could not sleep a bit, for it seemed to her that she heard the boards of which her bed was made in conversation with each other!

At last it seemed to her that one board said, quite plainly, "How are you, my brother?" And the other board answered, "Thank you, I am very well; how are you?" "Oh, I am all right," returned the first board, "but I wonder how our poor mother is in her dark dungeon! Perhaps she is hungry and thirsty!"

The wicked old queen could not sleep a minute all night, after hearing this conversation between the boards of her new bed; so next morning she got up very early and went to see the king. She thanked him for attending to her wish, and said she already was much better, but she felt quite sure she would never recover thoroughly unless the boards of her new bed were cut up and thrown into a fire. The king was sorry to lose entirely even the boards made out of his two favourite trees, nevertheless he could not refuse to use the means pointed out for his stepmother's perfect recovery.

So the new bed was cut to pieces and thrown into the fire. But whilst the boards were blazing and crackling, two sparks from the fire flew into the courtyard, and in the next moment two beautiful lambs with golden fleeces and golden horns were seen gambolling about the yard.

The king admired them greatly, and made many inquiries who had sent them there, and to whom they belonged. He even sent the public crier many times through the city, calling on the owners of the golden-fleeced lambs to appear and claim them; but no one came, so at length he thought he might fairly take them as his own property.

The king took very great care of these two beautiful lambs, and every day directed that they should be well fed and attended to; this, however, did not at all please his stepmother. She could not endure even to look on the lambs with their golden fleeces and golden horns, for they always reminded her of the golden-haired twins. So, in a little while she pretended again to be dangerously sick, and declared she felt sure she should soon die unless the two lambs were killed and cooked for her.

The king was even fonder of his golden-fleeced lambs than he had been of the golden-leaved trees, but he could not long resist the tears and prayers of the old queen, especially as she seemed to be very ill. Accordingly, the lambs were killed, and a servant was ordered to carry their golden fleeces down to the river and to wash them well. But whilst the servant held them under the water, they slipped, in some way or another, out of his fingers, and floated down the stream, which just at that place flowed very rapidly.

Now it happened that a hunter was passing near the river a little lower down, and, as he chanced to look in the water, he saw something strange in it. So he stepped into the stream, and soon fished out a small box which he carried to his house and there opened it. To his unspeakably great surprise, he found in the box two golden-haired boys. Now the hunter had no children of his own; he therefore adopted the twins he had fished out of the river, and brought them up just as if they had been his own sons.

When the twins were grown up into handsome young men, one of them said to his foster-father, "Make us two suits of beggar's clothes, and let us go and wander a little about the world!" The hunter, however, replied and said, "No, I will have a fine suit made for each of you, such as is fitting for two such noble-looking young men." But as the twins begged hard that he should not spend his money uselessly in buying fine clothes, telling him that they wished to travel about as beggars, the hunter – who always liked to do as his two handsome foster-sons wished – did as they desired, and ordered two suits of clothes, like those worn by beggars, to be prepared for them. The two sons then dressed themselves up as beggars, and as well as they could hid their beautiful golden locks, and then set out to see the world. They took with them a gusle and a cymbal, and maintained themselves with their singing and playing.

They had wandered about in this way some time when one day they came to the king's palace. As the afternoon was already pretty far advanced, the young musicians begged to be allowed to pass the night in one of the outbuildings belonging to the Court, as they were poor men, and quite strangers in the city. The old queen, however, who happened to be just then in the courtyard, saw them and, hearing their request, said sharply that beggars could not be permitted to enter any part of the king's palace. The two travellers said they had hoped to pay for their night's lodging by their songs and music, as one of them played and sung to the gusle, and the other to the cymbal.

The old queen, however, was not moved by this, but insisted on their going away at once. Happily for the two brothers the king himself came out into the courtyard just as his stepmother angrily ordered them to go away, and at once directed his servants to find a place for the musicians to sleep in, and ordered them to provide the brothers with a good supper. After they had supped, the king commanded them to be brought before him that he might judge of their skill as musicians, and that their singing might help him to pass the time more pleasantly.

Accordingly, after the two young men had taken the refreshment provided for them, the servants took them into the king's presence, and they began to sing this ballad:

"The pretty bird, the swallow, built her nest with care, in the palace of the king. In the nest she reared up happily two of her little ones. A black, ugly-looking bird, however, came to the swallow's nest to mar her happiness, and to kill her two little ones. And the ugly black bird succeeded in destroying the happiness of the poor little swallow; the little ones, however, although yet weak and unfledged, were saved, and, when they were grown up and able to fly, they came to look at the palace where their mother, the pretty swallow, had built her nest."

This strange song the two minstrels sang so very sweetly that the king was quite charmed, and asked them the meaning of the words.

Whereupon the two meanly dressed young men took off their hats, so that the rich tresses of their golden hair fell down over their shoulders, and the light glanced so brightly upon it that the whole hall was illuminated by the shining. They then stepped forward together, and told the king all that had happened to them and to their mother, and convinced him that they were really his own sons.

The king was exceedingly angry when he heard all the cruel things his stepmother had done, and he gave orders that she should be burnt to death. He then went with the two golden-haired princes to the miserable dungeon wherein his unfortunate wife had been confined so many years, and brought her once more into her beautiful palace. There, looking on her golden-haired sons, and seeing how much the king, their father, loved them, she soon forgot all her long years of misery. As to the king, he felt that he could never do enough to make amends for all the misfortunes his queen had lived through, and all the dangers to which his twin sons had been exposed. He felt that he had too easily believed the stories of the old queen, because he would not trouble himself to inquire more particularly into the truth or falsehood of the strange things she had told him.

After all this mortification, and trouble, and misery, everything came right at last. So the king and his wife, with their golden-haired twins, lived together long and happily.

The Two Brothers
(Bosnian)

THERE WAS A MAN who had a wife but no sons, a female hound but no puppies, and a mare but no foal. "What in the world shall I do?" said he to himself. "Come, let me go away from home to seek my fortune in the world, as I haven't any at home." As he thought, so he did, and went out by himself into the white world as a bee from flower to flower.

One day, when it was about dinner-time, he came to a spring, took down his knapsack, took out his provisions for the journey, and began to eat his dinner. Just then a traveller appeared in front of him, and sat down beside the spring to rest; he invited him to sit down by him that they might eat together. When they had inquired after each other's health and shaken hands, then the second comer asked the first on what business he was travelling about the world. He said to him, "I have no luck at home, therefore I am going from home; my wife has no children, my hound has no puppies, and my mare has never had a foal; I am going about the white world as a bee from flower to flower."

When they had had a good dinner, and got up to travel further, then the one who had arrived last thanked the first for his dinner, and offered him an apple, saying, "Here is this apple for you" – if I am not mistaken it was a Frederic pippin – "and return home at once; peel the apple and give the peel to your hound and mare; cut the apple in two, give half to your wife to eat, and eat the other half yourself. What has hitherto been unproductive will henceforth be productive. And as for the two pips which you will find in the apple, plant them on the top of your house."

The man thanked him for the apple; they rose up and parted, the one going onwards and the other back to his house. He peeled the apple and did everything as the other had instructed him. As time went on his wife became the mother of two sons, his hound of two puppies, and his mare of two foals, and, moreover, out of the house grew two apple trees. While the two brothers were growing up, the young horses grew up, and the hounds became fit for hunting. After a short time the father and mother died, and the two sons, being now left alone like a tree cut down on a hill, agreed to go out into the world to seek their fortune. Even so they did: each brother took a horse and a hound, they cut down the two apple trees, and made themselves a spear apiece, and went out into the wide world.

I can't tell you for certain how many days they travelled together; this I do know, that at the first parting of the road they separated. Here they saw it written up: "If you go by the upper road you will not see the world for five years; if you go by the lower road, you will not see the world for three years." Here they parted, one going by the upper and the other by the lower road. The one that went by the lower road, after three years of travelling through another world, came to a lake, beside which there was written on a post: "If you go in, you will repent it; if you don't go in, you will repent it." "If it is so," thought he to himself, "let me take whatever God gives," and swam across the lake. And lo! a wonder! he, his horse, and his hound were all gilded with gold.

After this he speedily arrived at a very large and spacious city. He went up to the emperor's palace and inquired for an inn where he might pass the night. They told him, up there, yon large tower, that was an inn. In front of this tower he dismounted; servants came out and welcomed him, and conducted him into the presence of their master in the courtyard. But it was not an innkeeper, but the king of the province himself. The king welcomed and entertained him handsomely. The next day he began to prepare to set forth on his journey.

The evening before, the king's only daughter, when she saw him go in front of her apartments, had observed him well, and fixed her eyes upon him. This she did because such a golden traveller had never before arrived, and consequently she was unable to close her eyes the whole night. Her heart thumped, as it were; and it was fortunate that the summer night was brief, for if it had been a winter one, she could hardly have waited for the dawn. It all seemed to her and whirled in her brain as if the king was calling her to receive a ring and an apple; the poor thing would fly to the door, but it was shut and there was nobody at hand.

Although the night was a short one, it seemed to her that three had passed one after another. When she observed in the morning that the traveller was getting ready to go, she flew to her father, implored him not to let that traveller quit his court, but to detain him and to give her to him in marriage. The king was good-natured, and could easily be won over by entreaties; what his daughter begged for, she also obtained. The traveller was detained and offered marriage with the king's daughter. The traveller did not hesitate long, kissed the king's hand, presented a ring to the maiden, and she a handkerchief to him, and thus they were betrothed. Methinks they did not wait for publication of banns. Erelong they were wedded; the wedding feast and festival were very prolonged, but came to an end in due course.

One morning after all this the bridegroom was looking in somewhat melancholy fashion down on the country through a window in the tower. His young wife asked him what ailed him? He told her that he was longing for a hunt, and she told him to take three servants and go while the dew was still on the grass. Her husband would not take a single servant, but mounting his gilded horse and calling his gilded hound, went down into the country to hunt. The hound soon found scent, and put up a stag with gilded horns. The stag began to run straight for a tower, the hound after him, and the hunter after the hound, and he overtook the stag in the gate of the courtyard, and was going to cut off its head. He had drawn his sword, when a damsel cried through the window, "Don't kill my stag, but come upstairs: let us play at draughts for a wager. If you win, take the stag; if I win, you shall give me the hound."

He was as ready for this as an old woman for a scolding match, went up into the tower, and on to the balcony, staked the hound against the stag, and they began to play. The hunter was on the point of beating her, when some damsels began to sing, "A king, a king, I've gained a king!" He looked round, she altered the position of the draughtsmen, beat him and took the hound. Again they began to play a second time, she staking the hound and he his horse. She cheated him the second time also. The third time they began to play, she wagered the horse, and he himself. When the game was nearly over, and he was already on the point of beating her, the damsels began to sing this time too, just as they had done the first and second times. He looked round, she cheated and beat him, took a cord, bound him, and put him in a dungeon.

The brother, who went by the upper road, came to the lake, forded it, and came out all golden – himself, his horse, and his hound. He went for a night's lodging to the king's tower; the servants came out and welcomed him. His father-in-law asked him whether he was tired, and whether he had had any success in hunting; but the king's daughter paid special attention to him, frequently kissing and embracing him. He couldn't wonder enough how it was that everybody recognized him; finally, he felt satisfied that it was his brother, who was very like him, that had been there and got married. The king's daughter could not wonder enough, and it was very distressing to her, that her newly-married husband was so soon tired of her, for the more affectionate she was to him, the more did he repulse her.

When the morrow came, he got ready to go out to look for his brother. The king, his daughter, and all the courtiers, begged him to take a rest. "Why," said they to him, "you only returned yesterday from hunting, and do you want to go again so soon?" All was in vain; he refused to take the thirty servants whom they offered him, but went down into the country by himself. When he was in the midst of the country, his hound put up a stag, and he after them on his horse, and drove it up to a tower; he raised his sword to kill the stag, but a damsel cried through a window, "Don't meddle with my stag, but come upstairs that we may have a game at draughts, then let the one that wins take off the stakes, either you my hound, or I yours."

When he went into the basement, in it was a hound and a horse – the hounds and horses recognized each other – and he felt sure that his brother had fallen into prison there. They began the game at draughts, and when the damsel saw that he was going to beat her, some damsels began to sing behind them: "A king! a king! I've gained a king!" He took no notice, but kept his eye on the draughtsmen; then the damsel, like a she-devil, began to make eyes and wink at the young man. He gave her a flip with his coat behind the ears: "Play now!" and thus beat her. The second game they both staked a horse. She couldn't cheat him; he took both the hound and the horse from her. The third and last time they played, he staking himself and she herself; and after giving her a slap in her face for her winking and making of eyes, he won the third game. He took possession of her, brought his brother out of the dungeon, and they went to the town.

Now the brother, who had been in prison, began to think within himself, "He was yesterday with my wife, and who knows whether she does not prefer him to me?" He drew his sword to kill him, but the draught-player defended him. He darted before his brother into the courtyard, and as he stepped onto the passage from the tower, his wife threw her arms round his neck and began to scold him affectionately for having driven her from him overnight, and conversed so coldly with her. Then he repented of having so foolishly suspected his brother, who had, moreover, released him from prison, and of having wanted to kill him; but his brother was a considerate person and forgave him. They kissed each other and were reconciled. He retained his wife and her kingdom with her, and his brother took the draught-player and her kingdom with her. And thus they attained to greater fortune than they could ever have even hoped for.

Silyan the Stork
(Macedonian)

I N THE VILLAGE OF MALO KONYARI lived a good and gentle man named Bozhin. He had only one son, called Silyan; he also had a daughter named Bosilka. Silyan was very spoilt by

both his parents because he was the only boy to survive out of the many they had born. For that reason, they let Silyan do as he pleased – they even let him marry Neda when he was only sixteen years old. By the time Silyan was seventeen, he had a son named Velko.

Because Silyan was so spoilt and immature, he tried his best to avoid doing any of the hard work that was needed in a village, such as ploughing the fields, digging the vineyards, harvesting the crops, and threshing. Silyan's father and mother, Bozhin and Bozhinitsa, were left to do all that as well as looking after the sheep and other livestock. Silyan's wife, Neda, together with his sister, had to do all the work in the household.

Silyan himself most enjoyed going off to the market in the nearby town of Prilep. He liked the idea of being a trader, and if he could, he would have hung around the market every single day, buying wine and brandy and lots of delicacies. In fact, every time he went to the market, the moment he dismounted from his horse, Silyan would rush directly to the bakeries where he would buy himself a warm loaf of the finest, whitest and sweetest bread. He would accompany this with a purchase of the best halva, and would dine in style on these luxuries.

"Ah, now seeing how warm, white bread and halva taste so good," he used to say to his friends, "why should I punish myself eating the coarse and sour home-made rye bread?"

Of course, his friends urged him on all the more to spend his money lavishly because it meant they would get to eat on his account as well! Sometimes when Silyan went to the market with some extra cash, he'd stay in town for two, even three days, ignoring the most urgent work at home in the village.

Many times Silyan's mother and father would scold him for being irresponsible, staying in town, and not helping with the work. That was all very well, but Silyan had wandered off the straight and narrow path and didn't take the slightest notice of his parents' words. As the saying goes, "once a dog has learned to hang out at the butcher's shop, it's very hard to teach it to stop"!

Silyan's father, with kindness and to the best of his modest ability, would often try and talk Silyan into changing his lazy ways, giving lots of examples of the terrible things that could happen.

"Oh my dear boy, Silyan. Leave off from your lazy, bad habits, my son. Stop mixing with that bad company. They're good-for-nothings. They trick you into throwing your money away, my boy. You'll end up penniless, just like them. Don't let them influence you, my child. Listen to me, listen to what your loving mother and I are telling you, because if you don't, bad luck will crush you. A curse of ours might come true. Believe me, son, all children who don't obey their parents are severely punished by God.

"Listen to the following story that I've always learned a lot from. It's about the two birds called Hark and Lark. You've seen and heard about those two birds yourself, son, in the plains where they live and sing among the hawthorns and other wild bushes. One of them sings 'Hark, Hark' and the other replies 'Lark, Lark'.

"You see, once upon a time those two birds were brother and sister. They were very naughty and misbehaved; they took no notice of their parents, who became very upset. Things got worse, as both the mother and the father were hot-tempered, and would often curse their wayward children. On one unfortunate day, their mother was cursing, 'My son Lark, and you, daughter Hark – May you be turned into birds and fly away from here. Fly away and go and live on the plains among the brambles and bushes, and forever seek and call to one another, but never succeed in finding each other'."

"So help me God, Silyan," continued his father, "you might think it's just a story, but I have always believed it. It's been handed down to us for generations, and you know that in the old days, the elders never lied, unlike the way young people lie these days. It's because I love you so much, Silyan, that I've been telling you this story. I hope it brings you to your senses and you stop mixing with that bad crowd who have been leading you astray; if you don't change, God might punish you in some terrible way. Finally, my child, I don't know how else to guide you, other than to remind you of my own father's wise words, may God keep his soul. Many a time he would say, 'if you jump from pole to pole, sooner or later, you will be impaled'.

"But I can see that you are not taking any notice of what I am saying, Silyan. Well, so be it, but the hour will come when these words will ring in your ears, and then you'll realize I've been speaking the truth. Let it be so, but as the saying goes, 'you'll become wise after the damage is done'. Now I've told you as much as I know, Silyan, so I have no more to say. Do what you like, but remember to obey your mother and father, lest you be afflicted by a curse in an evil hour and suffer terribly."

While Bozhin had been lecturing him, Silyan just stared up at the ceiling, or at the wall. His father's words made him furious, and he really couldn't bear to look at him.

"If I survive till morning, I'll show you what I'll do with all your curses and prattling that have given me such a headache!" Silyan thought to himself. "I can't wait to get into town. Ha! And when I do, you won't see me around here again too soon. I'm not going to get pushed into harvesting the fields in this heat when I could be sitting in some nice, cool, shady inn in town, enjoying myself with good company. Bless them, those townsfolk, they really know how to live. Not like we villagers killing ourselves in the heat, with rivers of sweat pouring down our foreheads. Tomorrow, God grant me health, I'm going into town and never coming back here again after all this stupid nonsense the old man has badgered me with! Why, if I thought my parents' curses would really come true and I'd turn into a bird, I'd gladly fly over the oceans, both white and black, but never ever would I return here. He's really pushed me too far this time. I'll teach him what sort of man I am. I'll show him how stubborn I can be too. Why, I'd rather eat a cellar-full of salt than bend to his wishes."

Silyan spent the night mulling over these and similar thoughts, and he set off for his usual inn in town even before dawn had broken. As luck would have it, that evening a man of the cloth from the Holy Land arrived at the inn. He had come on a fundraising mission, and he needed someone to show him around the Prilep villayet, so he asked the innkeeper to find him "the magic key to open all the doors" – in other words, a guide.

"Ha! Silyan, here you are. This is the very job for you," exclaimed the innkeeper. "You'll be able to spend all your time journeying around the villages." Indeed, that was exactly what Silyan wanted. His parents would just about burst on hearing that Silyan had left the town of Prilep. So the Holy Man and Silyan hopped off to the market and bought a bit of this and a bit of that; they were more or less prepared and set off early next morning to collect alms for the Holy Land.

All that summer and autumn, Silyan and the Holy Man travelled around. On Saint James Day they arrived back in Prilep. The Holy Man took out the agreed amount of money to pay Silyan. That was all very well, but Silyan refused to accept the money. Instead, he wanted to accompany the reverend to the Holy Land.

"Please, most Holy Father, I beg you; take me with you on your pilgrimage. I want to be a pilgrim too, so that when I die, I'll die in peace."

That was how Silyan pleaded with the Holy Man, and he begged with tears in his eyes to be taken along. But the Holy Man was not at all keen because the money Silyan had earned would not cover his passage and costs. The innkeeper got into the act as well and pleaded on Silyan's behalf. He argued that all the Holy Man need do was let Silyan sail with him to the Holy Land, and once there, Silyan could fare for himself. In the end, the Holy Man was persuaded.

They arrived at Solun and boarded the boat. The boat sailed along as it did, straight and true, but after a few days, a fearfully strong, unfriendly wind bore down on them, driving the ship willy-nilly across the vast waters. It seemed to skim like a hollowed-out gourd over the ocean breakers. Any moment now it appeared the boat would capsize there, here it would sink. For a whole week, the boat was lashed and driven by the storm, and finally one morning it was hurled towards an island. The boat was smashed on the treacherous rocks – smashed into tiny pieces. All those on board, save Silyan, were drowned. Silyan found himself clinging to a plank and was tossed to and fro by the waves before being dumped onto the shore.

For a long time after he was grounded, Silyan remained clutching tightly onto the plank, for it seemed to him that he was still being thrown around in the ocean. Finally, he realized he was on dry land. He stood up, made a sign of the cross and said a prayer of thanksgiving to God for rescuing him. He stood and waited at the edge of the water, staring out towards where the ship had broken up, hoping that perhaps the Holy Man

Might surface from the depths; but his wait was in vain, for not only the Holy Man, but every other passenger, had perished.

When it became clear to Silyan that no one else was left, he set out to explore the island. He walked on as far as he could, and found a freshwater spring and drank. Next to the spring was a tree, laden with fully ripe fruit, so he ate. A little way up from the spring, he discovered a cave. He went inside, planning to spend the night there. Well, if you had to spend the night there, you'd be as likely to sleep as well as Silyan did! The whole night he turned over and over in his mind thoughts about where he'd been and what had happened to him, and now here he was in this wilderness where neither a cock crowed nor a dog barked.

"Ah mother! Ah father! Ah my darling son Velko and my dear sister and my precious wife! Will you perhaps have some dream tonight where you see that I was saved from the wild sea that nearly drowned me? Will you see a dream where I am in a desolate land where no cocks crow? Oh, I'd rather have been killed by a bullet, mother, and at least had died at home and been buried in our village graveyard. Then at least, I know, mother, that you would have come to visit my grave and would have lit a candle for my soul. But here, mother, I will die in this desolate wilderness, and the eagles and crows will peck my bones clean. Ah father, father; why did you curse me so harshly that l should come to this desolate place?"

Silyan spent the night with these thoughts, and it was finally towards dawn that he managed to close his eyes and snatch a few winks. When he awoke, the sun was shining brightly.

"Thank you, God, thank you for making the sun shine from the sky in which it set. This will surely be a strange land," he said to himself. "Perhaps it is the Underworld! Alas, poor me. There will be no salvation for me from here, and I will never see my village again. Ah, oh precious village; ah, oh precious town Prilep. Will God ever grant that I should visit you again? If God grants me that, I swear that for three years I will pay homage to the Virgin Mary at the Treskavec Monastery. Oh, poor me. I am only deluding myself. How can I ever go home? Look at that ocean. It's water stretching as far as the eye can see. There's no way that I can return there ever again. My bones will rot here, nothing else."

Silyan resolved to investigate the land he'd found himself in to see what there was and what there wasn't. In order to recognize the place,

Silyan fashioned a cross from some dry sticks and perched it high in the tree. He figured that if he found no human traces, he could return to the spring and live off the fruit on the trees. He picked up a piece of wood, shaped like a walking stick, to have at hand in case he should have to defend himself, and set off up the hill. He had walked about an hour when he spotted another spring, and on his walk through the countryside he found lots of wild strawberries to eat. The only thing that was bothering him was the lack of any sign of a pathway or road, or some other human mark. But despite that, Silyan walked on with high hopes that he would find some sign of civilization. At about noon, he had reached the summit of the hill, and when he looked over in a particular direction, he saw some flat, open country, encircled by hills and mountains, which looked just like the landscape around Prilep.

"Praise the Lord," Silyan said to himself. "Is it possible that I am on our local mountain, and they are our plains that I can see over there? Or am I dreaming? I don't know. But there must be people living on these plains because I can make out fields and meadows."

Silyan set off down the mountain in the expectation of finding people. At about 10 o'clock, he came to the edge of the plain and found a footpath. "This is a sure sign that people live here," he thought to himself. "But then, who knows what sort of people they will turn out to be? If they are *my* people – that'll be fine; we'll be able to understand one another. But what if they are strangers, foreigners? How will we manage to speak to one another?"

Silyan walked along the footpath. It wound through some meadows full of wild spinach, which he picked and ate heartily. He'd been walking for nearly half an hour when he reached a small mound. He climbed on top of it and heard some voices, but he couldn't understand a word of what was being said. It seemed to him that it sounded like the clattering, clacking sounds of storks. Poor Silyan became awfully scared, because he thought that maybe the noise came from some fierce animals. He cautiously hid himself behind some briars, and from there he peered out and saw two people, a man and a woman who were mowing the meadow. Silyan wondered what he should do. Should he make himself known to them, or should he return from where he came that morning?

"Oh, poor me", he thought to himself, "whichever way I turn it's all hopeless. If I return, what am I returning to? If I make myself known to these people, I'm scared that they might hurt me. Maybe they're some savage types from the Underworld! What should I do, oh God in Mercy? No, I'll make myself known to them, and what will be will be. Either way, I reckon I'm done for!"

Silyan emerged from behind the bushes, and with his hands crossed and with tears in his eyes, he approached the couple. The moment the man and the woman laid eyes on Silyan, they dropped their scythes, said a few clacks to one another, then laughed heartily. Silyan thought to himself that it would be best if he remained silent and just bowed to them, seeing he hadn't understood a word they'd said. "How would these people understand," he thought to himself, "even if I said as much as a good evening to them in my own language?" So, he just bowed low before them, keeping his arms crossed over his chest and his head lowered. He didn't even open his mouth.

"Hey! Why don't you say something, Silyan! What about a 'good evening' or 'God keep you'?" exclaimed the man to Silyan. "Or maybe you lost your voice in the ocean when you were swimming!"

"I wanted to speak, sir, but I didn't think you'd understand me. And yet, not only do you speak the same language as me, but you even know my name," replied the astounded Silyan. "I beg you, sir, tell me how it is you know me; how do you know my name? I'm sure I've never seen you before, neither in any village nor town. During the summer, I accompanied a Holy Man through all our district, but I didn't meet anyone who even vaguely resembled you! Please, sir, I ask you again, won't you tell me how you know me?"

"Seeing the wind blew you to our land and you are the first man to ever come here," he answered, "I'll tell you what you want to know. You should realize that you were lucky to bump into me. I know you and I insist that you stay as a guest at my house. But, in the meantime, sit down and eat a little bread and cheese, and when it gets dark, we'll go home and I'll answer all the questions you have, and you can answer ours."

When dusk fell, the man and his wife finished off their work and took Silyan and led him back to their house. As soon as he entered the yard and the children saw Silyan, they started to yell excitedly and happily, "Ooh, ooh, here's Silyan from Malo Konyari. Here's Silyan! He's come to visit us!"

"In Heaven's name! Can this be for real, or am I dreaming? Even the children recognize me and know my name too! What sort of miracle can this be?" thought Silyan. "Ah well, the mystery will soon be revealed, God willing."

Silyan entered the house and the family followed, greeting him warmly. For dinner, they prepared the finest dishes, as is fitting for any special guest, and Silyan dined in style. He couldn't overcome his amazement at who these people might be and what this place was. He calculated that maybe he was somewhere near Prilep, maybe in the Struga or Ohrid region, because there was a lake there, and maybe the ocean had brought the ship into that lake, and maybe that's where the ship had been totally wrecked, and he was the sole survivor that was washed up on land.

However, he gave the matter a lot more thought. "No, I'm sure it can't be Ohrid or Struga, because no one there looks like these people. None of those people in those places have such long pointy noses and such long, thin legs. No, these people are very different from the people back home," he thought. "But then if they're so different, how come they all know me, young and old alike?"

Silyan had been left in the room by himself because all the family were busy with their chores, attending the animals and the like. All the time that he was alone, Silyan's mind was sunk in his own thoughts. After some time, the family returned, bringing with them a few of their neighbours.

They began to chat. "Hey, Silyan, how's your father's health?" queried his host. "And your mother Bozhinitsa and your wife Neda? And how is your sister Bosilka and your son Velko? All well and thriving, I trust? And you, Silyan, how are you getting on with your father these days? Better than before, or are you still giving him trouble?"

"You might say that I'm still giving him trouble, sir, rather than being a good son. And it's because I didn't listen to him that God has banished me to your land!" Silyan told his full story and confessed to the people all the wrong things he'd done and how he'd upset his mother and father. It was indeed very strange, as they seemed to be already familiar with most of what he told them. After he had finished talking about himself, Silyan begged them to explain how it was they knew everything about him and his family. It was as if his hosts had seen it all with their own eyes.

"You see, Silyan, dear boy," said the elders, "we have been settled in your village Malo Konyari even from before you were born. We've been living on top of your house and in your surrounding plains. That's how we know you and your family. In important ways, we are part of your family. We know every inch of your house, we know it probably better than you do! Do you understand our meaning?" they asked. "And although you might find a lot of what we're telling you hard to believe, once you hear the entire story, you'll believe us."

Silyan just sat there amazed at all he heard. What could it be about? People he'd never seen and never heard of telling him all about his house and about everything that happened in the village.

"Please, friends, tell me what this is about!" cried Silyan. "How can you know everything about my home? Are you angels from Heaven, perhaps, who visited us, or maybe saints? Or perhaps you are birds that flew over our village. Whatever you may be, I beg you, please tell me; let me know! My head is bursting and whirling from what you've told me so far!"

"We shall explain how we know so much," they replied. "It's because we live on the rooftops of the village houses. We are the storks who nest there and who fly throughout the whole region."

"But how and when do you turn into storks?" exclaimed Silyan. "You are people, even though you look different from my people."

"Yes, it's because we started off as people that we have the form of people now. The reason we transform into storks is because of a generations-old curse that our forefathers put on the people of this island. That curse prevents us from having human children on this island," explained his host.

"Won't you tell me about the curse?" asked Silyan.

"Well, it's like this," said his host. "In the old days, a saintly old man used to live on the island. In those days, the children here used to behave very badly. They never obeyed their parents. In fact, their parents didn't even make any effort to control them. So the children caused much mischief and were totally unruly. The pious old man alone tried to keep order. He attempted to teach the children and their parents to be more civil. If they continued to live in such a deplorable manner, they would come to great woe and calamity.

On one occasion, the old man was reproaching a group of unruly boys on the outskirts of town, underneath a big tree. As they were spoiling for a fight, they struck the old man and knocked him to the ground and kicked him, causing something inside him to burst. In his terrible agony, the old man cursed all the people on the island with his dying breath:

'God will judge you severely for killing me while I tried to teach you sense. I hope that you will be stricken by a deadly plague and all shall perish; children like you don't deserve to be born here. If your parents want children, they'll have to cross the black and white oceans, and bring their offspring here from distant places. God will judge all, for I am dying.'

"After saying those words, the old man died, and the islanders buried him under the tree. On the third anniversary of his death, two springs welled up at the burial site; they still flow to this very day.

"And the old man's curses on our forebears came true, Silyan. A few years not long after his death, all the children on the island died from smallpox. The place was like a ghost town; everyone was in deepest mourning.

"But God in His mercy did not want to wipe out the entire population, so he appeared in a dream to the old man's widow and told her what must be done.

"In the dream, God instructed the adults to go and bathe in one of the springs that flowed at the martyred man's burial site. The water, He said, would turn them into storks, and they could fly over the white and black oceans, to our land. There, the little stork chicks could be hatched and raised. When they were big enough, they could all fly back home and bathe in the other spring that would transform them back to people.

"And so you see, that is what we have been doing for thousands of years, and that's what we'll do till the end of time. So, Silyan, that's the whole story," concluded the host, and all fell silent.

"Praise the Lord; praise you too, sir! I am astonished at how dreadful curses can be," said the dazed Silyan, who could barely speak. "My father used to tell me about two birds that live near our village – Lark and Hark. He used to say they were a brother and sister who did not live according to God's will, and who, as a result of their parents' curse, were turned into birds, always calling for each other and never succeeding to find one another. And they really were changed into birds. And it is a well-known fact that such birds do live in our plains, forever calling to one another, but never seen together.

"I never used to believe him, but now after what's happened to me, and after what you've told me, I do believe it. He had always spoken the truth! But what am I to do now? How can I get home? There isn't a ship that comes here, is there, that I can sail home in? You said you know all that goes on here, sir. But please, might I know your name?"

"My name, Silyan," said the host, "is Lord Klack Klack, boy. With what sorrow one longs for one native land, Silyan but it's not possible for a boat to approach our land because of the craggy cliffs and rocks, and the dangerous seas. I'm quite an important person here – my position is a bit like a mayor in your region – so I've circled and explored our island completely, high and low, and I can assure you that it is impossible for any craft to land here. But, seeing you're my guest, don't worry. I won't desert you, and I'm sure we will be able to figure out some way of getting you home.

"Listen! This is what we'll do. When the time comes for us to fly to your land, you too must bathe in the spring and become a stork. You can carry a container full of water from the other spring around your neck, and then when we arrive, you can pour the water over yourself and change back into a man. Silyan, we'll get you there! You don't have to worry about that, at least. And until then, you can live at my house as my guest – eat, drink and be merry," said Lord Klack Klack, the most eminent citizen in that place.

Once they finished their discussion, they went to bed and slept. The next morning, Lord Klack Klack took Silyan to show him around the town and to also take him to the two springs.

"If you don't believe that a man can be turned into a stork", said Lord Klack Klack, "I'll prove it to you before your very eyes."

Immediately after saying this, Lord Klack Klack dived into the waters of one of the springs and, really, he was utterly transformed into a stork. He flew here, he flew there; he made clattering, tap tap noises with his beak like all storks do. Then he immersed himself in the other spring and became a man again. As fast as he could, Silyan tried it too, and was changed into a stork, then back into a man again. He was now convinced that he'd eventually make it back home.

Silyan stayed on the island for several months, during which he helped with all the field work. Could this be the same Silyan that never worked when he lived at his father's house? Here, he worked bareheaded in the burning sun, with boundless energy and enthusiasm.

The time neared for the storks' departure, and preparations started to be made. Lord Klack Klack sent messengers to all the young couples asking them to come and be transformed into storks. Over the following few days, everyone took it in turn to change into storks. They waited at the edge of the sea till everyone was ready. There was an extensive marsh there, where hundreds and thousands of frogs and other little creatures lived – a perfect banquet for the storks.

Silyan filled a bottle with the water which would turn him back into a man, and he tied it around his neck. Then after immersion in the spring, he changed into a stork, and together with Lord Klack Klack joined the rest of the storks. After they had all eaten their fill of frogs, his Lordship gave the order, and they flew higher and higher, ascending to the very clouds themselves. From there, they steered their direction straight for Silyan's native land.

They flew for exactly twenty-four hours and landed for a rest and a feed at another island. While they were dining on frogs and worms, two great sea-serpents struck out towards the storks, threatening to harm them. The storks quickly whirled into the sky, climbing high to safety.

Once they had risen above the clouds, they again set course for our land. They flew as far as they could and approached our coast, where they landed, rested, and nibbled on a few blades of grass, seeing that was all there was to eat.

Finally, they again took to the air and flew towards the regions where their nests were, each stork heading off to its own particular area. Silyan, his Lordship, and a few others headed towards Prilep.

When they approached the village called Pletvar, near the pass, Silyan saw the entire Prilep landscape before him, with all its familiar landmarks. He became terribly excited and started to descend quickly, planning to land near some boulders, pour the water over himself to change back into a man, then walk home from there. But, you know the old saying, "a person shouldn't get too happy or too sad, because trouble is guaranteed". And that is just how Silyan from Malo Konyari, and he was plunged from great happiness into great sorrow.

His landing was very heavy and clumsy, and the bottle around his neck was flung against the rocks, where it shattered into tiny pieces. The water flowed out over the rocks. Silyan rolled himself over the spilled water, but most of it had seeped into the ground. There simply wasn't enough. Silyan did not change into a man; he remained a stork.

He began to cry bitterly, thinking that he would probably end up spending the rest of his life as a stork and even dying as a stork.

"Serves me right, I suppose, for not obeying my parents and now suffering under their curse! I'm grateful at least to be in my own land. I won't be that upset if I die here." Thinking these thoughts, Silyan flew sadly from Pletvar to Malo Konyari and settled himself in Lord Klack Klack's nest.

"Silyan," said his Lordship. "Please don't take offence, for you are a good friend, but I'm afraid you cannot stay in my nest, for my nest is my bed too! It would be a better idea if you built yourself a house on the other end of the roof. Have no fear. I'll guide you back to our land, then back here again next year so you can return to your human form. It would have been better if you hadn't broken the bottle, but what's done is done – there's no use in crying over spilled milk. So long as you stay healthy, everything will work out."

Silyan knew that Lord Klack Klack was right, so he settled himself on the opposite end of the roof. Because it was still early in the morning, most of the household was still sleeping, and only his father was to be seen in the yard. Silyan wept from the grief that flooded through him when he first saw his father again.

After a little while, all the family appeared, busy with their tasks. His mother began to milk the cows, his wife went to milk the sheep; his son herded the pigs and sent the calves and donkeys out to pasture, his sister started to sweep the house and put out the rubbish. In the past, Silyan had managed to get out of doing any work, and now that he longed to help, he couldn't; anyway, there didn't seem to be any work for him to do. Despite Silyan's wishes, it had been fated for him that he must live through the pain of his parents' curse.

The date was the 9th of March, and Silyan spent much of it weeping as he watched his family. For he was unable to speak to them, even though he badly wanted to. With a heavy heart, he flew from the roof and across the plains to inspect his family's fields, meadows, vineyards, and pastures where the cattle were grazing. He wheeled over the entire Malo Konyari plain and even as far away as the Gurgling Brook on the edge of the marsh, where he fed on frogs, black beetles, grasshoppers, and lizards.

"Ah, poor me," thought Silyan to himself. "Fancy eating frogs instead of roast pork and crackling like I used to eat; fancy eating lizards and black beetles in place of the delicious fish and eels I used to order in the cool and shady inns of my beloved Prilep. It serves me right! I made my bed and now I'm lying in it, as my father would say. And he was dead right. He used to say that his words would ring in my ears, but it would be too late – and that's just how it is. Ah, Mary and Jesus, please let me live long enough to become a man again so that my mother and father can take me back in, and I will show them how hard I'll work and how obedient I'll be."

Whenever Silyan the Stork dwelt on these thoughts, he had become forgetful of his circumstances. Once, perched on the roof, he saw his wife milking the cows and thought he'd like to go and pet them because they looked so pretty. He flew down into the yard and started caressing them gently with his beak.

That was all very well, but how on earth was his son Velko to know that the stork meant no harm, and in fact was his own father Silyan! Velko happened to be holding a stick in his hands, and when he saw the stork rubbing its big, long beak over the calves, he was alarmed, thinking that the stork was going to harm them. He yelled out with agitation to his mother, "Mother, look at the stork. It's going to peck the calves!"

"Storks don't eat calves, son, though if it's bothering you, shoo it away."

When Velko heard his mother's reply, he threw the stick at the stork and hit it on the head, stunning him. Silyan wasn't able to fly away immediately, so Velko rushed towards him to collect his stick, and with both hands grabbed Silyan around the middle and called to his mother.

"Mother, mother, I caught the stork!"

In the meantime, Silyan's mother had arrived to help milk the cows, and Velko boasted proudly about how he threw the stick at the stork, and now he had it trapped. It was only then that poor Silyan remembered that he was a stork, and that his son could torture or kill him. Fortunately for Silyan, however, Velko's mother insisted that the stork be set free, thus saving him. It could have been quite possible for Velko to have chained Silyan by one leg and played with him, just like the boys play with birds and crows they have captured. Silyan the stork may have died in such custody!

"Let him go, Velko, my dear; let the stork go," said Velko's mother. "It's cruel to keep him. He's just a poor widower, like me, without your father. Do you realize it's been nearly two years since Silyan left? Ah, what bad luck I've had to have been left a widow so young!"

Velko reluctantly released the stork, and Silyan fled onto the roof of the house. He panted and panted. He could barely get his breath back from the fright he had felt when Velko grabbed him.

A few days later, Silyan decided he would like to fly out to the sheep pens to look at the newborn lambs. As he strolled around the pens, Foxy, their dog, spotted him and silently crept up behind him and sunk her teeth into his tail feathers. If Smille, the shepherd, hadn't ordered the dog to let go, Silyan would have lost all his feathers!

"Let it go, Foxy! You'll pluck the poor stork clean! Poor and lonesome stork," muttered the shepherd. And so this time, too, Silyan escaped from death.

A few weeks later, Silyan's father harnessed his bullocks and set out to plough a field. He took Velko with him, to do the job of guiding the team.

Silyan was keen to join them too, to watch the ploughing. They turned over one or two furrows, and Silyan positioned himself at the lower corner of the field, inspecting their work. As he was looking at the furrow, he noticed some small, red worms wriggling in the newly turned soil.

"Mmm," thought Silyan. "I'm very hungry. Some worms would be rather nice to eat." So Silyan stepped into the furrow and started pecking at the worms. He walked up the furrow pecking and because his steps were wide and fast, he came close behind his father. I don't know what made Velko turn around just then, but he did and saw the stork was only a few feet away.

"Grandpa! Grandpa! Look behind you! There's our stork," he cried.

"Never mind, child. Never mind. You just guide the bullocks," replied his grandfather.

They ploughed another strip and again Velko glanced round, and because he was only a little boy, he shouted out to his grandfather again. "Grandpa! Grandpa! Here's the stork behind you. Turn around and see him!"

"Come on, child, just guide the team and stop wasting time, because we have to have the work finished by lunchtime," said his grandfather.

They ploughed a little more, and because Silyan was following them closely along the furrow, happily pecking worms and imagining that his father was feeling fondly towards him, he forgot that he was a stork.

The third time that Velko said to his father, "Grandpa! Grandpa! Look at the stork! It's next to you!" his grandfather angrily replied, "I've had enough of that damned stork!"

As he said those words, Bozhin cracked his whip at the stork and hit him hard on the right leg, breaking it. Silyan reeled from the pain and flew off in a mad frenzy, like a horsefly, and landed on the roof of the house. He stood on his left leg and cried loudly in pain. I don't know how many days he suffered until his leg healed.

That evening, while they were having dinner, Velko told the family how the stork had been following them in the furrows, and how his grandfather had whipped him.

"That's terrible! The poor stork!" exclaimed Neda. "Fancy hurting him. It's sad enough that he's alone and a widower – like me – without you going and injuring him as well."

"Yes, I hurt him, and hurt him quite badly," mumbled Bozhin. "I broke his leg with the whip, but it's all Velko's fault. He kept staring at the stork instead of guiding the bullocks properly. After I hit him, I felt awful, but it was too late. May God forgive me for my hot temper. No matter how hard you try to be good, you still make mistakes." While this was being said, Silyan was squatting on the roof near the chimney and heard every word that was spoken.

It so happened that Silyan's sister Bosilka was engaged to be married. One day, she was sitting on a rug in the yard, stringing a necklace of coins to wear at her wedding. Everyone else in the household was at work in the fields. She was quite alone. At one point, she got up from her rug and went to check that the pigs weren't up to any mischief. Just then, it occurred to Silyan to fly down into the yard, steal the necklace, and hide it in his nest on the roof.

After a short while, Bosilka returned and sat down on the rug. When she went to take up her necklace, it was gone! She searched and searched. She couldn't find it anywhere and cursed terribly.

Not a few weeks later, Silyan's wife was left at home by herself, and she too was sitting outside on the rug in the yard, embroidering a widow's blouse with black thread. As she sewed, she wept, thinking how unlucky she was to be left without her husband. "It wouldn't have been quite so bad," she wailed, "if Silyan had died here. At least I'd know where his grave was and could tend it. But it's so much worse not knowing anything. He might have been drowned on that bleak pilgrimage."

Silyan heard his wife's lament, and his heart ached with sorrow. Nevertheless, it was his lot to live out his life as it had been fated. Neda rose to fetch something from in the house, and Silyan flew down from the roof and took the reel of black thread, together with her needle, and hid them in his nest, making sure they were well concealed. When Neda returned to the rug, she couldn't find her needle and thread. She searched, she became bothered, she swore; but no, they were nowhere to be found – not anywhere.

"Why are you pulling such a long face?" asked her mother-in-law, who just then arrived home from work. "What's gone wrong? Tell me and let me be the judge of whether it's worth being so upset about."

Neda told her what was missing and explained that someone must have stolen it while she was inside.

"And I'm glad that someone stole it," replied her mother-in-law. "You're sewing mourning clothes and forcing yourself into widowhood without good reason. Our Silyan is probably on the pilgrimage with the Holy Man, and you're carrying on as though he's dead and buried. It's a poor way to behave; it's as though you didn't want him back! You should be praying for his safe return, not weeping and mourning! Anyway, last week Bosilka lost her necklace too. It's not worth worrying about, I say. Why, people die and life goes on. But you, fancy crying and carrying on over a lost reel of thread!"

Not long afterwards, the wedding preparations for Bosilka got well under way, seeing the engagement had lasted a while already. Originally, they had meant to delay the wedding till Silyan returned, but the groom's side had grown impatient and insisted that either the wedding was on, or the engagement was off! Apart from this pressure, no one wanted to spoil things for Bosilka, so it was decided that the wedding would go ahead regardless.

Silyan's family invited as many guests as would fit in the house, and all was made ready for the following Sunday when the groom and his relatives would ceremoniously come to collect the bride.

On Sunday, the groom's party came in grand procession from the edge of the village. The best man was in front carrying a staff in his hands. Following him was the groom and all his family; then came the musicians with the bagpipes. They arrived at the bride's house with great ceremony. Guns were firing. The groom and his men were mounted on horses, and they came to a halt at the front door. They made such a fine sight in their white breeches. On their heads they wore fancy white turbans. They were decorated with all sorts of firearms, and on their feet they wore bright red boots. They were all young and handsome, and it was a joy to behold them. The bagpipes rang out till it seemed the very walls shook and the dust fell from the rafters. All the villagers had gathered in the yard to watch the fun; everyone was laughing and happy.

Only Silyan the Stork, high on the roof of his father's house, hung his head gloomily as he watched the festivities. "Ah, accursed be the hour when I disobeyed my parents and they swore that I should become a stork and end up nesting on top of our house," thought Silyan. "Oh, if only I was a man now, I'd be able to join in the party and welcome the guests. I could have been laughing and happy like everyone else."

All the guests went inside for lunch, except for Neda, who took Velko by his hand and climbed up into the barn. There she sat and cried and wailed because she missed Silyan.

"Don't cry, mother; don't cry for father," said Velko. "He'll be home for Easter after his pilgrimage."

Silyan heard their conversation and was flooded with such despair that he felt like throwing himself into the well and drowning. But life is precious, and he reconsidered.

Time had flown by, what with the wedding and all, and the moment approached when the storks had to return to their own land. All the young storks had been practicing flying high in the sky, and Lord Klack Klack sent word to all quarters that Saint Panteleimon's day would be the day of departure. He also told Silyan to get ready to leave too. During the few days that were left, Silyan flew over the entire Prilep plain, covering every hill and valley. He visited his own fields; he circled his house and finally flew as far as the Treskavec Monastery, which is dedicated to the Mother of God. There, perched high on the dome of the church, he prayed fervently, asking protection for his journey to the storks' island and praying that if he should come back and become a man again, he would give his services to the monastery for three years. From the monastery, he flew back to the village, and on Saint Panteleimon's day, the storks departed and arrived safe and sound on their island, as was God's wish.

For the entire summer, Silyan worked hard in Lord Klack Klack's fields, and they in turn looked after him as though he was part of their family. Again the time neared for the storks to fly to our land, and Silyan took pains to find a small flask. He filled it with the "person water" and tied it around his neck on the morning of the journey to our land.

The storks flew across to our land, following the same route as they had when Silyan first made the trip. There had been a recent bloody battle in our country, so when the storks reached that point when they normally separated into smaller groups to fly to their various quarters, the ground was strewn with corpses. Lots of eagles had gathered to peck at the bodies. There were as many eagles, you might say, as there were storks. Near the hill where the bodies were, there was a small plain hopping with giant grasshoppers – perfect food for storks. The storks landed there to eat, but as soon as the eagles saw them, they got angry. The birds began to quarrel, and soon war was declared. The older eagles and storks made the situation worse by trying to hold a peace summit – but all they did was make the quarrel worse! (As the saying goes, "the devil neither ploughs nor digs, but makes people quarrel"). The fighting began, and the birds swooped after one another on that damned hill. For three days and three nights the battle raged, and the plain flowed knee-deep with blood.

Silyan took no part in the war, as Lord Klack Klack took him under his wing, insisting that as he was a guest, he should not participate. Besides, the flask Silyan had tied around his neck helped him, as the eagles were frightened by it. Silyan spent most of the time in a cave he had found.

Finally the battle ended, and the storks took to the air and made their way to our parts. Each stork family was very happy to be flying into their own quarters, and Silyan and Lord Klack Klack and his family made it safe and sound to Malo Konyari.

This time, Silyan took more care and flew into the barn, where he undid the flask from around his neck and poured the water over himself. Lo! There he was a man – just the same as he was in the past when he lived with his mother and father, wife and son. He climbed down from the loft in the barn and made towards the house. It was still very early, and the weather was raining and windy. All the householders were inside warming themselves in front of the fire, staving off the chills of Granny March. The dog, Foxy, was lying on the front porch and at first didn't recognize Silyan, so barked at him angrily – woof, woof, woof.

"Hey, Foxy, fancy barking at me," said Silyan.

"Ooh, mother! That was Silyan I just heard speaking on the veranda," yelled Neda to Silyan's mother. They all jumped up and ran to the door to greet Silyan. The tears flowed as they kissed and hugged him and welcomed him. Silyan kissed his parents' right hands respectfully, and he begged them to forgive him and let him loose from their curse which held him.

His mother quickly put a pot full of brandy to warm on the stove, and Neda brought the most comfortable armchair in the house and sat Silyan down in it. After that, she took off his shoes and washed his feet, then dressed him in his best Easter clothes. Velko rose from sleeping, and Silyan embraced him lovingly, cuddling him in his arms.

The news of Silyan's return from his pilgrimage spread throughout the entire village. Everyone was delighted that Pilgrim Silyan had returned, and they ran over to see him and welcome him back. The house overflowed with villagers, mainly older folk, and they all said to him, "Welcome back, Pilgrim Silyan, welcome back!"

"Please don't call me Pilgrim, friends," replied Silyan. "I didn't have the luck to go on the pilgrimage because our boat was lost at sea, and the Holy Man drowned. And not only that, but I'm hardly able to tell you what I saw and what has happened to me in the past few years, and I'm sure you'll find it hard to believe too. Though, I deserved all that I got, as I didn't believe what my parents told me about curses and spells. But you? You? How are you friends? How has life been in the village?"

"Well, the village has continued as it was, Silyan, Praise the Lord," they replied. "But how did you manage in a foreign land? Tell us about your trip. Tell us about all the marvellous things you saw that we have never seen!"

"How did that poor Holy Man get drowned?" asked Silyan's father.

Silyan explained, "After we boarded the ship in Solun, a terrible wind blew up and the waves pounded the ship. For a whole week the sea seethed around us, and at the end of the week, the boat was hurled up against some rocks and broke apart completely. I was saved because I had the good fortune to cling onto a plank and float to shore. I found some fruit trees and fresh water, so I spent the night there. The next morning, I thought I'd explore the island and headed inland. I found lots of strawberries and managed to stave off my hunger with them. I walked for the entire day and at noon reached a plain, where a man and his wife were mowing a meadow. I was glad to see people, but they were strange looking people – they looked quite different from us. They had really long, thin legs, and their huge noses were at least twice as long as ours. But, as soon as they saw me, they called me by my name and took me home, where I was treated as a special guest."

"But how did they know you? Where did they recognize you from?" queried the villagers. "And they gave you such a warm welcome!"

"Those people are our very own storks that nest here, friends," explained Silyan. "In their town, there are two springs. If you bathe in one, you become a stork, and if you bathe in the other, you turn back into a person. How and why those people become storks – I'll tell you some other time," said Silyan, "but for the moment it's enough to tell you that I too became a stork twice. I nested here, on the roof of our house last summer. Mind you, I suffered for it. But something tells me that you don't believe me," concluded Silyan.

"Ha! Who would be silly enough to believe that story, Silyan!" cried the villagers. "As if you could have been a stork! Ha!"

It occurred to one old lady to say, "Listen, brothers, listen. Silyan is well travelled, and he's seen all sorts of strange lands – he's seen the sea. he's met all sorts of people, and he's learned these wonderful tales and stories to tell us too!"

"Of course! That's it!" replied the others. "God grant him a long life. He's certainly learned lots of clever ideas on his travels. He's probably got lots of stories to tell us!"

"No! I'm not telling you stories," protested Silyan. "I'm telling you what really happened to me and what I went through. I repeat – I was a stork, and I lived on the storks' island for two summers, where I worked Lord Klack Klack's fields. Lord Klack Klack and his family are the storks that live on top of our house! I know it might sound far-fetched, but I swear it's the truth. If I have to, I'll prove it to you, and you'll have to believe me.

"Listen, when I came here as a stork, I didn't want to be a stork, but I had no choice. I was under the power of my parents' curse – just like the birds Hark and Lark, who didn't obey their parents," explained Silyan.

"Yes, we all know about Hark and Lark – how they were a naughty brother and sister who turned into birds," said the villagers. "But that was in a different time, when God and the saints walked the earth and the people really listened to them. But nowadays, it's the devil that walks the earth. No, you can't expect us to believe that you were a stork!"

When Silyan saw that they didn't believe him, he began his story right from the beginning again. He told them about the awful things he did to his father; about how his father advised him, but he didn't listen; about his arrangement with the Holy Man; about how he ended up in the middle of the ocean; about how he thought he'd landed in the Underworld; about his conversation with Lord Klack Klack on the first evening; about the old man who was murdered by the children, and how he had cursed them; about the two springs that appeared after all the children had died from the smallpox plague; about how he became a stork and tied the bottle round his neck; about the flight from the island across the wide oceans; and about how he'd arrived at Pletvar and broken the bottle, and had remained a stork and lived on top of his father's house.

Silyan was aware that the villagers still thought it was all just a good story, so he started to tell them about all that had happened to him while he was a stork; and all that he saw and did.

"Ah, father, and you too, mother. Why don't you believe me when I tell you I was a stork and nested on the far end of our house?" asked the exasperated Silyan. "Was there or wasn't there a single stork there last summer?"

"Well, there was, son, but so what if there was?" they replied.

"That was me, father! I was that stork on the house," cried Silyan.

"Listen, mother, and you too Neda. Remember when you were milking the cows, and Velko hit me with his stick because he thought I was going to peck the calf? Remember, that's when Velko grabbed me because I couldn't fly, as the stick had stunned me? Velko didn't want to let me go!"

"Good Lord! You must have been watching from somewhere, or someone told you about it," said his mother.

"Alright, let's say someone told me about that. But what about when Foxy nearly plucked me clean and would have done so, except that Smille the shepherd saved me?" announced Silyan. Then he turned to the shepherd and said, "That's what happened, isn't it, eh, Smille?"

"That's right, that's how it was, Silyan," replied the Shepherd. "Foxy would have torn the stork apart – the single stork that nested on this roof."

"Ah, go on! Someone from town has told you all about these things that you're teasing us with," said his father.

"Ah, I see you still don't believe my story, father," said Silyan. "But what about when you were ploughing the big field? Velko was guiding the bullock team, and I was feeding on worms in the newly dug furrows – remember? Two or three times Velko wanted you to turn around and look at me. You got angry and cracked the whip at me and broke my leg. I was ill for quite a few days until it healed. That evening, Velko told the family, and everyone, including you, father, felt sorry for me. Isn't that what happened?"

"Yes, it was like that, Silyan," replied his father. "But I still can't believe that you could know about it any other way except by having been told by someone. Or maybe you saw it in a dream?"

"But how can you believe the story about Hark and Lark, father, but you won't believe what happened to me?" asked Silyan. Then he took off his right shoe and sock and showed them the bright red scar on his leg. "Here, look at this, father. This is the scar left from where you broke my leg!"

All the people, including Silyan's father, were amazed when they saw his leg, but even so they still weren't totally convinced that Silyan had been the stork.

"Though, who knows? Everything you've said and shown us makes me wonder. Perhaps you really were a stork," said his father. He really began to have doubts.

"It is true! It is, father. It is, all of you," exclaimed Silyan. "What happened to me sounds fantastic – a trip to the Underworld – to stork island – where no person had ever been before or will ever go again. You must believe me! There is no reason why I should lie to you! It's not as if I'd get something out of it by hoodwinking you. There's no reason for you to be skeptical. Besides, there's something else I've just remembered.

"One day my sister Bosilka was sitting on a rug in the yard making herself a necklace, and it disappeared. Not long after, Neda was embroidering a blouse in the yard, and her needle and thread disappeared too. That's what happened, isn't it?"

"Yes, exactly," replied both Silyan's wife and sister. "Though we still don't know who it was that stole them."

"Ha! It was me! I took them," declared Silyan. Then he turned to Smille the shepherd and said to him, "Climb up on the roof and poke around in the stork's nest. You'll find the missing items hidden in the straw. Bring them down so that everyone can see them. Then you'll believe what I've been telling you."

Smille climbed up on the roof, found the necklace and the needle and thread, then brought them down so that everyone could see them. All the villagers were astonished.

"Good Lord! It really must be true! The impossible has happened! Who could ever imagine a man being a stork!" they all exclaimed. Everyone in the village was quite convinced that Silyan had been the stork, and to this very day, storks are spoken about as though they are people.

So there it is, dear Reader – the story of what happened to Silyan from Malo Konyari. I know that you too think it's just a fantasy, but I know it is true, because my father told me this story – and that's just what he said when he first told it.

FLAME TREE PUBLISHING

In the same series:

MYTH, FOLKLORE AND ANCIENT HISTORY

Also available:

EPIC TALES DELUXE EDITIONS

flametreepublishing.com
and all good bookstores